FORTY LOADS

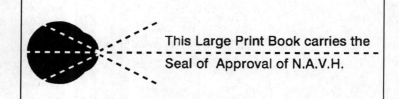

This Large Print Book carries the
Seal of Approval of N.A.V.H.

FORTY LOADS

BRETT COGBURN

THORNDIKE PRESS

A part of Gale, Cengage Learning

GALE
CENGAGE Learning·

Farmington Hills, Mich • San Francisco • New York • Waterville, Maine
Meriden, Conn • Mason, Ohio • Chicago

GALE
CENGAGE Learning·

LIBRARY OF CONGRESS CATALOGING-IN-PUBLICATION DATA

Cogburn, Brett.
    Forty loads / by Brett Cogburn. — Large print edition.
        pages ; cm. — (Thorndike Press large print western)
    ISBN 978-1-4104-7008-9 (hardcover) — ISBN 1-4104-7008-3 (hardcover)
    1. Large type books. I. Title.
PS3603.O3255F67 2014
813'.6—dc23   2014031920

Published in 2014 by arrangement with The Berkley Publishing Group, a member of Penguin Group (USA) LLC, a Penguin Random House Company

Printed in Mexico
1 2 3 4 5 6 7 18 17 16 15 14

This novel is for all my EOSC Aggie friends at old Johnston Hall: JD "Conroe" Roberson, James Bray, Lance Lewis, Mike Allen, Jesse Hotella, Craig Engles, David Banta, Glenn Lester, Justin Bray, Brian Kennedy, Mike "Grizz" Griswold, Joe Lane, Brian "Shoe" Shoemake, Todd Merida, Jay Payne, Greg Wilson, Marvin "Coach" Moore, Lance "Lucky" Hartsfield, Andy "Mushy" Antonelli, Bobby Pugh, Chad Speaks, Justin Harness, Chris Cormier, Brent Woods, Jason Moody, Les Rymer, Todd Pugh, Chad Mathis, Joe Bray, Larry "Mondello" Allison, Greg Davis, Karl Gentry, Tracy Rust, Johnny Rymer, Paddy Palmer, David "Iron Stob" Deaton, Kevin Clarity, Will Boatright, Frankie Young, Catfish, Chili, Lenny, Stoney, Donald, Jim, Abner . . .

Wild times, plenty of cards, plenty of stories, and good company.

PROLOGUE

The old Mexican stood long in the shadows of the balcony, staring at the lighted windows across the street from him. He waited unmoving, despite all the long miles behind him. Patient, yes, but that wasn't the only thing that kept him still. He was sure that he was being followed. Perhaps all that he had to do was to walk out into that street — so small a thing, dying, the matter of a few steps.

His weariness made it easier to wait. The journey had demanded much of him, and he wasn't sure how much more he had to give. There was only so much one could do out of loyalty. He was only a man, after all, and an old man at that. Terribly tired — the kind of tired that would take away a man's cautious edge, make him impatient . . . get him killed.

He scanned the mold black shadows carefully, but nothing was stirring except for the moths and mosquitos flittering in the pale light thrown from the row of windows and balconies lining that long ribbon of stone cutting through the old city. The gas lamps spotting the edges of the street glowed feebly, as if the hot, humid dark was too thick and heavy to allow light to pass through it.

Gut instinct, if nothing else, told him that trouble was near. He couldn't name his enemies, but twice, bandits had lain in wait for him along the trail. Maybe he was simply unfortunate enough to be the next traveler to come along after they set their ambush, or perhaps they waited for him in particular, some criminal sixth sense telling them that he carried a thing of great value. Gold will do that to wicked men, and oftentimes to men only a little wicked.

Quick footsteps sounded, and he sucked back tight against the wall. His hand found the butt of the ancient, smoothbore pistol tucked behind his broad belt. He pressed the trigger so that the hammer would make no sound as he thumbed it back, and then relaxed his finger when the gun was at full cock.

The white of his eyes followed the slave girl as she passed him by with her bundle of laundry clutched under one arm, her skirt hissing over the cobblestones. She never looked right or left in passing, as if she too realized the night bore bad tidings and wanted nothing more than to get behind the locked door of her master's home. He listened as her footsteps faded, and then to the sound of someone singing in French far up the street, accompanied by an instrument he could not name. The music was happy and light, and it was no way in keeping with the mood that had overcome the Mexican. A riverboat's horn bellowed from down at the docks.

It smelled as if it was about to rain, but then again it always smelled to him as if it was going to rain in the city of New Orleans. It rarely rained where he come from, other than the brief monsoon season in the fall that quickly lost itself in the parched sands. But the water in Louisiana seemed to swell up from the ground itself, and the black earth smelled like worms and rotten decay.

Travel overland to New Orleans from the west turned out to be a chancy thing at best, and his last weeks amidst the swamps had been a nightmare. Time and again, when he left the road for fear of pursuit, he found himself blocked by some dead-end bog or flooded quagmire. It seemed as if he had waded or swam most of his way to New

Orleans, but it was the loss of his horse that bothered him most. While crossing a great, stagnant slough, a giant alligator had taken hold of his good gelding's hind leg and drug it down into the oily, black water. The last he had seen of his loyal animal was when its head appeared one last time above the roll of churning water, with its nostrils flared wide and its eyes wild and wide with terror. He knew that it would have screamed if it could have.

The Mexican felt for the scabbard on his hip and was soothed somewhat by the long-bladed knife there. He could always trust his knife. All men bled when pressed against sharp steel. A gun might fail you, hearts and tongues might lie, but a good blade was always true.

He held the pistol before his eyes. Truly, it was a poor peon's gun, and there were far more modern and better weapons to be bought by a man with more money than he. However, it had always served him well enough, and it comforted him like an old friend. The three of them waited together: the knife, the gun, and the man.

He stepped from under the balcony when the moon passed behind a patch of slow-moving, smoky clouds. He was halfway across the street when he heard a horse coming. He started down the street in the opposite direction, but only made two steps before he heard the whispered talk of men moving toward him. He didn't have to listen long to determine that they were seeking him.

It started to rain, and not gently. The boom of thunder sounded like a starter's gun, and the dark sky opened up and poured forth big, warm drops slanting through the pale streetlights. He stood trapped in the middle of the lonely street with a steady stream of water running off the broad brim of his sombrero — a hat that marked him for the foreigner he was in a place where no men wore such things. He went back to the door he had studied so long and knocked on it. He knocked again and still no answer.

Stepping from under the balcony overhead, he craned his neck until he could see the second floor and the curtains of an open window billowing in the light breeze the rainstorm brought. He took the bag from his belt, and with a grunt, lobbed it through the open window and listened to the heavy thump of it landing on the floor inside, hoping that he had the correct address. Not perfect and not as he had envisioned delivering that which was entrusted to him, but

11

the best he could do.

In the end, that was all a man could hope for — to say that he had done his best. He started up the street, wanting to get as far away from the house as possible, so that maybe his pursuers wouldn't guess where he'd been or what he had left behind.

He didn't go far before he spied a lone rider coming toward him. The stranger rode a horse almost as dark as the night, and the Mexican could see nothing of his hands under the black, caped oilcloth overcoat he wore. Rainwater ran like glowing quicksilver down the silhouette of man and beast when they parked broadside before him.

"El Hombre Viejo de la Muerte," the Mexican whispered, half in fear that the dark angel would hear him, and half as if greeting an old friend.

He had talked to a man at a tavern back up the trail three days before that looked very similar to him that waited there and then. That man had asked too many questions about his journey. However, it had been daylight then, and never had he thought that the man was any more than a man — a cutthroat maybe, but at least a man.

Staring at the thing caped in black before him, the Mexican knew he was about to die.

He knew that, not just by the blackness that surrounded the thing, but also when he saw that single, Cyclops eye tilted down at him and the leering smile with the quicksilver rain parting around it, as if no moisture could wet those grinning teeth.

The Mexican gave the Devil no chance to ask for his soul, or time to make any demands on the bit of life he had left. He lifted his pistol and squeezed the trigger. His powder was too wet, and the metallic snap of the hammer fall was the only sound in the world. Misfire.

The one-eyed devil's coat moved, and a pistol appeared out of those dark folds. It was a ridiculously large revolver, and the rain made the charcoal blue barrel shine like polished ebony. The horse stamped nervously in the road and the pistol wobbled and strained to locate its target, moving in synchronization with the cold eye behind it.

The Mexican threw aside his own pistol and drew his knife. He could hear shouts and running footsteps splashing up the street behind him, but he ignored them and charged with his blade bared. Flames flashed before his eyes and the Devil disappeared.

The next thing the Mexican knew, he was lying on the street with water rushing down his sides and the rain falling gently onto his face. Couldn't move and didn't seem to have the will to. He was vaguely aware of a group of men standing nearby, silently watching him, faces devoid of all emotion. He looked up into the dark sky overhead until the Devil's face filled his sliver of vision and stared back at him with that leering eye. He knew what the Devil wanted to ask even before he asked it.

"You are a hard man to follow." The Devil cocked his head, his one good eye like a bird of prey studying its food for signs of life.

The Mexican smiled, although he didn't know why. For some reason, both his fear and his pain were gone. He felt light and careless, and found it amusing that the Devil spoke with a slight French accent. In all his life, he never would have guessed that. Living was full of all kind of surprises, and dying seemed no less adventuresome.

"I mean to have what I came for," the Devil said.

It took the Mexican three tries to speak again, and he felt his own blood on his chin, warmer than the rain, and seeping from him with every working of his mouth. "And you'll die for it, as I have."

The Devil's one eyebrow tilted down. "You could have given it to me back at the tavern, whatever this precious thing is that you carry. Who knows? Maybe I wouldn't kill you."

"I was never going home." The Mexican hacked up a ragged spray of the rainwater flooding his open mouth. "I knew it from the moment . . . the moment I said I would come here."

"Here? To this place?"

The Mexican tried to shrug, but only coughed again.

The devil eye staring at him was as wide and wild as a scared horse's, and the mouth below it parted like a cadaver's slowly contracting flesh into a patronizing grin, teeth wet and yellowed like varnished, aged ivory — an ancient smile, fallen, as old as the turning of the earth. "I've been here many times. This moment. Different places and different names, but still the same. Sometimes it pays; sometimes not. But this time . . . ah, yes . . . wouldn't be any other place since I guessed what it was you carried. Something very heavy in your purse."

The Mexican exhaled a groan.

The Devil held his stamping horse by one rein and squatted over his victim. He gestured casually and languidly with his pistol barrel for emphasis while he spoke — as if the Mexican wasn't dying, as if it wasn't

15

raining, and as if they were two friendly strangers who had met on the roadside with all the time in the world for pleasant, idle conversation. "And that is the true measure of worth in all things, old man. The world balances itself. Am I to blame for being willing to take your life for something that is so valuable that you are willing to die for it? I think not. You were simply here, as I'm here. There could be no other reckoning."

"Fool. *Pendejo!*" The Mexican was too weak to spit in the Devil's eye, but it still felt good to call him a dumbass.

The Devil laughed. "But there is a chance, and a good chance, *mon ami,* that I will die a richer fool than you. Tell me what it is you know, and about this thing you carried that is so precious to you. You've got my bullet in your guts. Big bullet, maybe busted your back from the way you're lying, no? Hurts, doesn't it? Tell me now, and I'll put another one in your head. Ease your suffering."

The Mexican was too close to death to feel any more pain, and the Devil's voice seemed to come from afar. He felt cold hands slipping inside his vest and tugging at his pockets. He tried to find the moon above him again, but it had long before disappeared somewhere into the smoky clouds drifting so low overhead. There was nothing but raindrops pelting his face and spotting his fading vision.

He took one last ragged breath. *The things men would do for gold — pack loads of dull, yellow metal waiting for the taking a thousand miles toward the setting sun. Fools.* Had he not been dead he could have told all who would listen that *el oro* was much easier to find than it was to keep.

CHAPTER 1

"I'll call." Faro Wells shoved a small stack of coins into the middle of the table and counted twenty heartbeats waiting to see the result of his decision. The swaying lantern above the table intermittently lighted half of his still, unreadable face.

Faro knew he was a loser, even before the riverboat captain showed his hand. The slow smirk building at one corner of the man's walrus mustache gave it away. He wished the fat man had been so easy to read earlier, then maybe he wouldn't have called.

"Tough luck," the captain said as he reached out with one hand and smeared the winning cards faceup across the table before him.

"Full house, ain't that the drizzlin' shits." The slave trader beside Faro let out a low whistle when he saw the captain's hand. He paused with a smoldering cigar suspended between two fingers before his lips and clucked like an old hen and shook his head somberly, as if he would have played Faro's cards differently.

The captain leaned forward to encircle the pot with both forearms. "Can't say as I blame you for staying on three jacks. I've risked more on worse hands."

Faro Wells watched stoically as the last of his fortune was slowly drug across the scarred oak table and into the fat captain's belly. He frowned at the pasteboards he'd just thrown down as if they'd failed him. He was dead broke, courtesy of another losing hand. And not just the no-money-in-your-pockets kind of broke, but the no-money-in-your-pockets, lose-everything-you-have, nasty-people-wanting-to-break-your-legs-for-what-you-owe, soon-to-be-no-roof-over-your-head, starving kind of broke.

Faro shrugged. He leaned forward until his entire face was in the light. It was a rugged face, with the angle of his jaw darkened with a two-day growth of whisker stubble. A round, seamed scar the diameter of a pinky finger dimpled the cheekbone just below his left eye. His lips parted to reveal a perfect row of white teeth, but the forced gesture fell short of its nonchalant intent. It was a pirate's smile that both those who knew him and those who didn't were never quite sure how to take.

"You know what they say, Captain. Sometimes the worst hand a man can have is a good one." Faro fought back the exasperated sigh that he so badly wanted to let escape his lungs.

"Better dig in your purse for some more coin." The clammy-skinned lunger beside Faro coughed into a filthy kerchief before gathering the cards to shuffle for his deal. "You win some, you lose some."

Faro merely grunted at the sickly cardsharp. Win some, hell, he couldn't remember the last time he'd walked away from a poker table a winner. A man could tell himself that his luck was bound to turn for only so long. He'd always been good with numbers, and he did a swift mental calculation of just how poor his luck had been for the past year. The answers he came up with were quite astounding — astronomical in fact — when considering that a man could be dealt so many poor hands and play what good ones he garnered so badly. It was a miracle of the worst kind, and the kind of miracle he believed in.

"No, I'm played out," Faro jerked a thumb in the direction of the slave trader to his left. "I haven't got the price of Fontenot's cigar on me."

The wick on one of the kerosene lamps adorning the papered walls was trimmed badly and smoking up the globe. Faro had spent half a decade in such dark, smoky backrooms, but suddenly he felt claustrophobic in the shadowed glow of such a den.

He rose slowly and straightened his coat. He raked back his coal black hair with his fingers and set his broad-brimmed straw planter's hat on his head, nodding to the men at the table. "Gentlemen, it's been interesting, if not profitable."

The slave trader rocked back in his chair with the cigar clenched between his snaggled teeth and his thumbs hooked in the armholes of his brocaded vest. "If it's a matter of money, my offer still stands."

"Fontenot, you'll have to wait in line with the rest of them if you want a piece. There's not one thing left on Royal Oaks that doesn't have a lien on it, including the slaves," Faro said.

The men at the table looked down or away, and the room, already quiet, grew uncomfortably so. Although there were no gentlemen present — the farthest thing from it — the group liked to think of themselves as such. And no gentleman liked to discuss another man's financial woes. It wasn't proper, even though they all knew that Faro's finances were in shambles. Social etiquette demanded that one avoid scandalous conversation, at least until the victim of the gossip had removed himself.

"I can stake you with a bit if you want to stay in the game. Your credit's good with me." The fat captain put a hand on a pile of money before him. "You've ridden my boat off and on for years, and you've always been good for your debts."

And well he could afford to be generous. The man had three riverboats plying the Mississippi from New Orleans to Missouri, and not even the war seemed to slow the man's profits. His knack for winning at poker proved just how lucky he was.

"Captain, your offer is kind, but I never gamble on borrowed money."

"Lady Luck can be finicky. You've just got to wait her out." The lunger had gathered control of himself after another round of coughing and sat pitifully hunched over the table, looking more like a beggar than a successful riverboat gambler, even with his suit, silk hat, and gaudy diamond cravat pin.

"You make your own damned luck." The captain pounded his fist on the table and glared as if he dared any of them to argue with him. "I've lost a quarter of a million dollars at one time or another to this old river, but I've made money too. I've seen my ships sunk and run aground and had the creditors howling at my door like a pack of hounds. A man's just got to keep picking himself up and coming back for more. Damn them all: drift logs, sandbars, and tight-fisted bankers. I'll die rich in spite of them."

Faro stood in the dark corner of the room, waiting for the circulation to return to his stiff knee after so long at the table. He looked down at his coat and plucked at a frazzled hole in the bend of one elbow. A tailor on the Vieux Carré had charged him eighty dollars to make the suit. Its style was supposedly the rage in Paris at the time it was made. When viewed from a distance, or in the dark confines of the room, it was a fine suit indeed, just like all the other dashing, custom-made clothes hanging in his closet at home. But up close, in good light, the suit was as worn and threadbare as Faro felt. It was as pretentious and fake as the empty wallet in his coat pocket, and nothing more than a hint of better times.

Faro started across the room. "I bid you all adieu."

The captain's bass voice stopped him at the door. "Faro, keep your chin up. You're the kind that will come through when all's said and done. You've just got to find something worth betting on."

Faro paused with one hand on the open door, his tall frame shadowing the doorway with the lights of the docks behind him. "I bet and won once."

"Hope you do again. The secret's staying afloat until something else comes your way." The captain studied the cards the lunger had just dealt him.

Fontenot looked over his own hand at Faro, the humidity of the room transferring itself to the sheen of sweat on his forehead. "I suppose I'll see you at the auction in two days."

"I'll be there," Faro said.

"I'll have my hired man there early to look over your bunch."

"You do that." Faro made no attempt to hide his disdain for the man. Fontenot was a greasy, shifty type, even for a slave trader. There had been a time when Faro was far pickier about the company he kept and the men he gambled with, but his latest string of bad luck had shortened his list of options. Playing cards with such riffraff was a side effect of his misfortune.

"Good night, Faro." The captain said absentmindedly, his mind already back on the game. "Give your father my best wishes.

He's always been a man of vigor, and it does many of us who know him no good to see him laid low with illness."

"I will." Faro tipped his hat to the room and went out the door.

Once outside, he rubbed at his aching eyes and took in the sun just beginning to peek over the city. He had no clue that he'd been so long at the table, even though the sun and a glance at his pocket watch told him he'd been at the game for better than thirty-six hours.

The riverboat on which he stood was docked alongside the riverbank. Every kind of watercraft imaginable stretched in a long line to either side of her. The great smoke stacks of steamships and riverboats and the masts of sailing vessels stood silhouetted in the dim light as far as he could see. He readjusted the leather and metal brace on his left knee and took the stairs down to the main deck. There was a slight limp to his gait, and he leaned heavily on his cane when he made his way down the gangplank to the dock.

Normally, a carriage or a buggy would have awaited him, but the high sheriff of the parish had impounded them, along with all the other chattels and property of Royal Oaks plantation. He would have had one of the captain's cabin boys or deckhands fetch him a cab driver, but he hadn't the price of a fare.

He crossed the breadth of the small wooden dock and made his way toward the low, earthen berm of the levee that lined the river some fifty yards back from the water's edge. The bare, silty ground was muddy from recent rains and high water, and a cypress plank sidewalk had been laid down for foot traffic. Once over the levee, stacked cotton bales, mule carts, and other piled goods created an alleyway with only a small view of the riverfront warehouses and a portion of St. Louis Street ahead. Faro paused when a black coach with high red wheels and polished brass lanterns halted at the end of that alleyway. The driver watched him with seeming unconcern, but it was obvious that he was waiting. The doors remained closed.

Faro felt for the Colt .31 inside the leather pocket sewn inside his waistband at a cross draw just in front of his left hip. The riverfront was no place to be for a man alone at night or so early of a morn. Better where he was than across the river in Algiers, granted, but still a place where bad things could happen to those less cautious. Regardless, most of those who would rob a man and roll his body into the river didn't travel in fancy coaches, but he had reason to worry anyway. Lately, his debts had grown, and many of those he owed money to were wealthy enough to afford such wheeled conveyance. More important, many of those gentlemen wouldn't be above sending a strong arm or two to collect for them . . . or make an example of him.

The coach waited in silence, except for the occasional stamp of the pair of fine bay horses' hooves upon the street. The window curtains were drawn, and he could see nothing of who might be inside. He was sure the coach's appearance meant no good for him, but he was too proud to turn back to the ship, and too stubborn to keep standing there like he was lost. He started toward the coach, keeping a close eye on the window curtains.

When he had closed to within a few yards of it, the near door swung open and a black man in a tall hat and a fancy red coachman's coat slid his long legs to the ground. He studied Faro carefully and there was more than a little hint on his face that he wasn't impressed with what he saw. He reached his right hand inside his coat.

Faro raised his cane and held it a foot

before the man's stomach. "I'd go easy there."

The black man didn't bat an eye. Instead, he ever so slowly produced an envelope and held it forward. "I have an invitation for you."

Faro kept a careful watch on the man as he leaned forward to take the envelope. His own name was written there in a fine, slanted, calligraphic script. He took two steps back and broke the wax seal. The envelope smelled of perfume. He read the brief invitation once, and then a second time more slowly.

Monsieur Faro Wells,
It has been brought to my attention that you are a bold man who can be trusted to be discreet. It is my wish to meet with you to discuss a small but challenging business venture pertaining to a shipment of gold bullion. Should you be willing to hear my proposal, my driver will bring you to my home.

Sincerely,
Rue McGaffney

Faro searched his mind for what kind of con was being worked on him and could barely keep from laughing. Was it a ruse to get him somewhere where there were no witnesses, or somebody's practical joke? He tried to decide who might be behind the matter. Offhand, he could think of no one who would bother with mysterious notes and carriages. It all seemed too theatric. Anybody wishing him harm could do so with far less extravagance, and there was no one he knew who would go to such great lengths for a joke's sake.

If the black man recognized Faro's conundrum, he didn't show it. "The coach awaits."

Faro looked up the river, past the team, in the direction of his home — a home that was only to be his for a few more days. He told himself not to be a fool grasping at straws.

Who was Rue McGaffney? The long hours without sleep and the perfume filling his head made it hard for him to think clearly. A desperate man with few options, the mention of gold had quickened his pulse. He knew what he was going to decide, even though he gave himself a thousand reasons to send the coachman on without him.

"Sucker," he whispered.

"What's that, sir?" the coachman asked.

"Nothing," Faro said as he went past the man and put a foot on the ornate, cast-iron step. "I was just saying what a fine morning it was for a drive."

He ducked his head and crawled inside the coach to recline on the overstuffed leather cushions on the rear bench. The door latch clicked ominously in place behind him. He was committed and tried to prepare himself for whatever was about to befall him. He was sure that his current run of bad luck would continue and that any fortune that fell out of the sky wouldn't land in his lap but would instead hit him on the head and kill him. Still, it might turn out to be an interesting morning.

The carriage rocked slightly as the coachman crawled up beside the driver, and the team took off with a lurch. Faro made small openings in the rear window curtains to either side of him so that he could keep his bearings, and sat back to enjoy the ride. However, he did lay his revolver in his lap. He might be a fool for a woman or gold, but he was a cynical fool.

CHAPTER 2

The coach traveled at a high trot up St. Louis Street, past the great warehouses lining the river, and then turned east, aiming for the heart of the oldest part of the city, the Vieux Carré, or what some were beginning to call the French Quarter. In the distance to the southeast, Faro could see the tall spires of the St. Louis Cathedral and the neighboring Presbytere rising above the city.

The clop of the horses' hooves on the street echoed as if from the bottom of a well. While originally settled by the French, the architecture of that influence had burned in a great fire long before and was replaced during the Spanish rule of the city. Buildings of brightly painted stucco and red tile roofs were jammed tightly against each other in an almost solid wall lining the thoroughfare. Multistoried balconies and galleries fronted almost every residence and shop.

The coach halted before a two-story, yellow town house, and the coachman opened the door for him. Before climbing out, Faro caught a flash of a white dress and a face equally pale disappearing from the balcony directly overhead.

The coachman waited patiently while he stood in the street to let the stiffness leave his bad leg, and then led him to the front door beneath the wrought iron balconies overhead. The coachman raised the hinged doorknocker and rapped gently upon the wood with it.

The door swung slowly inward. An elderly black woman in an apron and with her head bound in a scarf stood framed in the lamplight glowing behind her. The window curtains were drawn tight, and all that Faro could see of the apartment was the narrow strip behind her. She slowly stepped aside and bid him entrance into the house with a nod of her chin. The coachman remained behind when Faro removed his hat and stepped inside.

The house servant led him down a short hallway into a large parlor. A young woman sat before an open window across the room. She sat very straight and on the edge of a small couch with her hands hidden in the lap of her hooped skirt. Her eyes were wider than they should have been, as if her composed appearance was requiring effort.

And what lovely blue eyes they were. She could have been no more than eighteen, maybe twenty, with a luxuriant headful of blond hair gathered up high and a dimpled chin above a lovely neck. She gestured gracefully with one hand for him to take a seat in one of the two chairs across from her.

"Monsieur Wells, I presume?" Her voice had a slight French accent.

"At your service." Faro was distinctly aware of the awkward squeak of the hinged metal straps on either side of his knee brace as he walked across the carpeted floor. He suddenly felt shabby in his threadbare and wrinkled suit.

"I'm Rue McGaffney," she said.

"Pleased to meet you." He took a seat in a high-backed mahogany chair and studied the other expensive furnishings of the room. It didn't look as if she was hurting for money.

The black maid went into another room, leaving the ticking of a grandfather clock in the corner of the parlor as the only sound. Faro hung his hat upon one of his knees and watched the brass pendulum swing back and forth while he waited for the Mc-Gaffney woman to break the ice.

"Would you care for some hot tea?" She gestured to the kettle and cups on a silver tray on the small table before her.

"No, thank you."

"I can have some coffee brought."

Faro shook his head. "I would much prefer for you to explain the message you sent me."

Her eyes betrayed a slight annoyance, but she quickly covered it. "I was told you could be a brusque man."

One corner of Faro's mouth lifted in a smirk. "I admit, I'm usually far more content to while away the hours with a pretty woman, but the night was long and your message has intrigued me to point of impatience."

"Don't flatter yourself," she said with a hint of mocking in her tone. "I hear that you're quite the cad among the ladies, but I assure you that only business matters have brought you here."

"Is that all you've heard about me?"

"It is said that you're all but broke and about to lose your plantation because you gamble too much and too poorly."

Faro was more impressed by her candor than he was offended by it. "If you've heard such things about me, then why am I here?"

She sipped at her tea before answering, her eyes never leaving him over the rim of the cup. "I asked you here because it's also said that you're a man who knows mining and who has some knowledge of the western frontier."

Faro shifted in his chair and straightened his bad leg out before him. "You can hear anything in this city, but for the sake of conversation, why would those two things interest you?"

She set the teacup down on the table. "First, promise me that what I'm about to tell you won't be shared with others lest you agree to what I'm about to propose."

Faro was keenly aware of the silver brooch lying against the pale skin just below her collarbones, and he fought his eyes away from the where the square-scooped neck of her dress ended above the swell of her breasts. "You have my word as a gentleman, although it seems you may doubt I'm such."

She smiled again and leaned back against the divan, playing idly with one pearl earring dangling from her right earlobe. "What would you say if I told you my deceased father has left me a gold mine in the mountains of New Mexico Territory?"

The mention of gold was just enough to

break Faro's attention away from that earring. "I would say you're a fortunate young woman if the mine is producing profitable ore."

"And what would you say if I told you that he left me a good deal of refined gold in those very same mountains?"

It was Faro's turn to smile. "And I suppose this is the part where you offer to sell me this wonderful gold claim?"

"You're a very suspicious man."

"If you think I know something of mining, then you know I went west in the gold rush of '49. Stories like yours are a dime a dozen out there," he said. "Walk into any saloon in California and there'll be some sharp or drunkard trying to sell you a supposedly rich claim or a map to a treasure that doesn't exist."

The muscles in her long neck and those in her jaw tensed. She took a deep breath and turned slightly to look down the hallway leading deeper into the apartment. "Armand, could you come in here for a moment?"

Booted feet sounded in the hallway as soon as she spoke, and a massive man stepped into the room. No, he wasn't tall, almost short in fact, but he was wide of shoulder and carried that width down through a barrel chest and tree-trunk thighs. The only hair on his hatless, shaved head was a handlebar mustache waxed into curls at the corners of his mouth. He was dark-eyed and swarthy-skinned with a crooked pug nose and brawler's face marked with the kind of scars knuckles make. He stood there looking at Faro with the thumbs of his meaty hands hooked in the braided rope belt tied around the waist of his coarse spun cotton pants. The handle of a knife and the grip of a muzzle-loading pistol stuck out of the top of the belt between those fists. He spoke something to the woman in Cajun French.

Faro didn't speak French, much less the Acadian dialect peculiar to the swamps of south Louisiana. However, he could tell from the look on the man's face that a certain recent arrival, a particular gambler, might be in trouble.

Rue McGaffney studied Faro for a long moment, seemingly making her mind up about something. She finally sighed and leaned forward again. "Mr. Wells, you've insinuated that I might have brought you here for amorous reasons, and that my word is no better than a drunkard's. That's twice you've insulted me in my own home. If you do so again, I'll have Armand take you outside and use a buggy whip on you."

One look at the brawler and Faro had no doubt that he was more than capable of doing what she asked.

"My apologies. Have your man stand back, and I'll mind my manners," Faro said. "You must understand that it's not every day that I'm called to meet with a woman about a supposed fortune in gold she's inherited. It's only natural that I assume that I'm being played for a fool."

The squat Cajun remained where he was, his expression no friendlier.

"Forgive Armand. He's just very protective of me since my parents are gone," she said.

Faro tried to ignore the man glaring across the room at him. "I'm sorry for your loss, but just who was your father?"

"Gregory McGaffney. I believe he was known out west as Tin Pan McGaffney."

Faro let that soak in. "They say Tin Pan would have been rich if he had worked half the claims he located. Liked to hunt ore, the way I heard it, but lost his enthusiasm for a good claim once he found it."

She nodded. "He sold a promising gold claim on Feather River for twenty thousand dollars that it is said made its new owners as rich as kings."

Faro couldn't help but chuckle. Tin Pan was a legend in the far western mountains, and it was hard to imagine that the old sourdough sired the pretty young thing across from him. "They say he drank most of that money up in a week, with barely enough left to outfit himself to head back into the mountains prospecting for another find."

Her face grew hard again. "He sent a good deal of that money home to see to his family."

Faro could have kicked himself for thinking out loud. "I'm sorry."

"Never mind. Although I didn't lay eyes on him for the last six years of his life, I'm more than aware of my father's reputation and his wandering ways."

"And you would have me believe that the same man located another rich claim and invested the time and effort to make it produce in such volume? That doesn't sound like it fits Tin Pan."

"Why waste your time? Just show it to him." Another young woman shoved past the Cajun henchman and walked across the room to Faro.

Faro's knee had grown stiff again, but he struggled to his feet anyway, just in time to meet her. If at all possible, she was more beautiful than Rue, or perhaps her beauty was merely different — dark and sultry where her sister was as fair as white linen. She stopped before him and held out a hand. He grasped her fingers gently and bowed courteously, feeling even more at a disadvantage than he had with only one woman in the room.

"Come now, Mr. Wells, don't be disappointing. My sister has to threaten to have you horsewhipped, and yet you bow and act the gentleman when I walk into the room." She leaned back and clucked her tongue while she looked him over. "I might think you found me unworthy of any scandalous effort on your part."

Usually never at a loss for words when it came to the fairer sex, he found that he was tongue-tied. And for good reason; she was stunningly beautiful. She was almost as tall as he, and the house robe tied at her waist did little to hide her curves. Her hair hung wildly in long, natural curls. The shiny black of it was in sharp contrast to her olive skin and green eyes. Her mouth was wide and her lips were almost too full. He had the distinct impression, even when she wasn't speaking, that she was taunting him. It was plain to him that she had just come from her bed — too plain, and the thought wouldn't leave him.

"And so you meet my sister, Zula," Rue said dryly. "Forgive her, for she can be as forward as you."

Zula arched one eyebrow. She gave her sister a look and then she startled him with a conspiratorial wink. "Don't mind her, she can be such a bore sometimes."

Faro was under no false impressions that all women wore angel wings, but ladies of good reputation didn't usually wink at strange men either, nor meet with them half dressed. He noticed that she still held on to his hand.

"Let him go, Zula," Rue said. "My God, you're worse than a housecat sometimes."

The dark-haired beauty tossed her hair with a flip of her head and snorted softly through her nose. She let go of him and went to sit beside her sister, putting more than a little effort into the sway of her hips. She ignored Rue's straight-backed, proper posture, and flounced against the arm of the couch with one leg curled under her. She smiled at him again, and he had the disconcerting feeling that he provided great amusement for her.

"Show him the egg," she said.

Rue frowned at her but gave a nod to the Cajun bodyguard. "Show it to him."

The stout Cajun disappeared into the hallway for a few moments and returned with a small leather bag in his fist, which he laid upon the table. He stepped back and waited with his broad arms crossed over his chest. There was enough of a smirk on his mouth that Faro could see that he was missing a few of his front teeth.

My, but they are a smiling, smirking bunch.

The beaded leather bag was of Indian making, although Faro couldn't identify what tribe. Many a man on the frontier carried one for a purse or a wallet. It was a larger version of the small drawstring medicine bags many Indian men wore about their necks to carry their magic trinkets.

Rue reached inside the bag and pulled forth a small piece of tanned deerskin the size of a table napkin when she unrolled it on the table. He leaned forward and saw that it was a map with prominent landmarks laid out in a combination of paints and dyes. Portions of the map even seemed to have been tooled, or carved into the thin leather. In other places, it looked as if the mapmaker had written by stabbing a charcoal-coated awl into the leather, or used some other sooty black dye. The block writing was crude, smudged, and in some places barely legible. The mine or claim site was marked somewhere to the northeast of Santa Fe, but no specific directions to it were to be seen.

Faro took note of the smug looks on their faces, as if the map proved anything. "And how did you come by this map?"

"Before he died, our father instructed a trusted Mexican friend to deliver a message to us in the event of his demise. Two days ago, the courier from New Mexico brought us this," Rue said.

Faro spun the hide around until it was right side up, although he didn't have a clue about most of the landmarks. Many of the town or settlement names were in Spanish, and if Santa Fe and Fort Union hadn't been clearly marked he could have easily mistaken it for a map of anywhere — Mexico or South America for all he knew. However, that didn't stop him from acting like he recognized the represented geography and to nod his head occasionally. He was still sure that he was the focus of some kind of con, but thought it might be smart to act like he knew more than he did, at least until he'd heard them out.

"I take it you have detailed directions to the mine to go with this map?" he asked.

"We do," Rue said. "Do you think us foolish enough to give you that information?"

Faro waved a hand over the supposed map. "Is this all you've got?"

Rue smiled and reached once more into the sack. She came out with a gold ingot in the shape and size of a chicken egg. She sat it on the table with a gentle thump where it rolled and wobbled across the table for a moment before coming to a stop. "There are two more of these in the bag."

Faro couldn't take his eyes off of the egg on the table, and even the women who had obviously seen it before were quietly watching it. Zula ran the tip of her tongue over her upper lip.

The egg was dull and obviously crudely refined and containing impurities, but it was real gold. Faro reached out and hefted it — at least two pounds or more of gold worth over eight hundred dollars. Either they had gone through great trouble and expense to con him, or he was going to have to rethink the matter.

"There's enough of those eggs to fill the packsaddles of forty mules," Rue said.

"Forty loads," Zula repeated.

CHAPTER 3

"If you have a mine capable of producing these" — Faro tossed the egg in the palm of his hand like a ball, still sensing that he was being conned — "then why do you need my help?"

The two women locked eyes and passed an unspoken thought between them before Rue answered. "Within that same pouch was my father's last will and testament granting the mine and the gold to Zula and me."

"And?"

"Apparently, the pack train of gold has never left the site of the mine," she added.

"And?"

"As you know, transporting so much gold could be . . . well, difficult. We want you to hire a party of men and take us to go get the gold. While there, you can also ascertain the value of the mine and the financial feasibility of further work on it."

Faro set the gold on the table and leaned back in his chair. "For the sake of argument, let's say all is as you say it is." He made a temple of his fingers while he thought out loud, "How do you know the gold is still there?"

"We think it is still there," Rue's voice rose slightly.

It was plain from the looks on their faces that both of them had considered the question he brought up, and that it worried them.

"If this gold came from ore, then it required crushing and smelting, and that suggests a large enough operation that there's no way that you could keep the mine a secret." He paused to make sure they were really listening to him.

"What if the egg was melted down from gold dust?" Rue asked. "Father used the word 'mine' in his letter to us, but perhaps he meant it just as a term for a claim. I understand they wash gold dust and small nuggets from the streams out there."

Faro nodded. "Placer gold, maybe, but still you can't keep such a find a secret, at least not long enough to gather forty pack loads of gold. As soon as word leaked out, every miner and prospector in the West would have been drawn to the area like flies to sugar. And I've seen no such discovery or mention of a New Mexico boom camp in the newspapers."

"He worked the mine by himself and didn't let anybody know of the find except for his Mexican hired man."

"However secret he may have kept his claim, there's the high probability that you would find your gold claim jumped by others and your stored gold gone."

"It's still there. My father stated that the gold was well hidden, and that the mine was in a very remote location."

"Would you mind if I read the letter he sent you?"

The sisters looked to each other for a long moment before Rue turned back to him. "I'll read a portion of it to you. There are parts that I wouldn't care to share as a matter of protecting our interests."

"Fair enough."

Rue pulled a wrinkled piece of paper from the pouch and carefully unfolded it. Even from a distance, Faro could see that it was soiled and water-stained and beginning to tear along the folds.

Rue read the letter. Zula sat quietly beside her, often silently mouthing the words at the same time her sister read them, as if she had already memorized it.

The story was pretty much as they had told him, at least what they had shared with him. According to the message, their father had found gold in the mountains north of Santa Fe. The claim was located in a country of hostile Indians, and Tin Pan worked the mine alone for three summers, stashing his golden eggs until he had the fortune he wanted.

"And where is the Mexican who delivered this letter? What's to stop him from getting the gold?" Faro asked. "Maybe he has already."

Rue didn't seem to want to answer and made a point to look at the far wall.

"He left this package with us without our knowing three nights ago. The very same morning we found it, his body was discovered where he had been murdered just down the street from here."

"What happened to Tin Pan? You've said he died, but not how."

Again, Rue seemed reluctant to answer. "There was a brief letter from a priest that arrived a few months before we received the map —"

"The Indians killed him," Zula interrupted her.

Faro shook his head somberly. "Do you have any clue of how wild some of that country is?"

"You should've let me hire us a man," Zula said scornfully. "A real man."

Rue bit her lip and leaned forward again, as if her nearness could pressure him into the answer she wanted. Her eyes were big and soft. "Mr. Wells, I was told that you were a decorated officer and a hero of the Mexican War. And everyone in New Orleans knows the story of how you struck it rich in the gold fields of California, and how you came back here wealthy as sin and gave half your gold to the widow of the man who went west with you."

Faro looked away, uncomfortable with the story he'd heard whispered around him so many times.

Rue continued. "It's also common knowledge that everything you own is about to be sold at auction to pay your debts. It was my hope that I could entice you to help us. You're a professional soldier and a leader of men, and I hoped that your experiences in the war had given you a knowledge of New Mexico."

"Ma'am, I was in Mexico proper for only a few months, Veracruz to be exact. I never got anywhere near New Mexico Territory."

"We'll pay you well for your trouble. How does two thousand dollars sound?"

"Why should I settle for so little?"

Rue moved quickly back and leaned against Zula, failing to hide her shock. Zula passed her an I-told-you-so glance.

Faro chuckled. *Now you've got them listening.*

"Why would you say that?" Rue asked.

"How do you think I'm supposed to hire men who won't have the very same thought I just voiced?"

"Surely you know some honest men." From the way Rue was biting her bottom lip Faro guessed that she had already been worrying about "honest" men.

"Ladies, listen. I don't know if there's such thing as an honest man when it comes to gold." *Or a good-looking woman.*

"Including you?" Zula asked.

"Including me," he said.

Rue thrust her chin out a little and straightened her posture stubbornly. "All right, what if you were to take us alone. Just we three and Armand."

"Take you?" Faro laughed again. "Don't you know that there's a war going on? There'll be ten thousand ways to die between here and there: blizzard, desert, Indians, bandits, and just plain old bad luck. I'd as soon shoot myself in the head and save myself all the suffering rather than take

51

two women on that trail."

"Zula has heard that it would be no problem going by riverboat up the Mississippi and then along the Arkansas to Fort Smith," Rue said. "We could go overland to New Mexico along the Santa Fe Trail."

"Well, you might avoid trying to run the Union Blockade in the Gulf that way, but I hear the Union will eventually try to take control of the river. Our boys in gray aren't going to take kindly to that, and the last thing you need is to get caught in the middle of a battle. And for that matter, I hear all of the Indian Territory west of Arkansas is one big bloody fight. The civilized Indians out there are dressing up like soldiers and trying to exterminate each other."

"What are you saying?" Rue asked.

"I'm saying you need to find someone else to help you."

"And what if we can't find someone else?" Rue asked.

"You've got those eggs," Faro said.

Rue saw him looking around the fancy apartment. "The eggs might tide us over for a few months or even a few years, but as you can see, we're used to a certain standard of living."

"I wish you the best of luck, and be careful who you show that gold." Faro rose and went to the door. "I bid you both good day."

Rue seemed lost in thought but snapped out of it before he closed the door behind him. "Have the coachman take you home before he returns the coach back to the livery."

"Let him walk," Zula said.

"We brought him here. The least we can do is see him home."

"Have it your way, but I'd let him walk."

Faro shut the door behind him and gave the driver and the coachman directions to his home and climbed into the coach and shut the door for himself. The sun was already an hour up, and he was shocked to find that he'd been so long with the Mc-Gaffney sisters. But he'd always found that time flew when it came to pretty women or talk of gold.

Even if they were telling the truth, those two were in for some hard lessons if they thought hauling that much gold from New Mexico to Louisiana was going to be easy. He had his own troubles to attend to and told himself that the best thing he could do was to forget he'd ever met them or heard their story. And he'd vowed from the moment he walked away from the card table officially broke that he was done with gambling and taking foolish chances.

Despite his opinions, the coach was twenty minutes up-river along the road and he was still thinking about that golden egg rocking on the hard tabletop. Forty loads of golden eggs — what a story. A man could do a lot with that kind of money.

CHAPTER 4

Rue McGaffney played idly with the golden egg on the tabletop while she thought. Everything depended on getting the gold. Without it, she had few options, and all of them were distasteful.

Their mother had spent her life at the mercy of the whims of a wandering alcoholic and the feast-or-famine income he provided. Now, that same man, as if to make up for all he had done and hadn't done, dangled an absurdly rich inheritance in front of his daughters from beyond the grave. She could almost see his leprechaun smile and hear him laughing and daring them to dream as big as he always had. No more hardship and no more worries if they would just follow the rainbow.

"I'd say that went horrible," Zula said.

"Give him time to mull our proposal over. I hear his father is on his deathbed and will pass any day. Perhaps that's what's keeping him from going with us," Rue said.

"He isn't the only game in town. Adventurous men are two bits a dozen here."

"No, Monsieur Wells isn't the only man in town," Rue said, "but everything he said bears consideration, whether we want to hear it or not. The men who could get us there and back and not rob us blind are bound to be few and far between."

"True, but how much time do you think we have to wait around and do nothing? Someone may be stealing the gold while we sit here," Zula said. "We'll have to keep our wits about us, no matter who we hire, but I bet I can find someone."

"Who?"

"Let me think on it some more. I don't trust any man farther than I can throw him, but one thing I can guarantee you, it's going to take a man rough around the edges to help us get what we want. I've no faith in a fancy pants like Faro."

Rue threw a strange look at her sister. After so many years together, nothing Zula said should come as a shock. "Give Faro a couple of days. He's the only man I could find in the city that knows anything of mining, and even those who don't like him swear to his honesty."

"My God, Rue. He's nothing but a

crippled gambler." Zula whirled around with her green eyes flashing. "What makes you think a man that couldn't hold on to his own gold can take care of mine?"

"Ours," Rue said. "Our gold."

"That's what I meant." Zula stared out the window.

"He is a handsome man, once you get used to that scar on his cheek," Rue said absent-mindedly.

"Ah, sister. Who's the little cat in heat now?"

"You can act so trashy sometimes."

"Well, he's tall, dark, and handsome, I'll grant you that, and the fancy, mannerly kind that might make a schoolgirl like you warm between your thighs if you like that sort of man."

Rue resisted the urge to chastise her twin sister for the filth that came out of her mouth. However, she knew from past experience that to scold Zula would only cause her to say something even more impolite. Most of it was just an act meant to shock her and make her uncomfortable enough to give up an argument. Their French Creole mother had a sharp tongue like Zula's and a ribald sense of humor that would put a sailor to shame when no men or mixed company was around.

"I suppose Faro reminds you of the boys you met back East at that finishing school," Zula said. "Did they tip their hats and blush when they wanted to hold your hand on the porch swing? Did they stop every time you passed a window so that they could look at their own reflection and admire the cut of their clothes, or tell you how beautiful you were hanging on their arm?"

"I'm not arguing with you."

"Well, while you were reading poetry books and learning how to sit in a chair straight to sip tea, I was learning a thing or two about men," Zula said.

"You could have gone to school had you wanted to, and you don't mean that like it sounds."

Zula turned to her and smiled devilishly. "Wouldn't you like to know?"

"Sometimes, I don't know how we can be twins."

Zula got a funny look on her face. "True."

"We'll wait two days, and if Faro doesn't agree to help us, I'll listen to whatever you can come up with. Agreed?"

Zula shrugged. "They're opening the café down the street. I think I'll go get us some breakfast. I'm starving."

"Surely, you're joking. You aren't even

dressed. Let Sugar cook you some break-fast."

"That would be okay if there was anything to cook in the cupboard. In case you haven't noticed, the pickings are getting pretty slim." Zula screwed her lips into a pout. "I wish we could sell at least one egg."

"I've told you, we need that gold to pay for getting the rest of what Father left us," Rue said. "And besides, don't forget that the rent is overdue."

Zula glanced down at herself and a mischievous look spread across her face. She slid her robe and silk gown up her right leg and stretched out that long, white limb and rocked her knee side to side. "Maybe I could get us some free breakfast. That chef watches me like a puppy every time I go in there."

Rue refrained from saying anything else to egg Zula on. She'd already said too much. She rose and went to the kitchen. Maybe there was something left to eat.

She was pilfering through their pantry when she heard the front door closing. She felt sorry for that café cook. Zula was relatively harmless, except when it came to men, or for that matter, money.

CHAPTER 5

The man in the black great coat stood in the shadows of a balcony across the street and watched Faro climb into the waiting coach. He waited until it was almost a block away before he walked into the street and turned his one good eye upon the apartment Faro had just left. After a bit, he whistled loudly and two men appeared around the corner of the nearest street intersection behind him. Both men were mounted, and they were leading his horse behind them.

The one-eyed man took a last look up the street at the leaving coach before tossing his long, caped coat back over his right shoulder. He put a foot into his stirrup and swung a leg over his horse's back. The big black gelding pranced sideways in the road and pushed against the bit and the light pull of his hand on the reins.

"Boys, we might have to do something

about Faro Wells," the one-eyed man said.

A door opened, and he turned to see a woman standing at the edge of the street in front of the McGaffneys' home. She hugged herself with both arms and frowned at him.

"Want us to kill him, King?" one of the men asked.

The one-eyed man started his horse toward the waiting woman. "Maybe. I owe that bastard one. Let me see what that little darling has to say, and then we'll decide what to do and when."

CHAPTER 6

Faro had the driver let him off where his driveway met the road along the river. His knee hurt fiercely, but sometimes a short walk helped his discomfort. He waved the coach away and looked up the long row of giant live oak trees leading to the white pillars of his front porch. The limbs had been trimmed high until they were like an archway hung with Spanish moss. Such a canopy was tailor-made for triumphant marches home — a victory parade for the man of the house. Instead, he started down the lane beneath the shadowed limbs with a weary effort, unaware of the brooding frown on his face and the slight scuffing, dragging sound his game leg made with every step.

He reached for the silver whiskey flask in his vest pocket. A drink might cut the edge off his aching knee. Sometimes, he swore that he could still feel that Mexican pistol ball floating around inside it. To his chagrin, he found the flask empty and put it away.

He thought about the gold while he walked. Forty pack loads of refined gold was more than enough to tempt him, but life had made him all too aware of the price often paid for taking too many chances. His right hand involuntarily reached up to place a finger in the bullet dent in his cheekbone. Even in the years past, a woman had been as much to blame for his troubles as the war he'd gone off to fight. There was some unwritten law of the universe that stated trouble went hand in hand with women . . . and money.

His knee brace was still squeaking and creaking, and he promised himself to oil it when he reached the house. It was the damned humid swamp air that rusted the metal so quickly. He couldn't help but remember the sunny mountains far to the west and the high, dry air. It had been long since he traveled over that distant country, another lifetime.

"Mr. Faro," somebody shouted from the front porch ahead.

Faro pulled himself away from his thoughts. It was Lettie shouting for him and she seemed excited. He noticed the buggy parked before the house for the first time.

Lettie met him in the road, well before he

reached the porch, her fat legs churning to carry her great weight. She was breathing heavily. "Mr. Faro, it's your daddy. I called the doctor, but I didn't know where you were at to let you know."

"It's all right, Lettie. There's no way you could have known where I was. I've been on the river for two weeks." Faro put a hand on the old woman's shoulder for a brief instant and then climbed the stairs onto the porch.

He started to pass through his front door but paused when he'd opened it only a crack. He turned to look back at her. "Did you and the doctor get the pistol away from Daddy?"

Her eyes were wide. "You don't have to worry. Your daddy won't be shooting at nobody."

A dread built within him. He looked to the old bullet holes to either side of the door before passing inside. The house had seen better times. The furniture was covered in dust, and here and there green mold had taken hold on the wallpaper. He ascended the great, curved stairway leading up to the second floor.

He met Jethro carrying a bundle of rags and linens in the hallway above. The old slave merely nodded at him in passing. The doctor waited in the door to his father's bedroom. He already had his bag in his hand as if he were about to leave. He too nodded somberly in greeting.

Faro stopped before him and looked over his shoulder into the bedroom. His father lay there beneath his blankets, pale and dead.

"He passed about an hour ago," the doctor said. "The pneumonia was too much for his old lungs."

Faro looked away. "I'm sure you did all that could be done. Did he go peacefully?"

The doctor nodded again. "He mumbled some during the night, but never woke up until this morning when he asked for his old pistol and then went back to sleep."

Faro dabbed at his eyes before turning back to look in the doorway. "Thanks, Doc. Send me a bill."

The doctor patted him on the shoulder and walked away. "I'll put it on your tab."

Faro leaned against the doorway for a long time after the doctor was gone, staring at the withered old man lying on the feather bed. Both of his hands were laid on his chest, almost like someone had placed them there to pose him. The old flintlock pistol that he carried against the British in 1812, and that he treasured so, was clutched in one of his liver-spotted fists.

Faro went downstairs and sat on the bottom step. He set his cane aside and sailed his hat across the room at the stuffed black bear standing on its hind legs in the foyer. He missed landing the hat on the bear's head, but the sight of the ratty, moth-eaten taxidermy specimen and the thought of his father's pistol made him chuckle sadly. One of the bear's glass eyes was missing, and if he looked closely he would find several other bullet holes.

His father's mind had gone feeble in his last years, and he carried the flintlock pistol like some decrepit, elderly people clutched a walking cane. It was always in his hand or tucked into his belt. Nobody who lived or worked in the house entered without shouting out to the old man that they were friend and not foe. When it rained, his father's bedroom ceiling often leaked like a sieve where he'd fired upon imaginary redcoats or river pirates attacking him in bed.

And on those occasions when his father's mind had wandered even further from reality and into the past, he was known to stalk his collection of hunting mounts in the foyer of the house during the middle of the night. The black bear that he'd killed so long ago in Mississippi was his favorite target.

The house slaves, when there had been more of them, were terrified that his father would shoot them. Only old Lettie and her husband, Jethro, would brave the occasional gunfire. Faro tried to hide the pistol, but his father always found it before too long.

It had been Lettie's idea to steal his father's pistol in his sleep and to pull the ball and replace it with only powder and wadding. But that solution lasted only for a while. The old man might have been crazy, but he soon figured out that he was shooting blanks. Lettie kept stealing the pistol and unloading it, and the old man kept reloading when he discovered her ruse. They'd searched the house, but none of them could find where he kept his stash of bullets and powder. It was hard to believe that an old man who couldn't remember his own son's name sometimes could remember where he hid his pistol makings.

But the old man was gone now. He'd lived a long life, most of it spent on the Mississippi River. He'd been a sailor in his youth, and for a long time a riverboat captain. Faro's mother died giving birth to him, and his father raised him in the pilothouse of a riverboat.

It was hot in the house, and Faro went out the front door and sat in the porch swing beside Lettie. He could tell that she'd been crying. He started the seat swinging gently, and before long she started to hum. She was a singing woman, always with a tune coming out of her great lungs when working around the house. He liked to hear her sing.

In the distance, between his house and the river, black smoke filled the sky where slaves were setting a sugarcane field on fire. Such fields were lit prior to harvest to burn off the dead leaves and to drive away the snakes before the slaves went in with their knives to cut down the stalks.

That cane field had once belonged to Faro, but he had sold it two years previous. There had been a time when the plantation had been one of the best, but that was before he owned it. Now, after selling off the farmland a piece at a time, there was little left but the house, some swamp ground, and forty acres of prime farmland.

"You know there's going to be an auction tomorrow," he said.

"I know," Lettie answered. "The high sheriff was here yesterday afternoon checking what's left against the inventory on his list."

Faro could just make out the smokestacks on a riverboat passing downstream behind the burning cane field. "Daddy and I used to pass by big fancy houses like this when we lived on the river. We'd talk about how great it would be to live like planters, and I promised him that one day I'd buy him the grandest plantation in all of Louisiana."

"Mr. Faro, you never were cut out to be a planter," Lettie said.

"Well, Royal Oaks was a fine dream while it lasted."

Lettie sighed. "Maybe it was, but you never should have bought this place just to please your daddy. He didn't know anything about a plantation either. You should have bought you two a town house. He could have sat on the balcony with his old pistol and you could've gambled all you wanted and still had lots of money right now."

Faro reached inside his vest and pulled out a large envelope, which he handed to her. "That's for you and Jethro and the rest. I signed them a few days ago. You can read, so make sure that the others get the correct copies."

Lettie opened the envelope and shuffled through the papers within it. She finally held one of them out at arm's length so that her tired eyes could focus on the writing.

She soon tucked the paper back into the envelope with the rest and laid it in her lap.

"Do you know how much this means to me and Jethro?"

"Don't get all teary-eyed on me. Those papers might not be worth the ink I signed them with," he said. "The law says you're owned by Royal Oaks, and my creditors have a lien on all the property."

"But you've freed us before we could be auctioned off with the house furniture."

"According to the law, I have no right to free what I've given as security to my creditors."

"Then this paper really isn't worth anything?"

Faro patted her leg. "I've never given you much of anything besides empty gestures, but if you're brave, you might let me pay back some of what you did for me and my father."

Lettie studied his face. "You ain't telling me all of it."

Faro smiled, and felt a little better because of it. "Captain Smith has agreed to put you both to work in his kitchen. He's making a trip upriver all the way to Memphis. You'll get wages, and he won't pay attention if you two slip off up north. He's a got a sister there that is going on upriver to visit her husband. He's stationed with the Union Army in Iowa. You can travel with her to keep questions from being asked until you're far enough north of the Mason-Dixon Line to feel safe."

"You arranged all that for us?"

"Just say I've got a guilty conscious, and the captain's won enough money off of me over the years that he couldn't refuse me a favor," Faro said. "I wish I could've done more for the others, but they'll just have to slip off tonight and hope they can get somewhere where folks won't look too closely at their freedman's papers."

Lettie stopped the swing and leaned over and hugged his neck. "You never were cut out to be no planter. You ain't mean enough."

"Lettie, I don't know how you keep from hating me. I would if I was you."

"I don't hate you, and you hurt my feelings to say such a thing. Haven't I been good to you?"

"I don't mean outright hating me, but somewhere down deep you hate me a little. You can talk all you want about how good I've been to you."

"Maybe a little, but for all the bad things, there's good in you that pleases my heart."

Faro had never set out to be a slaveholder; they just happened to come with the vision that he had bought when he came back from the gold fields. He wasn't about to see Lettie and Jethro sold off to the likes of Fontenot or some other slave trader. Lettie and Jethro weren't blood family, but they were the closest thing he had left. Both of them were trustworthy, kind sorts and a credit to the human race, which was more than he could say for most people he knew, white or black, even himself.

To his shame, he should have given Lettie and Jethro and the rest of those remaining their freedom long before. That might have been the only good thing he ever did with the plantation, but now there was a chance he'd waited too long to do right by them.

"What are you going to do?" Lettie asked.

"For one, I'm going to miss you."

"You're just going to miss eating my cooking," she replied with a twinkle in her eyes. "But seriously, what will you do?"

"I'll think of something." He stood and looked at the toolshed out beside the carriage house. "But first, I'm going to find a shovel and dig Daddy a grave."

"You ought to let Jethro do that while you grieve. He's already built your daddy a pine coffin."

"No, you two need to pack your things and go on down to the docks this afternoon. The captain promised me that he'd head upriver in the night to help you out," he said. "And that goes for the rest of them. I don't want any of you hanging around here trying to shake my hand or thank me. Just get gone. Come daylight, I want to be the only one on this plantation when the auctioneer and the sheriff show up."

"Good luck to you, Mr. Faro. And God bless you."

"And good luck to you, Lettie," he said. "Don't think it's going to be easy. You've got a long road ahead of you, so don't be looking back."

"Mr. Faro, I feel at peace and like me and Jethro will be all right. But it's you I've got a funny feeling about."

"What kind of feeling?" He wasn't a superstitious or particularly religious man, but he'd long since learned not to totally ignore Lettie's premonitions.

"I had me a dream last night that you're going on a long trip that's liable to get you killed," she said.

"I'm not going anywhere, Lettie, unless it's gambling on a riverboat."

She shook her head at him like he was but a child. "I dreamed it, Mr. Faro, and if that dream is right like mine usually are, you're going to need a whole lot more luck than me and Jethro."

"Well then, you're a praying woman. Pray a little for me when you get the time."

"Oh, I will, Mr. Faro. I promise you I will." Her eyes were wide and soft like he'd seen them when she was worried over mending a chicken's broken wing or doctoring some child's scraped knees. "You see, I dreamed last night you was dead. As dead as your Daddy lying up there and nobody to dress your body and sing over you."

CHAPTER 7

Faro sat on the porch and waited until the heat of the day was over before finding a shovel and a pick. He walked down to a little hump of ground underneath a big shade tree halfway between the house and the cane fields. He took off his jacket and vest and stripped out of his shirt. His bare skin was fish-belly white after so many years without seeing the sun.

The rich ground gave way easily to the shovel, but he was long out of shape for such physical work. He sweated and heaved and stopped often to rest on the edge of the hole he was making. By the time he dug down above his head the sun had almost set. He pitched the last shovelful of dark earth up out of the hole and climbed out behind it. He knocked the worst of the dirt from his body with the flat of his hand and wiped his sweaty face with his shirt before pulling it back over his head and tucking it in.

He went to the toolshed once more and took the coffin and the little board tombstone that Jethro had made and put it on his shoulder. He carried the items to the grave and left them there. Back at the house, he lit a lantern and carried it up the stairway. The wooden steps creaked and groaned beneath his weight. It had been long since anyone but his father and Lettie and Jethro haunted the house, but even so, it was eerily quiet.

He went into his father's room and set the lamp on the bedside table. Lettie had already dressed his father in his best suit, although the pistol was still clutched in his hand. Faro started to remove the gun but changed his mind. His father would have wanted to be buried with it.

He scooped up the body in the bends of his elbows and was shocked at how light his load was. He always thought of his father as a big man, as he'd been in his prime, but he noted how the suit sagged on his bony frame. Carrying him was like carrying a child.

Even so, it was too much for Faro to carry his father and the lamp both, and he walked carefully along the dark hallway and down the stairs. Clouds had blacked out the moon by the time he crossed the lawn, but the cane field nearest the grave had started burning and cast a strange glow over everything. The light breeze had shifted a bit, and even the smoke floating across the lawn had a weird orange tint to it.

He set the body gently into the open coffin and studied the strange hue that the firelight gave his father's drawn face. One eye had come open, and he raked it closed with the tips of his fingers. He laid a palm against the thin white hair on his father's head and took one last look at him lying there with his pistol upon his stomach. He tried not to think of how much he'd been gone during his father's last years, but try as he might, he did anyway.

Faro wasn't a man that liked to cry, so he took up the lid and set it on the coffin. Jethro had done a fine job smoothing and pegging together the old pine planks. Faro didn't have the slave's carpentry skills, but he'd managed to locate a hammer in the toolshed. There were only two nails that he could find, and he used them to tack the lid to the coffin. He figured the dirt would secure it better and more permanently than nails ever could.

He managed to slide the foot of the coffin out over the grave and slowly let it pendulum downward until it touched the bottom of the grave. He walked it back and forth on end like he was moving some piece of furniture until he had the foot at the far end of the hole. Kneeling down, he lowered the coffin to the end of his 'arms and then let it drop the remaining distance to the bottom. The head of the coffin hit with a soft thump.

He stood over the grave. "They don't make 'em like you anymore, old man. I know you'd have liked a fancy funeral, but this is as good as I can afford or you're going to get. You can take it up with me when my time comes."

Faro picked up the shovel and pitched the first dirt into the grave. He heard something behind him before he could stab the shovel into the pile of earth again and turned with the tool held before him just in time to see a stranger standing with a pistol leveled at him. Something struck Faro a wicked blow in the chin and he fell backward into the grave in a blinding flash of light.

He landed flat on his back on the coffin, and it drove the wind from his lungs. His head spun dizzily and his face felt like it was on fire. He could see nothing in the dark grave except for the spots dancing before his eyes.

"I'll be damned. I think you hit him between the eyes," a voice from above said.

Even through the fog of pain, Faro knew that he'd been shot. His ears were ringing, but he could still hear more than one man moving around above. He didn't have long before one of them was going to come look down into the grave, and he'd left his pistol lying on his coat above.

"Get down in there and cut off one of his ears," another voice said. "King will want proof that he's dead."

"That ain't fair. King can go to hell."

"You tell that to King and see where it gets you. I've got the gun, and you've got a knife. I did the shooting and you'll do the cutting. Sounds more'n fair to me."

"Well, you ain't the one that's got to climb down in the grave. He's going to be messy, shot in the head like that."

"That's all the more reason for you to do it. I don't want to get my new suit bloody."

Faro kept a blurry watch on the smoke rolling across the rectangle of sky above him, afraid to move lest they would know he was alive and shoot him again, and afraid not to move for the very same reason. He dug in his boot top for the dagger there. It was a pitiful little weapon to defend his life — a T-handled, double-edged blade no longer than his hand — but it was all that he had. When the face appeared over the lip of the grave he closed his eyes to mere slits and pretended he was dead.

"Go ahead, Wes, jump down in there and fetch one of his ears. We ain't got all night."

The man stood on the edge of the grave, backlit and silhouetted by the glow of the cane fire. He drew a Bowie knife from his scabbard, the big blade hissing out of the tight leather like a snake. He shoved the flop hat back on his head and twisted around to look at the man somewhere behind him. "He looks deader'n hell, that's a fact."

"Well, hurry up. I want out of this damned smoke."

"If you're in such a hurry, you do it."

"Just think of your cut of that gold King keeps talking about. I'm going to bring up our horses."

"All right, but next time I get to do the shooting."

Faro heard the loose dirt falling down into the grave just before the man's booted feet landed atop the coffin to either side of him.

"Fellow, you're going to look funny without your ear, but I don't guess you'll mind." The man bent over and reached for Faro's head.

Faro's eyes opened wide and the little

push dagger stabbed upward for the man's throat. But the killer lunged backward against the end of the grave and the tip of the small blade only nicked the bottom of his chin.

Faro's heels scrambled madly to get a purchase on the coffin lid and to crab himself backward to the other end of the grave. He lurched to his feet and tried to make out his adversary in the dark. The big Bowie knife had him at too much of a disadvantage for reach, and his only hope was to close. He gritted his teeth against the sharp bite of steel into his flesh that he expected to come and lunged forward.

The killer's knife slid along Faro's side as they crashed together. Faro felt the razor edge grate across his rib bones, but he pinned the man's knife arm against his own side with his left arm. He kept the little dagger low and drove it in hard, and the air rushed out of the assassin's lungs in a sound that was somewhere between a groan and a growl.

Before he could bring the blade home again the man butted him in the forehead. Faro struggled blindly, furious to live, afraid to die, and knowing it was kill or be killed. It took every bit of his will to hang on to that knife arm, and they strained atop the coffin like two mad men in the dark. Savage curses formed on their lips but came out as no more than grunts between ragged gasps of breath. Faro fought to keep his own blade free and drove it into the killer's torso again and again until his muscles trembled and his arm grew numb with fatigue.

Die, you son of a bitch. Die. Faro's knees buckled and he fell backward with the great weight of the assassin's body falling on top of him. The coffin lid splintered and the center caved in, leaving Faro pinned on his back in the V of the broken lid. The killer groaned twice and tried to jerk the Bowie knife free one last time . . . and then he was still and Faro was all but smothered, pinned beneath the dead weight and the bulk of the man.

"Wes, what's taking you so long? You always was slower'n molasses in winter time," the other cutthroat called out, followed by the sound of a cocking pistol.

Faro managed to roll the body off of him and alongside the coffin just as he heard what sounded like horses walking through the grass. He stood on the foot of the coffin, his head barely high enough to peer out of the grave. A bullet struck the pile of excavated earth beside his head, stinging his face with debris.

He fell back into the grave, landing on his hands and knees atop the mangled coffin. Breaking his fall, his hands went through the broken lid and felt the flintlock pistol on his father's chest. He strained frantically to tear the gun free. At any second, that rider was going to look down into the grave and shoot him in the back. He pried at his father's cold, stiff fingers and wanted to shout at him to let go of the weapon.

Come on, Daddy!

The horses sounded like they were right above him, and he gave one last jerk and the pistol came loose from his father's death grip. In the instant before he rolled over onto his back again he said a tiny prayer that the gun was loaded with a bullet and not one of Lettie's wadding blanks.

CHAPTER 8

The horse's head appeared first, and then its rider showed beside it. It took a full second for the rider to make out Faro in the shadows of the grave. He pointed his revolver down into the dark hole at the same time Faro cocked the hammer on the flint-lock and thrust it upward at arm's length. The rusty weapon's flint struck home and the primer pan flashed and hissed. There was a great roar as both their pistols went off simultaneously, and the rider disappeared from view. The cane smoke and the black powder smoke was so thick in the grave that Faro was coughing and all but blind for an instant. His ears strained for more evidence of his attacker's where-abouts, and he soon heard the distinct sound of a body hitting the ground.

After a short wait, he stood and peered over the lip of the grave once more. The two horses had run off, but the man he'd shot lay on the ground not ten feet away.

He struggled out of the grave and crawled over to make sure the man was dead. The cutthroat's face was turned to the light of the cane fire, and it was just enough for Faro to see the neat round hole in his forehead. Faro sat and looked to the flintlock in his lap, and then back at the grave he'd just escaped. *Daddy, I guess I owe you another one. Glad I never could find where you hid your bullets.*

He sat there a long time catching his breath and fighting against the dizziness. Twice, he leaned over to retch and gag until there was nothing left to vomit up but painful dry heaves that made his head hurt even worse. His chin felt as if a mule had kicked him, and he could tell without even probing the wound in the dark that he was cut to the bone along his ribs. The weight of the blood he'd lost sagged his shirt and the waistband of his pants. He wrapped his coat around him, tying it tight with the sleeves to try to stanch the bleeding.

His face burned like it was on fire, and he touched it gingerly with his fingertips. The gunshot he suffered had come so close that his skin was powder-burned along his right jaw. There was also blood all over his chin, and he gently explored a deep cut there with his fingertips and remembered thinking that was where he'd been shot. He still couldn't explain how he'd survived a gunshot to the head at such close range, but there he sat, alive for the moment.

He wanted nothing more than to curl up into a ball and sleep, but people would be arriving for the auction in the morning and all he needed was to be found asleep with three dead bodies and an open grave. He got his good knee under him and lurched to his feet. He took the dead man by the ankles and dragged him alongside the grave.

Sorry, Daddy, it just keeps getting worse. He booted the body over into the hole. *Not that you were ever a saint, but they say Christ died with a thief to either side of him.*

He pitched the killer's hat and pistol into the hole and made a quick search of the ground for any other evidence before taking up his shovel and starting to fill the grave. It took him a long time to perform the burial. He stopped often on his knees in the dirt, leaning on his shovel and waiting for the world to quit spinning. When he finally finished filling the grave, he took up his shovel and raked back a small hole in the mounded earth at the head of the grave and set the end of the wooden tombstone in it. He packed the soil in tight around it with his hands. The fire in the cane field soon faded and he was left in the dark.

He awoke with his face pressed to the cool, damp earth, and his body stiff and aching. His mouth was dry and tasted of bile and guts, and his nose was full of smoke. He pushed himself up and found he had fallen asleep on the mound of the grave. The sky was already turning gray with the coming morning.

He took one last look at the little oak tombstone. Jethro had carved Faro's father's name and birth and death dates deep into the hardwood with a chisel. In time, even the oak would rot, but it was a pretty tombstone. Faro started for the house.

He noticed the hoofprints on the lawn and hoped that the horses had run back to their home and weren't hanging around the plantation to be found by someone looking for their owners. By the time he got to the toolshed it was coming on to real daylight. He was hanging the shovel on the wall of the shed when he noticed the bullet dent in metal. Thinking back, he could only guess that he'd flinched and thrown up the shovel in front of him when he turned around at the grave and saw the cutthroat aiming a pistol at him. The bullet must have ricocheted off the metal, driving it into his chin and knocking him senseless into the grave. Or something like that. Whatever the case, the shovel got shot and he didn't, and it was safe to say that he was alive by only the slimmest of margins. Lady Luck was a finicky, unpredictable bitch most times.

He built a fire in the basin of the forge in the blacksmith shed, and cranked the blower, feeding oxygen to the fire until the coal glowed red-hot. Stripping out of his bloody, tattered clothes, he pitched them on the fire and left them to burn. He walked to the well and pumped water over his head until he felt somewhat better. The burden of the pail he filled afterward tore at the cut in his wounded side as he carried it to the carriage house.

He washed the grime and blood away from his body as best he could, paying special attention to the knife wound over his ribs. After a bit of searching he located a needle and some heavy waxed thread used for mending harnesses. He rubbed the needle on the stone foundation at the foot of the wall until he'd ground a sharp point on it before threading a foot of thread through the eye. He then went to the sewn-up old boot top tacked to the wall that was supposed to hold a hoof pick and a horse brush. He reached down into it until his fingers felt the pint bottle at the bottom. Good old Jethro, you could always count on him to have a bottle stashed in his standard hiding places. He held up the bottle before his eyes and swirled the little bit of dark liquid in the bottom. It looked as if his medical supplies were pretty limited.

He doused the open wound in his side with a healthy dose of rum and then poured a trickle over the needle. He put a snort down his gullet, not for the pain, but just for the fun of it. The rum was nasty and burned his stomach about as bad as it did the knife wound. He gagged twice, but managed to keep the liquor down. There was some kind of justice in the fact that the liquor was almost as painful as being cut.

Taking a seat in a chair with the needle held between his teeth, he took hold of the open wound between his fingers and pressed it closed. Sewing himself up was going to hurt like hell, but all he needed was a doctor asking questions about how he'd come to be knifed and beaten. He ran the needle through both lips of the wound in the center of the cut and tied a simple double over-handed knot.

He was right; it hurt like hell. He took another slug of rum and made a second crude stitch. It still hurt, but running the needle through his skin got easier as he went, as if his body could only register so much pain. He managed eight stitches before his hands got so shaky he couldn't tie a knot. Another dose of rum didn't make him feel any better.

He soused the wound one more time, and the liquor ran down his naked side tinted with pink streaks of blood seeping from the sutures. The flesh along the knife cut was puckered in places where he failed to get the skin lined up properly, but he was satisfied and kind of proud of the operation. It was going to make a nasty scar, but he'd seen worse jobs done by army doctors and scars weren't anything new to him.

Carrying his boots, his pistol, and his knee brace, he crossed the lawn again and went into the house. He would have liked a hot bath but didn't have the energy to carry the water to fill the tub. He settled for scrubbing his face from a pitcher of water Lettie had left on his bedroom vanity, and glanced at his face in the mirror.

It was going to be a long while before he would even be presentable. The right side of his face was red and raw and specked with tiny black dots, but he didn't think it was so bad that it wouldn't heal quickly. The inch-long gash in his chin should have been sewn up too, but he didn't relish sticking himself any more. Along with his cuts and abrasions was a knot on his forehead that was going to make his hat sit funny for a few days. All in all, there had been days when he looked much better.

He bandaged his ribs with strips torn from his bedsheets and brushed the dirt out of his hair. He put on a fresh suit and buckled his knee brace in place before tugging into a pair of well-polished, high-topped black cavalry boots.

Somebody shouted outside, but he ignored them and took a leather valise and stuffed it with some extra clothes. Far in the back of his closet, he found his steamer trunk covered in cobwebs and a thick layer of dust. He dragged it to the center of the room and opened the lid. Rummaging through it, he set aside a brass-buttoned army uniform, pulled out an oilcloth bundle, and laid it on the bed and unrolled it until a holstered pistol was revealed. It was a .44 Walker Colt — a four-and-a-half-pound cannon made of dark blue and case-hardened steel. A normal charge for each chamber was fifty grains of black powder, and they were stout enough to take more than that. Beside the horse pistol was a coffin-handled, Sheffield-made Bowie knife in a crude deerskin sheath.

Faro rolled the weapons back up and put them in the valise with his clothes. He rummaged inside the trunk again and took out binoculars and a leather shoulder pouch containing a bullet mold and the makings for charging the pistol. He bagged those items before tossing aside a pair of worn-out moccasins and a few other souvenirs from his years out West. Finally, he found what he sought most — a little glass vial containing a gold nugget the size of his middle fingernail and half the thickness of a silver dollar. It was the first gold he ever found in California, and he tucked the vial into his jacket pocket and closed the lid on the trunk.

Shoving his Colt Pocket revolver in the leather holster at his waistband, he set a low-crowned, John Bull top hat on his head. He picked up his valise and took one last look in the mirror. The hat was the last new one he owned, and he had been saving it for a special occasion. He didn't feel particularly special at the moment, but he had to admit he rarely was cut and shot in the same night. Surviving that was certainly something worth celebrating. He tipped his hat to himself in the mirror. *Aren't you a dashing fellow? You look like something the dogs dragged in.*

Downstairs, he took up his cane and waved good-bye to the bear. "So long, sport."

There were already several people wandering the grounds looking things over, and more buggies and horsemen were coming up the drive to the auction. The high sheriff stood at the foot of the porch with a parish clerk and Faro's banker. The banker looked at him over his reading glasses and nodded before looking back to the ledgers the clerk was showing him.

"Morning," Faro said.

The banker was a little man, with a reputation for a lack of humor, especially where money was concerned. He looked at Faro with eyes that were stronger than his stature, and more fitted to a highwayman. "I don't suppose it's a good morning for you."

"Let's keep it civil," the sheriff said.

Faro paused at the foot of the porch steps. "It's all yours, Sheriff."

The lawman spat a stream of black tobacco juice on the ground and pointed a finger at the fresh mound of earth that marked the grave under the oak tree far across the lawn. "Your father?"

Faro nodded.

"Sorry to hear about him," the sheriff

brushed at some spittle that had managed to land on his string tie instead of the ground. "You look like somebody beat the hell out of you."

"You ought to see the other guy," Faro said.

The sheriff acted a little uneasy. "You aren't going to give us any trouble today, are you? I know how these foreclosure auctions can be."

"No trouble, Sheriff." Faro hefted his valise. "I've got my personal effects here, and whoever buys the rest of this place is welcome to it."

"Well, I hate to see you hit hard times, but I'm glad you won't give me any trouble."

Faro put a hand to the brim of his hat and started to leave when Fontenot, the slave trader from the card game the night before, walked up.

"Where are your slaves?" Fontenot asked.

"Slaves?" Faro gave him a dumb look.

"Yeah, the auction paper lists two house slaves and three field hands."

Faro looked around the yard. "They must be around here somewhere."

"I hope you didn't sell them. According to the court, they were to be disbursed to settle your debts," the banker butted in. The mention of missing property had his attention.

"I haven't seen them since yesterday evening," Faro said.

The slave trader was suspicious. "I came all this way to look at those niggers."

"I hate that for you, Fontenot. I really do. But maybe you and the sheriff and your banker buddy here can find them." Faro kept a straight face. "As for me, I think I'll run off before you boys decide to sell me too."

"Don't go too far, Faro. The sheriff might want to talk to you if we can't find those slaves," the banker said.

"Just look me up if you need me." Faro tipped his hat again to the smug banker and the frowning slave trader and started down the driveway.

Once on the main road, he turned back to look down the long row of oaks one last time. He could hear the auctioneer beginning to sell the first item. After a few hours of his chanting and whacking the gavel, Faro was officially going to be a property-less and penniless man. He lifted his hand to the plantation in parting, as if saying good-bye to an old friend. A mule-drawn cane wagon soon came along and he managed to hitch a ride. He did some thinking, but he never looked back all the way to the city.

CHAPTER 9

"Your face looks positively awful, Monsieur Wells. I didn't take you for a brawler." Rue smoothed the lap of her dress. "You seem, well . . . a little more civilized than that."

Faro took a seat in the very same chair he'd occupied two mornings earlier. "There was a disagreement, and it got a little out of hand."

"If he was any kind of brawler, his face wouldn't look like that," Zula McGaffney gave Faro one brief glance and then started examining her fingernails.

"I take it you've changed your mind and decided to help us." Rue rolled her eyes at her sister and shrugged at him.

"Maybe, but first off, let me get something out of the way," he said. "I want ten percent of the gold if I can get your treasure out of New Mexico."

"That's quite a share, Monsieur Wells," Rue said.

Faro leaned back in the chair and laced the fingers of both hands together over his chest. "Call me Faro, and I won't do it for a penny less. You might say I value my life pretty highly."

"I'll say," Zula said.

"That's my price," Faro said. "Take it or leave it."

"You're seriously going to discuss this?" Zula sighed like a spoiled child and flounced around in her chair and refused to look at him. "Ten percent of our gold for simply acting as a guide?"

"I get ten percent of whatever is there. You don't have any gold — not until you get it in the bank. It's just a gamble, and I'll be gambling along with you."

"What do you say, Zula? I think we should pay him his price," Rue said.

"He can fall in the river for all I care," Zula muttered.

"That's Zula's way of saying yes." Rue frowned at her sister. "How much gold do you think Father meant when he said there was forty loads of it?"

Her question got Zula's undivided attention, even if she tried to act like she wasn't paying them any attention.

"There's no telling. We'll have to wait and see when we get there," he said. "We'll load our mules lightly, say fifty pounds. We might need to travel fast. In fact, I'd say it's a guarantee that we'll have to run more than once before our trip is over."

"Are you still determined to do this alone?" Rue asked.

"I'd like to have an army to go with us, but that's the way it has got to be. There are few we could hire that I'd trust. Maybe I can find a man or two on our way west. Maybe not."

"Zula and Armand and I go with you, or no deal."

He thought her a silly woman who didn't have a clue what she was getting herself into, but he couldn't really blame her. He started to try to bluff her, but his gut told him that it wouldn't work. If it was his gold, he'd be damned if he'd trust anybody to go after it without him.

"All right, but don't say I didn't warn you."

"Would you like to have a contract drawn up?"

"Just how much good do you think a piece of paper is going to be worth when we're a thousand miles from the nearest settlement and with gold to tempt us and no lawyers or lawmen around? And do you want anyone else to know about your gold? Lawyers, especially?"

"Fair enough. Done deal. That wasn't so hard."

"It will get that way," he said. "Just give it time."

"When do we start?"

"Pack your things and be ready by daylight tomorrow."

"You work fast," Zula said. In contrast to Rue's anxious excitement, she looked positively bored.

"Pack lightly and with a mind on rugged travel. You won't be going to any dances or socials for a long time."

Zula rolled her eyes at him and hissed through her teeth. "Oh, Lord, I'm glad we poor little women have a big strong man like you to take care of us."

"We'll be ready," Rue said.

"With bells on," Zula added.

"What about the rest of the directions to go with the map? I can't very well guide you if I don't know exactly where we're going."

"We'll keep the rest of the map until you need it," Rue said firmly. "It's enough now for you to know that we need to get to Santa Fe. Once there, I'll give you the rest of the directions."

Faro didn't like it, but he had to admit it

was pretty cautious. "One more thing, I need the eggs to start outfitting us today."

"You just don't know when to quit, do you?" Zula asked. "I guess this is the part where we're supposed to give you the golden eggs and you walk away and we never see you again. Nice try."

Faro counted to three, waiting for patience to come to him. "If you can't trust me with that little bit of gold, you'll never trust me with forty loads of the same stuff."

Rue picked up a purse from the floor beside her chair and set it on the table with a clank and clink of the coins in it. She opened the purse and counted out roughly a third of the money and shoved it across the table to him. "That should do for a start."

It was plain from the look on Zula's face that she was shocked. "Where did you get that?"

Rue smiled coyly. "I sold the eggs yesterday."

Faro studied her, feeling that he may have underestimated her. "You plan ahead."

"I wasn't sure that you'd accept my offer, but I was sure that someone would." She stared back at him with a poker face that would have worked well over a riverboat card table. "Understand me, Monsieur

Wells, I mean to have my gold, and I will do whatever it takes to get it."

"Our gold," Zula said.

"Our gold," Rue repeated.

Faro put the money in his pocket and stood. "I'd best be going. We need to get out of New Orleans, and fast."

"What do you mean?" Rue asked.

"It won't be long until everyone in this city knows that there are two young women with a lot of gold."

"Don't be so melodramatic. I sold the eggs very discreetly to our banker, and he assured me that he would keep the matter quiet."

"You can't keep gold quiet." He started for the door but had second thoughts and stopped across the room. "I've got a lot to do, so do you think you could buy us tickets on the *Dixie Belle*? She's starting up-river tomorrow. I understand that she's to stop at Arkansas Post to unload goods, and that we might transfer to a smaller vessel there and go on up the Arkansas to Fort Smith."

"I can do that," Rue said.

"So, you decided to listen to me and take the river route to Arkansas?" Zula didn't try to hide her smugness. "Maybe you've got more sense than I gave you credit for."

"Maybe, or maybe I'm just thinking we need to get out of New Orleans in a hurry."

CHAPTER 10

The banker straightened his desktop before leaning back in his office chair to stare over his folded hands and half-lensed glasses at the man who had just walked through the door. There was something about the one before him that he almost envied — not quite, but almost. And it wasn't the black leather eye patch nor the bulge of the pistol barely concealed within the man's coat that impressed him. He'd seen plenty of tough, dangerous sorts come and go over the years while amassing his fortune. But this man was different — still a thug, but with some little something that set him apart.

The banker watched as his visitor took a seat and tossed his hat on the floor beside his chair. He was wraith-thin, with a bony face and hollow cheeks. There was something nasty about him, despite the fancy suit he wore, the smell of cologne, and a hint of fine manners, like a once-magnificent house overgrown with weeds and sagging in disrepair. His greasy hair hung about his bony shoulders like Spanish moss, and the fingernails at the ends of his slender fingers were blackened at the tips.

Yet, it wasn't the subtle filth of the man that both intrigued and repulsed. It came to the banker at that very moment as he stared at the man and noticed the impudent look on the slash of his thin-lipped mouth. It was death there in that one-eyed face — that and merciless, calculated efficiency.

The banker understood and respected efficiency. Neat columns and rows of numbers always led to an accurate count. But the man across from him didn't work in ledgers. No, his was another sort of efficiency. When you asked him to kill somebody, they died. And all that death had marked him. Yes, King Broulet had the mark of Cain upon him — death and mayhem in the flesh. Sitting across the desk from him was like being close to the Grim Reaper.

"It took you long enough," the banker said.

King Broulet propped his right ankle on his left thigh and flicked a wad of mud from his shoe onto the floor. He leaned back in the chair and twisted his head slightly to put the banker into better focus with his one eye. "Thought it was better to wait until after closing time. Nighttime suits me better anyway."

The banker lowered his hands to the desktop and began to drum his fingers on the wood. "You should know by now that I only send for you when it's urgent."

"You only send for me when there's money to be made, or when you want me to play dirty for you," King said flatly.

"I . . ."

King held up a pointer finger and waved it slowly back and forth. "I assume you brought me here to talk about the gold."

The banker kept drumming his fingers while he gathered his thoughts. King had a few loyal minions to aid him in his work, but there was no way he should know about the gold. "What gold?"

King slung his hair back behind his shoulders with a quick jerk of his head. "Don't play coy with me. Zula McGaffney told me that her father left her a gold mine."

"And why would she tell you, of all people?"

One corner of the slim killer's mouth lifted in what might have been meant as a smile. "She's liable to say the most profound things when I stick my cock into her."

The banker frowned. "Your vulgarities are

ever entertaining, but you're wasting your time and mine. It seems we both know that the girl has a modest inheritance that we might take advantage of."

"Modest? Come now. I roughed up the sisters' housemaid on the sly, and she told me she had overhead a far different story. How about forty loads of golden eggs? Do you trust me so little, or don't you know?"

The banker tried to hide his surprise at the added bit of information. The day before, Rue McGaffney had brought the banker three curiously shaped gold ingots to sell for her. What was of more interest to him was the notion that Rue McGaffney was up to something and trying to gather money for whatever it was. He had taken drafts for deposit over the years from the McGaffneys' bank in New York and was aware that the money came from the supposed mining finds of their father. Some of those drafts had been for healthy sums. That knowledge gave him ample reason to believe that there might be more of those odd golden eggs, but King's assurance that there was a *lot* of gold was more than he'd hoped for.

"Forty loads?" The banker didn't realize that his voice had lowered almost to a whisper.

"Why, you look positively pale at the thought of something you don't know." King's laugh came from far down in his throat, more like a croak. His deep voice seemed odd coming from such a scarecrow of a man.

"Tell me more."

"She hinted that she and her sister might hire someone to take her to it," King said. "She's thinks she's being crafty, but she'll play along with me or I'll cut her pretty throat."

The banker took a quick glance at the little pistol in the partially open drawer beside his right leg. He had to appear confident and in control, because there was nobody in the bank but the two of them and King's kind could smell weakness as quickly as a hound sniffed out a fresh trail. "I did some checking, and it seems that Rue McGaffney has been asking around town for a man that might know something of mining."

"She tried to hire Faro Wells, but I took care of that," King said.

It did the banker good to hear that he knew something King didn't. "I'd say you did a poor job. I saw Faro yesterday morning, and it looks like your boys didn't quite get it done."

King's cool vanished in an instant. "I'll have to handle that myself if he tries to meddle in this."

"It shocks me that you haven't handled that yourself long before now, considering the grudge you have."

"I've been busy, but I might have to make some spare time. He won't be any trouble, and the girl neither."

"Kidnapping or torturing a lady isn't something that will go unnoticed in this town, much less killing one. That isn't the smart way to play it. If we have to get rough, let's wait until they're away from New Orleans."

King's eye blinked a couple of times. "You're doing a lot of planning, but what makes you think I'm going to partner with you?"

"Because, you wouldn't be here if you didn't need me. I've got the money to outfit you and to pay the men you'll need. You aren't going to haul that much gold around without some help, not unless you don't want to keep it for long."

"I suppose you want things to be divided on the usual cut?"

"I'm feeling generous."

"By feeling generous, do you mean that you'll let me do all the killing and the work while you get the lion's share?"

"Getting that gold is going to cost a lot of money, and I want a sufficient return on the investment I'm making."

King stood and walked around the end of the desk to the bookshelf lining the wall behind the banker's desk. His hand brushed lovingly over the books there.

The banker didn't like King being behind him, and he was sure that the killer was purposely trying to intimidate him. He eased his hand closer to the pistol in the drawer. "Where else are you going to get the money to pull this deal off?"

King continued to look over the books until he slid out a copy of Herodotus' *Histories.* "Do you read history?"

"What the hell has that got to do with our business?"

King didn't seem to hear him. "Ever read about the Visigoths? Herodotus said they were a Scythian or Germanic tribe, and I've read elsewhere that they fought the Romans and later ended up fighting for them. Mercenaries. Did that for years, living and dying under the thumb of those caesars and senators using and abusing them."

"Are you just showing off that you can read? Reminding me where you came from? That you're still the southern gentleman?"

"It's nothing; nothing at all. I was just talking about history," King slid the book back into its place on the shelf and stopped at the end of the desk with his back to the banker, "I don't think you're so smart."

"Are you threatening me, or is this your way of bargaining for a bigger cut?"

"You know, you ought to keep your safe door closed," King said in a whisper. "I would venture to say that you might have more than enough in there to fund my treasure hunt."

The banker slid his hand inside the drawer, his fingers finding the pistol without looking at it. Despite his caution, he didn't see the knife that appeared in King's hand as if by magic, even though it was a long knife with a wicked double edge. King pivoted and nonchalantly buried the knife in the banker's throat and left it there, standing over him while he flopped on his back, choking and grasping the knife handle protruding from his flesh.

When the banker ceased to twitch, King plucked a handkerchief from his victim's breast pocket and used it to pull his bloody knife free and to wipe it clean. He went to the little safe with its door slightly ajar at the end of the bookshelf. There wasn't much in it but documents, but the single, heavy bag of coins on top of them caused a brief grunt of pleasure to issue from his lungs when he hefted it.

He sucked at a piece of meat stuck in his yellowed teeth, holding the money bag against his leg while he leaned over close to study Roy's face.

"There, now that's better," King said. "It's time a Goth took over."

CHAPTER 11

Faro crossed the street and headed toward the door tucked at the end of a narrow alleyway on the west side of Canal Street. The buildings in that part of the city were newer, if lacking the charm and beauty of the French Quarter. Some of the newcomers and fresh money in New Orleans found the older part of the city too mildewed and ancient for their tastes and had built up the west side of Canal Street until it outstripped the older part of the city along the river.

There was a painted sign on the door proudly proclaiming the modest establishment as a gun shop. Whoever had done the painting hadn't bothered with using stencils for the lettering, and had decidedly bad penmanship and a shaky hand. Faro chuckled. Sgt. Prometheus Pyle had never been much for a fancy appearance, and it was almost a shock that the words on the sign were correctly spelled, considering the one-time Kentucky backwoodsman thought you spelled "cat" with a "k." But he did know more about guns than any man Faro had ever met, and what's more, he had been to New Mexico back before the Mexican War.

"Hello, Sarge," Faro said to the rotund, balding little man in a shop apron hunkered over a workbench at the far end of the small room.

Sarge took his attention away from the rifle he was working on and looked up through his bushy eyebrows and scowled. "Look what the cat dragged in."

Faro ignored the jab and went across the room to where one entire wall was lined with long guns standing side by side on their butt plates. He tossed his cane on a short, glass display case containing pistols for sale, and took down a Colt revolving carbine and put it to his shoulder and aimed at an imaginary target on the wall.

"You never did know anything about guns." Sarge rose from his stool and hobbled over, his peg leg thumping on the floor.

"That's a hell of a thing to say. I saved your ass once with a fine rifle shot."

"You still had a little luck back then, but you couldn't do it again in a thousand years." Sarge pulled the carbine from Faro's hands. "And I've never forgiven you for not shooting that Mexican quicker before he hacked me off at the knee."

"It took me a while to get my aim."

"You just can't shoot for shit." Sarge put the gun back in its place and took down a '53 Sharps carbine from the rack. "Here, that Colt carbine looks fancy, but this Sharps breechloader shoots straighter. She doesn't have the primer feeder that the newer models do and she kicks a might, but she's a .52 caliber and will put down a buffalo."

Faro didn't even take the gun Sarge was offering him for examination. "All right, sold."

"Big shot, high roller, eh? You really must've been a winner last night."

Faro considered that. "It's going to be a while before I can tell, but I might be onto a good hand. I'll take two of those shotguns there too, but I want you to saw off the barrels."

Sarge ran a hand down the lovely, double Damascus steel barrels of one of the English shotguns. He frowned at Faro as if mutilating the original condition of such a fine weapon was sacrilege.

"Don't look at me like that. I want you to cut them off just past the forearms and shorten the butt stock about an inch on both of them," Faro said.

"Why not just buy a coach gun if you want a short scattergun?"

"You don't have any coach guns for sale and I'm in a hurry."

"It'll be a few weeks before I can get them finished."

"I don't have a few weeks."

"You're some piece of work," Sarge said. "Are you forgetting that you ain't my lieutenant anymore?"

"I need them now. Just hack off the barrels and stocks. I don't care how your work looks as long as the shotguns are short enough to be handy," Faro said. "And give me those two Colt Navys there, and bullet molds, and makings, and whatever else I need for a long trip."

"You taking up road agent work to offset your gambling habits?"

"I'm nervous, and enough guns lying around make me sleep better," Faro said.

Sarge was already laying out the guns on top of the pistol counter. He slid another pistol out of the case and held it up between them. "I bought this Colt Army off the widow of a Yankee officer who didn't come back from a duel down under the oaks."

"Doesn't sound like a gun I'd recommend. I'd say it was already poorly trained."

Faro scowled at the revolver, his mind on other things.

"It's a good gun. Nothing matches a Navy's balance, but a nervous man might want a bigger caliber than a .36 or that mouse pistol I see you're still carrying beneath your coat."

Faro waved one hand absentmindedly at the gunsmith. He was already busy sketching with his right pointer finger on the dusty glass top of the display case. He considered his work for a minute, made a few changes and additions from memory, and then looked at Sarge. "What do you make of that?"

"What's it supposed to be?"

"It's a map."

"Well, how am I going to know what it's a map of if I don't know the name of at least one point on it?"

Faro put his thumb down on the glass and twisted it before lifting it again. "There, that's Santa Fe."

Sarge pursed his lips and quietly looked at the crude sketch. He pointed out a few of the marks and reference points on Faro's map. "Then I'd say this here is Fort Union. These pointy marks at the top are most likely the Sangre de Cristo Mountains and the southern end of the Rockies. Those two

117

wavy lines to the south should be the headwaters of the Pecos and the Rio Grande. The other two rivers coming in from the east could be the Canadian and the Cimarron, or maybe some branch of the Arkansas."

"Most likely?"

"Can't tell for sure. You can't draw any better than you can shoot," Sarge said. "What's this map for?"

Faro moved his thumb and made an X in the middle of the mountains. "It's supposed to lead me to a lot of gold."

" 'X' marks the spot, eh? You don't smell like you've been drinking."

"I'm cold sober." Faro gave Sarge a quick run-down of the McGaffney sisters' situation.

"And those women won't tell you exactly where the gold is at?" Sarge asked.

"They're playing it safe until we get in the general vicinity. You want to go with me?" Faro lifted his left foot off of the floor and flexed his bad knee a time or two to work the stiffness out. "You in or out? I'm leaving in the morning."

"Ain't we a crippled pair?" Sarge asked. "If we'd found one more mad Mexican, it might have been the end of us."

Faro nodded grimly, thinking about the

gold, but also thinking about the day on the trail so many years earlier, in a mountain pass called Cerro Gordo. The hard-pressed Mexican army had opened up with a pair of little brass cannons on the patrol he was leading. The first ball went over their heads, and the second one killed Sarge's horse. Sarge was trying to untangle himself from the carnage of the dead animal when a thin line of farmer volunteers in straw sombreros and white cotton peon uniforms came charging down the trail right at him. Some of them had ancient muskets with bayonets almost the length of a man's arm, and some of them only had machetes. He got free of the horse just in time for one of those farmers to give him a lick in the knee with a machete. The Mexican was about to give him more than that when Faro shot him between the eyes.

"I'm too damned old and my stump pains me too much to go traipsing to New Mexico again," Sarge said. "Besides, I never found anything but trouble when I was out there the first time. I ended up trading my saddle horse to a butcher in Santa Fe for something to eat, and then took a job with an ox train just to get back to the Missouri."

"I found gold out West," Faro said.

"Yeah, and where's it at now? And how

much good's it done you? I think I'll just stay here and tend to my shop and leave all the fun for you."

"I need help. Good, steady men like you."

"Do you realize what you'll most likely to be up against?"

"Never said it would be easy. Somebody already tried to have me killed me the other night, and I heard one of them mention he was working for a man called King."

Sarge made a show of acting like he'd just noticed Faro's battered face, although he didn't hide the fact that he thought it was funny. "I thought maybe you slept in too late, and her husband showed up when he wasn't supposed to."

"What about this King?"

"You know who he is. You just don't want to admit it."

"Oh, that King."

"Yeah, that King, the Black Knight himself. You know, one-eyed, Creole fellow," Sarge said. "His family never was worth killing, especially after they went broke. Most don't do much worse than spend all their time trying to act like they're still rich, but King Broulet's meaner than all of them put together. He was bad enough before he decided to turn highwayman."

"The Broulet name's ringing a bell with

me for some other reason, even though there are enough by that name in this city that it shouldn't."

"It damned well should," Sarge said. "Whether you know it or not, you killed one of them."

It was Faro's turn to frown.

Sarge tapped his thumb on his chest, right over his heart. "His name wasn't Broulet, but you shot King's cousin right through the boiler with a dueling pistol, which, considering things, makes two lucky shots you shouldn't ever count on doing again."

"Byron Duphont was a liar, a poor card cheat, and fool enough to take offense when I caught him thumb-nailing an ace," Faro said. "I thought the matter done with, but the damned fool posted my name in the newspaper and a coward was the nicest thing he called me. It was a fair fight that I did everything I could to avoid."

"Well, that may be true, but King won't see it that way, distant cousin or not, and he doesn't have any honor and he doesn't forget who's made him mad. He'll shoot you just for fun."

"Sounds like a dangerous fellow."

"Scoff and smirk if you want to. Before King was blackballed among high society, he hung out down at Crokere's dueling school with all the other young dandies. They say his parents sent him to Paris when he was a lad to learn the rapier, and he whipped the *maître d'armes* every time they sparred with the blades. I hear he used to shoot coins out of his cronies' fingers with a dueling pistol just to show off."

"I'll keep an eye out for him."

"King's killed thirteen men in duels, but the word is that certain gentlemen in power have vowed to hang him if he dares fight another duel in New Orleans. So, he might be working other angles when it comes to you. Gold's a pretty good motivator, you know."

"I'll cross that bridge when I come to it." In truth, Faro wasn't as certain and confident as he tried to sound. King's men had come very close to killing him already, and everything about King sounded as if he might be an even worse proposition if he showed up in person.

Sarge could see that Faro was mulling things over and not liking the conclusions he was coming to. "King's bandit work has knocked him too far off his social pedestal for him to be making formal challenges. And he won't come alone if he can get a chance to catch you on the trail. They say he's got a gang of river pirates and knife men that specialize in taking what isn't theirs and leaving no witness behind to tell tales."

"If he's so bad, how come he's walking free?"

"Nobody's caught him at it. His family may be broke, but they've got just enough connections to the right people to keep the questions about his criminal activities to a minimum."

"I wish you would go with me. I don't know many that I could trust, and this deal gets harder by the minute."

"That's an understatement. You're going to get yourself killed, plain as that," Sarge said. "You remember the last time you started making plans around a woman? That like to have killed you, and she didn't even have any gold."

"Maybe you're right, but I could still use a good man or two to help me."

"You don't need an old one-legged soldier. You need an army and more luck than you've shown since you came back from California, but maybe I can help you out for old time's sake." Sarge turned his head toward the back of the room to the open door there and shouted, "Hey, kid, come in here."

Before too long, a gangly boy in homespun

clothes with a ratty hat on his head walked in. His hair was cut short, although it was plain that he was a whole lot Indian, even if Faro hadn't noticed that the boy was wearing moccasins.

"This here's Jim Tall Tree," Sarge said around the stem of the pipe he was trying to light. "He's Cherokee. Damn good worker, and claims to be a good horseman, although I've never seen him on anything other than shank's mare. I have seen him shoot, though, and he's brought me plenty of wild game when I loan him a gun."

"That right, Jim? Are you good with horses?" Faro asked.

"I am."

"What about mules? Do you know anything about them?" Faro asked. "I'm going west, and I could use a boy like you to tend my stock on the trail."

"I know mules."

"How old are you?"

"Seventeen."

Sarge puffed a couple more clouds of smoke out of one corner of his mouth, drawing so hard on his pipe that it made little hissing sounds. "He showed up here one day fresh off of the river, half starved and looking for work. I put him to cleaning up and giving me an extra hand when I

124

needed it."

"Are you game to go to New Mexico and back?" Faro tried his best to stare down the kid.

"I'm game," the boy said.

"How's a dollar a day and food sound to you, and I outfit you with what you'll need?" Faro asked. "And I'll give you two dollars a day once we get to New Mexico."

"What's my job, besides tending stock?"

"You'll be my bodyguard." Faro was a little put out that the boy didn't seem fazed by the danger he mentioned, and he thought it wouldn't hurt to try and scare him a little more. The kid looked young to be going with him.

"What if you get killed, who's going to pay me then?"

Faro made his mind up right then. "Have you been listening outside the door?"

The boy kept a straight face. "I have, at least I heard you talking about all that gold and that Black Knight fellow."

"You're smarter than you look. A boy that wouldn't eavesdrop has no curiosity to him, and I don't like dumb boys." Faro noticed that the kid was almost as tall as he. It was the fact that he was so gangly that made him appear smaller and younger than he was — all hands and feet sticking out of

125

clothes that were too small for him.

"You don't look like a guide and scout," the boy said. "I never worked for a man that wears purple coats."

"Well, Jim Tall Tree, you don't look like a bodyguard either, but come with me."

Faro looked over the bill Sarge held out for him and retrieved his wallet and counted out the coin. "There's no way guns should be that high."

"Good guns are getting harder to come by with the war going on. Be glad you got them," Sarge said as he put the money in the pocket of his apron. "And I stuck you some bullet molds and extra lead in the sack, plenty of Sharps fodder, percussion caps, and four pounds of black powder. I think you might need them."

"Good luck, Sarge." Faro held out his hand.

"Good luck to you. You're the one who's going to need it," Sarge shook Faro's hand, "Speaking of the war, your old friend Sibley was in the shop just two days ago."

"The Colonel?"

"He's a general now," Sarge said. "Seems like Jeff Davis himself promoted him to command troops in Texas."

"Was he sober?"

"Just drunk enough to talk more than he

should, and for me to figure out he's fixing to invade New Mexico."

Faro's grin made him look younger than his thirty-eight years. "That might be something to think on."

Sarge cornered a palmetto bug beneath the rifle rack and smashed it with his wooden leg. "Thought it might be."

The boy was still standing in the same place with a bland look on his face. Faro took up the Colt Army from where Sarge had left it on the counter. He pitched it across the room and the boy caught it.

"Load that and put it in your belt and meet me at midnight with the guns where the river road passes the north side of Bayou Black. Do you know where that's at?"

"No, but I'll be there."

"Good, Jim. I think I'm going to like you."

Faro nodded to Sarge and took up his cane and went out the door. He was feeling pretty chipper, even if he was busy trying to get himself killed.

The boy was left standing in the middle of the room. After Faro was long gone he turned to Sarge. "I don't know if I should've agreed to go with him."

Sarge grunted. "No, probably not. Fact is, I ain't liable to lay eyes on either one of you again."

127

"I wish I had me some fancy clothes like he was wearing. And he's about the purtiest-smelling man I ever came across."

Sarge grunted again. "Yeah, Faro's partial to his toilet water and highfalutin clothes. Always says that, if nothing else, he's going to leave behind a good-lookin' corpse."

CHAPTER 12

"I still don't understand why you're dragging us around in the middle of the night." Rue McGaffney rubbed at her sleepy eyes and clutched at the side of the open-topped carriage rocking and bouncing over the rough road.

There wasn't a cloud in the sky and the moon was bright, and none of that was to Faro's liking. "You hired me to do a job, and I'm doing it."

"We were supposed to leave by riverboat tomorrow morning." It was the first thing Zula had passed his way, other than a scowl or a hateful glare, since he'd shown up at their home and dragged them from their sleep.

"Call it a change of plans." Faro had his mind on the road ahead, and the roadside stretches where timber and swamp pressed in close and provided good places for ambush.

"Just because we hired you doesn't give you the right to make decisions without consulting us," Rue said.

"Just being cautious."

"I'd say you're being paranoid to the point you don't even trust us."

"I trust you some, but not enough to have any faith that you wouldn't slip and tell someone that we were taking the *Dixie Belle* upriver. It won't hurt at all to have anyone wanting the gold watching that riverboat while we go elsewhere."

"You seem to be well versed in the ways of deceit, Monsieur Wells," Rue said. "I don't know whether that means I've picked the right man, or that I should be worried about you."

"Worrying might do you and your sister both some good," Faro said.

"*Pas bon.* This is no good," Armand said, his chin thrust out and challenging the shadows at the edge of the road. "No good at all."

Faro wasn't surprised that Armand could speak English, nor that the first time he did it was to complain. He seemed a sour man. But Faro wasn't about to get his ears clipped voicing that opinion, and if the Cajun bodyguard was as tough as he appeared he might come in handy.

Faro had his own doubts about his decision to leave New Orleans in the dark by another route. Maybe he was being paranoid, but his experience told him that things would probably turn out worse than anything he could imagine. And being too cautious wouldn't hurt anything. Too many times he'd played the game of life too loosely, and he didn't intend to let a chance at a fortune slip out of his hands because he did so again.

The Cherokee boy stepped out in the middle of the road like a ghost, and the taxi driver pulled hard on the reins of his spooked team. The boy ignored the two horses rearing and sidestepping in front of him and went past them and opened the door to the taxi.

Faro noticed that the boy had the guns rolled up in an oilcloth under one of his arms and a flour sack duffel hanging from his other hand. He studied the road in each direction as he got down to stand beside the kid. "Has there been anybody by here?"

"Four or five riders went by half an hour ago, but it's been quiet as death since then."

Faro helped the women down from the taxi, and he and Armand unloaded their traveling gear before they motioned the driver on. The carriage managed to half-circle in the narrow road, and the five of them waited silently until it was gone. The big Cajun had a rolled blanket tied behind his back with a piece of rope, and he took up the handle of his own bag in one big fist and both of the ladies' in the other. He stood there waiting like his load weighed nothing. The scar-headed bruiser was as strong as an ox. It had been quite a fight to lighten the women's baggage down to so few things, despite his earlier warning to them to travel light. They had managed to narrow their luggage down to one valise apiece, but each one must have weighed fifty pounds.

"Jim, you and Armand follow behind us and keep an eye on our back trail." Faro led them along the road for a few minutes, and then turned off on a trail leading through the timber in the direction of the bayou.

They were only a few yards from the road when the sound of trotting horses became plain.

"You hear that, Mr. Faro?" Jim whispered.

"I hear it. Be quiet."

Zula McGaffney stopped in the trail and looked back. "The hour isn't so late, and I'm sure that there are many travelers along the river road. I don't see any reason to . . ."

Faro wrapped an arm around her shoulders and stopped whatever else she was going to say with his other hand over her mouth. She struggled fiercely for a moment, trying to break away and talking into his palm.

"Maybe so, but I'd just as soon you kept quiet," Faro whispered into her ear.

Zula twisted her face to him but stopped her struggles. It wasn't long before Faro noticed that she seemed to push closer to him and thought maybe his imagination was running away with itself, considering that one of her breasts felt uncommonly good against him. He jerked his hand away when he felt the tip of her tongue swirling in his palm.

"Listen to him. It's what we hired him for," Rue hissed.

"Yeah." Faro stepped well clear of Zula, trying to regain his composure. "I think it would be a good thing if we hurried down to the bayou."

He thought he heard Zula chuckle.

"Full moon. Easy to see us and easy to shoot," Armand said again. "*Pas bon.* I don't like this."

No more than I do, knucklehead. Faro rubbed at the damp spot on his palm left by Zula's tongue and tried to fathom what kind of women licked a man's hand at a moment they were all likely to get shot. He couldn't be certain that the riders on the road were looking for them. He'd been jumpy and nervous since sundown, for no reason other than his own instincts or worries.

They started along the trail more quickly, but the encumbrance of their baggage and the overhanging limbs and vines snatching at the women's dresses slowed any attempts at truly rapid progress. Faro looked back and could see torchlights winding through the thicket behind them.

"It's just a little farther down to the bayou," Faro said, stopping to let all of them pass him. In fact, he could see the gleam of moonlight on the water just ahead of them.

"They went down here!" Somebody shouted behind them, followed by the sound of horsemen crashing through the thick jungle of the river bottom.

"Must have a boat down there," another voice answered.

The woodland ended and the trail crossed ten yards of waist-high marsh grass to where the shadowed form of a man stood waiting at the bayou's edge.

"Hurry now." Faro was several steps behind the rest of them, and his legs fought at the mud and ankle-deep water. He hacked ahead of him with his cane, and lifted his knees high and lunged against the push of the thick vegetation.

A gun bellowed from somewhere behind him, and the bullet clipped through the grass nearby. His bad knee screamed at him from the strain on it, and the knife wound in his side felt as if it were ripping apart. He gritted his teeth to cover the last few yards to the boat.

"Get that bastard!" The voice behind them was followed by another gunshot and another near miss.

They were all getting in the boat when Faro finally arrived on the narrow strip of firm ground, heaving and sweating.

"Looks like you've brought company with you." The man who had been waiting for them stood alongside the boat with his hands resting on his hips. He was taller than Armand, and almost as big, even if he was only a shadow under the moonlight.

"You won't be so funny if one of those bullets hits you." Faro pushed by him and started helping the women into the boat.

The cypress wood boat was what Cajuns called a pirogue and was so narrow that they all had to sit single file. The boy took the bow, Armand sat behind him, and the women behind them. The big man was already standing in the stern and ready to push off the bank with a long pole.

Faro pitched his bag into the boat and followed it in. The gunfire had ceased and the moon had climbed higher and grown even brighter, and he could plainly see several horsemen stirring around at the edge of the marsh grass, partially lit by the torches some of them carried. They were trying to get their mounts to wade out, but the suck of the mud was spooking them. However, one man sat his big horse calmly at the edge of the timber. A horseman with a torch passed close enough to the still man that, for an instant, Faro swore he saw a white face with a dark hole in it.

Faro fumbled at the Pocket Colt at his waistband and managed a good grip on it after a second try. But the pirogue was already moving across the water and he held his fire and scrambled to sit down before he fell over the side.

"Give me the women and that map, and I'll leave you be," the man on the big horse shouted across the distance.

"Go to hell," Faro called back.

The pirogue's hull glided along the water with each push of the big man's pole. Faro noticed Rue trying to stack some of their bags behind her for a shield. Zula had sat up a little straighter since the shooting had stopped. The moonlight plainly lit her face, and she didn't act overly scared; she looked more angry than anything, as if she could eat nails at that moment.

Their pursuers must have truly given up, for the pirogue was soon turning a bend in the bayou and leaving the bandits behind without any more guns popping. The boat slid quietly along with the only noise the ripple of the boatman's pole as it lifted again and again, propelling them over the black sheen of the water and stirring and distorting the reflection of the moon floating there — dark water, swamp water, the kind of inky blackness that things sink into, never to be seen again. The crickets and tree frogs soon started to sing again, and a gnat buzzed irritatingly around Faro's head.

"You must have really pissed somebody off this time, Faro," the boatman said.

Faro didn't answer. He was sure that was King back there, but he couldn't figure out how that cutthroat had known where to find them.

A bull alligator groaned somewhere along the banks and vibrated the water with the trembling bulk of his body. The sides of the pirogue were only inches above the bayou, and Rue sat lost in thought and trailed one hand over the side with her fingers dragging in the dark water.

"Better pick up that hand," Faro said.

He heard her snort her disdain. It was plain that being shot at was making her doubt his capabilities. She continued to drag her fingers in the water.

"Fine," Faro said. "But that old gator out there sounds like a big one. Those fingers of yours might make a pretty good fishing lure if you want to catch him."

She tossed her head and mumbled something but did jerk up her hand and put it in her lap. He also noticed that she kept a sharp watch on the water to either side of them after that, occasionally shrinking back from the dark line of a log protruding from the water or an odd shadow.

After a half hour's travel they came to a point where the open water of the bayou was blocked by scattered cypress trees. The knotted knees and trunks of those trees and the moss hanging down from the limbs overhead looked eerie in the moonlight.

The great river lay just beyond the flooded timber and the boatman poled them out into the main channel. He laid his pole in the bottom of the boat and took up a long-handled paddle. The lights of a steamship glimmered above the water at midstream several hundred yards downriver. Five minutes later, they pulled alongside the high hull of the ship.

A rope ladder was dropped down from above, and they threw their luggage up on the deck. The men stayed in the boat to steady it and hold it in place while the women climbed the ladder. The boatman, Jim, and Armand were next. Faro was the last to go, and he was reaching a hand over the side at the top when a big boot on the hull in front of him blocked his vision. He looked up and saw the boatman standing above him with his hands once again resting on his hips. His captain's cap was shoved back on his head to reveal a broad face and a frown.

"Get out of the way, Tom," Faro said.

The boatman shook his head. "Pay me first."

"Can't it wait until I get off this damned torture contraption you call a ladder?"

"My money." The man held out one calloused hand burned shiny over a lifetime of handling coarse ropes and lines.

"I'll fall off the ladder trying to get it out of my pocket."

"Just take a chance. You're going to be swimming anyway if you don't pay me now."

Faro managed to hook one elbow in a wooden rung and reached inside his coat while he fought against the swaying and twisting rope ladder. He pulled out the remainder of the money that the Mc-Gaffneys had given him and counted out a hundred dollars, which he placed in the man's waiting palm.

"Damned, you've gotten mistrustful in your old age." Faro climbed past the man and onto the ship. "And expensive too."

"I don't normally have to get shot at or paddle a pirogue through miles of swamp to pick up my passengers."

A couple of crewmen came along the deck and one of them went over the side to tie the pirogue so that it could be hoisted onboard. Faro and his party followed their host to the center of the main deck and inside the ship's deckhouse.

Hurricane lamps lit the galley, and the big man stopped just inside and turned to them. Faro noted that the he still had that damnable, cocky, smug look on his face.

"Ladies and gentlemen, meet Captain Tom Kellogg, the greediest smuggler to ever run the Union blockade, the vainest sailor to ever lie to a lady, and the owner of the SS *Jamaica Royal*," Faro said. "And, Captain, this is Miss Rue and Miss Zula McGaffney of New Orleans, Jim Tall Tree from up in the Indian Nations, and the talkative one is Armand."

Captain Tom was a handsome, broad-shouldered, narrow-hipped man tanned to a golden brown that set off the curly blond hair showing beneath his cap and the pale blue of his eyes. He nodded to the men gravely, but changed his expression to a smile and bowed and tipped his hat to the women. "It's my pleasure."

"Hello, Captain." Rue was blushing.

"Yes, hello." Zula dabbed at the dew of sweat on her throat with a lace kerchief and batted her long black eyelashes in a way that didn't match her usual haughty behavior.

"You'll have to pardon my demand for payment," the captain said. "It's just that Faro and I go way back."

"Way back." Faro gave him a smart-aleck smile behind the ladies' backs.

"You own this ship?" Rue asked.

"I own a share with certain British interests," the captain said. "She's not as fancy as a passenger liner, or as big as a freighter, but she's long and lean and the fastest ship in the Gulf."

As if to prove his point, the twin propellers of the ship kicked in and the vessel began to churn downriver. The clank and chug of the steam engine's pistons and drivelines could be heard from belowdecks.

141

"She sounds wonderful." Rue seemed to have gotten over the scare of alligators and men trying to kill them, and suddenly appeared quite chipper, despite the fact that they were all wet and tired.

"She's a screw steamer, one hundred sixty feet long and twenty-four feet across the beam, with an iron hull and a coppered bottom to keep her fast and free of barnacles. Her two engines can crank out 250 horsepower apiece when we can get good coal."

"She sounds fast," Zula cut in before Rue could say anything.

"She'd better be if she's going to outrun the Union Navy," Faro said.

Both of the women gave Faro a disappointed frown.

"We southern ladies would have to make do without some of the comforts of life if it weren't for brave men like the captain running the blockade," Rue said with a tone that was more than a little patronizing. "And not to mention the arms and supplies they deliver to support our troops."

Captain Tom winked at Faro when the sisters weren't looking and stepped between them and hooked elbows with them. "Ladies, allow me to show you to your rooms. We haven't much in the way of accommodations, but I'm housing you in the bosun's

142

cabin and he'll sleep with the crew. You'll find the windows on the second deck catch a nice breeze when there is one."

The McGaffney sisters were both smiling like cats that swallowed a canary, and neither one was doing a good job hiding the fact that she found the captain very interesting. Faro, Jim, and Armand took up the girls' baggage and followed them to the foot of a stairwell.

The captain stopped with the ladies three steps up the stairs. "My cabin boy will attend to that."

Faro dropped the bags he was carrying with pleasure and put a foot on the stairs.

"Oh, no, we've only four officer's cabins, and one common room for the crew. There isn't a spare bunk, and you three will have to sleep on the deck," the captain said.

Faro noticed that the captain was really enjoying himself. "I suppose you'll refund a portion of the ticket price I paid you?"

The captain smiled again and looked to each of the sisters. "The price was for passage only, and you never asked about accommodations."

"This isn't about that inside straight I drew into the last time we played, is it?" Faro asked. "No . . . I know, you're still upset about me inviting you to play with

143

those flatboat men at Natchez Under the Hill."

"I wish you hadn't brought that up."

Faro winced. "I thought they were good sports. How could I know our cards were going to run so hot and that they were such sore losers?"

"You ladies should be proud of yourselves for traveling with Faro," Captain Tom said. "If there's a man who knows trouble, it's him. Lord knows, he's gotten himself into enough of it. And his friends too."

Faro watched the trio disappear up the stairwell, followed by the cabin boy toting the McGaffneys' bags. Faro took up his own bag and turned to one of the deck hands. "Good man, would you care to show me to my quarters?"

The sailor's wry smile was dotted with black teeth. He stepped aside with an exaggerated bow and a broad sweep of his greasy hand. "Your quarters await. Captain said nothin' but the best for gents like you."

The men's quarters turned out to be a section of hard deck near the bow, where the heat from the dual smokestacks toward the stern wasn't as bad, and forward of the worst of the noise from the steam engines. At least there was plenty of room, as the ship was running empty and the decks were clear.

"This here isn't what I'd call a luxury room," Jim said.

"Captain Tom can be a little vengeful, sadly one of his less admirable traits."

Faro took a blanket from his valise and spread it out on the deck for some padding. Armand and Jim did the same, and Faro could hear Armand grumbling under his breath.

"Go ahead, say it," Faro said to the Cajun.

Armand pushed his hat down over his face to shield it from the mosquitos, and his voice was muffled because of it. *"Pas bon."*

Faro couldn't argue with that. The deck was a damned hard bed, and no good was exactly what it was. He tossed and turned long after Armand and Jim were asleep, still too grumpy over the captain's treatment of him to sleep. He lay on his back, staring at the moon overhead with his leather valise for a pillow. True, he and Tom had been in a scrape or two, but both of them were still alive to tell about it. Some people were just too high-strung.

CHAPTER 13

The rise and fall of the ship's hull riding through the waves awakened Faro at dawn. He staggered to the railing and found they had left the river behind and were far out in the Gulf of Mexico with no land in sight. The sun was just emerging from the water on the eastern horizon, smearing the low band of clouds with orange, as if the door to a hot stove were slowly being opened.

Faro had always loved the look of being at sea, but his stomach hated the motion and his legs could never seem to match the roll of the deck, no matter how long he spent aboard ship. Hoping to settle the queasiness he was beginning to feel, he went to the deckhouse in search of breakfast. Jim and Armand were already sitting at a table in the galley, devouring leftover baked chicken and hot cups of coffee. Neither of them appeared bothered by the rough seas. Armand had no more to say than ever, but the

Cherokee boy seemed happy.

"I've never been to sea before," Jim said. "Walking around without staggering takes some practice, but I like it."

"I promise you, the new will wear off before we get to Texas." Faro tried not to growl at the kid, but he never was a morning person, especially when seasick.

He took up a cold chicken leg and washed it down with a mug of strong coffee. He had already lost the appetite he woke with, but knew he needed something in his stomach. Being confined by walls made his motion sickness worse, and he decided to go to the bridge where he would have a view of the horizon.

He took the first set of interior stairs he came to and went up to the next level. He was about to move down the hallway he came to when he saw a cabin door come open aft of where he stood. Captain Tom stepped into the hallway tucking in his shirt and trying to free himself from the clutching hands reaching from inside the room he'd just left. He said something to whoever was inside the cabin, and almost made it to the stairs before he looked up from buttoning his pants to see Faro standing there.

"Morning, Faro." Captain Tom looked sheepish.

"Morning, Captain. I was just going to the bridge for a better view." Faro stepped slightly to one side to try and see around the captain's shoulder.

"You look a little pale around the gills." The captain shifted a little to stay in front of Faro but couldn't help glancing back to his cabin.

Faro leaned just enough to see Zula appear from the captain's quarters. Her black hair was wild, and she leaned for a moment against the doorjamb, wrapped in nothing but a sheet. She acted as if she didn't know Faro was there at first but paused long enough to let him know that she didn't care. She passed them a sultry smile before disappearing into the cabin.

"I see you're still taking payment for our passage," Faro said.

Captain Tom had lost some of his bashfulness at being caught. "Rank has its privileges."

Faro already had the impression that Zula was a wild one, but her lack of shame and flagrant flouncing of her feminine wares was more in keeping with the prostitutes walking the streets of New Orleans than a southern lady.

"You aren't going to make an issue of this,

are you?" Captain Tom asked like he gave a damn.

Faro knew it was none of his business how much fornicating went on, but he couldn't help but wonder if Zula was going to keep up her antics all the way to New Mexico. "I'm sure you did everything to avoid taking advantage of her."

"Like hell." The captain grinned and started past Faro and down the stairs. "Believe me, she's one of a kind."

Faro glanced at the captain's cabin door and noticed that it still stood open as if she were taunting him. Everything in him shouted a warning when Zula was around, but he knew that for a brief moment he had felt jealous of Captain Tom. He also knew that the open door looked to him like an invitation, and it shouldn't. The sight of Zula standing there with that smoky look in her eyes was hard to forget. Beautiful women were scarce where they were going, and women like Zula were rare anywhere. A slut for certain, but she had a body to die for, and a way about her that men would lie, steal, or kill for. It didn't matter that he'd long since sworn to never again let a woman get him in trouble, because there he was with one on his hands like none he'd seen before.

Rue McGaffney stepped out of the room next door and came down the hall to him. Her hair was gathered high with a pearl-jeweled comb and she was wearing a fresh dress that would have been more at home in a fine restaurant rather than aboard a smuggler's ship. She even seemed to have found a way to iron it.

"Have you seen Zula?" she asked. "She must have risen early."

Faro shook his head and avoided looking at the captain's open door.

Rue paused at the head of the stairway. "Who's the Indian boy?"

"Jim works for me."

She made an odd face. "Can he be trusted? I hear all kinds of things about Indians. People say they're sneaky."

"People say a lot of things. Jim's as civilized as you or me. I don't think he'll scalp you in your sleep, if that's what is worrying you."

"I suppose you'll tell us of our route over breakfast?"

Faro glanced in the direction of the wheelhouse, but his nausea hadn't gotten any worse and he decided it wouldn't hurt to go back below and let them all in on the plan — or at least what they needed to know. He let Rue go first and couldn't help but notice the sway of her hips as she started down the stairs. And to think, he had to travel with two such women.

He followed Rue down to the galley and leaned against the wall while she took a seat at the table. Captain Tom was standing in the doorway nursing a cup of coffee.

Rue took a plate and picked daintily at her food for a minute but couldn't wait any longer. "It's pretty plain by now that we're not going upriver to Arkansas."

Faro nodded. "We're going to Texas."

Rue looked to the captain.

"Just like the man says. I was going to Indianola to pick up a load of cotton and cowhides and didn't mind making a little extra hauling you there," Captain Tom said.

Zula came down the stairs at that moment, dressed, but with her hair still wild and uncombed and looking exactly like she'd just spent a wild night of lovemaking. She took a seat at the table beside her sister and began to strip the chicken carcass between them as if she were famished.

"You look terrible," Rue said.

Zula glanced up at Captain Tom between bites with a catlike smirk at one corner of her mouth. "Well, I feel wonderful, if a little sore."

"Yes, I scraped my hand badly on that

rope ladder last night, and my legs are sore from sloshing through that swamp." Rue didn't notice the look her sister was giving the captain and studied her injured hand.

Faro noticed that Armand was staring suspiciously at the captain, and it was a little different expression than his usual sour demeanor. It might not hurt for Captain Tom to keep a watch on the cranky Cajun if he was going to continue his late night dalliances with Zula.

"How many times have you run the blockade?" Rue asked.

"Enough times that I can tell you it isn't easy. It won't be long until the Union has so many ships at sea that the odds won't be worth it."

"I gather that you and Monsieur Wells are old acquaintances," Rue said.

"Faro and I go way back, but I try not to hold it against him."

"You're breaking my heart," Faro said.

"Monsieur Wells, what are your plans for our overland journey once we reach Texas?" Rue asked.

"I've asked you to call me Faro."

"Very well, Faro."

"We'll go to San Antonio and play it by ear from there." Faro's stomach was churning again, and he was beginning to get dizzy.

"You give me such faith in your planning skills," Zula said.

Faro started to reply with something snappy, but the ship went over a roller and the falling sensation he felt cut off anything he was about to say. He was suddenly sure that he needed to puke.

"Are you all right, Mr. Faro?" Jim asked. "You look a little peaked."

"It's nothing. The chicken just didn't sit well with me." Faro intended a smile to assure them that he was master of the moment but had to put a fist over his mouth and fight back the urge to gag.

Captain Tom stood there smiling like some sculpted statue, perfectly at home on the rolling deck of his ship and not the kind to get sick in front of ladies. Faro hated to appear less of a man.

"I'm fine," he said, willing the contents of his stomach to stay down for a little longer. "I think I'll take a walk about the ship to stretch my legs."

"I'll go with you," Jim said.

Faro held up a hand to keep Jim in the galley but couldn't manage to speak again. Suddenly, the smell of chicken grease was more than he could bear. He started across the room trying not to stagger, concentrating on making it outside without making a

153

fool of himself.

"You ought to see the engineer about some lubricating oil," Captain Tom said. "All that swamp travel has you squeaking like you're all worn out."

Faro was sick enough that he let the captain's comment lie. The brace on his left knee squeaked and protested out the open door and up the deck until he was sure he was out of sight of the galley door. His willpower beyond its limit, he hung his head over the side and let go of his breakfast. The sight of the rolling water below him made him even sicker, and he continued to gag until he expected to see his intestines pitch overboard.

He hung there on the handrail for a long time, liking the feel of the cool spray splashing off of the ship's hull and the breeze on his face. He tried not to think about how much more time at sea he had to endure before they reached Texas. He somehow found the energy to curse the day he'd met the McGaffney sisters and heard about their gold. He vowed to start keeping count of how many times he regretted his decision just to remind himself of what a fool he was.

"You'll get your sea legs before we reach Indianola," Captain Tom said from behind him.

Faro wiped at his mouth with the back of his sleeve and gathered himself before he turned around. He did his best to strike a dignified pose and to appear as if he'd only been sightseeing.

"What do you mean? I feel fine."

The captain's laugh told just how much he believed Faro's bluff. "Is that the way they taught you to stand at attention at West Point? Even so, all your spit and polish has left you. You're seasick, and somebody beat the hell out of you."

"I was just admiring the scenery."

"Same old Faro. Stubborn as ever. I remember when your daddy told us not to be jumping off the Texas deck into the river, but you did it again anyway."

Faro couldn't help but laugh, even as sick as he was. "Broke my arm on a drift log that time."

"We had some good times."

Faro thought back to those long years before when Captain Tom had been one of the deckhands on his father's riverboat. "Remember when we snuck into that cathouse in Memphis just to peep through the door curtains?"

"And I remember you telling me that big black kid at Choctaw Landing wasn't as tough as he looked and that I could take him easy," the captain said.

"You made a decent showing for a little while; he just had the reach on you. I'm going to miss that old river."

"You sound like you aren't coming back."

"Not if I can help it. I think I'll go on to California once I've gotten this business taken care of. I liked it there. Rarely rains too much, not too cold, not too hot, and nobody's fighting a war out there."

"Are you after gold again?"

Faro was too quick to answer; maybe a little too quick. "What makes you think that?"

"I don't know. You send word to me that you want to sneak out of New Orleans in the middle of the night, and you've got that look like you had when you went to California the last time. Not to mention that you and the women obviously have something somebody wants." The captain put both hands on the rail. "I heard one of those highwaymen ask you for a map."

"I guess you immediately went to thinking about buried pirate treasure or something, just like when we were kids?"

"No, but you're supposed to be some kind of mining expert. I don't know where those women fit in, but nobody's willing to kill for a map unless it leads to money. Are you going back to your old gold claim?"

Faro and Captain Tom had been like brothers at one time. Maybe that was why Faro decided to admit what he'd never admitted before, at least to no one east of the Mississippi and not in the last decade. For too long he'd let the story of his gold find build and build by the retelling of strangers until it was something it never was.

"I don't know a damned thing about mining or prospecting, at least not enough to make any money at it. I nearly starved to death in California and never found more than a speck or two of gold pilfering through the mountains for more than a year with every other damned fool with gold fever."

Captain Tom looked like he was waiting for the punch line to some joke. "Everybody knows you and Piggy Barton struck it rich. You came back to New Orleans with enough gold to anchor this ship."

Faro spat into the ocean. "California wasn't like everybody thinks. That last winter, Piggy and I were fifty pounds lighter than we were when we left New Orleans. We barely had any shoes left on our feet or clothes on our backs, and not the price of a drink between us. We decided to come back to New Orleans the next spring and holed up in a cabin another hard-luck fellow gave us before he pulled out for good. By mid-winter we were tired of carrying water from the creek way down below, and me and Piggy started digging a well."

"Where'd you find the gold?"

"There shouldn't have been water where we dug, much less a pay streak of gold, but there it was. We'd dug into a wide vein of ore — high-grade stuff."

"I heard you took a hundred and fifty thousand out of that claim."

"We never took more than a couple of bags of ore out of that hole. We rode down to town to have it assayed, and I sold the claim to some real mining men for seventy-five grand two days later. I heard afterward that the gold vein ran out less than five feet from where we exposed it, and the buyers never could find it again."

Captain Tom couldn't hide his surprise, but he recovered quickly. "That sounds like you, but you've still got that look again. You and those women are after something, and you wouldn't be sticking your neck out if you didn't think there was money in it."

"I remember you being a whole lot dumber when we were kids," Faro said. "If anybody asks, we're going to Texas to look over some property . . ."

Faro didn't get to finish, for Captain Tom

shaded his brow with one hand and suddenly looked very concerned over whatever he was seeing far in the distance. Faro looked in the direction the captain was staring and soon made out a ship trailing them a couple of miles off and a little to their north. It was another steamer, as there were no sails to be seen.

"That could be nothing or it could be trouble," the captain said.

"Will they fire on us if that's a Yankee ship?"

"They're still way too far off for accurate gunnery, and the reason there are so many patrol ships is that the captain and crew get to split the auction price of any ships and goods they can seize. A lot of them won't fire unless they have to. They'd risk sinking their profit if they did."

"You still have a good lead, and I thought you said this ship was fast."

"We'll outrun her. I can do thirteen knots empty on a perfect day, but we're lucky she isn't one of the fast boats they've confiscated. That might make it interesting."

"You mean some of the patrol ships used to be blockade runners?"

"With everybody wanting in on the profit, it stands to reason that the Union Navy buys the fastest captured boats at auction to

159

turn against us."

Captain Tom started shouting orders to his small crew to put on more steam and to adjust the engines and look sharp.

"If I was you, I would take cover if that ship gets close," the captain said as he ran for the pilothouse.

"I thought you said they wouldn't fire on us," Faro called out as he went after him.

Captain Tom stopped halfway up the outside stairs to the pilothouse. "I said they probably wouldn't."

"It just keeps getting better," Faro said as he hobbled inside the galley.

CHAPTER 14

Faro poured himself an enamel pan full of
water from one of the ship's kegs and borrowed Captain Tom's room to clean up. He
brushed his teeth and stripped down and
did his best to scrub himself clean with a
rag. The knife cut in his side seemed to be
knitting nicely, with no signs of infection or
busted stitches. He'd bought some poultices
from a Creole woman in New Orleans and
put the last one on the puckered red line of
the wound and wrapped his ribs with a fresh
bandage. The trip through the swamp had
left his clothes less than presentable, to say
the least, and he took another suit from his
bag and dressed. The fabric was wrinkled,
but at least it wasn't so stained and smelly.
He dunked his head in what was left of the
water and combed the tangles out. After a
look in the captain's mirror he was satisfied
that it was the best he could do.

The first person he saw when he went

downstairs was Rue.

"You look every inch the gentleman again," she said.

"I don't know about that, but I at least feel better."

"Would you be so kind as to take an evening walk on the deck?"

They went out onto the main deck and he offered her his elbow. They made a circle around the deckhouse and Faro focused on making sure his limp was less noticeable. Captain Tom waved at them from the wheelhouse window.

Jim Tall Tree was sitting against the wall just below the wheelhouse with a fiddle on his shoulder and sawing a tune that lifted even above the sound of the ship's engines. Faro hadn't even known that the boy played, much less with such skill. His head was bowed over the scarred wooden instrument as if his melody were a prayer, and the scuff of his foot on the deck kept time to the music. The waltz tune was catchy if sad, and his tightly closed eyes and the sway of his head in perfect unison with the back-and-forth motion of his horsehair bow showed that he was just as much lost in the music as Faro found himself.

Walking with Rue on his arm and music in the air made Faro feel like he was promenading through the salon of a great river-boat again, or strolling along the walkways of an evening through New Orleans or Charleston. Her bare forearm brushed against his hand once, and the soft coolness of it reminded him of old touches from another time and another woman whom music had also made smile. It had been a long time since he felt like he did right then, and he looked to the boy once more to fathom what Indian spell he was weaving with his battered old fiddle.

He and Rue stopped along the port side near the stern and leaned against the hand-rail. The sun was shining, and the seas had calmed to nothing more than a glassy ripple. To the north was a narrow strip of sandy land that appeared to be a peninsula paralleling the mainland coast, and a great bay lay on the north side of the barrier. All manner of birds and fowl dove and lifted from the marshes, their strange cries filling the air.

"It's a beautiful day," Rue said. "Captain Tom says that's Texas you're looking at."

Faro grimaced at the other steamer still riding their wake, a day later. The sight of it reminded him of the predicament they were really in. "I think they're gaining on us since the seas have calmed."

Rue looked up at him with a frown that wasn't really a frown. "Why must you always rain on the parade? We don't even know that it's a Yankee ship."

"Habit, I guess, but I'd like to think I'm just realistic." He wished he hadn't let his worries slip out of his mouth. Truly, it was a beautiful day.

"A man who knows the odds? Cold-minded cardplayer, seeing what's coming so he can fold or stay in the game, never surprised even when you lose, is that you?"

"If life isn't a game, I don't know what it is."

"Seems a sad way to think about it. Did you get that scar on your cheek in the war?"

"You might say that."

"And the knee? Was that how you won your medal? Did you storm the enemy cannon, or lead a great charge?"

"I zigged when I should've zagged, but they missed my heart."

"Are you having fun teasing me?"

"What about that little scar on your chin?" Faro asked. "You haven't told me about *your* war wounds."

"That's not a very subtle way of avoiding my questions, but I'll tell you just the same." She lifted her chin a little to further reveal the inch-long, faint scar splitting the cleft of her chin. "I was home from school for the summer, and Zula and I had a fight. We couldn't have been more than thirteen or fourteen at the time, and I've even forgotten what we were fighting about. She threw a rock at me and clipped me on the chin."

"I've noticed she has a bit of a temper."

"You don't know the half of it. Don't ever make her mad."

"You went to college?"

"No, I went to Catholic school in New Orleans, and then Rogers Hall in New York. It was a finishing school for girls."

"How long were you away?"

"Five years. I stayed at the finishing school for a year after I graduated and taught arts and literature. I only came home for good a year ago."

"Did Zula go off to school?"

"She could have, but she stayed home. And then Mother got sick, and she and Mother were very close. I thought maybe she'd go after Mother died, but she didn't. Anyway, there was no money for schools by then."

"Did you like it back East?"

"New Orleans will always be home, but New York was grand. So many people and things to do, and so much more civilized."

"A man can starve or get himself killed in

a dark alley in New York just as quickly as he can in New Orleans. And I bet you could find a lot of poor people up North who won't swear to you that they live in the land of milk and honey."

"Maybe, and maybe I just like all the trappings and all the people coming and going and talking about something other than living and dying, or the price of cotton and molasses, or how much it's going to rain and whether the levees will hold."

"You make us sound pretty boring."

"I'll always love New Orleans, but I'm going to buy myself a home in New York, or maybe in Boston. The winters there are cold, but you've never seen so many colors as when the leaves change in the fall. And the snow is beautiful if your stove is warm and you can watch through the window."

"Okay."

She leaned closer to him. "Get me my gold, Faro. Can I count on you?"

Somebody on the bridge sounded the ship's steam whistle, and Faro heard his name being called from the wheelhouse.

"What's the matter?" Rue asked.

"Captain Tom must want me for something."

He led Rue to the galley where he left her with her sister before he went upstairs to the wheelhouse. Captain Tom handed Faro a spyglass and pointed out the starboard window.

Faro aimed the spyglass and focused the fine German optics until the ship in the distance was in clear view. Now that it was much closer he could tell that it was indeed a steamer like the *Royal,* although almost half again as big. The second thing he noticed was the two cannons on her foredeck and what looked like more cannons along her sides and at the stern. The last thing he noticed was the Stars and Stripes flying in the wind above it.

"I thought you said yours was the fastest ship in the Gulf."

"That's a screw steamer like us, and I wasn't thinking about the likes of her when I said it."

"You said yourself you don't have anything onboard. Why not let them board us and then be on our way again?"

Captain Tom got that sheepish look on his face like he had when Faro caught Zula in his room. Faro had known him too long not to suspect what the captain was hiding.

"What have you got belowdecks?"

"Ten cases of Enfield rifles promised to the Texas Rebels."

"And you waited to share this with me

until now?"

"Didn't seem important at the time."

Faro handed the captain his spyglass. "You know, we're really going to have to renegotiate the price of my passage."

CHAPTER 15

Captain Tom went below deck to the engine room while Faro kept watch on their pursuer. A half hour later, he came back to the wheelhouse wiping his hands with a grease-stained rag. They stood together and watched the Union ship plowing through their wake.

"She's a fast one," the captain said. "I can't seem to outrun her, even though my engineer has got our pop-off valves pinned open and we're running all the steam pressure my boilers can stand."

"How far is it to Matagorda Bay?"

The captain pointed to the body of water on the far side of the peninsula. "You're looking at it."

"How long until we reach Indianola?"

"Maybe a half hour, maybe less. There's only one entrance on the southwest end of this barrier," the captain said. "The Rebs have got a little fort on the east end of Matagorda Island overlooking the pass, and that Union gunboat won't risk sailing before the fort's cannon to follow us into the bay."

"That's if we can make it to the pass."

Tom passed Faro a faked grin. "I could always depend on you to see the sunny side of things."

A seaman shouted something down to them, and was waving wildly to get their attention and pointing at something to their southwest. Both of them followed the line of his arm to see what had him so excited. The sun on the water made it hard to make anything out, but Faro's watering eyes were the first to discern what it was that had the sailor so stirred up. Another ship was coming down the peninsula from the opposite direction.

Captain Tom took his spyglass and studied the vessel for a long time before handing the optics back to Faro. "I'll kiss your ass if that isn't a Texas flag on that side-wheeler."

Faro could only tell that the flag flying from a mast of the ship was red and white. "It doesn't look like a warship. It's loaded with cotton."

"She's been refitted as a cotton-clad. Those cotton bales stacked around her deckhouse are there for armor. See where an extra bulwark has been built up along her hull amidships? I bet they've got cotton bales between that bulwark and her main hull to protect her paddles and her boilers. I've seen that before."

"She doesn't look like much as a fighter."

"I wouldn't sell that cotton-clad short, and any kind of help is welcome." The captain turned to the seaman on watch in the wheelhouse. "Go run up the Stars and Bars so they'll know we're friendly."

The watchman took a Rebel flag from a cabinet and went out of the wheelhouse at a trot. Captain Tom took the wheel from his pilot and turned the dial on his ship's telegraph to signal the engineer below for more speed.

"I thought you said you were making all the speed you could?" Faro asked.

"I've got one last trick left in my bag. By now that engineer is stuffing our ovens with cotton soaked in turpentine to give us a little extra kick."

"Is there anything else you Rebels can do with cotton?"

"Rebel? Hell, I'm just a war profiteer," the captain said, "But let me know if you think of something else to use cotton for. It's about all that Jeff Davis's boys have to fight this war."

"Don't you run the risk of blowing us up?"

171

"My engineer is as crippled as a three-legged dog and old as Methuselah, but he's forgotten more about a steam engine than most'll ever know." The captain studied the lay of the water ahead, adjusting the wheel slightly and trying to get all the speed out of his hull he could. "If you hear a big boom and start seeing angel feathers floating around, you'll know he pushed the boilers too far."

The Rebel cotton-clad was veering away to pass on their port side, giving them room to plough straight ahead. At the same moment, a cannon boomed from behind the *Royal,* and a cannonball flew overhead and splashed just forward of their bow. The Yankee steamer was only two hundred yards behind them now.

"You'd better go tend to your people. Have them packed and ready if we have to abandon ship. The next shot might not miss," Captain Tom said. "And Faro, I'm having my men load those rifles in the lifeboat. If something happens, take care of those guns. They're worth a small fortune."

CHAPTER 16

Jim Tall Tree flinched when the cannonball ball whistled over the ship. He saw Faro and the McGaffney sisters running for the quarters, and the ship's crew scampering to take cover wherever they could at their stations. And yet, he stood frozen upon the open deck, his legs refusing to run and his heart pattering like a rabbit's. The roar of the Union steamer's cannon brought back memories all too recent. Scenes of torn limbs and men screaming and maimed, horses kicking on their sides flashed through his mind, and he was a coward once more. He wanted nothing so much as to curl up in a ball with his fingers in his ears and wait to die.

He tried to slow his breathing and told himself to be brave just like his uncle had told him up in Missouri when the Union artillery rained down hellfire on their camp.

Another cannonball skipped over the

water along the Royal's port side.

He told himself that he was a Cherokee warrior and the son and grandson of brave men. He gritted his teeth and tried to will his legs to move — just one step.

A third shot from the Union steamer's bow guns knocked over Captain Tom's flagpole and it crashed to the deck. Jim continued to stand as if he were rooted to the planks below his feet, taking in the terror that surrounded him.

Another cannon fired, and he was surprised to see a cannonball strike the Union steamer's hull. He looked to port and saw the Rebel cotton-clad passing alongside the *Royal.* She was a hundred yards off and swinging a little to the south to put the majority of her guns broadside to the enemy when they soon should pass each other on opposite courses. Her side-wheels churned up whitewater, and muskets and rifles went off in one long crackle as the men on her raked the Union steamer's decks with small arms fire. Two more cannons went off, and great clouds of black powder smoke rolled out of the gun ports in the cotton bale wall on the Rebel ship's main deck. The first shot went so wild that Jim couldn't spot it, but the second one destroyed one of the cannons on the Union steamer's bow. He saw a body fly overboard amidst the flying deck debris and cannon carriage.

A barrage from the gun ports along the Union steamer's side struck the cotton-clad's port paddle wheel and knocked a great hole in her deckhouse. The Union ship tacked slightly north and closer to the barrier in order to keep a parallel course with the approaching Confederate warship. A cannonball from the cotton-clad clanged off of the Union ship's reinforced steel hull like someone beating a plowshare with a hammer.

Jim changed his focus just in time to see a round smash into the deck in front of him, but the impact of the second one cracking open the hull beneath him drowned out any sound he managed to make. His body flew through the air with his arms windmilling, and he crashed ten feet farther up the deck.

He could hear Captain Tom sounding the ship's whistle and the first mate shouting orders to the crew. Smoke was rising from somewhere, and soon tendrils of flame were licking out from belowdecks and the ship was slowly listing to the stern. The *Royal*'s bow swung slowly to the south, and her speed had slowed to a crawl. He was vaguely aware of the crewmen dragging wooden boxes to the starboard side and heaving them into the single longboat suspended there. And for an instant, he saw Rue Mc-Gaffney's face staring at him through the smoke and her hand beckoning him to get up and run. He laid his face against the warm deck and prepared to die.

CHAPTER 17

Faro helped the McGaffney sisters and their luggage into the longboat just as two of the ship's crew heaved the last of the crates of Enfield rifles into its hull. Rue hugged Zula and both of them flinched as artillery fire sounded again. Armand was cursing and helping a sailor prepare to swing the longboat over the side.

Captain Tom stood in the door of the wheelhouse with his legs braced wide and his cap tugged down on his head. The look he gave his slowly sinking, burning ship was more one of hurt than battle fury.

"Abandon ship!" he yelled down to the longboat. "I'm going to try to swing her around and ground her!"

The captain disappeared back inside the wheelhouse.

"Hurry, Faro!" Rue shouted.

Faro was only half listening to her, for he was looking for Jim. It was hard to make out anything through the curtain of smoke hanging over the deck. The wind gusted a little, and through a hole he made out the Cherokee kid sprawled on his stomach toward the stern. The ship was listing badly in that direction and to port, and Faro ran for Jim with his bad knee swinging with each stride to compensate for the downhill grade.

He took hold of Jim's arm and tried to pull him to his feet. At first he feared that the kid had been hit by debris from the rounds that had struck the ship, but he could see no injuries on him.

"Get up." Faro managed to get Jim to his knees.

Jim was conscious, but his face was drawn with terror and his wide eyes had the blank look Faro had seen on battlefields.

"Come with me if you want to live."

Not only did Jim not stand, but also his body seemed to resist Faro's pull. Faro grabbed the kid by his waist and ducked to heave him over his right shoulder. He started back up the incline of the deck carrying Jim. They were downwind of the fire, and the smoke was so thick that Faro coughed with every step and his eyes watered and a stream of tears rolled down his cheeks.

He almost ran into the longboat before he saw it, and he dumped Jim unceremoniously over the side and climbed in behind him. Armand and the sailors working the boat sling wasted no time getting the longboat over the side of the hull. The drop to the water below was greater than usual, due to the list of the ship to port. The pulleys on the rope tackle blocks screeched as the longboat was slowly lowered.

The boat settled on the water with all of Faro's party and three of Captain Tom's crew aboard. Two of the sailors used the oars to push off from the hull of the ship, and then mounted them and started to row toward shore. The surf carried the boat away quickly, but not so quickly that they weren't still in the middle of a dangerous fight. All of them grimly watched the dying *Royal,* and the naval battle being carried out between the Union steamer and the Rebel cotton-clad.

The Union ship and the cotton-clad were passing each other broadside with only a pistol shot's distance between them. The cannons along the decks of both warships fired in a long, ragged volley from bow to stern, as if someone were setting off fireworks in a linked chain. Hunks of wood and steel flew from both vessels as the marksmanship of the gunners took deadly effect. Rifle and musket balls raked decks, and occasionally the high whine of a ricochet mixed with the din of battle. Black powder smoke drifted over the water like fog.

A ragged cheer sounded from the Confederate crew as the Union ship seemed to shudder and slow. The cotton-clad peeled away after it completed its pass and started a long clockwise circle to the south to bring it back for another try. Captain Tom was trying to turn the *Jamaica Royal* back to port, but the flooding hull had the ship setting far down in the water and a portion of the stern almost submerged. His path put him at the mercy of the Union ship, and she raked him again with cannon fire as she passed behind him. Some of the Union steamer's port guns had been knocked out of the fight, but there was still enough firepower left to blast the crippled blockade runner as if giant, invisible teeth were ripping her to pieces and spitting out the chunks.

The sailors were rowing the longboat furiously, as the Union steamer was coming right at them, threatening to run them down. The water rolled up in a V of froth and wave before her sharp bow, and they looked up in terror at her hull looming over them. One of the sailors shouted something none of them could make out, and then he leapt over the side. The last thing Faro saw of him was the man bobbing on the waves just before the prow of the Union ship sunk him.

Another oar stroke and the longboat scooted ahead just enough that it avoided being crushed and only slapped against the steamer's starboard side. Water washed over them, and the longboat rose high and tipped precariously atop the wake of the ship. For a moment it seemed as if they would capsize, and everyone grabbed wildly for a handhold.

Somehow, the longboat righted itself and skimmed along the side of the steamer until they passed through the backwash of its churning props and watched it sail away. Smoke was pouring from somewhere on her starboard side.

The cotton-clad was on fire too, and Faro watched as her crew fought to shove a burning bale of cotton from her main deck, lest the fire spread. He followed the course of the ship until it made the slow circle around the *Jamaica Royal* and headed straight on for the crippled Union steamer. The Yankee cannons bellowed and recoiled back into their gun ports, but the Union ship was running too slow, and the cotton-clad was coming hard with her smoke stack pouring out a black cloud. It was then that Faro noticed the iron-and-oak reinforcement on the cotton-clad's bow.

"She's going to ram them," he said.

The oarsmen had them pointed for shore and Faro twisted on his bench to await the impact. Three minutes later, the cotton-clad buried her bow in the Union steamer's side with a groan and rending of wood and steel. Men from both ships fired upon each other at point-blank range with all manner of weapons. The cotton-clad reversed her engines and began to try to back herself free. Her paddle wheels chopped the water furiously, but the two ships were locked together. More fire broke out, and men could be seen on both decks fighting hand to hand. The Union steamer was taking on water, sinking fast, but it seemed as if she was bound and determined to take the cotton-clad to the bottom with her.

By then, the longboat was nearing the peninsula shore, eighty yards away from the locked ships, and three times that distance from the *Jamaica Royal.* Captain Tom's once-swift blockade runner had all but stalled at sea.

"She's too crippled to turn," Zula said.

"Why won't he just abandon ship?"

"This was the only lifeboat," one of the sailors said.

The remaining crew aboard the *Royal* had managed to put out most of the fire, but Zula was right — the ship was done for, and her captain was never going to be able to beach her and save her from sinking.

"Look," Armand said.

Something flew over the *Royal*'s side and hit the water, followed by two men diving overboard.

"Somebody got the pirogue into the water," Faro said.

After a few minutes two men were plainly visible trying to paddle the little swamp boat to shore. The man in the stern was bailing water from the hull with his cap, as even the smallest waves cleared the pirogue's shallow hull.

"That's Captain Tom and the engineer," the sailor on the oars cried.

Faro's heart leapt at the sight of his friend. He had almost written him off. Tom had always been a good swimmer, and even if the pirogue capsized, he could make it to shore.

The longboat's hull grated along sand and came to an abrupt stop. The sailors and Armand were quickly out at its side, in surf above their knees, trying to drag it farther up on the beach. Faro helped the women out and shoved Jim after them.

"I'm glad Captain Tom made it," Zula said.

It was if the Devil had waited until that exact moment to pull his prank. The *Jamaica Royal* exploded in a ball of fire and the concussion was so great that it knocked them flat where they stood.

Faro gathered his senses and found himself facedown on the beach. He spat the sand from his mouth and looked dumbly around at his surroundings, trying to remember where he was and what had happened. Pieces of the *Royal* were scattered on the beach around him, and soot and ashes rained down from the sky. He stood shakily and looked to the burning remains of the blockade runner's hull out on the water. Despite his dazed mind and the ringing of his ears, it came to him that one or both of the *Royal*'s boilers had exploded.

One by one, he found the members of his party and checked them for wounds and helped them to their feet. One of the remaining two *Royal* sailors was dead from a piece of shrapnel burying itself in the back of his skull, and it looked like Jim's arm was broken when he was thrown to the ground.

Armand was walking back and forth on the beach crossing himself and clutching his rosary beads. Both of the McGaffney sisters stood hugging each other and looking hypnotized by all the destruction.

The explosion had torn much of the stern off the cotton-clad, and nothing was left of the deckhouse but charred timbers and lumber, looking like nothing more than a blackened, smoldering skeleton. The Union steamer had sunk to the bottom, but the water was shallow and the top half of it was still visible. Flames engulfed both ships, and men could be seen leaping over the sides. Those already treading water and swimming were crying for help and latching onto anything that floated. Debris littered the surf, and bits and pieces of the three ships were already washing ashore. Here and there, some burning piece of lumber bobbed on the waves like a wick floating in a pool of oil.

There was no sign of what happened to Captain Tom. As close as he'd been to the *Royal* when it exploded, Faro had no doubt his friend was dead.

"It's awful," Rue whispered.

It was one of those times where Faro was sure that words couldn't be found to sum up the moment.

Jim walked up beside Faro, clutching his injured left arm close to his chest. He flopped on the sand and sat there cross-legged with the same blank stare he'd had on his face when Faro rescued him from the *Royal.*

"My uncle used to say that every journey exacts a price from the traveler," Jim said.

"I'd say your uncle was a wise man," Faro said.

They kept the rest of their thoughts to themselves and sat alone on the beach trying to wrap their minds around the tragedy and mayhem they'd just witnessed. After a half hour had passed, a low-hulled riverboat flying another Lone Star flag came chugging up the Gulf side of the peninsula. The riverboat put off two longboats full of men before going on to troll through the debris of the burning and sunken warships, looking for survivors at sea.

Other survivors from the wreckage of the battle were beginning to wash ashore, along with a few bodies of those less fortunate. Faro got up and went to help several men near him, wading waist deep into the surf and half dragging and half carrying them to the security of dry land. Many of them were only exhausted from their swim; however, there were those with severe burns or other wounds well beyond anything Faro could do to help them. Rue and Zula soon joined him and did what they could to comfort the wounded while Faro waded out after more.

During a lull, Faro paused to gather his strength. He looked down the beach and saw the walking wounded scattered for a mile or more — stunned men coming to terms with the fact that they were still alive when so many weren't. Some of them rested on the sand, while others walked in dumb circles, muttering to themselves or talking to God.

Rue called to him, and Faro went over to where she was tending to a wounded Union sailor. Faro could see that the sailor, little more than a boy, was dead. His clothes were literally burned off of him, and in places his skin hung in charred tatters.

"I was talking to him to try and calm him," she said. "I was just rambling on about nothing, and looked down and he was gone."

Faro took off his coat and covered the Yankee boy with it. He gathered up Rue as gently as he could. He knew that there was nothing he could say to her that would make any difference, not really. "You tried."

"This is the most horrible thing I've ever seen." She was trying hard to present a tough front, but her chin still trembled and her voice quavered.

"It's probably going to get worse before it gets better. Take a walk to gather yourself, or find someone else that needs your help. That's all you can do; help the living."

She leaned against him for a moment, and then started off to where another man nearby was trying to wrap his head with his shirt for a bandage. Faro turned to look for Zula, and found her coming toward him lending a shoulder to one of the wounded.

"Do you need help?" he asked.

"If you want to help, get yourself back in the water and see who you can find," she snapped at him.

The longboats had landed on the beach, and the troops that unloaded began attending to the wounded and rounding up prisoners. Faro waited for the infantry patrol coming down the beach. They wore a mixed lot of civilian clothing and mismatching uniform pieces, both blue and gray, and carried long muskets with bayonets propped on their shoulders. Faro's group gathered close and waited. The Confederate officer at the front of the troop stopped short of them and doffed his hat to the women and held it wide to the side of him. He was very young, and the peacock feather in his hatband fluttered in the breeze.

"I'm Captain Dickinson in charge of the Confederate forces at Fort Washington," the officer said. "And who might you be?"

"Survivors of the blockade runner *Jamaica Royal,*" Faro answered. "We were out of New Orleans bound for Indianola."

The officer set his hat back on his head and studied the gore and destruction all around them. He seemed to be hunting for something appropriate to say.

"Welcome to Texas," he said in a southern drawl that was so soft and slow that it was in no way in keeping with the morning. From the look on his face, he was well aware that his greeting fell far short of his good intentions, and was wishing he hadn't said anything at all. He even blushed a little.

Armand grumbled something, unintelligible and probably in his native tongue, the first thing he'd said since he hit the beach.

"Don't pay any attention to Armand," Faro said, "He's not much of a traveler, and we're all having a bad morning."

CHAPTER 18

Faro squinted out the window of his hotel room, the morning sun already high in the sky. The street below was teeming with early risers. A long string of Mexican *carretas* was headed out of the city bound for San Antonio and then on west and south to the silver mines of Chihuahua City or northwest to Santa Fe. Each of the wooden-wheeled carts was pulled by four or six oxen and mounded high with goods. The Mexican bullwhackers laughed and cracked their whips over their oxen's backs. They tipped their sombreros to the passing freight wagons of their American counterparts headed down to the docks, bound in a common fraternity by the southwest trade routes both nations traveled.

The Casimir Hotel lay at the eastern end of the street, a stone's throw from the beach where two long wooden piers ran far out into Matagorda Bay. Several riverboats, ships, and smaller vessels were tied up there, and a steady stream of goods was being carried up and down those docks. Bales of cotton and sacks of pecans, salted steer hides and beef, kegs of tallow and oysters, and various other goods from the coast and far into the interior of Texas and Mexico lined the beach around the port proper.

Faro looked to the corner of the room where Jim still lay asleep atop the rifle crates with his blanket pulled up over his head. The previous day's events and the laudanum the doctor had given Jim after he set his broken arm must have knocked the boy out. Faro dressed quietly, locked the door behind him, and went downstairs. The lobby was crowded with people, most of them still excited and disturbed by the previous day's naval battle ten miles to the south. He searched the crowd for signs of his comrades, as he hadn't seen any of his party since the afternoon before when the steamship, *Matagorda,* had hauled them to Indianola. The McGaffney sisters had gone immediately to work helping set up a field hospital for the wounded, and Armand was probably with the women, wherever they were.

"Where's that Indian? You better not have him up there in your room," the little old lady behind the hotel desk spat at Faro. "I won't have him running around here disturbing my customers. It could cause quite a scandal if anyone thought we served his kind."

The hotel manager wasn't really that old, but she was a battle-ax nonetheless, one of those fussy, huffy types always shocked or outraged by something. Despite assuring her that Jim was his manservant, she was adamant that no Indians were to stay in the hotel. He was quickly learning that Texas had little love for Indians, even civilized boys like Jim Tall Tree.

"He didn't pee on the floor or scalp anybody when he was standing in your lobby," Faro said. "I doubt his appearance would hurt your business."

"Why . . ." She held her mouth open in a tiny circle and shook like a leaf. "You're no gentleman, not at all. I ought to throw you out . . . call the city marshal. If the owner weren't gone to France, I'm quite sure he wouldn't tolerate such indecent behavior."

Faro tipped his hat to her and walked off before she had a chance to get really riled up. He went first to the City Bathhouse and paid two bits for a bath and some hot water to shave with. He left a half dollar and his dirty laundry with a washwoman and went back on the street somewhat cleaner, even if he was down to his last suit of respectable clothes. He was a man that liked to look his best, but swamp travel, naval battles, and little space in his bag made it very hard to keep up a dapper wardrobe.

After a meal at a nearby restaurant, he started down the street toward the docks. A Confederate sergeant followed by two privates stopped him on the boardwalk before he made three steps.

"Captain Dickinson sent us up here to get those Enfield rifles," the sergeant said.

Faro wasn't exactly in a good mood, nor was he surprised. "I told your captain that I'm taking those rifles to the Confederate forces in San Antonio."

The sergeant acted like he wanted to get tough. "I'm just following orders."

"You go back and tell your captain that I won't turn those rifles loose, no matter how hard you try."

The sergeant was obviously a man caught between a rock and a hard place. His commanding officer had sent him on a simple errand that wasn't turning out to be so simple.

"How about me and my men just carry those rifle cases down to our camp while you and the captain haggle some more over the price? That way, you and me both avoid having a bad day," the sergeant said.

Faro was already out of the little patience and goodwill he started the morning with. "Have it your way then. You go on up to my hotel room, but I'd be careful if I was you. I've got two men up there sitting on those crates with scatterguns in their hands and instructions to pepper anybody who might come for those rifles."

"That's no way to be, Mr. Wells. Captain Dickinson needs those rifles to outfit his troops. That could have just as easily been a Union landing force yesterday morning instead of one patrol ship, and we don't have enough good rifles right now to go on a squirrel hunt." The sergeant was already glancing at the second floor of the Casimir Hotel across the street as if he didn't relish knocking on a door with two shotguns aimed at it.

"You tell your captain that those rifles are already earmarked for another outfit," Faro said.

"All right, but I'm afraid this ain't the last of this. Captain Dickinson really wants those rifles."

"Just repeat to him what I've already told him two times. Those guns aren't for sale."

"How about you tell him? He took a boat back over to Matagorda Island to look over the fort, but he'll be back before too long. I imagine he'll want to talk to you. He ain't a patient man."

Faro couldn't have agreed more with the sergeant's assessment of Captain Dickinson. He seemed young and out to take the world by the horns. In Faro's experience, such men of duty never took no for an answer when they didn't have to. He had accosted Faro about the rifles the instant Faro stepped foot on the Indianola docks, never mind the ordeal that Faro had just been through.

"Sergeant, my answer isn't going to change." Faro was relieved his bluff seemed to be working. "How about the search?"

The sergeant looked to his privates and then shrugged. "No sign of any more survivors, not since yesterday evening anyway."

"Bodies?"

"Two, but neither one of them was your ship captain. Just two Yankee boys," the sergeant said. "The sharks had already eaten most of them, but there was enough blue left on them to show they were Yankee sailors."

Faro brushed by the sergeant, his mood growing blacker. He knew in his heart that Captain Tom was dead, but that didn't stop him from wishing. There had been a time when Tom and he were close, although they'd grown apart over the years. Faro had spent all of the day before helping with the search, but no sign of his old friend could be found, not even the pirogue Faro had last seen him in.

He located Rue in the lobby of the Smith Hotel. Two soldiers stood outside the front door as guards and nodded at him as he entered. Cots for the wounded had been thrown together out of planks, and some of the injured sailors, Yankee and Rebel alike, were laid out on simple pallets on the floor. From all the comings and goings up and down the stairs he presumed that all the guest rooms were full of patients too.

Rue was leaning against the clerk's counter nursing a cup of coffee. Her sleeves were rolled up to her elbows and her wrinkled and torn dress was the same one she'd worn the day before. One look at her bloodshot eyes and sagging stance told him that she'd been up all night.

"How's the nursing business?" he asked.

"We've got a few that won't make it, but there's many that will," she said. "I never imagined anything could be so horrible as what I've seen."

"Maybe once you've finished helping the doctors, you ought to think about going back to New Orleans."

For a moment she seemed to soften but fought it off and stood straighter and shook her head. "No, nothing's going to stop me from going on to New Mexico."

He knew that none of them, including him, were in any mood to argue. He could wait until she had some sleep and things calmed down to bring up the matter again. If he said anything more, it would just come out as an "I told you so."

The sinking of the *Jamaica Royal* was an especially bad turn of luck, but he knew that the journey ahead could hold more such nasty surprises. And he had heard enough about New Mexico to know that it was no place for ladies. The best thing the Mc-Gaffney sisters could do would be to wait in New Orleans or Texas for him to get their gold for them. The more he thought about it, the better it sounded. He'd never thought it a good idea to bring them along.

Zula came down the stairs with a pan of bloody water pinned to her hip. She handed it off to Armand, who was working as an orderly. The Cajun frowned at him as he passed out the front door. Zula put both hands to the small of her back, stretching the kinks out of her muscles as she came over to them.

"Any sign of Captain Tom?" she asked.

Faro shook his head. "It doesn't look good."

"He was a brave man," she said very quietly.

"He was one of a kind. I'm going to miss him."

For once, Zula didn't seem her usual, saucy self. The smirk usually playing at the corners of her mouth had disappeared, and maybe she seemed a little harder around the edges. The day before must have upset her more than she was letting on, and the kind of strength it took to hide it so well surprised him in such a genteel young woman. If life had taught him one thing, it was that you had to get back up when you got knocked down.

"Why don't you two let me walk you back to the Casimir so you can get some sleep? The doctors and Captain Dickinson's boys can handle this."

"Why don't you leave me to my work," Rue said testily. "There's only one doctor, and he hasn't slept any more than we have. I'm going to help him up until the very moment you tell us that we are ready to leave for Santa Fe."

Faro could see that Rue was in no mood to reason with. He held up both palms in

198

supplication. "All right."

"I wish I had a drink," Zula said.

Rue gave her sister a little frown before patting her hair with her palms and starting across the room without another word. She went over to one of her patients and began to bathe his fevered forehead with a wet rag.

"Don't get your feelings hurt," Zula said. "She's just upset right now like the rest of us."

"What?" he asked.

Zula managed a little of her old smile and leaned back against the counter with her elbows resting on its top. "Don't try and kid me. Your eyes get big and you go to acting silly every time you're around her."

Faro scoffed. "I assure you I haven't made eyes at your sister."

She clucked her tongue against the roof of her mouth. "That's a shame, Faro, a real shame. Always the gentleman."

Faro left the hotel before any more was said. He knew good and well that he'd made eyes at both the McGaffney sisters, but it was only the natural interest of a man in two very beautiful women. They were both most certainly very easy to look at, but Zula was mistaken if she thought he was infatuated with her sister. He was half again Rue's age, and even if he was thinking along those lines, he doubted that she'd have any interest in a broke riverboat gambler. She was too much of a lady for that.

But Zula was right about one thing; a drink was just what the day called for. A toddy, or maybe two, would calm his nerves and settle his mind.

He found the nearest saloon and knocked down two shots of the best whiskey the bartender could bring him before he bought the whole bottle and took it to a table in a back corner of the room. He worked that bottle slowly, swearing himself to just one more drink. The more he drank the more he thought about his father, Captain Tom, and other bad things long before — things he usually didn't think about and things that always made him want to drink or fight. By late afternoon the bottle was almost gone, and he was barely sober enough to realize that he was drunk.

Two sailors were playing poker with a slick-looking gambler in a tall hat sporting a ring on every finger of his hands. Faro didn't need to watch him long to see that he was a professional, at least compared to the skill level of the men he was gambling with. Faro had seen many of the cardsharp's kind on riverboats and in gambling houses from New Orleans to Memphis. Truthfully, there were many along the river that would throw Faro into that same class.

"Care to join us?" The jeweled gambler paused his shuffling of the deck to look at Faro.

The old urge to gamble crawled up Faro's spine and whispered in his ear. He told himself that he shouldn't play poker with the McGaffney sisters' money, and that he was smarter and more honest than that. And still, the little devil on his shoulder kept whispering to him.

After another drink he went over and took a seat in the game. A Johnny Reb standing at the bar followed him and took the remaining empty chair.

"Looks like we're finally going to have a full table and a real game," the gambler said around the ivory toothpick working around in his mouth.

"Deal," Faro pulled his wallet from his pocket and laid it on the table.

"All right, let's gamble. Ante up." The gambler passed a sly look around the table to let the rest of them know he was tolerating a drunk.

Faro acted like he didn't notice and took another drink of whiskey. Let him catch a few good hands and he would show that backwater cardsharp a thing or two.

The cards never came. Four hours later his whiskey was gone, and the last of his money was in the pot. He blinked twice to focus his eyes on the hand that Ring Fingers had just laid out on the table. The two pair Faro had should have been enough, but it wasn't, at least not against the three tens Ring Fingers was grinning over.

"Tough luck," the Texas cardsharp said. "The cards just aren't running for you today."

Faro tapped his cane on the floor a couple of times while he considered the fact that he had lost everything Rue had trusted him with.

Ring Fingers saw the brooding look on Faro's face. "We aren't going to have trouble, are we?"

The other men in the game leaned back or scooted away from the table. Ring Fingers was smiling, but his right hand had disappeared from the table. Faro assumed it was resting against the ivory-handled knife showing from the top of his waistband.

Rue and Zula stepped into the saloon and it took Faro a moment to change his attention from the cardsharp to them.

"Ladies, you shouldn't be in a place like this," he slurred.

Zula smiled, but Rue pointed at the

money Ring Fingers was raking his way. "I hear you've been in here all day playing poker."

Faro could see no sense in denying the truth. "I have."

"I see you're drunk as well."

"You're very astute. I most certainly am."

Rue's nose and lips wrinkled in disgust. "Dare I hope you're a winner?"

Faro couldn't meet her stare, and lowered his eyes. He noticed that his boots were absolutely filthy and could use a good cleaning and polishing. They had once been such good-looking boots.

"Don't tell me you lost everything I trusted you with," Rue said.

"My luck's no good tonight, but I'll win it back . . ." Faro's mind drifted off. A million thoughts and a million things to say fluttered around in his head, but they wouldn't stay still long enough for him to catch a one of them.

Rue gave the seedy room a glance and frowned at the men at the card table, her disdain landing back on Faro when she was finished. "You, Faro Wells, are a no-good gambler and a crook."

She turned and stormed out of the door before he could answer. Zula gave him a sad shake of her head before she followed her sister out.

The room had grown quiet and strained. The saloon was full of men that late in the day, and he could feel all their eyes on him, judging him and laughing at him. Not only had he let a tinhorn gambler best him, but two women had followed him and scolded him in public.

"Women, huh?" Ring Fingers said.

Faro staggered to his feet and went out of the saloon swaying and leaning heavily on his cane. The breeze off of the Gulf felt good on his face and he took a deep breath to gather his wits. He was going to have to figure out a way to get their money back. It was as simple as that.

He wandered along the street with no destination in mind, mumbling occasionally to himself. With his coordination dampened by booze, his limp was more pronounced than usual. Campfire light showed at the edge of town, and although he wasn't sure how he arrived there, he soon found himself inside its glow. The Mexican teamsters around the fire only stared a moment before greeting him and offering him their hospitality. One of them passed a bottle of tequila his way, and he took a healthy slug.

"Cómo se llama, hombre?" the oldest of the group asked.

He was short and wiry with skin like oiled leather and an Indian's eyes. He was hatless, and the hair on his head was black and without the gray a man of his apparent age should have. Something about the lay of it above his forehead seemed odd to Faro.

Faro's Spanish was terrible, but he could tell by the man's actions what he wanted. "Name's Faro Wells."

The old man stood and smiled to his friends. "Ah, you are the *capitán* who came in from the big fight on the water."

"I'm no captain." Faro's eyes were acting up on him, making it hard to focus on anything, but he couldn't pull them away from the old Mexican's hair.

The Mexican noticed and pointed to the top of his head. "You are wondering about *mi cabello,* no?"

Faro took another pull from the tequila bottle when it was passed around the fire again. "No offense, but it doesn't look right."

Faro was just sober enough to realize that insulting a man in a camp full of strangers was a good way to get "educated" about manners. He tried to smile away any insult the man might have taken and wanted to hit himself again with his cane.

The Mexican seemed pleased instead of

offended. He leaned forward over the fire toward Faro and gave a quick jerk and held out all the hair that used to be on the top of his head. He laughed while Faro took in the scarred and puckered scalp where the hairpiece had once been.

"Don't feel bad. We all have our troubles, some more, maybe some less," the Mexican said. "Do you look at me and think I was once always a man who walks beside oxen? Am I only a man who was once the best *cargador* and mule handler between here and Chihuahua City? No, I was another thing before any of that."

Faro couldn't hide the creepy feeling watching a man remove his scalp gave him. He'd seen men with hairpieces, but there was something about the firelight and his drunken vision that made the sight a little odd — that and the Mexican's awful scars.

"That looks like it might've hurt." Faro nodded at the Mexican's mangled head. "Don't blame you for wanting to cover it up."

The Mexican shrugged and tipped up the tequila bottle. His eyes twinkled in the crackling firelight as his Adam's apple bobbed with three long swallows. He smacked at the sticky liquor left on his lips and put his hairpiece back on his head, taking the time to attach it with whatever setup held it in place.

"A hairpiece, yes, but it's my hair, not the hair of some other man, not some fake hair. It's mine, and was once taken from me." The Mexican walked a half circle around the fire and then back to his original spot.

"Let me tell you story, a true one. *Eso es la verdad,* my true life." The Mexican looked to his audience around the fire as if to make sure they were listening. "Do you know the Apache, señor?"

Faro had heard something of such Indians, but his mind was too foggy to try and recall what it was he knew.

"They are *Indios,* terrible savages, *muy feroz.* Maybe more terrible than the Comanche the Tejanos fear so much. They can kill a man quick, or maybe they kill him slow if they can capture him," the Mexican stabbed at his chest so hard it thumped, and then slowly drew the edge of that same hand back across his stomach like a knife. "When I was young some Apaches came to my home. None of them had horses, and they looked like they had traveled far. I thought maybe they were hungry or wanted to trade. I sent my wife to fetch cool water for them and offered them tobacco."

The Mexican paced to one of the ox carts

behind him and paused there with his back to his audience.

One of the other men at the fire said, "Tell us what happened, Caesar."

The old Mexican stormed back to the fire with his eyes wide and wild. "*Los diablos,* devils, they wore no war paint on their faces. But what could I see of their foul hearts? They killed my woman and pinned me to the wall with an arrow."

The Mexican held up his right hand so that his palm was plain to see in the firelight. An ugly, knotted, spiderweb scar was there in the center of his hand. He stood there with that hand held wide as if he were posing as some crucifix — martyred by the witness of the camp and the flames dancing off his impassioned face.

"They laughed at me and beat me until I wanted to die. They killed my oxen and gathered my horse and my mules. Then one of them took me by the hair and scalped me." The Mexican pantomimed a strong fist jerking upward on his hair, and his other hand acted the part of a knife again, slicing slowly across his forehead. "I was a weak man to let them kill my woman and treat me so, but as I watched them ride away I swore I would one day have my vengeance. I spent many years hunting for the warrior who took my hair and the same one who murdered and defiled my wife. I wanted to kill him, but most of all, I wanted to take back from him my shame. I wanted my hair. It was all I could think about when I was awake, all I dreamed about when I slept."

"Are you telling me you're wearing a hairpiece made from your own tanned scalp?" Faro asked.

"Maybe I was a fool; maybe I was crazy. But I vowed to have my own hair back."

All of the men around the fire nodded at the wisdom of what he said, each of them somber, although Faro had a feeling it was a tale that many of them had heard before.

The old Mexican continued. "I wandered the mountains and the desert until I walked the sandals off of my feet and the clothes on my back were replaced with grass and tree bark. Sometimes I stopped for a while to take a job so that I could resupply myself, but always I went back to the hunt. You see? I was driven. I killed my first Apache with a rock from ambush, and the next ones I killed with the bow and arrows I took from the first one. I sold their scalps to the governor in Chihuahua and bought a musket with the money. People who saw me said that I would never find the Apache I sought, and that I should accept my scars and give up. But I didn't listen to them. Ten years I searched."

The Mexican went quiet as if he were finished with his tale, or perhaps waiting for something. The eyes around the fire stared at Faro as if expecting him to play some part.

"Did you ever find him?" Faro finally asked.

The Mexican bullwhackers nodded in unison, as if he had done well to ask the man that question.

The Mexican leaned forward over the fire again until it looked as if his skin would be seared. Beads of sweat slid down the deep lines of his cheek. He pointed again to the hairpiece.

"Did I find him? What do you think this is on my head?"

"Where did all of this happen?" Faro asked.

"Do you know Mora? Santa Fe, maybe, or Taos?"

"Heard of Santa Fe."

"I lived in Mora. *Muy pequeño.* Tiny village in the mountains. My woman is buried there."

Faro had to admit the story was a good one, but the Mexican was getting more intense by the moment. He thought it good

to ask no more questions and contented
himself with a sip from the tequila bottle
that somehow ended up in his hands again.
He closed one eye to better focus on the
old man who was starting to blur before
him, and a while later, he barely realized
that he had slumped lower down the cart-
wheel he was resting his back against.

He thought again about losing the money
the McGaffneys had trusted him with, and
the thought made him tap his walking cane
against his head. He had heard certain
Catholics flailed themselves with straps or
switches for punishment and penance for
their sins. He tapped himself again, harder,
but it gave him no relief, and in fact,
brought on a headache. His chin slowly fell
to his chest and one of the Mexicans slipped
the tequila bottle from his grasp.

CHAPTER 19

Rue McGaffney stood on the second-floor balcony and listened to the surf. It was hot in her room and the fall Gulf wind blowing across her sweaty skin cooled her. She knew it wasn't only the heat that made her restless. Things weren't going according to her plan. Another day waiting and not going anywhere. Getting the gold hadn't seemed easy back in New Orleans, but she had been sure that she was equal to the task.

And now? The terrible sinking of the *Jamaica Royal,* the death of the handsome Captain Tom, and all the others dead and dying weighed her down with doubt and worry. She should have been happy knowing she was about to be rich, but the treasure seemed farther away than ever.

Faro was to blame. Not only had he lost a great portion of her money, the fact that he wouldn't share his plans with her showed that he didn't understand she was his employer. He probably thought her to be some foolish girl too fragile and weak-minded to be bothered with manly business, and that a woman should be seen and not heard. He was nothing if not a difficult man.

The smooth-talking, well-dressed man who would risk his life to save an Indian boy didn't match with the man who would get drunk and lose her money. She wondered if he wasn't more con artist than the type of man she needed to get her gold. He was charming at times, but her father had been charming as well, even when he was in his cups or about to leave his family again for another year, or two, or God knows how many. If there was one thing she had learned from that Irish rogue, it was that she wanted no part of a drunk nor an undependable man.

Despite the warning bells that went off in her head when Faro was around, she had to admit that something about him made her feel funny when he looked her way. Maybe it was the touch of deviltry about him that slightly intrigued her. There had been times on the ship when she found herself looking around for him, and it was hard to hide the smile on her face when he did appear.

She didn't like it that he made her feel

that way against her wishes. A woman could never totally trust any man. She believed in love, because she knew that her mother had loved her father. But she had also seen that trusting a man broke her mother's heart. Her mother had always said that even the best of men were only little boys trapped in grown bodies. They never quit playing, and only the games they played changed. The man Rue envisioned for herself one day had none of Faro's faults. She wouldn't tolerate his games, whatever they were, nor wait demurely to suffer the consequences of them. There was enough gold waiting for her in the mountains somewhere far to the west to see to it that she had the life she wanted, and she wasn't about to let such as he ruin it for her.

Still, she couldn't find the anger she wanted when she thought of him. He wasn't exactly a handsome man. His looks were too rakish and rough around the edges for that. There had been many men who had courted her, some far better-looking, well groomed, young and old, smelling of cologne, and smiling like wealthy princes.

Faro probably didn't have the price of a meal left in his pockets. But there was still that something about him. Even the little scar on his face and the slight limp he walked with sometimes seemed charming. And then there was the fact that he was possibly the first man to ever look at her more than Zula when both of them were in the room. For once, she felt prettier than her sister, and it felt good.

The gold. She had to keep her mind on what was important, and nothing could come between her and that treasure, not some drunken gambler with lots of big talk. Not anyone. Come morning, she was going to tell him just what she thought of him, demand he sell those rifles and pay her back, and then she would get Armand to take them on to San Antonio. She would find the gold herself if it came to that.

CHAPTER 20

Faro was glad that the old woman who managed the hotel wasn't in the lobby when he limped into the hotel at sunup. He had a headache to beat the Devil and was in no mood to be questioned about "that redskin boy" again. He took the stairs up to his room slowly, the liquor from the night before making his heart race, and the taste of bile in his mouth. Nothing sounded so good to him as drinking a couple of pitchers of water and then going to bed and sleeping the rest of the day away.

The first thing he saw when he opened the door was the McGaffney sisters waiting for him. Jim and Armand were sitting on the rifle crates. None of them seemed especially pleased with him. He considered offering them his cane, but he already felt beaten and battered.

"Good morning," he mumbled because he could think of nothing better to say.

"Sit down, Faro. We need to talk," Rue said.

"I believe I'll take this standing."

"As you will." Rue smoothed her dress over her lap and looked to her sister before continuing. "Did you lose all the money I trusted you with?"

"Every bit of it, except what I spent for a few supplies and our ship passage."

"I told you not to trust him with the money," Zula said.

"I'll make it up to you," he said. "I was drunk, but it won't happen again."

"Do you drink often?" Rue asked.

"Occasionally."

"Do you have a drinking problem?"

"Only when I drink."

"What makes you think that I could trust you after this incident?"

"You thought I was the man for the job back in New Orleans, and I haven't changed any since then."

Rue looked to her sister again before going on. "Even if you are the man for the job, how do you plan on getting us to New Mexico? We barely had enough money before, and now half of it's gone."

"I'll think of something. We'll just play it by ear."

"I've heard you say that before," Zula said,

"and so far, your planning has been at best, let's say, quite eventful."

"Are you holding those rifles for Captain Tom's next of kin, or for his business partners?" There was a cunning look on Rue's face.

"Tom was an orphan. His folks were killed in the Creek Indian wars, and I don't know who his British partners were."

Rue seemed to be trying to figure out how to word what she wanted to say. "Captain Dickinson said you were very stubborn, despite his repeated requests to purchase those rifles."

"I've got other plans for those rifles."

"Are you going to gamble those away too?" Zula asked.

"Captain Dickinson has hinted to me that, should you be interested, he would be more than glad to pay you top money for those rifles," Rue quickly added. "His quartermaster will pay you on the spot in Confederate scrip."

"No deal, and that's it," Faro said.

"And what if Zula and I were to tell you that unless you sell those rifles to him we're going to travel to Santa Fe without you?"

"I wouldn't like it, but I'd say 'best of luck' to you."

Armand said something to the sisters.

Faro's head was hurting bad enough that his patience was worn thin. "Armand, if you want to say something to me, then say it in English so I can understand you."

Armand stared right through him.

Zula cocked her head and gave one of her catlike smiles. "He said that if we wanted him to, he would beat you within an inch of your life."

Faro frowned at Armand and went to the dresser and poured himself a cup of water from the pitcher there. After another cup he turned back to the women.

"It would seem that we should go our separate ways," he said.

Zula leaned close and whispered something in Rue's ear. She wasn't as quiet as she had intended, and Faro caught the gist of what she said.

"That's right. I've seen your map, and I know about your gold."

Rue's mouth tightened into a thin line and Zula's eyes were flashing fire. Armand looked to them as if awaiting the okay to take hold of Faro.

"Correct me if I'm wrong, but what you're saying is that if we can't trust you to lead us, then how can we trust you not to go ahead of us and steal our gold," Rue said.

"I didn't say it, but that's what you're

thinking."

"You can't threaten us into keeping you hired," Zula said.

"I never threatened you," he said. "What you're thinking is what's threatening you."

"It would be a much simpler thing for us to forgive and forget if you would just sell those rifles. Such firearms during wartime should bring a good price, and that money, combined with what I have left, should give us what we need to purchase mules and supplies," Rue said. "Can't you see?"

"If I'm to lead this party, then what I say goes," he said slowly. "And I say I hang on to those rifles for a while."

"You're a pigheaded man," Rue said.

"And that's why I'm the man for the job."

The sisters stood together.

"We've some thinking to do, Faro. Perhaps we can talk again in the morning," Rue said at the door.

"Nothing will have changed by then. I won't sell those rifles to Captain Dickinson, and I promise you I won't drink anymore."

Armand shoved past Faro and followed the women out of the room. Faro drank another glass of water while he studied the open door they had just passed through.

"They won't fire you, Mr. Wells." Jim looked exactly like the vagabond he was sitting there with his arm in a splint and sling and his too-short pants revealing his ankles and the bottoms of his calves where his feet dangled off the floor.

"And why's that, Jim?"

"Because they need you, and because they're too scared you'll steal their gold to let you out of their sight."

CHAPTER 21

"Mr. Faro, wake up," Jim hissed.

Faro opened his eyes when he realized that someone was gently shaking his shoulder and calling his name. He could see the window from his bed, and it wasn't even daylight yet.

"What do you want?" he grumbled.

"Get up. I think those soldiers are going to come take the guns," Jim whispered again.

Faro came out of the bed with a start. "How do you know?"

"There are two of them standing across the street, and I think they're watching the hotel and waiting for others."

Faro went to the window and looked down through the gray twilight at the street below. The entire town was cast in black and white, as if it were a tintype photograph and not a moment from real life. Sure enough, two Rebel soldiers were leaning against the awning in front of the wagon shop. They were trying to look nonchalant, as if they stood around town so early for fun, but not doing a very good job of it. Several times they stared at the upstairs of the hotel where he stood. Farther up the street, were the two soldiers standing guard at the infirmary inside the Smith Hotel. They too seemed to be keeping more than a casual watch on the Casimir. The boy was right; Faro had a feeling that Captain Dickinson and more troops wouldn't be too long showing up.

"Wake Armand up and you two take those rifle crates downstairs and out the back door," Faro said as he tugged into his clothes. "And be quiet about it."

"What if Armand doesn't want to help? He might even try to stop me. Those women might like to see those rifles confiscated and you forced to sell what you can't get back."

"Convince him."

"I don't want to shoot him."

"I didn't say shoot him; I said to convince him."

"You tell me how I'm supposed to convince that big mean bastard. Better yet, you do it and I'll watch."

"Don't cuss," Faro said. "It's unseemly in a boy your age. Just get those rifles out the

223

back door."

Faro eased the door open and peered down the hall. Nobody was in sight.

"Where are you going?" Jim asked.

"I'm going to get a ride for us and those rifles."

Faro went down the hallway and knocked softly on the McGaffney sisters' door. It took a couple more knocks, but Rue's sleepy voice finally answered.

"Get up. We're leaving," Faro said as quietly as he could.

He soon heard quick footsteps across the floor inside the room, and then the door opened a crack to reveal Rue's face. Zula's head soon popped up behind her.

"What do you mean we're leaving?" Rue asked.

"Just what I said. Get your things packed and meet me out the back door."

"You're running from something, aren't you?"

"I think Captain Dickinson has decided he's tired of waiting for those rifles."

Rue opened the crack a little farther, far enough that her entire face was revealed. There were dark rings under her eyes as if she hadn't slept well, and she was even madder than he thought she would be.

"Sell the rifles, you fool," she said. "We

need the money, and we don't need the Confederate army chasing us."

Faro didn't have the time to dally and argue. "You can come along with me or not. It's your call."

"I could just as easily go tell the captain and you won't be going anywhere."

"Do what you've got to do. If there's any way possible, I intend to be headed toward San Antonio before the sun rises."

"My, so assertive this morning. And sober too," It was the first thing Zula had said, and she was giving him that look again.

Faro looked down the hallway to avoid meeting her gaze. What did you say to a woman like that?

"Make your minds up," he said.

He went down the stairs and across the lobby and through the kitchen to the back door. He had no clue where the manager slept, and was careful not to make too much noise. He gave silent thanks that his knee brace had decided not to squeak for once.

Once out the back door, he walked as fast as he could. He wasn't sure if the Mexican freighters would still be camped outside of town, or if he could convince them to haul his party to San Antonio should they still be there. Like it or not, he didn't have many options at the moment.

The Mexicans were yoking their oxen and packing gear at the very moment he arrived. It wasn't hard to find Caesar, and it seemed he was some sort of leader of the freighters. The old Mexican met him at the edge of the camp.

"*Que tal,* Señor Wells?"

Faro didn't have much time, and he decided to lay all his cards on the table. "Have you got room in those carts to haul six big boxes?"

Caesar didn't hide his curiosity. "*Sí.*"

"And how about taking me and four others with you as far as San Antonio?"

"The pay?"

Faro reached into his coat pocket and pulled out the glass vial containing his lucky gold nugget from California. He held it out to Caesar.

Caesar took the vial and held it up close to his eyes. "Is this a real gold nugget?"

"It isn't worth more than five or six dollars, but if you'll take my friends and I to San Antonio, I think I can see to it that you're paid whatever you think is fair."

"You think?"

"I can't give you my word that I'll be able to pay you more, but you do have my word I'll try," Faro said.

Caesar thumbed his sombrero back from

his forehead a little and there was no sign on his face whether he found Faro's offer insulting or simply funny. Faro had little hope that the man would take them on. It was just another long shot.

"You must be very anxious to get to San Antonio," Caesar said.

Faro cast a glance back over his shoulder. There was no sign of any Confederate troopers, but they could already be inside the hotel.

"I was pretty drunk last night, but didn't I hear you say that you were once the best mule packer between here and Chihuahua City?" Faro asked.

"I was. I miss working with mules. Prodding oxen with a stick is no job for a man of skill . . . a man who knows how to handle mules and how to get the most out of the *arrieros* who pack them."

"What if I was to say I might give you a job overseeing a forty-mule string?"

"You have these mules?" Caesar cocked one eye.

"I intend to buy them."

Caesar held out the vial in his open palm. "You will buy forty mules, yet this is all you have?"

"It is. It's my lucky gold piece; the first gold I ever found in California. I've had it for almost ten years, although I can't say that it's been that lucky for me lately," Faro said. "But if I can get to San Antonio, I have another option or two that should pay out."

"And if your plan works out, will you hire me to be the *cargador* of this mule string you are going to buy with these *options* of yours?"

"If my plan works out, you can pick the mules yourself," Faro said. "And I'll go you one better. I'll give those mules to you once we finish our trip."

"And you would give this, your last money, to have me take you to San Antonio?"

"I would."

Caesar pitched the gold back to him and offered his hand. "Then we have a deal."

Faro couldn't believe his ears. "You're a trusting sort. We might make it to San Antonio and find out I can't pay you a thing more, much less buy any mules."

Caesar smiled. "I don't risk much, but I'll take a chance on any man who believes so much in himself that he'll offer everything he has to see things through, especially for a chance to own forty mules."

"Caesar, you're a gambler."

"Aren't we all? Nothing in life is certain. *Quién sabe?*" Caesar shrugged and looked up at the sky. "Who knows? And besides, I miss mules."

Faro took another look behind him. "I don't mean to look a gift horse in the mouth, but can we hurry this deal a little?"

Caesar tried to see what he was looking for back toward town. "Are you wanted by the law?"

"No, but there are those back there who want those boxes I'm asking you to haul."

"These boxes, they aren't stolen?"

"No. A friend died at sea and left them to me. Trouble is, there's a certain man in town who thinks he ought to have my boxes."

Caesar smiled even bigger and patted him roughly on the back. "Let's go get your goods."

"We'd better hurry. I've got the boxes waiting behind the Casimir Hotel, but they might not be there for long."

Caesar turned to the men and women around him. *"Ándale, mis amigos. Vámonos!"*

Caesar shouted a few more things in rapid Spanish. All the oxen were yoked and the caravan of carts was soon lining out to the northwest. Caesar started his own ox cart in the opposite direction and toward town. Faro followed along, and the cart's high wooden wheels rattled and screeched on the cottonwood axles, even over the smooth ground. He felt as if all the noise was like beating a drum to let Captain Dickinson know what they were doing.

The sky had lightened even more, and Faro could plainly see the McGaffney sisters and Armand waiting for him with Jim beside the rifle crates at the rear of the hotel. It seemed Rue hadn't sent for Captain Dickinson, at least not yet. He and Jim immediately began to load the rifles in the cart as soon as Caesar stopped before the door. Even Armand helped.

"Are you two coming or not?" Faro said to the sisters when the rifles where stashed beneath a stack of housewares and a canvas tarp tied over the load.

Rue simply stared at him, biting her lip as if she were still making up her mind.

"And let you get our gold and never see you again?" Zula said as she tossed her bag into the cart. "Not a chance."

"We'd better hurry," Jim said.

Faro rapped on the cart with his cane and Caesar coaxed his oxen and began to circle it. Faro and Jim walked alongside the cart keeping a sharp eye out. Zula set in right behind them, and Rue only took a few more seconds before running to catch up. Armand threw her and Rue's bags on top of the cart

230

and went with the group without saying a word.

"I'm sorry, but I have no horses or buggies for you to ride," Caesar said to the McGaffney sisters. "Perhaps we can make space later for you to ride atop one of the carts."

"That's all right," Rue said, "I'm sure Faro wouldn't have it any other way. Buying horses for us to ride would have made too much sense."

The need to be quiet prevented them from motivating the oxen with the crack of a whip or shouted urging, and the animals moved at what seemed to Faro like a snail's pace. The coastal plain was as flat as a sheet of paper, and fifteen minutes later they were still within sight of Indianola. The top of the sun was showing above the eastern horizon.

"Maybe Captain Dickinson wasn't even coming after the guns," Jim said. "I could have been mistaken."

Faro shook his head. "I don't know him, but he struck me as the kind that's bound to come sooner or later."

"But you don't know that for sure."

Faro pointed behind them. The entire group turned and looked back toward town, and every one of them could make out the squad of soldiers coming up the street with

Captain Dickinson leading them. It was too far to make out much detail, but the peacock feather in his hat fluttering in the breeze was as plain as day.

CHAPTER 22

The train ride was a short one, but Faro still managed to wiggle his shoulders into a more comfortable position against the hardwood back of the passenger car's bench seat and go to sleep. He was dog tired, and the sway of the coach and the steady clump of the iron wheels passing over joints in the rails was a lullaby he couldn't resist. It had taken them three days of walking to get to Victoria where they had left the company of Caesar's cart freighters and bought tickets on the railroad that connected Victoria to San Antonio. Caesar was good company, but Faro and the rest of his party had all the plodding along on foot beside oxen that they could stand. Besides, Caesar said he would be in San Antonio in about six days and promised to look up Faro when he got there.

The locomotive's steam whistle awakened him after what seemed like a very short while, and it took him a bit to realize that the passengers were unloading while he rubbed his eyes and yawned. He stood in the aisle and waited his turn to step out onto the depot's wooden deck. All of his party was waiting there for him except for Jim. Faro left them and went down the line of train cars until he found Jim working one-handed with an express agent to unload the rifle cases from the open door of a boxcar. Rue paid for a wagon to haul them and the rifles, and by the late afternoon of their third day out from Indianola they arrived at the Menger Hotel.

The stucco front of the hotel with its second-floor iron balcony and high, arched windows topped by an imitation classical peaked pediment stuck out like a sore thumb among the dull, lumber-framed, adobe-and-stone buildings scattered along the thoroughfare. Somebody had planted some young saplings along the front of it, but they were as scraggly and parched as the dust that blew along the street.

The men carried the rifle cases into the lobby while Rue arranged for rooms. The clerk and staff were looking only a little less carefully at the rifle boxes dumped unceremoniously on their floor as they were at Jim Tall Tree.

The clerk looked up from his ledger over the tops of the glasses resting on the end of his nose and scowled at Jim and Faro standing across the room from him. It wasn't long before he walked around the end of his counter and approached them.

"Sir, Indians are not allowed inside this establishment." The clerk made a point not to look at Jim and focused his attention on Faro.

"Indians you say?" Faro twisted around as if searching the room for what had the clerk so upset, finally stopping to point a finger at Jim. "Do you mean my little brother? If so, you are mistaken. He's half Mexican, but a far shot from an Indian."

It was plain that clerk wouldn't have been much more impressed had Jim been a Mexican. He pointed to the lobby door. "I take it that you won't force me to call the city marshal to resolve this matter."

"What's the problem here?" a deep voice from behind them said.

Faro turned to see two Confederate officers coming down the main stairway. The first to reach the lobby floor was a man of medium height with dark ringed eyes, long sideburns that hung past his jaw, and a bristly mustache that didn't want to lay in one direction. He was hatless, which was odd in a country and a time of hats, and the cowlicks swirling his wiry hair were every bit as unruly as his mustache. He ignored the clerk and offered his hand to Faro.

Faro eyed the three stars on the collar of the man's coat and shook his hand. "General Sibley, is it now? I see you've moved up in the world."

"And I see you're still making trouble for yourself," the general's voice was decidedly Deep South and betrayed his Louisiana heritage. "Only you would be trying to house an Indian in the best hotel in town. But then again, the best way to get you to do anything was always to tell you that you couldn't."

"It's just the world that's difficult, not me."

"I thought I heard you went to California and got rich."

"It was fun while it lasted."

General Sibley glanced down at the brace on Faro's knee. "You're getting around better than the last time I saw you."

"I won't win any footraces, if that's what you're asking, but considering all things, I'd say I healed fairly well."

"This is Captain Lacey." The general twisted to indicate the officer behind him.

"Captain Lacey, this is Faro Wells, formerly one of my lieutenants down in Mexico; the hardest-headed man I ever met, but at one time, the best junior officer in the Second Dragoons."

Captain Lacey nodded at Faro, but seemed far more interested in the McGaffney sisters standing over by the clerk's counter. He doffed his broad-brimmed Mexican sombrero and bowed genteelly to the sisters before turning back to Faro. He was a short, bowlegged man, no more than thirty, with a meticulously trimmed sandy beard and mustache. His foxy blue eyes were narrow, set to either side of his thin nose, and a cigar stub poked out of one corner of his mouth.

The brass buttons on his short-waisted, gray, wool uniform jacket were polished until they shined like jewels, and a broad red sash was wrapped around the waist of a pair of Mexican pants with conchos laced onto the outside of the legs amidst an embroidered floral pattern in yellow thread. Some boot maker had tooled a single white star in each of the captain's boot tops, and every time he shifted his feet the big rowels on his rusty Chihuahua spurs rattled like a wagon's trace chains and thumped the floor.

Faro appraised the captain's outlandish

garb and his rooster-like stance, while at the same time noticing the McGaffney sisters doing the same thing. Certainly not the epitome of latest fashion, yet he grudgingly had to admit the captain had a certain flare to him. He was also beginning to think that given time, he might not like Captain Lacey at all.

"Mr. Wells, what brings you and your friends to Texas?" Captain Lacey placed special emphasis on the word "friends" and cast another glance at the sisters. The ash fell from his cigar when he smiled.

"We're headed west," Faro said.

"You didn't come to join up with me, did you? I could use a man like you on my staff," General Sibley said.

Faro noticed the general eyeballing the rifle crates. "No, but maybe I've got another deal for you."

"Is it something that will get me court-martialed?"

"I don't think you'll mind doing a little horse trading after you've heard me out."

The general looked quizzically at Faro and then walked over to the rifle crates. His gaze passed from them back to Faro. "Are these what I think they are?"

"Maybe."

The general propped a foot up on the

boxes and leaned one elbow on his upraised knee, pointing to Jim. "I suppose this young man is your scout?"

"He's a bona fide Cherokee chief and can track a shadow."

General Sibley looked to the clerk, who was still standing there with an impatient frown on his face. "I've just employed this young man for the day to stand guard over my conference room while I meet with Mr. Wells. You won't have a problem with that, will you?"

The clerk tried to conceal his displeasure. "General, you know I'm grateful for the rooms you've rented for your headquarters staff, but I don't know if the hotel can tolerate such an outrage. What would my other guests think?"

"How about if I promise you that he will spend the night in Colonel Green's camp across the river?" General Sibley looked to the boy. "What say you? Maybe after a good hot meal and night's rest you'll want to sign on as a scout for my brigade."

Faro started to butt in, but Jim cut him off with an anxious shake of his head. It was plain that the Cherokee kid didn't want him to make trouble.

"Just make sure that the Indian stays in your conference room where the other guests can't see him until he leaves." The clerk plainly still had his feathers ruffled, but he nodded to the group and went back to his desk.

"And who might these two young ladies be?" the general asked, stepping past Faro.

Rue and Zula smiled at him and offered their hands, which the general politely held briefly in turn by their fingertips. Captain Lacey stepped up beside the general and doffed his hat for the second time. His hair was styled into a big curl at each of his temples and his bangs into another one. The smile he gave them would have melted butter.

"The pleasure is all mine," Captain Lacey drawled. "Rarely has such beauty graced this fair city."

"Why, Captain," Rue said.

Faro noticed her coy smile. He'd never seen her do that. Normally, she was far too levelheaded for such foolishness.

"Gentlemen, this is Rue and Zula Mc-Gaffney of New Orleans. They've hired me to guide them west," he said.

"You're a fortunate man," Captain Lacey replied.

"And the talkative one over there is Armand," Faro added.

The Cajun had his handlebar mustache

turned down in his usual frown, and it didn't bother Faro at all that he was looking at Captain Lacey like he'd just bitten a sour apple.

Captain Lacey didn't seem to notice the look Armand was giving him. "If you two should become bored with your stay here, I'd gladly show you about town. I trust you've both heard of the Battle of the Alamo?"

Zula's expression was noncommittal, but it seemed that Rue had suddenly become interested in history.

"I'm sure you saw the old mission next door, and should you ladies wish, I'll have a buggy brought by to take you on a tour," Captain Lacey said with another one of his smiles.

The general cleared his throat. "If you ladies won't mind, I'll steal Faro for a while."

"Keep him if you want," Zula muttered.

"What's that?"

Zula did a perfect imitation of the coy smile Rue was still giving Captain Lacey and spoke with an exaggerated southern drawl. "We'll manage to get by without him if he isn't gone too long."

General Sibley looked from her to Faro, measuring the byplay he felt. "Captain

241

Lacey, relay my messages to Colonel Green and we'll talk again later this evening."

Captain Lacey jammed the cigar stub back into his mouth and saluted the general crisply. The spoked rowels of his spurs raked the floor as he went out the door.

The sisters headed up the stairs with Armand carrying their bags, while Faro and Jim followed the general to a first-floor room where the bed had been removed and a writing desk mounded with maps and paperwork sat in its place. Several chairs were scattered before it.

General Sibley took a seat behind the desk and motioned for Faro to do the same in front of him. Jim remained standing just inside the door.

"A courier from Indianola showed up here earlier this morning claiming you had stolen six cases of rifles," the general said bluntly.

"I didn't steal those guns from anybody, and I was bringing them to you," Faro answered. "Sergeant Pyle back in New Orleans told me you were mustering a brigade here."

"Since you've turned gunrunner, what's your price?"

"I hear you're going to New Mexico."

"That's the rumor."

"Well then, I want you to grant my party

passage with your forces. You get the rifles at half price for your troubles."

"And what if I confiscate those guns and arrest you?"

Faro leaned his chair back on two legs. "You won't. You're too damned honest for that, and you know me well enough to know I'm not a thief."

"I understand a down payment was placed on those rifles."

"Deduct it from the agreed upon price and pay me half the difference."

The general leaned back in his own chair. "Why are you taking those women to New Mexico?"

"It's a private matter."

"I seem to recall that it was a woman who got you in trouble in Mexico."

"That was a long time ago. Have we got a deal?"

"If you join up with me, I'll make you a lieutenant and hire the kid there as a scout."

"That'll be the day. But for conversation's sake, what've you got planned?"

General Sibley got a sly look on his face and unrolled a big sheet of paper on the desk. He ran a finger around various points on the map. "I'm forming a brigade to march west to Fort Bliss, and then I'm going invade New Mexico. The Union forces in the territory are scattered thin, and the Mexican population there poses no threat to us. You and I know that poor Mexicans have no military spirit and will most likely stay out of our way."

Faro didn't recall a lack of spirit on the Mexicans at Veracruz and Cerro Gordo, but he didn't argue with the general. "What else?"

"Before winter's out I will take Fort Union on the Santa Fe Trail and the territory will belong to the Confederacy lock, stock, and barrel, with nothing to stop us from driving on to the mines in Colorado Territory or west to California. Those rich mines and a wide open route to the Pacific to break the Union blockade could be the key to winning this war."

"You're biting off quite a bit there. How many men have you recruited?"

"Almost three thousand."

Faro let what he'd just heard soak in. General Sibley had been a laconic man in the past, but it was easy to see his excitement and to hear it in his voice when he spoke of the upcoming campaign.

"Like I said, that's an ambitious plan," Faro said.

"Faro, I've got almost a full brigade of Texans bivouacked around San Antonio, and every one of them is chomping at the bit to ride west with me and fight some Federals or Mexicans, or whoever else I point them toward. They may be a little undisciplined and unschooled, but they know how to fight. They've been doing it on their own for a long time, and they'd smack their own mother to get a crack at New Mexico."

Faro recalled the Texas volunteers and Ranger scouts who he had fought alongside during the march from Veracruz to Mexico City — rough, rowdy men handy and quick with pistol or knife, and as merciless as the frontier that raised them. They had long memories of the revolutionary times, and remembered their fallen brother Texans at battlefields like Goliad, the Alamo, San Jacinto, and the failed filibuster attempt of the Mier Expedition. The general was right, most Texans had about as much use for their south-of-the-border neighbors as they did Indians. Mexicans were considered a treacherous race, and fighting them seemed to be sort of a hobby in Texas.

What Sibley didn't say was that the hatred cut both ways. Mentioning a Texan in parts of Mexico was like mentioning the Devil. It was a grudge almost forty years old. Mexico had never forgiven Texas being taken from her, and the gringos across the river were a hated symbol of that conquest. Border warfare was a constant, and years of night riding and raiding back and forth across the Rio Grande by both sides was just as much a blood feud as a disagreement between two nations. There had even been a time back in the early '40s when a force of Texans had unsuccessfully tried to invade Santa Fe. New Mexicans or regular Mexicans, it wasn't going to matter. Faro wasn't so sure that the natives of New Mexico would stand aside for another Texas invasion, much less welcome them with open arms.

"Faro, I need good officers."

"No, thanks, but I wish you luck."

The general stared at him for a long time, unblinking, but finally gave up. "I don't guess there's any way I can threaten you into joining me?"

"Not a chance. You can take those guns, and I'd still find my way to New Mexico without your army."

As he was saying it, Faro was wondering how was he going to get through seven hundred miles of Indian country with two women and a small party without getting all of them killed. General Sibley held all the cards, even if he didn't know it. The stage to El Paso usually ran once a month, but hadn't even managed that since the Indians

246

learned that the Union pulled its troops out of the forts along the Rio Grande. Faro needed the safe passage Sibley's army could grant him, but had no desire to entangle himself in the man's military schemes. Faro knew next to nothing of New Mexico, but his experience elsewhere told him that the bigger the plan the more that was likely to go wrong.

He studied his former commanding officer closely, trying to gauge just how sincere the man was with the elaborate campaign he'd presented. Maybe he was simply putting on a sales pitch and overblowing things. That, or the man had grown more ambitious over the years — far more ambitious.

And then there were other things to take into account. Sibley's cheeks and bulbous nose were permanently flushed red, a sure sign of a hard-drinking man, but he seemed sober enough at the moment. The booze had never been known to make Sibley silly, even if it had been known to make him disappear from duty a time or two.

The general sighed. "All right, you win. I get your rifles for half price, and you get safe passage with my army to Fort Bliss."

"To Santa Fe."

"Santa Fe it is."

"If you make it that far."

The general brushed that thought away with a wave of his hand. "Jeff Davis himself made me a brigadier general because he believed I could do just what I told you I'm going to do. I tell you, here and now, there's half a country for the taking, and I'm going to see that we take it, come hell or high water."

"Well, old Jeff Davis ought to know."

CHAPTER 23

The next morning, Faro put on a set of clothes more suited to the trail. He kept his cavalry-style boots, polished to a high sheen by the hotel's shoeshine boy, and tucked his new, cotton canvas pants into the top of them. He slipped the suspenders over the shoulders of his last white shirt and studied himself in the mirror. The clothes might be practical, but he felt underdressed. His other self smirked back at him in the glass. *Asshole.*

He retrieved the pair of flap-holstered Navy Colts he'd bought in New Orleans from his closet and slung them around his waist, high up on each hip. The Bowie knife from his California days was scabbarded just in front of his left-hand gun. The old blade was a little rusty and the antler handle had shrunk below the brass bolsters after so long in storage, but it still had an edge that would shave. He cinched the gun belt down tight and then shrugged into the suit coat that he couldn't bear to part with, fastening only the top button. The little Pocket Colt was under his pillow and he stuffed it down his right boot top with the pearl grip handy should he need it. Taking up his cane, he put his John Bull hat on. The storekeeper had tried to sell him another hat, claiming it would better shade his face from the sun, but he kept his fancy New Orleans felt. Its three-inch brim might not make much shade, but he couldn't abide by a poor-looking hat. He would stick to his old one, even if it was beginning to get a little dingy.

He went downstairs, hoping to find the rest of his party for breakfast, but the hotel clerk hadn't seen any of them. He assumed the sisters were still asleep.

There was a thousand dollars in Confederate graybacks from the quartermaster on his person, and he had hidden in his closet another nine hundred dollars in American coin from General Sibley's own personal fortune as payment for the rifles. The Confederate scrip, although only issued six months earlier, traded at seventy-five cents on the dollar in San Antonio, as many of the merchants were leery of the currency and some of them had already sold too many supplies to the mustering brigade on credit. The town was wholeheartedly in support of the war effort, but that didn't stop folks from worrying about the financial security of promissory notes from the Rebel government in Virginia.

Faro intended to spend the Confederate money first and where he could. He needed to purchase supplies, a buggy or wagon to haul the women, and horses. And then there was the matter of the pack mules he was going to need.

Jim Tall Tree came down the sidewalk, red-eyed and looking like something the dogs dragged in. It was also plain to see that the Cherokee kid was more than a little peeved at Faro.

"You look like you slept in a barn," Faro said.

"I did."

"Thought you went out to Colonel Green's camp."

"Even though you volunteered me as a scout without my asking, I thought you might need me. I caught a ride on a wagon the ten miles back to town and slept in the livery stable down the street."

"Sorry about that, but . . ."

"Yeah, I know. It's just the way it is. Is that what you were going to tell me?" Jim said like it didn't matter, but it was plain he

251

wanted to spit.

"Have you had any breakfast? Some food in your belly might lift your spirits."

"No, but I could use some." The kid's clothes were ragged, and he was shivering in the north wind without a jacket. The weather had gone from warm to cold in a matter of a few hours.

"Feels like fall is here," Faro put his hand on the crown of his hat and turned and faced the gusting Texas wind that was sending waves of dust down the street. "How about we go get a meal out of the wind and then see if we can find you a new set of clothes?"

Jim hunched his shoulders against the cold. "You won't hear any argument from me."

Faro noticed that Jim might be cold and shabby, but the pistol he'd given him looked clean and well oiled. The kid was obviously proud of the gun, and it was probably the first pistol he'd ever owned. Faro remembered what it was like to want to wear a pistol as a sign of his manhood. Nothing made a young man feel as tough as a chunk of iron weighing down his waist.

Jim gave Faro a curious look while they walked. "Why did you join up back in the Mexican War?"

"It's just like a lot of things that happen to a fellow. You look around one day and wonder how you let yourself get where you are. I went to West Point because my father wanted me to. You know, soldiering sounded exciting enough, and the girls like men in uniforms." Faro's smile vanished. "Seemed like a good idea at the time, but I got all those kind of thoughts knocked out of me down in Mexico, and damned quick. Life's a hard teacher like that."

"I know what you mean about ending up in places you never guessed or things turning out different than you expected. Some things are hard to imagine."

"Jim, that's the wisest thing I've heard you say." Faro noticed that the kid was sounding down-in-the-mouth again. "What's eating at you? You've had something in your craw ever since the *Royal* was sunk."

Jim shook his head and his face turned stoic and unreadable like only an Indian's could. "It ain't nothing. Nothing at all."

An hour later their bellies were full of steak and eggs and Jim was carrying a new set of clothes and a pair of shoes under his good arm, and a brand-new slouch hat on his head. They stopped by the livery long enough for him to change, and when he came out of one of the horse stalls again he didn't look like the same kid. He had on a pair of striped California pants and a red shirt with a blanket coat with the left sleeve hanging limply because of his bad arm slung against his chest. He lifted the lapels of his coat on the other side so he could look at himself and wiggled his feet around in his new shoes.

"You know, this almost makes me forgive you for making me sleep in a barn."

"Don't get all mushy on me, kid. Word will get out that I'm an Indian lover." Faro handed him a twenty dollar gold piece. "There's your wages."

Jim eyed the gold coin in his open palm. "That's more money than I've seen at one time in four months, and more than I've earned by a far shot."

"Call it an advance, or interest on the two dollars you loaned me back in Indianola."

Jim shoved the coin down deep in his front pocket. "Mr. Faro, I don't know if I can go on with you. You never said I'd have to be a soldier."

"You don't have to be a soldier. General Sibley needs scouts, and everybody knows you Indians are supposed to make good ones."

"I don't know anything about New Mexico."

"Study the sky, sniff the wind, and put on a show about reading the tracks you see in the dust. The officers will think you know what to do, and there probably won't be any call for you to do anything other than ride ahead of the column and report back anything you see that needs mentioning."

"Sounds like I'd be the first one to get shot in an ambush."

"I thought nobody could sneak up on an Indian."

Jim chuckled. "Don't believe everything you hear. I just like the idea of soldiering even less than you do."

"Stick with me. I don't have any intention of being a hero myself," Faro said. "With any luck, the New Mexicans will run from Sibley, and we'll go get that gold without having to be shot at. Besides, you can draw wages from both the quartermaster and me until we get to Santa Fe. Double pay ought to motivate you."

"I'm not a coward. You might think that after you had to drag me off the ship."

"I never thought you were a coward."

Faro wasn't sure if Jim had been stunned by the impact of a cannon round on the *Jamaica Royal* or if he had merely been locked with fright. He'd seen men on the battlefield, normally brave men, let fear and confusion get the best of them, and he'd seen timid men fight like berserkers. There was no way of telling who would fold under fire and who would fight, not until you had been in the trenches with them. It was plain that the kid had something riding him hard. Jim just stared at the ground, and Faro could tell their conversation on the matter was at an end.

"How about we go see if we can find some supplies for the trail?" Faro asked.

They didn't get too far along the street before Faro saw Zula coming down the boardwalk. She was enough to make any man look twice, but she wasn't what held Faro's attention. No, it was the thin man in black that made Faro look twice. His back was to Faro, and he laid a hand on Zula's arm and leaned close to her ear, as if he were whispering something. And when he turned his head to glance down the street Faro saw the lantern jaw and hollow cheeks and the black eye patch. It was the very same man who'd fired on them in the swamp, and if Faro wasn't mistaken, he was none other than King Broulet, the Black Knight of the South himself.

CHAPTER 24

Zula pulled her shawl tighter about her shoulders and wished she'd thought to buy a coat in Indianola, or maybe one of those brightly colored Mexican wool serapes to keep her warm. Fall in Louisiana was never that cold, and the wind didn't blow so hard there that it swept the street as smooth as a house floor. Texas was a strange country where it was summertime one day and winter the next. She'd gone to the store to see if she could purchase clothes more suitable to the trail than her fancy dresses and it was a long walk back to the hotel with her purchases. She stopped several times behind the corners of buildings or in the mouths of alleys to get out of the cold wind and wipe the dust from her eyes.

She was halfway back to the hotel and across the street from the Bullhead Saloon when she saw him walk out the front door of that establishment. He stood on the boardwalk and stared up and down the street like he was hunting something or someone. He stopped looking when he finally saw her. She quickly walked on, but he took an angle across the street that soon put him beside her.

"Miss Zula, you're looking chilled," King said in the gentlemen's voice he used when he was being sarcastic, as if he had come all the way to Texas just to smile at her and talk.

"What kind of fool are you? We don't need to be seen together." Zula's mind was racing a mile a minute.

"*Ma chérie,* afraid you'll ruin my snow-white reputation?" he asked with a leer. "Where's that broke-down gambler at?"

"Are you going to shoot at me again when you find him?"

"I didn't know you were in the boat until it was too late."

"Liar."

"Don't play the angel with me." The fake smile left his face as if it had never been there.

"You and I had a little fun once, but you assume too much. What's more, I never asked you to come along."

"We might not have come to terms, but I bet you were counting on it. It's just that

258

you're scared now and having second thoughts. Worried I'll take more than you bargained for."

"I have more sense than to ever trust you to do anyone's bidding but your own. You don't mind well, and that's a fact."

"That's too bad, but I seem to recall you worrying about that gambler robbing you blind, and a sister who might do the same." He spun in a circle with his arms held out from his sides as if he were on display. "And here I am."

"Am I supposed to be impressed?"

His eyes narrowed and he paused long enough that it was plain he didn't like that. "Don't make me get mean, Zula. I've come a long way to Texas, and I intend to be paid for my trouble, one way or another."

"You think too much of yourself if you think you scare me."

He grabbed her arm and stopped her. His eye wandered over her body brazenly. "You like it rough, don't you? What do you say we go up to that hotel room of yours? I've been a long time on the trail without a woman."

She jerked away from him and cast a glance up and down the street to see if anyone was watching them. "Go back under whatever rock you crawled out from under and leave me alone."

King caught back up to her and angled into her until he stopped her again. He didn't lay hands on her, but pinned her between his body and the wall to her left. "You can keep that hot little pleasure box of yours to yourself, but I intend to have a share of that gold."

"This is what I get for talking too much."

"What about that sister of yours? Are you still afraid she'll cut you out of your fair share? Maybe I ought to bargain with her. Seems like she'll pay a man for his services."

"I can handle her." Zula gathered herself to push past him, not sure if he would yield the way. His eyes were locked onto hers, and she took that moment to reach inside the little purse dangling from her wrist. She tried not to yield to the violence she saw in his eyes, lest he think her weak. He'd had his way with her more than once, but not again.

King laughed in her face. "Is the little rich girl scared? Do you think I'll mount you right here on the street and everybody will see what a slut you are? You like to play with dirty boys. Gives you a thrill, doesn't it? Like to think you can make men do your bidding, but you're really just a spoiled little tramp and Creole whore. *Petite pute.*"

"Get out of my way, King."

He grabbed her by the upper arm again. "You listen here, bitch, I'm not playing games with you anymore. You like bad boys? Well, you got one, here and now. You're going to tell me where that gold is. You'll give me that map and then you're going to ride with me to find it — no ifs, ands, or buts about it. Best-case scenario is that I screw you all the way to New Mexico and leave you somewhere afterward with a little gold for your services. Worst case is that I kill the whole damn lot of you and take all the gold myself. Your call."

"You bastard," was all that Zula could manage from her trembling mouth.

"I like it when you talk dirty."

His face was only inches from hers, and she thought he was either going to slap her or kiss her, maybe both. The angry pressure in her chest threatened to burst her, and knowing that she was still a little bit attracted to such a vile man made her even angrier.

She licked her lips while her hand slid past the drawstring of the purse and slipped inside. "I've got just what you need, big boy."

King straightened and the sneer came back to his mouth. "Just what have you got for me?"

Bootsteps sounded on the boardwalk, and both of them turned to see Faro getting out of a buggy and coming toward them.

"Is there a problem here?" he said as he stopped about twenty feet away.

King faced Faro with his thumbs hooked in his waistband and his forearms holding the front of his coat open. "No problem here."

Faro saw the big revolver at a cross draw on King's left hip; couldn't miss the god-awful thing. It was one of those LeMats, a nine-shot .42 caliber with another 20-gauge single-shot shotgun barrel below the regular barrel. King kept his thumbs hooked behind his waistband, but was tapping the LeMat with his left pinky finger.

"I think the lady would rather be some-where else," Faro said, conscious of the fact that his own pistols were beneath his coat and not at all handy. *He's ready for you, wanting it.*

"She's free to go. I saw her walking, and just thought I'd pay my respects. You know, she and I go way back."

"She doesn't seem to be enjoying your company."

King tapped the grapeshot revolver again. The look on his face was many things at once: sneering, pompous, calculating, and even amused. "You must be Faro Wells."

"I take it that you're King Broulet."

Tap, tap. King sucked at his upper front teeth and grunted as if Faro had just told a joke. "I never shot a cripple before."

"I hope you shoot straighter than your cousin did." Faro felt his temper rising when he should have been nothing but scared, and his mouth moving when he should have kept it shut.

Tap, tap, tap, like a little woodpecker hammering against the Lemat's walnut grip. King took a cautious glance over his shoulder, as if he couldn't believe Faro was so bold as to insult him and thought perhaps that there was somebody sneaking up on him from behind. "Me and you have some things to settle."

"Go back to the hotel, Zula," Faro said, not daring to take his eyes off of King.

Zula stayed where she was. Her bottom jaw was trembling and she was breathing heavier than she should have been.

"I'll make you a one-time deal, gambler. You can walk away scot-free if you give me that map. I'll settle for the gold, and you get to live." King stepped away from her, but in doing so forced Faro to turn where he was facing right into the sun. "I didn't like my cousin so much. Just a pretty boy like you . . . nothing to him. Maybe I could forget that little matter if I didn't have to lay eyes on you again, and with enough gold in my pockets to keep me occupied."

Faro didn't need anyone to tell him that the man before him was deadly, but it didn't matter. He was there and King was there and that was all it sometimes took for a killing — two of the wrong people meeting up at the wrong time. He was going to be slow getting to one of his pistols under his coat, and there was no avoiding the fact that he was going to take lead. It wouldn't even help him to back down, for he was sure that King would put a bullet in his back. *Front or back, you'll be just as dead. Take it in the front like a man if you're going to die. Throw the cane at him to buy some time while you reach for your pistol.*

He never had been much good with a rifle and was only a little better with a pistol for that matter. Regardless, it was point-blank range between them and just a simple matter of pulling your pistol and shoving it toward the other's gut and squeezing the trigger until they weren't there anymore. *You're going to get hit and it's going to hurt. Take your time. Trying to be fast will just make you bobble. Steady and smooth. Make that one shot count and take the son of a bitch with you — if you get one shot.*

Faro gently patted his chest with his right hand, his left holding his cane. "No deal."

Staring into the sun like he was, Faro's eyes began to water with the strain. King kept tapping the LeMat with his pinky, *tap, tap, tap,* like an undertaker rapping on his window glass, studying Faro's face as if he were counting blinks.

Damn that sun. A wagon passed by them, and the driver gawked as if it were plain the two of them were about to bleed each other. In addition, half the people along the street and in the main plaza must have felt something, for they peered from open doors or windows and stood whispering on the boardwalks.

"You just say the word, Mr. Faro, and I'll let fly at him," Jim's voice sounded from Faro's left.

Faro dared to look away from King long enough to take a glance at the kid out of the corner of his eye. Jim was standing behind the trunk of a shade tree on the far side of the street with just his head and right shoulder sticking out behind the trunk.

King shifted his feet slowly until he was pointed between the two of them. He frowned at the crossfire he was caught in.

He couldn't even see if Jim had a gun or not, and the Cherokee's arrival gave him time to notice the crowd watching them.

"Perhaps another time, Monsieur Wells, when we don't have such an audience."

"Another time," Faro answered.

"You think you're good, don't you?" *Tap, tap.*

"Good enough."

"Suppose you think the army and your general buddy will protect you?"

"It won't hurt my chances, and I don't mind having you outnumbered." *Not at all. Wish I had a whole damned company behind me right now to haul your sorry ass off to a firing squad.*

King moved his chin back and forth as if he had a crick in his neck, and slowly let out a big breath like a boiler letting off steam. "You talk big in front of Zula, but we'll see what you're made of before long."

Take your chances or he'll get you later. Right now is about as fair as it's going to get. Faro's pistol butts felt a long way from his hands even though they were just under his coat. His eyes watered until his vision was a greasy blur. *Do it now.*

King went across the street, walking wide of Jim. When he had disappeared inside the Bullhead Saloon, Jim came out from behind the tree and started toward Faro. His Colt Army was dangling from his hand.

Faro looked down at Zula and caught a strange look on her face before she could hide it. He expected the encounter to have her upset, but for an instant he swore she looked more excited than scared. And then he noticed the tiny rimfire derringer in her hand. It was almost hidden hanging at arm's length alongside her dress. *Now, how long have you had that out, Zula dear?*

"You can put that peashooter away now," he said evenly.

He heard the click of the hammer as she let it down and watched as she tucked the tiny pistol back into her purse. She handled the weapon like it wasn't the first time she'd held a gun.

"Do you think I can't handle the likes of him?" she asked.

"What I'd like to know is how you two are acquainted. I wouldn't think he's the sort young ladies would be associating with."

"Why, I hardly know the man."

"Did you tell him about the gold before we left New Orleans?"

She made a point to stare across the street and avoid his eyes. "I might have mentioned it accidentally in polite conversation."

Faro jabbed a thumb at the saloon. "Polite conversation with the likes of him? If ever there was a neck born for hanging, it's his."

"I admit he's not quite what I thought at first. I never thought he would come after me."

"I'd say you never thought at all."

Zula's face went cool and blank. "If he's so dangerous, why didn't you kill him while you had the chance?"

"It didn't look like an easy proposition."

"Is that another way of saying you were scared?"

"That's another way of saying I don't particularly care to die if I can help it. So far in life, I've found that money spends much better when you're alive to enjoy it."

Zula hissed through her teeth and twisted her mouth. "When I saw you coming down the street I was thinking maybe there was hope for you after all. King is a no-good, but I think he might be right. You're just like a painting of a man, nice to look at, but not much good for anything else. And to think, you're supposed to be the war hero and a duelist. What's going to happen when we find that gold and King comes back around again? Are you going to talk him to death? Convince him that he's wrong? If you were half the man we thought we hired you would have put an end to that worry when he was standing right here."

Zula hurried off in a rustling of her dress before Faro could say anything else. He frowned after her and took three slow, deep breaths.

"She's kind of bloodthirsty, ain't she?" Jim asked.

Faro thought some about the gun she'd been holding. "I wonder if King knows just how close he came to getting shot by a woman? Hate to think I saved his life."

"How do you know she had that gun out for him and not for you?" Jim's face was unreadable.

"I don't, but I thought it prudent to keep my eyes on King. He seemed the most dangerous, but I'm not so sure about that now."

"I had him," Jim said matter-of-factly.

Faro glanced at the kid and was surprised at the fierce look on his face. He also noticed that Jim was still holding the .44.

"And who's the bloodthirsty one now?" Faro pointed at Jim's pistol.

Jim hefted the Colt and examined it with a chuckle before shoving it back in his holster. He jerked a thumb at Faro's waist. "I don't mean to tell you your business, but wearing your pistols on the inside of your coat is damned unhandy."

"Jim, are you some kind of kid pistoleer?"

"Naw, I was just thinking." Jim looked skittish again instead of ready to fight.

"How many guns am I wearing, Jim?"

Jim kicked at the ground bashfully, but slowly looked up with a sly grin on his face. "From the bulge of your coat and the way you move I'd say you're wearing one revolver on each hip, and you've got another one just peeking out of the top of your right boot."

"I suppose you noticed all that by chance?"

"I'd also say that you've got a blade on you somewhere. Any man that will carry a boot gun strikes me as one that likes a backup and's going to have himself a good sharp knife somewhere on him."

"You're a quick kid, Jim, maybe too damned quick. What school did you say you went to?"

"I spent some time in the boys' seminary at Tahlequah. You know, an Indian school, Cherokee academy. But I had to drop out by the time I was eleven. The math was all right, but I never did see any use for all that Latin and philosophy stuff."

"Must have been some school. Did they teach you about guns there?"

Jim smiled slyly again. "Mr. Faro, you know schools don't teach the kind of stuff that matters. I've been around some."

"Jim, one day you're going to have to sit down with me and tell me a story or two."

CHAPTER 25

Zula's heart was still beating too fast when she closed the door to her hotel room. Her anger had yet to cool and her hands still trembled with excitement. She knew she was no angel, but it sometimes worried her that she liked to watch men fight so much. She couldn't explain why she enjoyed it so, she just did. Sometimes it seemed as if everything that she liked or that excited her was supposed to be bad. But if it was wrong, why did being bad usually feel so good?

Her father had been a gentle man when he was at home, full of laughter and always a kind smile on his face, especially if he had a good supply of the blarney hidden somewhere in the cupboard. Anyone watching him during those family hours would never have guessed that he could hurt a fly. But an old memory hovered in the misty recesses of her mind, and in it she was a small girl again, walking along the docks between he and her mother and holding their hands while they went to see him off on one of his long trips. There had been a big deckhand unloading a riverboat who'd said something when they passed. The rest of the workers had laughed and made no attempt to hide the way they were looking at her mother, nor the fact that the deckhand had said something rude and ribald. Looking back, it was no wonder, for her mother had been a beautiful woman.

Her father had never said a word, simply letting go of her hand and picking up a shop hammer left lying on the dock. He made a few quick strides and the hammer thumped into the deckhand's ribs before he could even drop the load he was carrying or utter another word. Her father kept swinging that hammer while Zula squeezed her mother's hand and flinched with every blow. She remembered how he and the deckhand had grunted like two mad, sweaty bulls, and the sound of that hammer burying itself in flesh and the sharp strike of fists against skin. Her heart had beaten fast then just like it had when she watched Faro and King facing each other. It wasn't the potential for blood and the gore that excited her, but something more complex than that, something that spoke to some part of her that she couldn't shape to words.

"Don't let it upset you, child. A man that won't fight for you is no man at all," her mother had said quietly, never turning away while her husband beat that flirty fellow to a bloody pulp.

Nothing Zula had learned since did anything but confirm to her that men were brutes, but she liked them that way. Maybe that meant she was bad. Rue would say it did, but Rue wasn't her. And even if Rue liked to watch men fight she would never admit it. Not high-and-mighty, ladylike Rue. She would have shrieked and cried for their father to stop, and he would've patted her head when he was through and carried her home promising her a new baby doll or something because he'd scared her. Rue always could find a means to get her way — to go off to school and leave Zula alone, and then have the gall to come back and lecture her on how she should act more like a lady and go back East with her, no matter that their mother wasn't well and had no one to comfort her. Rue didn't know anything, nothing at all about men or what made a lady.

Zula went to her bag and pulled out a copy of the map. The two of them couldn't agree on who should carry the map and the letter, so they'd made copies to satisfy both of them. Zula studied the strange marks, reread the letter, and thought about the gold. Rue believed that riches would make everyone see her as what she wanted to be, but she was wrong. The material things you could buy with enough money weren't what mattered; it was the money itself. If you had enough of it, people wouldn't say a damned thing, however you chose to act.

She loved Rue, but that didn't stop her from thinking her sister overlooked the life lessons all around them, just like that Faro. Both of them playing by rules not of their own making and pretending like the rest of the world played by the same ones. Zula knew better. Nobody looked out for you like you would yourself, and there was always somebody willing to break the rules or make some new ones up to their advantage. That somebody usually won, and at the very least, they had more fun.

Dallying with King hadn't been her brightest moment. She had played with fire there, and it would have been so much simpler if Faro had just killed that blackhearted bastard.

CHAPTER 26

Faro stood at the edge of the street and scowled while he rubbed his face and squinted distastefully at the morning sun, as if he bore a grudge against sunlight. He grumbled and gave everything around him a dirty look, from the old spotted sow and her litter of pigs rooting around in the mud beside a water trough at the edge of the street to a loose advertising sign above the boardwalk, squeaking and thumping in the breeze. He never was what one would call a morning person, and the whole damned world usually grated on his nerves until he had a couple of cups of coffee and ample time to come awake. He would have been the first to admit that too many years of sitting up all night over cards and sleeping into the afternoon had given him the habits of a hoot owl. He had too much to do and too much to worry about, and sleep was as scarce as rain since he'd come to Texas.

The brigade was preparing to head west, and Faro had ridden down two different rented livery horses traveling the surrounding countryside searching for horses and mules to purchase for his party. It had been a long time since he had ridden, and to say he was saddle sore would be an understatement. And all for nothing. He hadn't found a single decent animal to purchase yet. Sibley's army had sucked them all up.

While he stood there wishing he had taken the time to knock back one more cup of coffee before venturing out, Captain Lacey came out of the front door of the hotel with none other than Rue on his arm. She and her bowlegged Texan escort were both smiling like it wasn't so early in the morning, and whatever the Texan captain was saying seemed to be the funniest thing in the world. Faro didn't know which grated on his nerves more, the laughing or the smiling. He was of a mood to pick up a rock and throw it at the old sow grunting nearby. On second thought, after glancing again at the smiling couple, he thought they might use a good rocking too.

"Good morning, Faro," Rue said cheerfully.

Faro half mumbled and half growled something that neither one of them could understand. His mind was too thick to think, and the last thing he wanted to do was talk.

"What was that?" she asked.

"I said that they oughtn't to allow pigs on the streets. It's a travesty of civilization if you ask me."

"Mr. Wells, you look like you had a hard night and could use some more sleep," Captain Lacey said.

Faro didn't even consider taking that as anything but an insult; he was in that kind of mood. Furthermore, the comment made him instantly conscious of the fact that he hadn't bothered to shave that morning and that his clothes were wrinkled and smelled of dust and sweat.

The bowlegged captain obviously found it funny that Faro was bedraggled, and also must have thought that the strange blend of frontier garb that served as his own uniform looked quite dashing. That was easy to tell by the way he twirled the waxed ends of his mustache and failed to hide the smart-ass smile working around just beneath those whiskers.

There was a smell hovering around the captain like a fog that was somewhere between cologne and surgical disinfectant. Faro quickly identified it as Beecher's Hair

Tonic. He used the brand himself and had found it lived up to its label, "Not a hair out of place, anytime, anywhere." It had a pleasant smell without being too oily, yet his own supply had long since run out and he hadn't been able to find a single bottle anywhere in Texas.

Captain Lacey smelled like a whorehouse. *No, I'm pretty sure now. I don't like him at all.*

"Captain Lacey is taking me over to the Alamo Mission. He says it is the most heroic site in Texas," she said.

The old adobe mission and fort lay just across around the corner. Faro knew it to be hallowed ground for Texans.

"I'm sure you'll enjoy yourself," was all Faro could manage to say.

"I get absolutely bored in my hotel room, and it has been so nice of Captain Lacey to show me around the last few days." She seemed to be measuring Faro for something. "Why yesterday, we had the most delightful buggy ride along the river and a picnic."

"I'm surprised that Captain Lacey has so much spare time on his hands with the demands of his company weighing on him." Faro immediately regretted his words.

Captain Lacey stiffened. "I assure you, Mr. Wells, my men will be ready to ride when the general gives the order, and as to training, any one of my men is worth ten Mexicans or Federals."

Faro noticed that the Texan had a quick temper. "Never said anything to the contrary."

Rue quickly butted in. "We are going to church later this morning, and you're welcome to join us."

"No, thank you, I've got other things to attend to," Faro said. "Besides, lightning might strike the church and burn it down if I was to set down in the pews."

Captain Lacey looked pleased and Rue looked disappointed. Faro tipped his hat to them as they walked away, and then headed down the street in the opposite direction. His mind was elsewhere when he ran into Caesar, the muleteer, in the middle of the broad street. The Mexican smiled and offered his hand.

"You look like you could use some sleep," Caesar said.

"I've only got myself to blame."

Caesar nodded as if he understood. "But you do look more prosperous than you did the last time I saw you. Do I dare hope that your *options* worked out?"

"They did, indeed."

Caesar smiled slyly. "Do you still need a man who knows mules?"

"I do, but I need some mules first. Haven't had a bit of luck finding any."

Caesar smirked like he had a secret. "I just arrived last night, but I did have the good fortune to camp beside a man who has mules for sale."

"I need a wagon team and some saddle stock as well."

Caesar glanced around him as if someone might be eavesdropping. "This man I know, he's got horses too. Fast ones, strong ones."

"How about we go talk with this friend of yours?"

"I get to be your *cargador,* and you will give me the mules when you are through with them?"

"That's the deal."

They rented a buggy from the livery and Faro followed Caesar's directions out of town. The rutted two-track the old Mexican put him on left the main road and wound through the scrub brush and oak tangles an hour's drive from town. They eventually came upon a small clearing hacked out of a mesquite thicket. There was a cedar picket hut at its middle with a large brush corral alongside it. Whoever had built the corral obviously hadn't invested much money into its construction. A few crooked and leaning posts were set into the ground at random intervals, and the iron headboard from a bed was tied up with bits of old rope to serve as a gate. Thorny mesquite limbs and other brush with the limbs still on were stacked and woven together between the wide-spaced posts and leaning against an occasional cedar rail. Saplings and cacti and vines had grown up amidst the brush walls until the thing would have held a mad elephant, despite the builder's lack of effort or skill.

Faro looked around suspiciously. "Caesar, no honest trader operates from the middle of a thicket."

Caesar smiled his conspirator's smile again and shrugged. "That army has bought every available horse and mule within sixty miles of here. I didn't think you would be so picky."

The coals from a campfire in front of the *jacal*'s door sent a trickle of smoke into the sky. The sagging front door creaked against the support of its rawhide hinges and the bottom of it grated on the ground as a Mexican shoved it open and stood in the doorway. He was carrying a rifle resting in the bend of his left elbow, and he gave them a hard look and searched the trail behind them for signs of any more company.

"He is my cousin's husband, a good man,

but not one who likes towns," Caesar said.

Another rough-looking sort, a white man with a sagging leather hat and a beard down to his chest, was coming around the corral with a rusty shotgun dangling from his hand and a mongrel dog padding along at his heels.

Faro studied the mixed pen of mules and horses either sleeping or browsing around the bare ground of the corral in search of a blade of grass. They were all a little on the thin side, but some of them looked to be of decent stock.

"How many of these animals are stolen?" he asked quietly.

"Stolen?" Caesar did his best to look offended. "Amigo, let us say that there is a possibility that these mules were ransomed from across the Rio Grande. All Texans know that the Mexicans steal their stock, and that it's no crime at all to take a midnight ride when the moon is right and take a few of those animals back."

"That's a surprising defense for your in-law, considering that you're both Mexicans."

"I'm a practical man. Were we in Mexico, I would tell you that that all Mexicans know that the Texans ride across the river and steal them blind, and that those horses and mules were ransomed back from Texas."

"That's all I need, some Mexican rancher hunting me down and hanging me for being a stock thief." Faro started to turn the buggy around.

"The mules are some of the finest I've seen, the horses aren't too bad either, and the prices are cheap," Caesar said. "Very cheap."

Faro waited while the two strangers made their way to the buggy. Truly, riding and wagon stock was in short supply. What had his father once said? Beggars can't be choosers?

"I guess Caesar brought you out here because you're interested in them there mules," the white man said.

"Buenos días." His Mexican counterpart rested his rifle on his shoulder and looked Faro over as if he were deciding how much was in his pockets.

From the grime caked into their skins and the smell of them it was plain that neither man had taken a bath in a month, if then. One look at them was all Faro needed to decide that both of them were just one step ahead of a hanging. The little mutt at the white man's feet trotted around the buggy growling and stopping to urinate on every wheel with his hackles standing straight up on his back.

"How many mules have you got?" Faro asked.

The Beard and his Mexican partner shared a smile between each other before the Beard answered. "There's twenty mules and about three horses that might fit you if you're riding east or north."

"What if I'm going west or south?"

The Mexican said something in Spanish and the white man laughed and rubbed at his matted whiskers. "Well, there's three mules and four or five horses that might suit you."

Faro didn't know much about livestock, but even from a distance his untrained eye noticed the scabbed-over, fresh brands on several of the animals' hips or shoulders. It was plain that the two "horse traders" had blotted over old brands with new ones.

Faro knew that a good man would go back to San Antonio and tell the law where the camp was located. *Damn that gold.* "How about we look at those three mules and horses?"

He got down from the buggy, making sure to walk behind the duo and to keep an eye on the dog. He nodded to Caesar and the muleteer followed his Mexican in-law into the corral while Faro and Beard stayed at the gate.

"Care for a chew of Tar Baby?" Beard held out a plug of chewing tobacco as black as its brand name. When Faro shook his head the man tore off a chunk of the plug with a vicious jerk of his teeth. He smiled and those teeth were as black as the tobacco.

The animals bunched together and pressed against the far side of the corral. None of them had to be roped, and they came out of the herd willingly enough when haltered.

The first three led out were two little brown mules with tan noses and another flea-bit gray with a dead limp on his left hind leg and one injured ear that flopped limply at half mast. Caesar waved a disgusted hand at the gray and examined the brown mules closely, checking everything from their hooves to their teeth, lifting and flexing legs, and watching the way they traveled while his in-law led them around.

"These two mules will do just fine. He says they both pack well," Caesar called across the pen.

"Two mules is a long way from the forty we need." Faro had no love for mules, and that, coupled with the felt need to keep an eye on the bearded man beside him made it hard to pay attention to the purchase process. Anyway, Caesar was supposed to be the mule expert.

"There is one more mule that might work for you," the Mexican in-law said in broken English. He scanned the penned animals for a long moment, finally focusing his attention on a black rump pointed at him.

The Mexican didn't attempt to walk up and halter his next selection, but chose instead to take up a braided rawhide riata. He threw a high, soft, backhanded loop across his body and it dropped over the black mule's neck just as it flinched and picked up its head from where it had it down between its front legs and jammed up against the corral wall, as if it were hidden by the fact that it refused to look at the men. As soon as the loop tightened the mule kicked twice at the rope with one back leg faster than Faro thought was possible. The dog raced in barking and trying to bite the mule's heels.

The Mexican took a gentle pull and turned the mule and coaxed him through the crowd of bodies until it stood alone in the middle of the corral. The dog was still darting in and out under the black's feet, and the mule leisurely bided his time until the right moment and effortlessly kicked the dog through the air. The whimpering mutt hobbled to its feet, gave the mule one last look, and crawled through the brush fence with its tail clamped. The mule looked half asleep, despite his dog kicking.

Faro found mules to be especially homely beasts. Horses were unpredictable and flighty animals at best, but at least they had some eye appeal about them. Painters loved to try and capture the sleek, classical lines of a good horse, but to Faro's knowledge, no artist yet had found anything worth capturing on canvas when it came to an old flop ear. Mules were just plain ugly, with their big ears, chug heads, and short, rounded little hips.

But he had to admit, the black John mule that the Mexican led out of the herd had something that bordered on impressive about him. First, he was twice as big as the rest of the little Spanish mules, as big as the farm mules back east, maybe fifteen and a half hands tall and weighing easily over half a ton. His hide was as black as a chunk of coal, and his hooves were exceptionally big and broad for a mule.

The Mexican eased up the riata to the mule with a halter in his hand. The animal stood with its head hanging, but when the Mexican started to slip the noseband of the halter over his nose he cow kicked at him with a back hoof and sent him scrambling backward. Even standing at the black mule's shoulder, it had been a close call, the hoof brushing the Mexican's shirt. That was one nasty thing about mules that Faro knew — they could kick you with a back hoof without turning their hindquarters to you, even if you were standing beside or in front of them. The damned things could fold up like a Barlow jackknife when they were of a mind to.

A second cautious attempt saw the mule haltered, and he came along docilely enough, his sleepy eyes hiding the fact that only minutes before he had tried to maim the man leading him. Caesar circled the big mule and clucked his tongue and shook his head a few times when his in-law stopped near the gate.

"That's one fine mule," Beard said and spit a big wad of tobacco juice into the dust. "Big bastard. Pull a plow or carry a hell of a load. Jerk out a stump if you're of a mind to."

Caesar put a gentle hand on the little spots of white hair on the John mule's neck, just in front of the crease of his shoulder. "He's definitely pulled a plow or a wagon before. Got the collar marks on him to prove it."

Even Faro knew that horse and mules

forced to pull loads with ill-fitting collars or harnesses often were rubbed raw and bruised until the fresh hair that grew back over the wound came in white instead of the color of the animal's hair coat. Saddle horses did the same thing over their withers when a saddletree's shape didn't match their backs or insufficient blankets or pads were used beneath the saddle.

"He's very broke, either to pull or to ride," the Mexican trader said.

"Big Missouri mule." The other spat through his beard again. "From the size of him and the look of those feet I'd say he has more than a little draft horse blood in him."

Faro was quickly losing interest in the mule. "What about those horses over there?"

He left the gate and started past the mule to get a better look at the horses intermingled with the mules. The black giant was standing on three legs with his lower lip sagging as if he were asleep, but when Faro passed by he came alive in a split second and snaked out his neck. His teeth snapped the elbow of Faro's left coat sleeve hard enough to jerk him off balance.

Faro took a quick couple of steps away from the mule and passed dirty looks back and forth between the hole torn in his coat sleeve and the mule who was standing there with a piece of cloth still held in his teeth and that sleepy, lazy, innocent look written all over him again.

"He can be a little cantankerous, but he's broke to death once you put him to work." Beard took a third spit and then wallowed the tobacco around in his jaw like a cow chewing its cud. "I'd call him about the finest mule in Texas, if I do say."

Faro was amazed that the stock trader could even spit, considering that his whiskers all but covered his mouth. "A devil is more like it."

"That's what Julio there calls him, Old Scratch." The Beard's tobacco juice landed dangerously close to Faro's foot. "Sorry there, I'd hate to stain those fancy boots."

Faro gave the black one last look. Old Scratch seemed an appropriate name for the hateful mule. He was glad he wouldn't be having anything to do with him.

The horse selection was limited, but there was a pair of mismatched wagon horses that looked like they might work — an ancient-looking bay and a sorrel that looked as if he might have a little Belgian blood in him. There wasn't a saddle horse in the lot that was sound to ride, or that the traders would vouch for the safety of riding them around

San Antonio without somebody trying to take them back.

"You said you needed a team to pull a wagon, and those three mules would be a start on putting together a pack string." Caesar leaned against the gatepost and rubbed his jaw as if he were enjoying the prospect of doing some trading.

"What the hell do you want with that black mule?" Faro asked.

"I think he'll be fine. Maybe he's a little spoiled to the collar, but give me time and I'll make a good pack mule of him. And maybe I'll ride him."

"You're the mule expert. It's whatever you think as long as I don't have to get within ten feet of him. Seeing you try and ride that black mule might be worth whatever he costs."

"You'll see. Won't be long until you'll wish you had taken him for your own mount."

Just to prove him wrong Faro pointed to a gray mare across the corral. She was standing by herself, as if she didn't have the energy or the gumption to join the other animals. She was thin to the point that he could count her ribs and her hipbones stuck out like horns. But he was sure she would look fine once she had some regular groceries. "What about that mare? Nobody's mentioned her."

"She's as gentle as a lamb." Beard started to spit again, but noticed Faro glaring at him and made an obvious adjustment to aim his juice safely away from Faro's boots.

"She's very old," Caesar said.

In the end, Faro bought the three mules, the mismatched team, and the old gray mare. For a few dollars more, the traders sold him a rickety army ambulance with a weather-rotted canvas top and in bad need of a paint job. While Faro paid the sellers, Caesar hitched the team to the wagon and tied the mules and the mare behind. The dog came a little ways out of the hut he'd been hiding in, just far enough to growl. Old Scratch cocked one ear at the mutt and slowly lifted a hind leg as he was led past. The dog yelped like it was scalded and fled back inside the hut.

"Caesar, you and that dog have different opinions about Old Scratch," Faro said. "Me, I think I agree with the dog."

CHAPTER 27

Jim had about finished painting the ambulance when Faro walked over to the livery. He'd painted the wagon box and was applying touch-ups of black paint to the wheels. When he noticed Faro he pointed to the wagon with his paintbrush, a proud smile on his face.

"What do you think about that?"

"I'm at a loss for words."

"Well, it's different; there's that."

"If it was any brighter I'd swear it was a circus wagon." Faro picked up an almost empty bucket of paint. According to the label, the color was supposed to have been red, but the wagon was more faded pink than any kind of red.

Jim squinted and rubbed at the blotch of paint he could feel on his nose with the back of his wrist. "Yeah, can't do anything about that. It looked red until the paint dried."

"Paint over it with that black. I'd rather it

look like a hearse, and I'll be danged if I'll travel all the way to New Mexico with two women and a pink wagon. I'd be the laughingstock of the army."

"Better get used to it." Jim tried to keep a straight face, but it was plain that he thought the whole thing funny. "I don't have enough black left, and that was the last can of paint I could find anywhere."

"An eyesore is what it is." Faro scowled at the sickeningly pink wagon. "At least it looks to be in traveling shape."

A new white canvas top was stretched over its bows and a new shaft, wheel repairs, and a few rotten planks replaced made it look like a different rig. Faro circled the wagon to scrutinize the improvements. He paused when he reached the back end and looked a question at Jim.

"What?" Jim shrugged.

Faro couldn't hold back the smile he felt building. The boy's sense of humor seemed as dry as his own. There on the tailgate, hand painted in neat, black letters were the words NEW MEXICO OR BUST.

Armand showed up with a pail of axle grease. He set his load down and stared at the wagon while he rolled his shirt-sleeves up. "I don't like it."

"Give it a chance. Pink might be your

color," Jim said.

Faro raised an eyebrow. "Maybe it will grow on us."

The three of them pitched into the work of completing the wagon's repairs. Faro oiled and mended harnesses while Armand greased the axle skeins and Jim finished painting. Two of Sibley's regiments were already on the trail west, and the general had informed Faro that his headquarters staff and the last remaining regiment would start west the next morning. Jim was smiling and laughing and apparently his worries and concerns over serving as a scout had left him for the moment. Even the gruff and surly Cajun surprised them both by chuckling or smiling once or twice at Jim's youthful antics and jokes.

They finished their work just before dark and the three of them went down the street in search of a meal. Faro buttoned up his coat and listened to Jim tell another one of his stories of farming in the Indian Nations while he looked ahead to the warm glow of lamplight coming from the restaurant windows ahead. They kept to a section of boardwalk on the upwind side of the street, using the building walls and porch awning to shelter them from the wind that was steadily picking up.

They were still a city block away from the restaurant when the shadows of two people came around a corner on their side of the street and ducked into an alleyway. Shortly thereafter, a woman called out for help. It wasn't exactly a scream, but it was plain that she was in trouble. Faro thought is sounded like Rue's voice, and he ran to the alley's mouth with Jim and Armand on his heels.

The evening light was poor in the shadowed alley, but the first thing Faro saw was a man holding a woman pinned by the throat against the left-hand wall. They were too deep into the dark to make out who they were.

"Help me," the woman said pitifully.

Faro started forward, fumbling with the buttons on his coat to free his guns. "Let her go!"

The man in the shadows slowly stepped away from the woman, moving deeper into the alley. Faro took two more steps forward as the woman ran by him and out of the alley without another word.

Faro could feel Jim and Armand and his back, so he knew good and well that they too had heard a side door open into the alley behind them. Couldn't miss it. And just like him, they had to see the other two men rise up behind the man who had held the women. Faro chanced looking away from the three in front of him to see how many were coming out of the side door behind him. Three more, six against three — it was a neatly laid trap. He wondered how much they had paid the woman to lure him into the alley. The thought of being played for a sucker bothered him almost as bad as the thought that he was about to get killed.

The evening was cool enough that he had his coat fastened all the way up. His hand was still fumbling with the buttons when one of the ambushers in front of him raised his arm. It was just a shadowed thing, little more than a flicker of movement some part of Faro's brain or gut instinct registered as dangerous. He didn't need daylight to know that there was probably a pistol or a knife on the end of that arm, so he charged forward, trusting that Jim and Armand would take care of those behind them. And if they didn't, it wouldn't matter for long, because he was going to be very, very dead.

There was no getting to his pistols in time, and he slid the sword cane from its sheath and slashed right and left with the thin blade as he stepped into the middle of the men before him. He felt the sharp steel slice into flesh just as pistol flame passed over his left shoulder. Deafened by the gunshot and half blinded by the flash, he thrust at the man farthest to his right with the blade and swung a backhanded blow with the sheath at the man who had shot at him. The hardwood sheath smacked a skull, sending the gunman crashing against the far wall of the alley. The man in front of Faro grabbed at the sword piercing his thigh and the blade snapped as he twisted to the ground.

The remaining man in front of him rushed forward, and Faro flung the grip of his broken sword at him. He chopped down with the sheath in an arcing, overhand stroke, but his attacker was coming too fast and ducked under the blow and crashed into him. Faro was driven backward until his shoulder blades were pinned against the downspout of a gutter and a stack of shipping crates.

Two quick gunshots sounded in the alley, but things were happening too fast for him to keep up with what was going on. He was wondering who had been shot when something clipped him hard on the chin — harder than a fist, maybe a club or brass knuckles. Bright spots danced before his eyes and he could already taste the blood in his mouth where he had bitten his tongue. He grasped wildly and blindly with his left hand and managed to block the next blow. They were tangled together, each of them trying to free a blade or a gun to finish the fight.

Faro managed to get his forearm across the man's throat and raised his right leg as much as he could, reaching for the little Colt in his boot. The killer's hot whiskey breath was in his face and there was no room to raise the pistol when his fingers finally closed around its butt. He took another blow on the shoulder just as he eased back the hammer on the pistol hanging at the end of his right arm and pinned between them. His finger convulsed against the trigger at the shock of the blow and the pistol went off unintentionally. His attacker groaned and cursed and staggered away.

Faro slid down the wall to the ground, his chest wheezing for air and groping for the pistol he'd dropped. By the time he found it the three men he'd fought were helping each other out of the back end of the alley, two of them limping and the other with his head clutched in his hands.

More thumping and knocking was going on back the way Faro had come. He rested the Colt on an upraised knee and waited for someone to come along who needed killing.

The alley went quiet — too damned quiet, like death.

"You all right, Mr. Faro?" Jim finally called out, his boyish voice out of place coming on the heels of such violence.

"I'm still kicking. What about you two?"

"We're still standing."

Faro didn't think he had anything broken or that he was seriously wounded, but it took him two tries to get to his feet. His right arm was still half numb from the blow he'd taken, and the fresh scar on his chin felt as if it was broke open again.

A crowd had gathered in the alley and lanterns were shining by the time Faro got to his feet. He didn't recognize any of the faces other than Jim's in the feeble lamplight.

"You look like hell." Jim held a lantern high and leaned forward out of the glow to peer at Faro.

"Get that light out of my face." Faro took the lantern himself and used it to examine what had been a battlefield only moments before.

Jim bent over to pick something up and soon handed Faro the grip of his broken sword cane. "Now that's a sneaky trick you've been packing around."

"A man ought to keep a little insurance,"

Faro said. "Not that I did a whole lot of good with it — stuck one of them through the leg and gave another a bad headache. What about you? You aren't shot, are you?"

Jim looked down at his pistol in the lantern light and chuckled before he shoved it in his holster. "I don't need but one arm to get this old bang-bang out and busy. I hit one of those behind us hard, or I'll be a suck-egg hound."

Armand shoved into the light, holding something out to them. "Looks like this Indian did hit something."

They all leaned over to peer at the bloody pinky finger lying in the Cajun's palm.

"Anybody you know?" Jim asked.

"I don't recognize him," Faro answered.

"He seemed taller in the dark," Armand growled.

"I suppose you didn't like this either. *Pas bon,* huh?" Faro thought for once he'd beat Armand to the punch.

Armand grinned like he was the happiest man in the world. "*Non, c'est bon. C'est si bon.* Good fight."

"Go figure," Faro scowled at the Cajun.

"You should have seen old Armand here," Jim said. "He grabbed two of those fellows and smacked them together like they were rag dolls. Hit one so hard I swear he skidded on his back when he hit the ground."

The lantern light was enough for Faro to see that Armand was also bleeding from a wound in his side. Blood was steadily soaking through a hole in his coat.

"You shot?"

Armand shook his head. "Stabbed, but the blade, it didn't go in too deep."

"Lucky."

Armand took a lantern from one of the gawkers and squatted in front of the gutter downspout and examining the ground. "You don't fight too bad for a gambler."

"I only touched off one shot. A big fellow had me pinned to the wall there and I let my pistol go off into the ground."

Armand pointed to the thick pool of blood smeared into the dirt. "Your aim must've been better than you thought. Looks like you bored him in the leg or the foot."

"You got any idea who they were, Mr. Faro?" Jim asked.

Before Faro could say that he didn't, a man from the crowd of gawkers at the mouth of the alley butted into the conversation. "I saw a handful of rough-looking men and a woman hanging around here about a half hour ago."

"Did you recognize any of them?" Faro asked.

"Naw, never saw them before except for the woman. Bulldog Mollie, she's a whore around here. Got a shack down on the creek."

"You don't have to worry about questioning Mollie," another voice in the group said. "They just found her down the street with her throat cut. Must've been a sharp knife, because they danged near cut her head off."

Faro looked up from searching his body for wounds. "One of those men you saw, he didn't happen to be wearing one of those caped coats, long hair like a woman's, all in black?"

"He was one of them. One-eyed, tall fellow."

Jim took the lantern from Faro's hand. "Mr. Faro, maybe I ought not say it again, but you better start wearing your pistols on the outside of your coat."

"I think you're right, Jim. I think you're right."

CHAPTER 28

It was a leisurely departure for an army with so far to go, but a little after high noon General Sibley came out of the hotel and stood in his buggy and gave a little speech to his troops and those civilians gathered around to see him off. It might have been a fine speech, but the wind had picked up again, drowning out his words, and the nervous roan filly hitched to his buggy spooked from something in the crowd and threw a run away before the general even got good and started. His arms windmilled wildly until he fell backward in his seat, and he scrambled to gather his reins and to check the filly's speed. An empty whiskey bottle bounced out of the buggy as it sped away.

The crowd waved at him and gave a ragged cheer, apparently thinking that the general's departure at a high gallop had been done on purpose for effect. Everyone in town knew that the general could be a little dramatic, especially when there was the smell of whiskey on his breath, or maybe they were simply more than ready to get the parade over with so they could get out of the wind.

Fifth Regiment's band took the general's fast departure as their cue and marched down the road after him, beating drums and blowing the dust out of their instruments. The rest of the soldiers mounted their horses or put their shoes and boots to the road and followed along, most trying to put to use the close order drills that they had been practicing for weeks to show off for the town folks. A few men waved at wives or sweethearts, and some even bragged that they would be home in a couple of months with the flag from the governor's palace at Santa Fe. Few there doubted that the Army of New Mexico, as it had been dubbed by General Sibley, would be back to celebrate a victory by the following spring. Texans were widely known to be the toughest men on the face of the Earth, at least in the opinion of other Texans, and all could agree that a few Yankees and piss-poor Mexican rabble didn't stand a chance against such fine sons of the Lone Star State. All the hoopla excited the pack of town dogs and they darted in and out of the band barking and howling.

Captain Lacey's lancers popped their pistols into the air, and kept their wild-eyed horses in check and two by two down the middle of the street. They were indeed an impressive lot with their brightly colored lance pennants, red sashes, and a standard bearer riding at the head of their line toting a flag the ladies of San Antonio had sewn for them.

Faro studied the troops in their mismatched uniforms and outsized smiles, and thought them all proud fools. But he couldn't blame them. Going off to war was a lot more fun than war itself.

Regardless of his scoffing and complaining about the parade, and regardless of the fact that he wasn't a soldier, he had gone through the trouble of making sure his clothes were brushed, and he replaced his abused suit coat with a waist-length Mexican jacket and a wool poncho made from a brightly striped serape. He had even bought a new saddle to throw on the back of his flea-bit gray mare. While she was too old to prance like the lancers' mounts, he still felt taller as he rode between the lines of people gathered at each side of the street. *Well, look at you. Strike up a marching tune and have a parade, and you think you're really something.*

The pink wagon was a big hit with the crowd, and more than one of them pointed at it as it passed. Jim acted like it was the funniest thing in the world, although Armand on the wagon seat stared straight forward and looked madder and more embarrassed by the moment.

The motley procession of would-be conquerors soon disappeared into the dust, and eventually even the sound of the band and the barking dogs faded away from the ears of those left behind. Faro eyed the afternoon sun glowing feebly through the cloud of dust raised up by the long line of supply wagons and carts following in the wake of the army, and thought about all he'd heard of the trail ahead of them during his stay in San Antonio. After a traveler left the Devils River nothing called that country home except for snakes and horny toads and an occasional wandering Indian. Most of the supposed waterings were little more than wells and springs or run-off tanks that would barely keep up with the thirsts of thirty men and horses, much less a brigade of soldiers and its supply train. That was the reason Sibley had been trickling his troops to Fort Bliss a regiment, or sometimes even a company or a squad, at a time.

Rue McGaffney rode up alongside him sitting sidesaddle on a good bay gelding. She wore a caped long coat over a green dress, with silk gloves, and a small derby hat with a lace band that made her look as if she should have been following the hounds on a fox hunt back East rather than about to set out across half of Texas. Her cheeks were flushed and her smile was the first true one she'd given him since he'd gotten drunk in Indianola and lost most of her money.

"Isn't this kind of grand?" She leaned over to pat the sleek neck of the bay and looked along the line of their march.

Faro cast a glance out of the corner of his eye at the bay. It was a fine horse indeed, but it rankled him that Captain Lacey had given it to her. There was nothing that he could put his finger on, but something about that cocky Texan captain bothered him. Maybe it was his foxy eyes, or the strained chuckle he used for a laugh. Then again, the fact that he had found a good horse for Rue when Faro couldn't do better than an old gray mare might have been what rankled him most.

"Be careful with that horse. He looks a little flighty," he said.

She laughed. "He's a sweetheart. I used to

ride often when I was in New York. Horses are such wonderful creatures, aren't they?"

Faro didn't think she wanted to hear his thoughts on horses. She was big on keeping things upbeat, and he hoped he didn't sound too droll. "They can certainly be spirited."

She gave his gray mare a once-over. "How old did you say that mare was?"

"She'll be just fine." He didn't tell her that Caesar had examined the mare's teeth and guessed her at over twenty years old, more like thirty, the equivalent of ancient in equine years.

"He doesn't like horses," Zula called from the spring seat of their pink wagon. Armand was sitting beside her and driving the mismatched team.

"I bet you that mare won't make it halfway to New Mexico," Jim chimed in. The general had supplied Jim with a lanky little blue roan mustang, and the kid rode as if he were born on the back of a horse.

Go ahead and laugh. They could say what they wanted to, but horses were damned unpredictable creatures, and that was on the best of days. They could kick you, bite you, buck you off, do everything but what you wanted them to, and worst of all, some of them had a damnable habit of running off every time something scared them. He'd long since had his fill of horses in the army and going to the gold fields in California. The less he had to ride the better, and he tried not to think of all the miles he was going to have to ride to New Mexico. The old gray mare suited him just fine.

"You ought to be ashamed of riding that poor thing." Caesar sat astride one of the little mules, his legs dangling comically below its belly and near to the ground.

Faro started to point out that Caesar's mount wasn't exactly the romantic image of a cavalier's charger but stopped short. The Mexican was fond of mules, and more touchy about insults thrown their way than he was about his own self.

"She'll look better once she's had some more groceries and proper care." Faro had already found the gray mare to be fairly predictable, at least as horses went.

As if in response, the gray mare stumbled and lowered her neck until her drooping bottom lip threatened to drag on the ground. Even though the ground was level and smooth, she came close to falling to her knees.

"Must have tripped over a rock," Faro said.

"I'm going to ride ahead and see if Captain Lacey wants to race me." Rue tapped her bay across the hip with a leather bat and tore away at a run up the side of the column.

"Steady often wins the race." Faro called after her.

"I'll tell you what steady is: It's boring," Zula said.

In contrast to Rue, Zula was dressed for the trail. She wore a wool skirt and a white shirt so tight that it looked like it barely had room to button over her ample chest. Her hair was braided into a single thick rope hanging down her back and somebody had given her a buffalo-fur cap to wear. A heavy, sheepskin coat lay on the seat beside her. She might have been dressed like a man, but nobody was going to mistake her for one. Already, several soldiers had made a point to match pace with the wagon, infantrymen and cavalrymen alike, all of them casting glances at Zula and looking like they were trying to get their courage up to talk to her.

"You folks need to remember who your leader is. You know, the one you hired to get you to New Mexico," Faro said. "Hey, Jim. Did you get me those cigars I asked for?"

Jim kicked his mustang up beside Faro and reached into his coat pocket and pulled out a handful of stogies. Faro only took one, bit off the end, jammed it into his mouth, and lit it. He puffed away and made a point to stare ahead of him.

"The old gray mare ain't what she used to be, ain't what she used to be," Jim sang in a fair voice, looking straight ahead like his boss, but keeping a watch on him out of the corner of his eye.

"Aren't you supposed to be scouting ahead of the column?" Faro asked.

Faro's growling didn't wipe the smile off Jim's face.

Zula puffed out her chest and took a pose on the wagon seat that was a fair imitation of Faro's posture in the saddle. "Oh, you look very much the picture of a fearless leader, Don Quixote, but I'd suggest you'd be better off tilting windmills on that old nag, cause you sure aren't going to impress Rue with her."

"You'd be better off riding the black mule than that old mare," Caesar added.

Faro eyed the big black tied alongside the remaining mule to the rear of the wagon. "It'll be a cold day in Hades before I ride that black John. This mare's just fine."

"Suit yourself," Caesar said. "But she won't make it a week on the trail."

"We'll show them, won't we?" Faro

313

reached back and rubbed the top of the mare's hips to praise her and bumped her with his heels, intent on loping away and showing them just what a good choice in mounts he'd made. The gray mare farted in surprise and only managed a trot until he kicked her twice more as hard as he could.

"Keep an eye out for windmills, bold knight," Zula called after him.

He wondered where she had come across *Don Quixote* and made a mental note not to travel again with educated women who read Cervantes and were too smart for their own good.

CHAPTER 29

"I thought you said you saw a herd of buffalo?" Faro asked.

"I did. Give me time to find them again."

"We've cut a five-mile circle. How do you lose a herd of buffalo?" Faro asked. "We haven't even seen a track."

"Maybe they're around that point yonder. I might have taken us too far west to go to them the way I came the first time."

"I thought Indians never got lost," Faro said on the side of the butte where they'd stopped to scan the country.

"An Indian never told you that."

Faro scowled down the length of the red, chalk-streaked mountain. He tried to search out their camp at Fort Stockton in the midst of all the miles and endless miles, but couldn't find it. Nothing but brown, brittle grass underneath a gun-smoke sky, and the only green an occasional cactus or yucca bush dotting the desolation.

"Let's turn back. We aren't going to find anything," he said.

"There's us some meat." Jim pointed down the mountain, and half whispered, "She ain't a buffalo, but she'll do."

It took Faro a full minute to spot the mule deer doe Jim was trying to point out. The animal had come out of a dry wash some one hundred yards below them. It was wary and stopped with only its big-eared head showing over a clump of boulders, looking back up the butte in their direction.

"You better shoot quick," Jim whispered. "She's getting spooky and will run for sure."

Faro fumbled at the string his rifle hung from, but finally managed to ease the Sharps to his shoulder. The deer must have winded them, for it trotted twenty yards farther away from them before stopping broadside and looking back again.

"Bust her," Jim whispered again.

Faro took a long time aiming, fighting the wavering front sight and trying to draw a careful bead just behind the deer's front shoulder. He knew he'd missed just as soon as he squeezed the trigger. The deer whirled and ran away in high, bounding leaps.

"You kicked up dirt ten yards in front of her," Jim said.

"My sights must be off."

"No, I sighted that gun in for you. Hold a fine bead and it's dead-on at that distance."

"I guess I'm just not used to it, or maybe the sights got knocked off hauling it around on my saddle."

"Maybe." Jim's voice didn't sound like he believed that.

Faro knew it had been a poor shot, but hearing some smart-alecky kid say it rankled him. "I guess you could have done better?"

"Maybe. I've made harder shots."

"Oh, you have?"

"We haven't had anything but tough beefsteak since we left Devils River. Don't get touchy just because you missed our supper."

"I thought Indians weren't supposed to talk so much. You chatter like a bird." Faro shoved another paper cartridge into the Sharps breech, closed it, and capped the nipple. "Why'd I hire you in the first place? You got any of those cigars left?"

Jim reached in his pocket and passed them to him. "I guess you hired me to pack your cigars and unsaddle your horse at night. You just didn't say nothing about how much I could talk."

"The least Sarge could've done was point out a kid to go with me that wasn't so sassy." Faro hung his rifle back on his saddle horn and started down the butte, cocking his head away from the cigar smoke that the wind was blowing by his face. "I should've known not to take you along. Could tell right off that you didn't know how to respect your elders."

They were halfway back to camp when a jackrabbit burst from a clump of grass right under their horses' hooves and zigzagged at high speed away from them. Faro had taken to wearing his Navy Colts outside his coat, and he thought he drew his right-hand gun quickly, or at least what he thought was quick. But Jim's pistol went off before he even had time to raise his own. Startled, he swiveled around to study the kid, his right ear ringing from the concussion.

Jim shoved his pistol back in its holster and smiled. "A little rabbit stew ain't quite buffalo meat, but it'll do in a pinch."

It dawned on Faro that the jackrabbit had disappeared. "Are you trying to tell me you hit him?"

"I am."

"Horse crap."

They kicked their horses up and rode to look for the rabbit. Faro was sure the kid was just bragging. There was no way in creation that anybody could snap off a shot that quick and hit anything, much less a snot-nosed, know-it-all teenager.

"I didn't lead him enough. Might have missed his head." Jim stepped down from the saddle and made a show of searching the grass.

"You might have missed his head? On a running rabbit? You're something else." Faro tried not to gloat, and was wondering how long Jim would keep up the act before he admitted he missed.

"What do you call this?" Jim held up a limp, dead rabbit with a bloody hole busted through its rib cage.

"Luck."

"I call it a dead rabbit."

Faro went on ahead. It was obvious Jim wanted to rub it in, for he quickly mounted and caught up. They rode in silence for a little ways, Jim still smiling over the stringy rabbit, as if he had killed a bear with his bare hands.

"How come a man that doesn't shoot any better than you is wearing two pistols, plus one in his boot and another one on his saddle?" Jim asked after a while. "That's kind of like a man that never rides a horse wearing spurs."

"I guess you could say it's because I'm not a trusting sort. No more friends than I've got, I figure the more guns the better."

"That might not be a bad idea at that." Jim said.

"Where did you learn to shoot like that?" Faro asked. "You aren't even dry behind the ears yet."

"I've always kind of had a knack for it, but my uncle taught me a bit too."

"This uncle of yours sounds pretty tough."

"I don't know. There's some salty folks back where I'm from that walk wide around him."

"Does he shoot like you?"

"Better."

The more Faro came to know Jim, the more he realized how little he knew about him. "Are you on the run from the law?"

Jim shook his head. "Naw, I ain't wanted for anything."

"Did you shoot somebody back there in the Indian Nations?"

"Told you, I ain't ever been on the scout."

"That isn't exactly an answer," Faro said to Jim's back as he followed him.

"Maybe I'll answer if you'll tell me how you got that bullet scar in your cheek and that bum knee. I heard Sarge mention something back in New Orleans about you having trouble over a woman, and General Sibley hinted at the same thing."

"That isn't any of your business."

"There you go. No disrespect, Mr. Faro, but I guess some stuff doesn't need talking about."

Before Faro could answer, gunshots sounded from the direction of the fort — a lot of gunshots. Seemed like everyone was in a shooting mood. They could just make out the shape of the fort's buildings in the distance. The gunfire continued, and they could hear men shouting.

"They aren't shooting at us." Faro wondered if he and the kid's own gunfire had alarmed the Confederate pickets. The last thing he wanted was for some antsy guard to shoot them by mistake.

"They ain't shooting at jackrabbits either." Jim pointed to a dust cloud retreating a quarter mile from the fort. "I think it's Indians. It's hard to make them out, but it looks like they're driving horses. Probably our horses."

CHAPTER 30

Jim's eyesight was impressive. Faro could only make out the cloud of dust to the south. "How can you tell they're Indians?"

"Indians don't ride like white men."

Faro kicked the gray mare up to a lope, and they kept a watch on the fleeing Indians, or whatever they were, while they rode for Fort Stockton. They were met by half the camp pointing rifles at them and shouting warnings.

"Don't shoot! We're friendly!" Faro shouted back.

Men were running every which way, gathering and saddling horses and calling out to each other. It was pandemonium, but a couple of officers were forming the calmer sorts into defensive lines, sergeants cussing them into a little discipline and having wagons rolled up to provide a barricade. An artillery crew was straining to roll two field pieces to the edge of camp.

"Damned Indians stole our horses," a soldier said to another as they passed.

Faro didn't slow down until he reached the McGaffney sisters' tent on the creek bank just below the big spring that watered the fort. The sisters met him at the door, both of them watching the confusion of the camp with big eyes.

"Are you two all right?"

"We're fine. Are we under attack?" Rue asked.

"From the sound of it, I'd say some horse thieves raided us."

"I heard men shouting about Indians, and I hear the savages do awful things to their captives," Rue said. "No offense, Jim."

"None taken. If it was Indians, they weren't Cherokee. This ain't our country. Maybe Comanche or Apache." Jim turned his horse away. "I'm going to go have a look-see and talk to a couple of the Kickapoo scouts. I need to talk to another Indian to make sense of this."

Caesar came running through the crowd leading their horses and mules. "The Indians got away with about twenty horses and mules and tried to drive off some of the beef herd."

"Any casualties?" Faro asked.

"They snuck in and were almost gone

323

before anyone knew they were here. One of the guards took an arrow in the foot, but nobody else got scratched," Caesar said.

"Looks like you made sure all of our stock was still here. Good job."

Caesar wiped the sweat from his forehead. "They're all here except for Old Scratch."

Faro hadn't even noticed the hateful black mule wasn't among those Caesar was leading. "Can't say that I'll miss him."

"That's a good mule we lost. I don't know if there is a better one in this camp, or a horse that can match him either."

"None of us has even worked him or ridden him. All I've seen is that he can kick dogs and bite men."

"I know mules. It's what you hired me for."

Faro noticed for the first time that Zula was holding her peashooter pistol. "That isn't much gun."

Zula turned her hand to study the pistol in it, holding it as if weighing it or balancing it on a scale. "It's what I've got."

"Maybe it's time we fixed that." The Indian raid, while not a full-fledged attack, made him think about something he'd intended to do before they left San Antonio.

He went to the wagon and climbed in. Shortly, he came out carrying the two shotguns he'd purchased in New Orleans. He offered them to Zula and Rue.

"What's this for?" Rue looked askance at her shotgun.

"We're going to be passing through some rough country, and I'd feel better if you two were armed."

Rue was holding the shotgun awkwardly, and eyeing it like it might bite. "Do you want me to carry this on my person?"

"Carry it if you want, but I'd settle for you just making sure it's always nearby and handy."

"Is it loaded?" Zula was already shouldering her shotgun and aiming it at an imaginary target.

Faro noticed that she seemed pleased with the gun, as if she were a child with a new toy, as if she were as gun crazy as that Cherokee kid.

"It is. There are those that say a loaded gun is dangerous to keep around, but don't ever forget that an empty gun is useless too. You don't want to use it, but if the time comes that you need to save your own life, you'll probably find that the bad guys aren't going to give you time to load."

"I want to shoot it." There was more than a touch of demand in Zula's voice.

"You might ought to wait. You shoot that

thing off, and you'll have everyone in the camp thinking the Indians are back."

"It feels kind of awkward." Rue imitated her sister and was aiming her gun too, swinging it around with a little less caution than Faro would have liked.

"Careful where you point those things, ladies."

Both of the women passed him looks that told him that they weren't really listening and thought he was patronizing them.

"I've never seen shotguns this short," Zula was squinting one-eyed down her barrels as if she were a sharpshooter with a Kentucky squirrel gun.

He tried to keep an eye on both women and their guns. "I had the stocks and barrels cut off to fit you two. If things get up close and personal, you just aim it in the general direction and touch it off. I guarantee you it will get someone's attention."

"You really think we might need this? We've got a whole army to guard us," Rue said.

"Those Indians stole horses right out from under this army's nose. What if they had wanted to steal women?"

It was plain that Rue hadn't thought of that. "I see your point."

"Do they kick bad?" Zula asked.

"It will give you a little punch, but you won't notice it if you ever have need to use it."

"What about spare loads? I want to learn how to load mine," Zula said.

"Me too," Rue added. "I'm still not sure I need this, but if I'm going to have it, I want to know how to load it and operate it."

"No, you've both got two shots apiece. Loading a shotgun can be tricky. Load it wrong and it's more likely to maim you than who you're shooting at."

"You just said that an empty gun was useless, and that you might not always be around," Zula said. "I'd like more than two shots."

"If you ever need that gun, I suggest you take your time and make sure those two shots count, because two shots is all you're going to get."

"Anything else we need to know?" Rue asked.

"Keep it dry and keep it handy," Faro pushed the barrel of Rue's gun away from where she had it pointing at his feet. "And don't point it at yourself or anything else you wouldn't want to shoot."

"I'm sure we're smart enough to safely manage our weapons," Rue said.

At just that moment, a gun blasted behind

Faro. He turned to see Zula with her shotgun still to her shoulder and admiring a mangled clump of prickly pear not ten feet from her. The green, platelike sections of the cactus were shredded, bits of white, pulpy meat blown everywhere. Her mouth was moving, apparently talking, but he couldn't hear a thing.

"What the hell?" Faro cupped both hands at the sides of his head. He could hear a little bit again, but his ears were ringing wildly.

Zula smiled proudly. "I like this gun."

"Let me try." Rue cocked both shotgun hammers.

With his impaired hearing, it took a bit for what she said to register with Faro. Before he could stop her or make sure he was out her line of fire, she let off not one, but both of her barrels simultaneously. He was standing even with her gun muzzles, and the concussion of the shots made him so dizzy that his knees wobbled.

The double charge staggered Rue backward a step. She rubbed her shoulder gingerly but smiled and pointed at the cactus she'd finished off. The gunshots had Faro addled to the point that all he could do was stare at her.

Bang! Zula emptied her last barrel into

the pitiful stump of the cactus. He staggered around to face her, mouth open, but his head swimming too much to curse.

"Good shot, Sis," Rue said.

In such a state, it took him a few seconds to realize that soldiers were running their way with rifles at ready. He fought to get his bearings and waved them back. "Nothing to worry about. Just a little target practice."

A big-eyed private skidded to a halt in front of Faro, panting from the exertion of his run. "For a minute there I thought the Indians were back."

Faro gingerly wiggled a finger in his aching right ear. "Huh?"

"I said I thought we were under attack." The soldier raised his voice several notches.

"Huh? Back?" Faro's voice sounded strange to his own ears, and as if it were coming from the bottom of a well, slowed down and garbled. "Oh, yeah. You boys can go back. Nothing wrong here."

The soldier shook his head and leaned close, all but shouting, "I was saying, a man in Indian country can't be too careful."

Faro heard him that time, barely. He scowled and turned for another look at the two women behind him, holding their shotguns and smiling sheepishly. "Don't worry about Indians. It's white women with guns that should scare you."

CHAPTER 31

Rue awoke shivering somewhere past midnight and found that her sister had pulled the covers from her. She regained her share of the blankets, but by then she was wide awake and could only stare up at the ceiling, feeling her heartbeat through her chest with her fingertips. The dark confines of the tent seemed too tight, crowding in and smothering her. Zula mumbled something incoherent and rolled over on their feather mattress pallet, threw out an arm that flopped across Rue's face, and shoved a knee into the small of her back. Too restless and bothered to sleep, Rue rose and put on a coat over her gown, then slipped quietly from the tent.

The camp was quiet, and the stars overhead seemed even clearer in the brittle air. There were no skies like that where she came from, at least not so much of it. She strolled along the edge of the camp, the ground cold against her bare feet. The wind whistled through the buffalo-chip campfires, and she could just make out the sleeping soldiers ringed around the coal-red glow of each such fire, snuggled up to its warmth like puppies to their mother. Occasionally a sentry challenged her, but merely mumbled shy greetings or pleasantries when they recognized her voice.

For the most part, she was alone, and that was what she needed — time to herself, time away from Zula and her constant fussing and judgments, and most of all, time to refocus on her goal and to get things straight in her head. The gold was what mattered. Everything she wanted to do depended on the gold. It had all seemed so workable, if not easy, back in New Orleans, but the farther she traveled the more she came to realize just how hard it was going to be.

She made a half circle around the camp, and by the time she backtracked to their wagon a man's silhouette was thrown against the wagon sheet by the fire he sat before. It was Faro, sitting on a camp stool, staring into the flames with both elbows resting on his knees and his palms supporting his chin, as if he were lost in worries of his own.

She knew she should have already apologized for shooting her gun off next to his ear, but she hadn't. He wasn't an easy man to apologize to. Plus, she had more than few bones to pick with him — some she could put a finger on, and some she couldn't.

Even with so much riding on his shoulders, he seemed in no hurry at all. Planning? It was plain to her that he merely winged it from the moment he woke up until he lay down for the night. She could see no reason why they had joined up with the army, when they could have made much better time alone. It seemed silly to her that they should swing so far west instead of cutting a beeline from San Antonio to Santa Fe. Oh, she had heard all the Indian scare stories and the claims that only a handful of scouts could find their way across the Llano Estacado without dying of thirst, but Captain Lacey said he could do it. Then again, the captain didn't have a very high opinion of Faro.

True, she was used to her suitors belittling other men in her presence, but Captain Lacey did seem to know what he was doing. He was as rugged as he was charming, even if that charm seemed a little strained at times. She hadn't told him of the gold, but she had questioned him about the best way to get to Santa Fe.

Studying Faro's profile, she tried to remember what had made her feel such confidence in him back in New Orleans. Sitting there like that, he didn't look at all like the confident, arrogant rake that had walked through her town house door. Why him? It was becoming plain that he wasn't what she needed.

She took a deep breath, intending to discuss their journey, to make him agree to the demands that were too long in coming, to remind him who was paying him, and once and for all to take charge as she should have done from the beginning. Instead, she found herself standing silently at his shoulder, feeling silly and uncomfortable in a strange way.

He looked up and smiled. "Can't sleep either, huh?"

"No."

He was rubbing his right ear tenderly, the same one she'd injured with her gun. Before she knew what she was doing, she reached out and laid the back of her hand against it.

"I hope I didn't bust your eardrum."

He stiffened but didn't pull away. "No, and it's already better."

"Still, I'm sorry." His hair felt nice against the back of her hand.

She could tell what he wanted to do, so it came as no surprise when his arms reached for her waist and pulled her onto his lap. He tried to kiss her, but she pushed against his chest and leaned back.

"Somebody might see us."

She made her best pouty face. "All the time we were in San Antonio, and you never even spent any time with me."

"A thing like that is hard to judge. You might have slapped me rather than kissing me."

She liked it that she made him unsure. "I still might slap you."

"And you and that Captain Lacey have been as thick as thieves lately."

"Jealous?"

"Some." He gave her the same smile — the smile that always made her feel that he thought he knew something she didn't.

He tried to kiss her again, but she pushed away out of his lap.

"There is no telling who is watching. We'll be the scandal of camp if someone sees us."

The look on his face told her he didn't give a damn about propriety, but he stayed seated. "Maybe once we get back to civilization I could take you out on the town. A fine restaurant, then to the theater, or maybe an afternoon at the horse races."

"Do you like to dance? I love music." She immediately chided herself for the excitement in her voice.

He patted his knee brace. "I'm not the glider I once was, but I can still find my way around the ballroom floor."

"Maybe you could come to New York. I could show you around and we could see all the sights together. I promise that you would love it. Maybe we could find the time when this is all over."

"Yeah." His voice changed.

"What's the matter?"

"Those Apaches have me worried."

"Captain Lacey says it was nothing, just a small band making a horse raid." She held her hands out over the fire.

"Maybe, but there are a lot of those small bands between here and where we're going, and other tribes as well. And this war isn't going to be as easy as Sibley lets on," he said. "Perhaps not one of my best plans, dragging women off to war."

"We could leave the army when we get to Fort Bliss and strike out on our own." She turned her back to him, palms out over the warm fire, waiting for his answer.

"That's a thought, but be patient."

"Patient? Do you know what that gold means? To me and to you? No more worries. Everything you ever dreamed of, New York, the things you just spoke of."

"Gold doesn't last forever, even if you can find it. And there's more to think about than just the gold," he said.

"You said yourself, this deal is worth taking chances. You talk of taking me places, and the things we might do, but both of us know you left New Orleans with nothing. Aren't you willing to gamble a little for what you want? For the gold? For me?" She knew she was trying to manipulate him, admitted it to herself. It seemed like something Zula would do, but she had to be strong. It was a strange mix, the feelings he stirred in her and the need she felt for the gold; wanting him to protect her, and, at the same time, not trusting him to do so.

"Why don't you two stay at Fort Bliss when we get there? Let me go up into the mountains and find your gold," he said.

She whirled to face him. "That's right. My gold."

"All right, your gold, but you don't have to die for it. You're paying me, so why not let me take all the chances?"

"Do you think you're the only one with something riding on this? Do you think I would trust anyone? Trust even you?"

"I get the feeling that you're used to getting your way."

"I'm paying you to get my way." She folded her forearms across her chest.

"Come back over here." He offered his hand.

"No, not until you get me my gold. If you really care for me, you'll get me there before anyone else beats us to it."

She charged into the tent, too mad to make any effort at being quiet while she undressed and crawled under the covers.

Zula stirred. "Where have you been?"

"That Faro Wells, sometimes I'd rather slap him than look at him."

Zula yawned and stretched her arms over her head, a sleepy smile on her face. "Those are the best kind, aren't they? I think I might get up and go have a bite of him for breakfast."

Sometimes she hated Zula, but sometimes she wished she were more like her too.

CHAPTER 32

Jim considered the tracks left in the bottom of the sandy wash. Tracking in the woodlands he normally called home was a bit different than the treeless semidesert country he found himself in, but he was pretty sure that the Indians who had stolen the army's horses were long gone and not likely to be caught. The mishmash of horse and mule tracks were already losing their shape in the windblown, powdery sand, and he guessed that the stolen herd had passed that way sometime in the night. He wasn't familiar enough with the country to have any opinion of where the raiders might go, ruling out the possibility of taking a gamble to race ahead to a waterhole or a likely camping spot and hope they were there. The only thing left was to try to work out the sign left behind and trail the horse thieves down — a slow process, and all the while the raiders were getting farther away.

The Kickapoo trackers both felt that the sign suggested Apaches, pointing out the moccasin tracks above Comanche Springs that indicated that the horse thieves had arrived at Fort Stockton on foot. Apaches rode horses when they were available, but could travel just about as far and as fast on foot.

Apaches had reputations as fighters, and cornering a bunch of them was a good way to get killed. And like Jim, the Kickapoos had little hope of running the raiders down, didn't really want to, and were out more to make a showing for the soldiers than anything else. They would all ride back once they had been out long enough to make it look like they had made an honest effort to either recover the stolen stock or locate the hostiles' camp. White folks liked for a man to look busy. Even the dumbest Indian knew that.

The Kickapoos had rode on ahead, lethargically cutting for more sign, but Jim was weary of the game and sat his horse in the shade of a bluff. Despite his looking forward to visiting with the Kickapoos, the night and half a day he'd spent on the trail with them hadn't been what he'd hoped. It seemed he had little in common with them, but then again, they weren't Cherokee.

He would have loved to talk to someone about which girl would be the prettiest at the next stomp dance, whether the acorn crop was going to be heavy that fall, how fat the deer would be for hunting, how much rain would come with the spring, or what the rows of corn would look like green and waving in the wind. The Kickapoos didn't know anything about cattle standing belly-deep in lush bluestem grass, or walking behind a mule with the dark river-bottom ground rolling up before the plow like biscuit dough. They didn't know the sound of a tom turkey's spring gobble with everything green and wet and blooming.

The two other scouts only grunted or stared at him when he spoke of such things. The Kickapoo were rumored to have become a wandering people, white men and red men alike running them from land after land until they had no roots. Maybe that was why they didn't listen. If they had their own dreams of a perfect place somewhere in their memories, then they kept it to themselves, hiding it behind a seeming contentment with the desolate, dry country around them.

If his uncle was there, the Kickapoos might have talked to him. At the very least, they would have listened to him. He was a

Cherokee war chief, a Raven, and leading men was as natural to him as breathing. Jim didn't even have a warrior name, just his boyhood name, a nobody. He'd left before that could happen, impatient and head-strong.

He tried hard to quit thinking of home or the things he should have done, because there was no going back. What was done was done. Unc' said a man had to live with the things he did and make the best with what was left. His mother had called that sleeping in the bed you made.

He wished he'd never heard of Missouri or of the white man's war. If he had only listened when Unc' said he was too young to follow the warriors, instead of sneaking off after them once they were well on their way up north. Then nobody would know his weakness, and he could ride back to his family without them having to duck their heads. He was a coward, and none of his tribe would ever forget that, nor could he.

Unc' had also once said that no matter where he was that he was comforted by the fact that he was Cherokee, but Jim had no people left to him. All he had was his place among the treasure party, and there was no one among those strangers who he could talk to of such things.

Faro Wells seemed a good man, if a little hard to figure out. Jim might have talked to him, but despite being a Fancy Dan clotheshorse, Faro was like Unc'. He didn't seem to fear anything, not exploding ships nor professional killers like that one-eyed Frenchman. Not even cannonballs flying around and whistling like spirits kept him from charging ahead. He didn't ride well or shoot well, and had a poor sense of direction, yet didn't seem to fear or worry about striking out beyond the frontier with a crazy Mexican, and two white, city women.

Jim had seen what kind of men the world contained while coming down the Mississippi to New Orleans — shifty-eyed predators, pirates, pickpockets, confidence men, gamblers, thieves, and whores. Bankers, lawyers, and stump-speech politicians, all watching to see who passed by and estimating what could be taken from them. The worst kind of opportunists. Trash. It took a brave man indeed to set out after so much gold when there were so many who would ride a week to kill you for much less. No, he couldn't talk to Faro about fear.

And the Mexican mule hand? How could he talk about cowardice to a man who'd spent years hunting Apaches to get his scalp back?

And the women?

Rue was headstrong like some women he'd known, his own mother included, scared and stubborn all at the same time, with definite ideas about how things should be and never happy unless life was moving the way she wanted it to. She was always levelheaded, yet at the same time, a little too quiet and distant, almost too calculating in spite of her smiles. Folks seemed to consider Zula the feisty one, but Jim wasn't so sure that Rue was as soft and gentle as was supposed.

Zula? Now she was a horse of different color, yet just as unfathomable and unsettling. Who ever thought that there was a woman who looked like that? Dangerous is what she was, and as sharp-tongued as a crow.

He waved a hand to get the Kickapoos' attention and signaled them that he was going to scout for sign to the west, up a broad canyon of jumbled rock and bare, red earth. Both of them waved and went back to their business of tracking without paying him any more mind.

The canyon was really more of a pass or a wide break between two almost sheer walls of mountain hovering above him. He had no sooner gotten into its mouth than he heard hooves clattering over the rocks, and it was plain that a horse was racing his way. He drew his pistol and turned his horse broadside in the mouth of the pass, waiting. He debated whether to run or take a stand in the rocks. The pass rose hundreds of feet higher as it cut through stone on its way northward and deeper into the red mountains, but the terrain was too broken for him to see more than a hundred yards or so ahead.

As if by magic, the black mule came up out of a gully or a fold in the ground, running hard with its head cocked to one side to avoid stepping on the rein of the hackamore trailing from its nose. A cloud of dust big enough for a whole herd of mules boiled up behind him. Jim moved his horse to block Old Scratch, not sure the beast didn't intend to run him down, while looking for Apaches or whatever was chasing the black devil.

Old Scratch slid to a stop not a foot from Jim's frightened, sidestepping horse, and Jim was quick enough to snatch the rein before the mule could whirl away. He bailed out of the saddle and fought to keep the frightened mule facing him. The big black seemed terrified, the whites of his eyes showing, and those great pupils rolling and straining in their sockets to look behind him. He danced his hips side to side, kicking out at thin air, as if he were seeing phantoms sneaking up behind him.

Jim tried to gather and coil the rein so that neither he nor the mule would become entangled in it, but it was either hung in the rocks or something was weighting it down on the other end. The dust had finally settled some when he managed to put a soothing hand on Old Scratch's neck, and it was when the mule quit fighting that he noticed the dead Indian tied to the rein.

Jim took his knife and cut the rein free of the corpse's wrist and led Old Scratch over to his horse and tied him to his saddle horn. He walked back to the body and rolled it onto its back with the toe of his shoe. It was plain that Old Scratch had drug the body a long ways, for there wasn't much hide left on the Indian's carcass, mainly just raw meat, the head smashed and warped. Considering the moccasins on the naked body's feet, he assumed it was one of the Apaches who'd run off with the stock.

He studied the weird positions and bends of the dead Indian's limbs, and looked back the way Old Scratch had come from. He toed the body again, noting how it flopped like jelly, as if every bone were broken or dislocated. High up on the Apache's fore-head was a strange-looking dent. Jim studied it closer, and when he was finished he was sure that it wasn't a rock that had caved in the Apache's skull like that. It looked more like the shape of a hoof — Old Scratch's hoof.

He went back to the mule and un-cinched the rope the Apache had tied around the animal for a girth. He ran his fingers lightly over the bloody quirt welts cut into the mule's neck and flank. He took one more glance at the dead Indian and then back at the wild, murderous look in Old Scratch's eye.

"Apache killer, are you? Looks like you don't like to be rode any more than we thought you might."

Old Scratch gave a halfhearted kick at another ghost and tossed his head hard enough to shake his big ears. He bared his teeth and threatened to bite, but Jim was too quick and ducked aside before rapping the mule on the nose.

"No, you don't, not this Indian."

CHAPTER 33

King Broulet could tell that the bartender was scared. The little beehive fireplace in the corner of the adobe trading post barely put off any noticeable heat, yet the pimple-faced trader was sweating profusely, and he'd been swiping nervously at the plank bar top with a filthy rag for the last five minutes.

"You say some soldiers came through here two days ago?" King made a sour face at the glass of tequila he'd just thrown down his throat.

"Those Rebels have been filtering through here for weeks headed upriver to Fort Bliss. Those were just the last ones."

King reared his chair back against the wall and propped his boot heels on the table at the far end of the room. "What about the women?"

"I've done told you. I saw two white women with them. One dark-haired and one fair."

King laid his LeMat pistol on the table beside his legs and opened the book in his lap. He looked up from time to time to keep his eye on the trader.

Stuttering Willie came through the door, followed by the rest of the gang. They lined up at the bar and ordered drinks.

"That's two bits a glass," the trader said after all of them had knocked down two glasses apiece.

Willie ignored him and jerked the bottle from his hands. "S-s-s . . . sounds kind of s-s-s . . . steep to me for this Messican turpentine you're serving."

"Two bits a glass. A man's got to make a living."

The trader wiped his palms on his stained leather apron. King thought it looked more suited for shoeing horses than it did for tending bar. And the trader had good reason to be nervous around the likes of the men standing in his place of business. Every one of them looked like just what they were, scum. King had purposely picked them for that very quality. One or two of them he had picked up along the way, but most of them had worked for him back in Louisiana.

"Wuh . . . wuh . . . what's that you're r-r-r

349

. . . reading?" Willie turned his back to the bar.

King marked his place in the book with his thumb and closed it. *"Beowulf."*

"What kind of wolf?" Black Jack asked. He was twice as big as Willie, but only half as mean, and not near as ugly.

"It's an ancient tale about heroes and villains. A poem."

"Where does the wolf come in?" Black Jack asked. "I like wolves."

"Beowulf is the hero and Grendel is the monster, or maybe it's the other way around, depending on how you read it."

"Monster, huh? Must be a pretty good story. You've been reading it off and on ever since we left San Antonio."

King gave up on reading and set the book on the table beside his pistol. The trouble with riding with most cut-throats wasn't that you had to watch your back. It was the fact that they were so damned dumb.

"This is the third time I've read this book," King said. "Black Jack, have you ever seen any of those Indian paintings on rocks or the like?"

"I seen some a few days back, down there along the river."

"Well, books like this are civilization's way of painting on cave walls. The bard that put this story together took a lot of time doing it. Time that he could have spent biting and scratching and screwing and making sure his belly was full. That's the mark of civilization, that we can do something the animals can't. Think of it like building a fire. Not because it's cold or you need it, but just because you can."

"I never build a fire 'less I need it, and I never learned to read."

"Well, read this one if you ever do. The fellow that wrote this knew more about men than most. Knew that the man who doesn't let things get in his way is the man that matters."

"Just what kind of monsters are in that book? Bet it ain't got me in it," Black Jack said.

"Black Jack, not even the great bard himself could have imagined you," King said.

Black Jack looked perplexed, but the grin that soon spread across his face told that he finally took it as a compliment. "I ever tell you that I've been shot twice, and hung and left for dead onest?"

"Qu . . . quit your bragging, Bl . . . Bl . . . Black Jack," Willie said. "No . . . n-n-n . . . nobody cares that you've been huh . . . ung."

A short little Mexican woman, middle-aged, came from the back room and wove her way through the leering men, her eyes downcast. She set a plate of beans and a stack of tortillas on King's table.

"Hey there, trader man. How much you charge for that woman?" Black Jack purposely stepped in her way and made her walk around him, slapping at her bottom as she passed by.

"There's no call for that," the trader said, but didn't look Black Jack in the eyes.

Turtle Ketchum snickered. He did look like a turtle, no chin, and his flabby neck too long and sticking up out of his buffalo coat collar and craning around like his namesake. The hand he was holding the shotgun with was wrapped in a filthy bandage, and a fever sweat dotted his face.

"You got whiskey *and* a woman," Turtle leaned his shotgun against the wall, pouring himself a drink and eyeing the Mexican woman setting plates of food on the bar top.

"I get her first," Black Jack said.

"You two mind your manners," King said. "We don't want our host here thinking we're uncivilized, do we?"

The trader was all the way to the door to the back room. King froze him there with a sharp look and his pistol floating over that way. "How much do we owe you for the food and liquor?"

The trader seemed to relax a little at the mention that he might get paid. "Two bits a man times twelve, and I'd say you've drunk about two bottles of tequila. That's ten dollars more. Let's see. Oh, yeah, two bits for that cigar the stuttering one's smoking. Thirteen dollars and twenty-five cents."

"Too damned high, trader man." Black Jack said. "Maybe you could throw in your woman to round things off."

The trader pulled a shotgun of his own from inside the room behind him. He pointed it at King. "All right, you men, it's time to leave."

King adjusted the patch over his eye with his left hand and his right hand held the LeMat pointed at the trader. "We're both at full cock. Say you get me first, you've just got one barrel there for the rest of these boys."

"I don't want any trouble. You just need to leave. Go find those white women you're so hot after."

"I'm not going to leave, not until you put that shotgun down," King said.

"You guessing I'm a fool? Soon as I put this gun down the lot of you will fight over who's going to kill me," the trader said. "Should have took up this scatter cannon and barred the door when I first saw the likes of you riding up."

"So, we are at an impasse?"

"What's that?"

"A road of no return. You shoot me, and I shoot you. No winners."

The trader readjusted his grip on the shotgun. "I reckon that's how it is."

"All right, what say you we both keep our guns handy and these men and I ease out of here? Nobody hurt."

"Fair enough." The trader's shotgun barrel trembled like his jawbone.

The men began to back toward the door, every one of them looking for a chance.

"Careful," the trader said. "Nobody move too fast."

"You wouldn't let me leave without paying, would you?" King asked. "Don't shoot. I'm just going to pull your price from my vest pocket here."

"You had better move slow. I can't miss at this range."

King eased a twenty-dollar gold piece out of his pocket, slowly showed the coin for what it was, and then flipped it with his thumb in a high arc across the room.

The trader didn't grab for the coin; didn't even flinch. It landed at his feet and rattled on the hard-packed dirt floor. "You just get on out of here."

King nodded to his men. "Let's leave this man to his business."

"Easy now."

King uncocked the LeMat and shrugged, gesturing with his free hand toward the door. *"S'il vous plaît?"*

The trader took a half step backward. "Go ahead."

King eased the front legs of his chair down. "Been a bitch of a day, hasn't it?"

"It's getting better."

King recocked and fired the LeMat at the same time his boots slid off the table and hit the floor. The .42-caliber bullet struck the trader in the Adam's apple and his head flopped forward and then back. The shotgun went off into the ceiling, raining down dirt and grass. Bits of spiderweb floated in the gun smoke.

The trader gargled and slumped against the wall. King thumbed the selector on his pistol hammer and put a 20-gauge buckshot load into the trader's chest. He watched as the little man slid down the wall to the floor, his back leaving bloody skid marks on the pale adobe.

"Well, that's the end of that two-bit sumbitch," Black Jack said.

King picked up his twenty-dollar piece.

"Load up anything we might need."

Black Jack was already at the door leading into the back room. "What about the woman?"

"I don't kill women. It's against my rules."

"First time I ever recall you having any rules, King," Black Jack said. "You mean you expect us to leave her alone?"

"No, I mean *you* kill her. I don't want any witnesses."

Willie rushed to Black Jack's heels. "Luh . . . look. She thinks she's huh . . . hiding behind that little old cot."

"If she knew what I'm fixing to give her, she'd be acting a hell of a lot happier." Black Jack stuck his big knife in the wall, hung his pistol belt on it, and started taking off his coat.

"I d-d-d-d . . . don't want to k-k-k-k . . . kill her, Black Jack. How about you duh . . . do it? You can have firsts if you want to, buh . . . but killing women always makes me feel kind of bad." Willie pushed Black Jack into the back room. "Watch out now, don't let her s-s-s . . . stick you with that little old knife."

King rummaged around behind the bar until he found a small, steel cash box on a shelf. Most of his men were busy carrying away anything they might need, and some things just for the sake of stealing. He opened the box and shoved the meager contents into his coat pocket — no more than a hundred dollars at best. The woman screamed in the back room.

"Give me that can of kerosene," King said to one of his men. Opening the lid, he began to slosh it on the bar. "You two back there had best hurry, or I'll burn you down."

King struck a wad of matches on the door face and lit the thin cigar in the corner of his mouth. He puffed on the stogie twice and then pitched the matches on the bar as he left. Smoke was already pouring out of the trading post by the time he made it to his horse.

A gunshot sounded from inside, and Black Jack and Willie came running out of the smoke. Black Jack was coughing and trying to get his suspenders over his shoulders at the same time he ran.

"You d-d-d . . . didn't give me enough time for my turn, King," Willie said. "I did all the holding, and Black Jack got to have all the fun."

Black Jack scowled at King as he tightened his saddle cinch. "Hard to concentrate on pussy with you setting fire to the place."

"You should have let Willie go first. He's always bragging about how quick he is,"

King said.

"I'm greased lightning, by . . . by God, with either a gun or my puh . . . puh . . . pecker," Willie said.

Black Jack rode by the burning trading post and spit onto the low sod roof. "King, you must be feeling mean today. That was a sweet little brown woman in there, and you didn't even give me proper time with her."

King turned his horse and started along the trail. "I kind of like this western country. A man can be the hero or the villain either one, and nobody to stop him."

"You feeling like a wolf?" Black Jack asked.

"I'm feeling like a monster."

Chapter 34

The month spent on the trail from San Antonio to Fort Bliss was more than enough to give winter a chance to take hold. Since arriving at the fort two days before, Faro had done little but listen to the wind howl and hunker close to his stove. A light dusting of snow still lay on the ground beneath the weak winter sun when he decided he was sick and tired of being cramped up in the room in the post barracks that General Sibley had let him use. He hadn't seen a sign of the McGaffney sisters since their arrival. The sisters had rented a house in Magoffinsville at the edge of the military post and were probably holed up out of the weather just like everyone else. Armand was probably with them, Jim was busy scouting, and Caesar stayed in camp a little ways upriver with the livestock.

The rumor was Sibley was about ready to move his army north, and they all needed to be on the same page and ready to travel. He went to find Jim and Caesar first, his breath smoking in the frosty air, and well aware that he was stalling and giving himself time to think of what he'd say to Rue when he got around to her. Pretty women were usually damned easy to talk to. Rue Mc-Gaffney was a different story, and that bothered him.

Jim was nowhere to found when he came into sight of the pink wagon, but Caesar was in a rope corral with the black mule. Faro leaned against the wagon and watched the Mexican mule tamer work with Old Scratch. There was an aparejo lying on the ground in the center of the pen, and Caesar was rubbing a hand over the mule's body and talking softly to him in Spanish. The haltered mule had both of his ears pinned back in displeasure but was standing quietly for the procedure.

Unlike the American sawbuck pack-saddles, which consisted of a bare wooden tree that was cinched down on a mule's back with panniers or a top dressing lashed on over it, the Mexican-style packsaddle was more like a padded blanket with pockets. Old Scratch seemed to be taking things better than usual, no matter what kind of pack gear it was. Caesar obviously thought so, for

360

he picked up the aparejo and swung it on the mule's back.

Just as quickly, Old Scratch bucked the packsaddle off, kicked it a few times, and proceeded to chase Caesar out of the corral. The muleteer barely had time to roll under the rope fence before Old Scratch's teeth could snap a chunk out of him.

Caesar looked up at Faro and grinned, apparently unbothered by the mule's antics. "He's a little wild, no?"

"You're the mule man. I'm just watching."

Caesar stood and dusted himself off. "It's not that he's afraid, but he is soured to work. I just have to be patient and as stubborn as he is."

"Is that so?" Faro couldn't fight back a smirk. "Like I said, I'm watching, but I think you're going to have a hard time if you think you're going to out-stubborn that mule."

The muleteer ducked back under the rope and approached Old Scratch again. Despite the fact that the mule had tried to kill him only moments earlier, he stood calmly and sleepy-eyed as if it had never happened. Caesar took up the lead rope and began the whole process over. He rubbed the mule until he thought he would stand still for the saddle, and then put the aparejo on his back. Old Scratch threw the thing off again and kicked it several times to make sure that it was dead. Apparently he wasn't sure if he had killed it, for after taking a good sniff of it, he pawed it a few times for good measure.

"I guess you could say he's improving," Faro called out. "He didn't run you out of the pen that time."

Caesar ignored him and tried again.

"Why don't you blindfold him?" Faro asked. "That's the way the army mule packers do it."

"I want him to see what's coming and learn to accept it. Be dependable," Caesar said. "A mule who always needs to be blindfolded to be saddled is not a trained mule."

"I don't know anything about training mules, but I do know that a teacher can't teach anything to a student who won't listen."

"This one will listen. He's smart. Give him time and he will decide that none of his fighting is worth the trouble."

"Maybe he just likes to fight. That's an outlaw if I ever saw one."

Caesar smiled and shrugged. "Maybe he does have a little outlaw in him, but I'm going to make a fine saddle mule out of him. You need something to ride."

"You're crazy as that mule is if you think I'm going to ride him," Faro said. "You'll have done something if you can just make a pack mule out of him. The gray mare suits me just fine."

Caesar grimaced and pointed behind Faro. "I didn't want to tell you, but the gray mare is dead."

Faro turned and went to another corral behind the wagon. Truly, the mare lay on her side, her open eyes already glazed over and her body stiff with rigor mortis.

"What happened to her?" he called back to Caesar.

The Mexican shrugged. "Who knows? It was cold last night and she has little fat to keep her warm. Maybe she froze to death, or maybe she just died of old age."

Faro tried not to look at the mare again.

Caesar took note of the look on Faro's face. "You say you don't like horses, but I think you cared for that flea-bit mare."

"It's a damned shame. She was a pretty good sort as far as horses go. Never did me anything but right."

"She was a grandmother horse. *Tenía muchos años.* Ancient," Caesar said.

"Find somebody to bury her. She looks pitiful lying there like that, and I don't want the coyotes getting to her."

Caesar nodded. "You need something else to saddle if you don't want to ride in the wagon."

"I'll find something."

"Old Scratch will make a fine mount. Mule or not, he would run circles around that gray mare, even in her prime."

"You ride him. A man that will ride a mule doesn't care how he looks. Riding a mule is like wearing an ugly hat." Faro took a seat on the wagon tailgate, waiting to see how long it took for the mule to outlast the Mexican.

Caesar kept repeating the process, an hour's worth of work, and getting the same results. The mule didn't seem all that scared of the packsaddle, but he was positively unwilling to bear it.

"I see what you like about him," Faro said. "He's a real quick learner."

Just to prove him wrong, Old Scratch finally stood with the aparejo on his back, even if he had one ear cocked and his head turned to keep a skeptical eye on it. Caesar took the rig on and off a few times until the mule seemed relaxed and acceptant of the whole process.

"This might be interesting," Caesar said as he tightened the cinch.

Old Scratch flinched a little and blew his

belly up against the cinch, but didn't explode like Faro expected him to.

Caesar kept a sharp eye on his trainee for a long moment, but finally turned to Faro with a look of triumph on his face. "See? Not so hard."

At that very moment Old Scratch put his nose on the ground and went to bucking. His first jump almost landed in the middle of Caesar's back, and the Mexican barely ducked out of the way. Old Scratch went past him lunging high into the air and kicking at the cinch around him with every stride. He hit the rope corral like it wasn't even there and headed off toward town dragging rope, stakes, and fence posts. He passed by several other mules and horses tied to picket lines and caused most of them to break free and charge off after him.

Caesar stood and dusted himself off once more. "I'm going to have that mule broke to pack before sundown. In a few more days he'll be riding and as gentle as a lamb."

"As a lamb?"

Caesar smiled sheepishly. "Well, maybe not a lamb. It may take a man to ride him for a while, until he gets used to the whole idea."

Faro watched the stampede hit the edge of town. A pack of dogs had joined the melee. Their barking mixed in with Old Scratch's braying, and he could already hear women screaming where the herd had torn through someone's clothesline, taking several loads of laundry with them. "You'll be doing good not to get your neck broke or your head caved in if you try and ride that mule."

"Why are you here instead of getting ready for the fiesta?" Caesar asked.

"What fiesta?"

"The one at Magoffin's house. It's New Year's Eve."

"I forgot what day it was."

"Many people will be there, and I'm sure Señorita Rue will be also." Caesar smiled slyly. "And I bet the men will ride for miles for a chance at a dance with her or Señorita Zula."

Faro kept a poker face. "I need to talk to Magoffin. They say if you want mules or horses, that trader's the man to talk to, and I've still got to find you a string of pack animals."

"Yes, that would be one reason to go. Business."

"Never took you for a nosy sort."

Caesar started toward the military post and Faro fell in beside him.

"Perhaps there is time to get ready for the

fiesta, no?" Caesar asked.

Faro frowned. "Let's go catch that mule. The most fun I've had in a while is seeing him humble you. Maybe we could get a few others I know to try and ride him."

By nightfall, Faro had made himself somewhat more presentable. He polished his boots and paid a laundress to sew up the holes in his favorite suit coat and give it a good brushing. A bath, a shave, and a liberal dose of hair tonic finished up his pruning. He missed his fancy sword cane but settled for a fake diamond ring that he bought from the miller's son. He slipped it on his finger, admired its shine, and then stuffed his little Colt in his pocket and headed for the New Year's celebration.

James Wiley Magoffin, or Don Santiago, as he was known on the border, made a fortune sending trade goods up and down the trails to Santa Fe, Chihuahua, New Orleans, and St. Louis. At one time, he had operated south of the border, but Mexican claims that he traded firearms to the Comanche in exchange for safe passage for his wagon trains, and imprisonment during the Mexican War for espionage, had soured his relationship with his neighbors across the river. After the war, he had settled on the

American side of the Rio Grande. Soon, a settlement grew around him, and eventually the military post that was to become Fort Bliss joined him. His home was a large, Spanish affair right off the edge of the post and surrounded by several lower adobes forming a plaza known as Magoffinsville.

Dozens of lanterns had been lit and were hanging from the eaves of the long front porch. A chorus of children and a priest had come across the river and were singing hymns on the street corner. Faro followed the stream of people into the house. The large front room was decorated with bunting and more candles than Faro had ever seen in one place lined the walls. A Mexican band was playing from the rear of the room.

Magoffin's home was packed with locals and soldiers; however, beyond a few officers' and merchants' wives, the party mostly consisted of men. It seemed that many of the young women of the country were attending similar parties south of the Rio Grande, downriver at Ysleta or San Ignacio, or in the new community between the post and the river that some were beginning to call the American El Paso. As a result, bachelors lined the walls staring enviously at those fortunate few men who had found dance partners.

Considering the shortage of pretty, eligible females, it was no wonder that when Faro spied Zula a crowd of men already surrounded her at the punch table. She was wearing a light blue dress and whatever her suitors were saying caused her to throw back her head and laugh. Her beauty mesmerized him for a moment, as it did the men gathered around her. The black-headed wench had a way about her.

He took a stance against the wall and looked for any sign of Rue. After a half hour of waiting, he still hadn't seen her and had done little other than to swap stories with some of the Rebel officers. He soon learned that General Sibley's staff had purchased every single mule and horse Magoffin had for sale.

The music was lively and the atmosphere friendly, but Faro couldn't put a damper on his impatience. Admitting that he had gone through the trouble to make an appearance at the party for nothing more than a chance to see Rue rankled his pride and made him edgy. The fact that she hadn't even bothered to show up made him feel like even more of a fool.

Just when he was about to leave he caught a glimpse of Rue twirling around the dance floor. He shifted his position until he could better see through the crowd. One of the Texas boys had brought a fiddle and was giving the Mexican musicians a break. The tune he chose was wild and fast, not at all suited for a genteel southern reel or promenade, but Rue was more than capable of ad-libbing to the music at hand. In fact, the cultured southern belle was enjoying herself immensely. The steps she performed seemed to come from the music itself.

Faro moved again to get a better look. Through a crack in the crowd he saw that it was Captain Lacey she was dancing with, and damned if that Texas dandy couldn't dance as well as she could.

Now I'm sure I don't like him.

An artillery sergeant beside Faro must have noticed him staring at Captain Lacey. "Don't look so down in the mouth. As soon as she figures out what he is she'll get shuck of him quick. Then we can all get a dance with her."

Faro gave half of his attention to the little sergeant beside him while he continued to watch Rue dance. "How's that?"

"The captain is a little rough around the edges to be courting the likes of her. Those lancers of his are as wild as Comanches. Fighters they are, but most of them should have been hung back in Texas. They say that

Captain Lacey recruited most of them from every saloon and watering hole on the frontier. Renegade Indian fighters and no good malcontents for the most part, and he's the roughest of the lot, no matter what kind of airs he puts on."

The song ended, and Rue and the captain moved toward the far side of the room while Faro debated what to do. He could stand there and pose like a fool, hoping that she would notice him, or he could take the bull by the horns. There wasn't a gambler who ever won anything unless he threw his bet into the pot. Faro smoothed down his coat front, lifted his hat to give his hair a quick finger combing, and moved to intercept the couple. He might not dance like that Texan, but he was more than capable of stealing Rue for a song, or maybe two or three.

Wading through the crowd took time, and the closer he got to her, the less courage was left to him. By the time he had crossed the dance floor, Rue and Captain Lacey were already to the far side of the room. He slowed his pace while he tried to think of what he would say to her. He was three steps away when Captain Lacey kissed her. She smiled and laughed and moved away with the captain's arm at her waist.

Faro stood in the crowd watching them

go, until he became aware that people were staring at him. He headed for the front door.

"It's a good party." Caesar appeared in front of him with a pretty young Mexican girl on his arm. He was limping and obviously a little drunk. He also had a black eye and one side of his face was scraped raw.

"Happy New Year," Faro mumbled. "You look like you've been in a fight."

"I rode Old Scratch." Caesar smiled like he was proud of his black eye. "If only for a little while."

Faro tried to think of how he could end their conversation without offending Caesar.

"You don't look happy. You should try the yellow punch," Caesar said. "Then you will have some fun like me."

The girl on his arm laughed and had obviously been in the spiked punch herself.

Faro shoved past them and continued toward the door, but his eyes caught a gap in the crowd at the punch bowls. He was still telling himself that the last thing he needed to do was to get drunk when he poured the first sweet cupful down his throat.

Across the room, a patch-eyed face appeared in the crowd for an instant, and then was gone.

CHAPTER 35

Faro crashed into something, stumbled, and almost let the neck of the tequila bottle slip out of his grasp. It took him a long moment to realize that he had run into their pink wagon, even though he couldn't remember how he had gotten there or why he might have wanted to be there. He took another pull from the bottle and pitched its empty carcass into the weeds.

Something moved in the dark and he blinked, trying to focus on the large shadow. The snow on the ground reflected just enough light from the sliver of moon overhead for him to recognize Old Scratch's head hanging over the rope corral. The mule yawned and shook his head, big ears flopping.

"Hello, you son of a bitch," Faro slurred.

Old Scratch bobbed his head up and down and flopped his ears again.

"You don't scare me," Faro stepped closer,

373

catching himself against the single strand of rope when he stumbled again. "Just a mean old mule. I've been to war and I've seen worse things than you."

Old Scratch turned half away.

"Don't turn your backside to me," Faro said. "She may not know what a man I am, nor that Mexican mule lover either, but I'm the bull of the woods in this camp. You hear me? I can ride anything with hair. I'm a ring-tailed terror, that's what I am."

His saddle stood on its end next to the rear wheel of the wagon, and he grabbed it and pitched it into the corral, lurching under the rope with his bridle in hand. "You or no damned Texas horse soldier is going to make a fool of me."

He fell against Old Scratch's neck, but managed to get the bit in his mouth and the headstall over his ears. "I'll show you. That's what I'll do. You can take this easy, or you can take it hard."

He heaved the saddle up and slammed it down on Old Scratch's back, resting his forehead against the mule's rib cage while he groped for the cinch hanging on the far side. Finally getting a hold of it, he took a few wraps of the latigo through the cinch ring and tugged it down so tight that Old Scratch grunted.

Gathering his reins, Faro managed, after three wobbly tries, to stand on one leg long enough to get his boot in the stirrup. Two more tries and he was able to get in the saddle, although he almost fell off the other side. Old Scratch bent his neck and looked back at him.

"There now. What do you think of that?" Faro belched, attempted to straighten his coat front, and booted the mule's ribs with both heels.

Old Scratch went off like a Chinese fire-cracker. One moment he was standing still and the next minute he was six feet off the ground. He bucked and kicked and twisted with Faro clawing at his saddle. Man and beast were two erratic shadows under the stars — the larger shadow a storm, and the smaller shadow swaying wildly like a young tree limb in the wind.

Time and again, Faro's seat loosened and he was far off center and almost thrown. Yet, somehow, as if by some fortune or perfect alignment of the cosmos he flew from the saddle only to land back in it again for the next jump. In two more leaps the mule had already busted out of the rope corral again. He bucked so hard that he lost his footing on the slick ground and went to his knees. Scrambling back to his feet, he crashed blindly into the side of the wagon, caving its side in and becoming entangled in the wagon sheet in the process.

Faro wasn't sure which end was up, and he clawed at his saddle horn with his free hand and gritted his teeth against the impact of the giant mule's hooves hitting the ground. There was only pain and strain and the feeling of being caught in the middle of a bad dream. He wanted nothing more than to get free of the black mule, but there were no options to escape that didn't look more painful than the beating he was enduring staying in the saddle.

The wagon's sideboards cracked and splintered, and loosened bolts and freed nails screeched as Old Scratch jerked loose from it. The man thing was still on his back, and it infuriated him. He made two more great lunges and then tore off down the road toward the lights in the distance, crowhopping in stiff-legged lunges, with his hooves thumping on the road like mallets on hardwood.

A gunshot cracked out in the night, and then another, but Faro's roaring ears barely registered the sounds. Nor did he have time to think on the matter, for it was quickly dawning on him that Old Scratch wasn't just trying to throw him. The damned beast seemed dead set on killing him.

CHAPTER 36

King Broulet paused in the dark, his eyes searching the area around the wagon some thirty yards in front of him. It was high time he took Faro Wells out of the picture, and he had recognized a good opportunity to do just that when he saw the gambler stagger drunkenly from the New Year's Eve party. He impatiently fingered the grip of the double-edge knife in his hand. He should have caught Faro long before reaching the wagon, but for a man highly intoxicated, Faro walked extremely fast. He had rushed ahead and to the side several times, hoping to head Faro off and ambush him, but every time he appeared on the path the gambler was already past him.

He could hear Faro stumbling around the wagon, and he took a couple of quick steps nearer. The Arkansas toothpick in his hand was razor sharp and would cut through a man's neck like butter. He knew that because Faro wouldn't be the first one he'd used it on. All he had to do was to get within arm's reach and the blade would take care of the rest.

He was finally close enough to realize that Faro was preparing to ride off, and he realized at the same time that he was too far away for the knife in his hand to do anything about that. He sheathed the blade and drew the LeMat in its place. It was hard to make out Faro in the dark, but it looked like he was already in the saddle. King trotted forward, telling himself to hurry, but not so fast that he bungled the kill. Faro had already escaped him twice, and he had no intention of letting it happen a third time.

King was only ten yards away when he decided to stop and shoot. It was too dark to use his sights, but Faro's shadow atop the mule was a target hard to miss at such close range. He eased the hammer back on the LeMat. It was just too damned easy.

Before his finger could tighten on the trigger, the mule started bucking. He could barely make out anything, but he saw enough to be sure that he had never seen an animal fight so fiercely. Faro wobbled around in the saddle like some kind of circus clown, yet somehow he stayed on. In those occasional moments where King felt he could see well enough to shoot, the mule and the gambler were moving too fast. And then the mule crashed into the wagon and was blocked from King's view. He ran forward, hoping to catch Faro on the ground. Dark or not, he couldn't miss if he shoved the LeMat against Faro's ear and pulled the trigger.

The big mule charged past him just as he rounded the corner of the wagon, almost bowling him over and knocking him to one knee in the process. He pivoted and fired at Faro's back, but knew he had missed the instant he pressed the trigger. He fired again, more out of frustration than anything, but the mule was running by then instead of bucking.

King's last look was of the tangled wagon sheet trailing behind Old Scratch like a ghost floating on the breeze as they disappeared into the night. He listened to the sound of the mule's hooves on the road and cursed.

CHAPTER 37

Somewhere, minutes, maybe hours, or maybe an eternity later, Faro realized that he wasn't moving anymore. Whatever nightmare he'd been in was over. Every joint in his body ached, and he was soaking wet, terribly cold, and out of breath. But at least he was no longer rising and plunging with his head snapping forward and back until it felt like it would separate from his neck. He felt so limp and drained that he expected any minute to melt and trickle away.

Raising his chin from his chest, his head bumped into something. He grimaced and craned his neck around to stare dumbly at the ceiling rafters just above him. He squinted in the feeble glow of lamplight that he found himself surrounded by, and after a few more heartbeats, his head ceased to spin enough for him to barely recognize that there were faces staring at him. Surrounded by strangers, he also recognized that he was still sitting on Old Scratch. The mule's head hung so low that his nose almost touched the floor and his sides heaved like great leather billows. The remains of several tables and chairs lay scattered about his legs.

He wasn't quite sure how he ended up in the room, and it didn't come to him to ponder how the mule got there with him. A hand touched his leg and he looked down into a shadowed face with a glowing smile. Soft, friendly laughter, whispers, and even what sounded like drunken cheers came from all around him. It felt like an invitation.

He attempted to dismount, but his left leg fooled him and he tumbled from the saddle. Hands lifted him from the floor.

"You one crazy gringo," the voice said.

"What a ride!" somebody shouted.

There was more welcoming laughter as he was guided to a cottonwood log bar. He was too weary to resist and the room was warm and relaxing. The lamps on the wall barely lit the room, and it felt like he was in a deep, dark cave. The only thing connecting him to the real world was the soft touch on his arm. He looked down at the brown hands touching him and followed the arm up to its owner's face — eyes soft and brown and laughing.

"Juanita," he whispered.

The face smiled again, lovingly and familiar. "My name isn't Juanita."

Rougher hands patted him on the back and a guitar began to play. Somebody shoved a clay cup into his hand.

"Salud, caballero!" the voices said. "Somebody give the mule some tequila. I'm sure he is thirsty too."

The liquor went down Faro's throat like fire. The burn felt good.

"Mr. Faro!" Jim said.

Faro shoved the hand away that was shaking his shoulder and squinted painfully at the pale morning light while he tried to get his bearings. He found that he was lying in a haystack in an alley. There had been a New Year's party, of that much he was certain. Maybe a cantina, maybe two, but the rest was hazy. He felt like he had been in a fight, but couldn't recall it.

His hand found a bottle of mescal in the hay beside him, and understood why it felt like he had been drinking kerosene. There was a swallow left in the bottle, but he didn't have the stomach for it. He checked his pockets to see if he had any money left, and surprisingly, he still had most of it.

After a moment of debate, he summoned

the will to fight his stiff limbs and aching body and got to his feet, his head swimming. The insides of his thighs felt like they had been beaten with a hammer, and he'd knocked a fingernail off during his holiday festivities.

Jim was leaning against the far wall of the alley. "I didn't think you were ever going to wake up."

"Where am I at?"

"You don't know? Man you must have really hit the sauce last night," Jim said. "You're south of the river in Mexico."

"I don't remember emigrating." Faro noticed the mule for the first time. Old Scratch stood three-legged, his head hanging and his winter hair matted and caked with chalk-white sweat marks, despite the cold. He was tied under the roof eave to one of the rafters of an adobe shack and the saddle was still on his back. A wagon sheet was tangled on the saddle horn and stretched out on the ground behind the animal.

Faro found his John Bull where it had lain beneath him in the haystack. The poor thing was crumpled like an accordion and the top of the crown was torn open. He put a fist through the tear, studied it for a moment, and removed it and jammed the hat on his head.

"What do you want, kid?" he croaked, his throat and mouth as dry as dust.

"Thought you might like to know that the pox has hit Sibley's army."

"Smallpox?"

"One of the soldiers died last night, and Sibley has ordered everyone inoculated to try and head it off."

Faro considered that. He had been vaccinated years before in the army, but many of the Texas troops born on the frontier might never have had the chance. Whole bands of western Indians had been wiped out by the disease, as well as entire Mexican villages. It was liable to run through Sibley's army like wildfire.

"All right, we're all going to get sick and die," Faro said. "Did you have to wake me up at daylight? I'm perfectly capable of dying in my sleep."

"General Sibley wants us to move north tomorrow, but he found out this morning that those supplies he was counting on from Mexico aren't coming," Jim said. "The Mexican merchants wouldn't take Confederate scrip as payment, and some of the soldiers are saying we'll be eating our horses before winter's over."

"So we're going to starve too. Have you got any more good news?"

"Looks like it might snow again."

Faro glared at the gray clouds overhead. "Figures."

Jim turned his attention to the mule. "Can't believe you rode him. Never would have thunk it."

Bits and pieces of the previous night were beginning to come back to Faro. "You aren't the only one. Must have seemed like a good idea to me at the time."

Faro folded the wagon sheet and tied it behind the saddle and then led Old Scratch down the alley following Jim. The black mule pinned his ears for a moment, but did no more than that. Faro kept a close eye on him, nonetheless. He'd done some dumb things in his life, but for the life of him, he couldn't imagine why he had ridden Old Scratch or how he had done it.

"I still wouldn't trust him. You didn't see what he did to that Apache," Jim said.

Faro's head was starting to pound worse, and his heart raced if he moved too fast. Jim's horse was tied just at the end of the alley where it met a north-south street. He watched as Jim mounted.

Jim looked from Faro to Old Scratch and then back again. "It's a pretty good walk back to the fort, and you don't look in any shape for walking."

Faro studied the mule. *I'd rather have my teeth pulled.* Sober, a second go at Old Scratch seemed worse than insane. *Must have been the tequila.* He stored that for future reference. *No tequila. Stuff makes you crazy.*

"Well, walk or ride," Jim said. "Your choice, unless you want me to see if the general will send an ambulance across the river for you."

Faro looked Old Scratch in the eye, and didn't like anything he saw. More of the night before came back to him. He straightened the leaning saddle and tightened the girth. "I imagine this is going to hurt."

Jim nodded. "Yep. This I've got to see."

"Don't act so happy." Faro put his left foot in the stirrup. "Makes me think you get a kick out of watching me try and get myself killed."

"Maybe you rode the rough off of him last night."

Faro swung a leg over the saddle and eased into the seat. His sore butt, and the tender contact of the inside of his thighs with the saddle instantly told him where most of his bruises had come from. Only a quick pull on his reins kept Old Scratch from taking a bite out of his left leg. Just the simple act of mounting left Faro feeling like he might pass out, and a biting mule was just a little bit more than he could take. He drew his right hand Colt and pointed it at the back of Old Scratch's head.

"I see you looking out the back of your eye at me," he said. "I'm a little off my game this morning and you're trying my patience. The first time you cut up on me again I'm going to make a good mule out of you. Understand?"

"You realize that you're expecting a mule to understand a death threat, don't you?" Jim asked.

"This is between me and this damned, no-account mule."

"Are you going to shoot him, or are you waiting for him to answer you?"

"I'm just too kindhearted, or I'd shoot him and save myself whatever misery he's going to cause me."

"He's acting about halfway social."

"Give him time. I'm sure it will go downhill from here." Faro holstered his pistol and gave Old Scratch a gentle bump of his calves.

"Damned if I don't think he understood you," Jim said.

Faro was a little shocked himself. Old

Scratch stepped out quietly, as if he had been ridden all his life. He even responded lightly to the bit instead of like a green-broke mule.

"I think Old Scratch has been holding out on us," Jim said.

"I think you're right. He knows more than he's been letting on."

The wind was whipping dust and trash and gravel down the street when they started toward the river, and people stopped to watch them pass. Many of them whispered to each other and pointed at Faro on the giant black mule.

"Looks like you're the talk of the town," Jim said.

"They're probably just poking fun at a fine-looking Louisiana gentlemen having to ride an ugly mule." Faro put a hand on top of his hat, trying to keep it from blowing away.

"I don't think so." Jim pointed to a little man standing in front of a store.

Faro couldn't understand what the store-keeper was saying, but his angry gestures and spitting passion, along with the fact that he kept pointing at the broken hitching rail in front of his place of business, made it plain that he felt Faro was to blame for his property damages.

Another group of men scowled at Faro as he passed. They were trying to replace a busted wooden post supporting the roof in front of a small cantina. Not only was the roof sagging, but the front door also lay on the ground, torn from its hinges. Little was left of the doorway framing and facing other than busted, splintered daggers of lumber, and several of the adobe bricks either had their plaster knocked off in chunks or were lying on the ground.

"Call me silly, but it looks like something way too big tried to fit through that door," Jim made a point not to look at Faro.

An old woman gave them equally nasty looks and shook a rake at them while she attempted to salvage a trampled garden. A little boy amidst a group of children had an old broom handle for a stick horse, and pointed at Faro and Old Scratch and mimed a wild, bucking ride.

"I don't speak much Spanish, but I'm getting the feeling that you and Old Scratch put on quite a show down here last night. Looks like a storm hit," Jim said.

They passed a group of women carrying laundry baskets from the river, and two of them made the sign of the cross and veered wide to avoid them.

"Never would have guessed it when I first

390

met you, but you're a regular showman. What possessed you to come down to Mexico to put on a riding exhibition?"

"All I remember is winding up in some cantina."

"Well, they sure remember you. Most folks tie their mule out front instead of riding him inside."

"Blame it on Old Scratch. He must have been thirsty too."

At about that time a curly-tailed mutt of a yellow dog ran out of the crowd and darted for Old Scratch's heels. The dog's teeth never bit home, for as quick as lightning, the mule cocked a hind leg and busted his attacker a sound lick in the ribs. The dog sailed back in the direction he came from.

"I don't guess Old Scratch has totally reformed his ways," Jim said. "He's pure poison for dogs."

"As long as he isn't trying to kill me, I guess I can't hold kicking a dog against him. Everybody's got to have a vice or two, and I'm feeling like kicking one myself this morning."

"Does he ever miss?" Jim grimaced at the whining dog crumpled on the side of the street. "It's like he's got a set of rifle sights on his back legs."

"Let's ride on. I don't want to find out

what else this broncy mule tore up, and it feels like the natives are growing restless." Faro tried to keep his eyes focused straight ahead.

"They do look a little peeved." Jim pointed to a man on the side of the street who had produced a piece of paper that he was angrily pointing at. "I think that storekeeper has got a bill for you."

"What's he saying?" Faro asked.

"I think he just insulted your mother."

Faro tugged his big Walker Colt out of his saddle holster.

"My gosh, but you're testy this morning," Jim said. "First you pull a gun on Old Scratch, and now you're waving it around at citizens."

"I'm not going to shoot anyone. I'm just letting them know I intend to get back across the river in one piece."

The two of them didn't slow until they reached the ford across the Rio Grande. Jim threw a look back over his shoulder to check for any pursuit and then started to whistle.

"Do you have to do that?" Faro asked.

"Does it bother you?"

"I wouldn't ask of you to quit it if it didn't." Faro rubbed at his temples and swore to himself again that he was never going to touch another drop of liquor.

They splashed across the shallows and came out on the far bank, and at that moment the wind gusted harder than ever and Faro grabbed wildly for his hat as it was jerked from his head. He threw a glance down the river just in time to watch his good John Bull disappear on the current. "I've been to Mexico twice now, and it's been like this both times. I'm going to miss that hat."

CHAPTER 38

Faro finished saddling old scratch and then helped Caesar to harness the team while Jim loaded the last of their camp into the wagon. Already, the line of soldiers was marching northward.

"Have you seen the O'Hell sisters?" he said over the horses' backs to Caesar. "We'd best be moving if we don't want to be left behind."

"I saw Rue down by the parade ground an hour ago." Caesar said. "Don't know where Zula is, or Armand either."

"Speak of the Devil," Faro said.

Armand came walking up with two armfuls of the sisters' luggage. "That's quite a hat you've got there."

"You're real funny." Faro readjusted the sombrero on his head. The post merchants were short of anything in the way of proper headwear, and that morning he had been forced to settle for the Mexican hat. Even though he had picked the smallest one available, the thing still felt ten times too large on his head, and no matter how he tried to shape the wide, felt brim into a dashing shape, within minutes it was drooping down over his eyes again.

"Where are the girls?" Faro asked. "Sibley's headed north, and bent on taking Fort Craig before February is out."

Armand shrugged. "I haven't seen Zula, but Rue said she will be along in a bit."

Faro swung into the saddle, keeping a good part of his attention on the volatile mule. "I'll see about that. She'll come now, or I'll leave her."

Armand gave a rare smile. "You think? I think you tell her that and you get a different answer."

Faro headed Old Scratch toward the military post. He passed by the barracks and spied Rue bundled up for the cold and standing on the far side of the parade ground.

"Nice hat," she said when he dismounted in front of her.

Faro ignored the jab at his headwear. "It's time to go. We're loaded and waiting on you."

"Waiting on me? Since when did you get in a hurry to do anything?"

"The sooner you come with me the sooner we can make it to Santa Fe."

"If this army that you've put us with ever gets there. A new mount?" She nodded at Old Scratch.

"Don't ask."

There was more than a bit of devilment in her eyes as she appraised him and the mule. "He's not so ugly when you really take a close look at him. And I think your dispositions might match."

"Go ahead. Tease me all you want."

Something else had her attention, and he followed her gaze across the parade ground. Captain Lacey was riding toward them leading her horse.

The captain smiled at Rue. "Are you ready to ride?"

Rue gave Faro what he thought was an apologetic look. "That's why I had Armand take my things to the wagon. Captain Lacey has asked me to ride with him."

"Don't worry, Wells, I'll take good care of her," the captain said, saving his smirk until Rue had her back to him while she gathered her horse's bridle reins.

Faro held the horse for Rue while she climbed up on a mounting block and put a foot in the stirrup. She hooked her right leg over the sidesaddle's post and straightened her dress. "I guess I'll see you in camp this evening."

Faro nodded and let go of her horse's bridle and went to stand by Old Scratch.

"Nice mule," Captain Lacey said. "Fits your hat."

Faro started to spit back a quick retort, but Rue riding away distracted him. He was watching her leave when he finally noticed that Captain Lacey lingered behind.

"You're really no competition at all, gambler," the Texan said.

Rue had stopped her horse and was looking back at them.

Faro guessed that she was too far away to hear anything he said, at least if he said it quiet enough. "The first man to bet doesn't always win the pot."

Captain Lacey wet his fingertips and twisted the ends of his mustache. "And just what kind of pot are you after? That woman there is a fine piece of flesh, but surely you could have stayed back in New Orleans and found plenty to wet your wick."

Faro clenched his teeth.

Captain Lacey noticed the effect his words were having. "You look like somebody just drove a hot poker up your ass. Are you fixing to challenge me over the maidenhood of that fair damsel?"

"You son of a bitch."

"Careful there, gambler. A fight with me is the last damned thing you want. There isn't a day that I can't best a tinhorn priss like you in any kind of fight. But you just go ahead and insult me one more time. I'll shoot you in the guts and leave you for the buzzards."

"Come on," Rue called out. "I'm getting cold sitting here waiting."

Faro adjusted his coat lapels and pulled a cigar from his pocket. He jammed the stogie in the corner of his mouth and talked around it while he gathered a match. "You're an easy man to dislike. Perhaps we can continue this discussion at another time."

"You're going to hate me worse when I bed her." Captain Lacey stuck the spurs to his horse and scattered dirt and gravel as he left.

Faro watched them leave and told himself that he didn't give a flip what Rue McGaffney did. He also told himself that he wasn't going to let that arrogant Texan get to him when he struck the match on side of his thigh. He lifted the flame to his face, but the cigar fell to the ground just before his cupped hands reached it. He stared at it lying between his dirty boots and realized that he was grinding his teeth so bad that he had bitten his last good cigar in two. He finally spit the other end of it on the ground and put the match out, quenching its flame between his thumb and forefinger, liking the sting of his skin and the feel of the charred wood crumbling and crushing beneath his grip.

I'm as cool as ice, Captain. You couldn't make me mad if you wanted to.

CHAPTER 39

Zula sat under the Ramada and watched Rue and the captain riding across the plaza. She glanced at Faro standing there so stiff and trying to act like he wasn't hurt, and then turned her attention back to Rue.

A group of Mexican children flocked around Rue's horse as she passed in front of the little adobe church, calling out to her, "Doña Rue, Doña Rue."

Rue stopped her horse long enough to reach in her purse and pass the children a few coins, and for the padre to bless her before riding on. The children waved and smiled at her as if she were an angel.

Zula took a sip of tequila from the small bottle she kept in her coat and watched the children coming her way when her sister was gone with the captain, laughing and still talking about the wonderful, generous charity of Señorita Rue. One of the smallest of the girls, a pretty thing, finally noticed Zula sitting at the table underneath the brush arbor and stopped the group. All of them looked at Zula with expectant, hopeful faces, as if the dark-haired sister might give them money like the fair-haired one had.

The little one smiled and said, "Señorita Zula, how are you today?"

"Go away, kid."

The children awkwardly scuffed the ground with their sandaled feet. One of them looked like he might cry.

"Get out of my sight, you little orphan beggars."

The children may not have understood all that she said, but they understood the tone. They scrambled into each other until they finally untangled and ran back across the plaza. A priest met them at the church door and stretched his arms out as if he could enfold them all, his flock of little apostles. They all spoke to him at once, and although Zula couldn't hear what they were saying, she did notice how the priest finally looked her way and scowled at her before making the sign of the cross and taking the children inside.

"Same old Zula," a voice said from her left. "Tongue as sharp as a knife."

She recognized the voice even before she turned her head. Her hand had already found the derringer in her right-hand coat pocket before she looked at King Broulet leaning there against the roof post, his arms folded and one leg crossed over the other.

She laid the pistol on the tabletop, still holding it. "You've got a lot of gall."

He laughed. "Don't let that little temper of yours get the best of you. You might get me if you're lucky, but I won't die quick and I'd shoot you right in that pretty little face of yours before I went."

She rattled off a string of French and turned the pistol until it was pointed at his belly, although it was still on the table.

"You come crawl in the sack with me again, and I'll make you speak in tongues like those backwoods preachers. Make you talk gibberish like the workers on the Tower of Babel," he said.

"Did you come over here to tell me something, or do you just love to hear yourself talk?"

"I'm going to offer just once to do this the easy way."

"You must truly think me a fool."

"I'm offering you two thousand for the directions to your mine. You take it and go back to New Orleans." He reached slowly inside his coat and pulled out a handful of coins. "That gold of your father's may not even still be there, and there's a strong chance that somebody will kill you for it if it is. You know, somebody like me. Why not take the bird in hand that I'm offering?"

"It'll be a cold day in hell before I sell out to you," she said. "I'm sure you've already figured out a way to get my gold and to keep the money you're promising me too. I wouldn't trust you farther than I could throw you by your tail."

"Easy with that pistol." He stepped slowly to the other table in front of her and set the coins down in two neat stacks. "Consider this a token of my good intentions, and as a down payment while you consider my offer."

"Who did you kill to get that money?" she asked.

He shrugged. "A dear old friend and business partner left it to me."

She cocked the pistol. "You're boring me."

"Maybe I should try and deal with your sister."

"Good luck. She wouldn't give you so much as a look."

"Maybe she's got more sense than you do."

"What if I just shoot you now and take your money to go with my gold? Isn't that the way you would do it?"

"Oh, you are a little witch, aren't you, Zula dear?" He tipped his hat and turned away in a swirl of his long coat.

She kept the pistol cocked until he was out of sight and she was sure he wasn't coming back, for the moment anyway.

Moments later, she saw Armand coming across the plaza looking for her. She stood and gathered the coins and dropped them into her coat pocket. She resumed her seat before he spotted her.

"What are you doing, Zula?" he asked. "It's time to go."

"I was just sitting here thinking."

"Worrying?"

"Just weighing my options." The money in her pocket felt heavy and real.

"I think you worry about only one option, and that's your father's gold," he said. "Don't look so sad, *honey chile.* Gold makes everyone dream of being rich, but wanting so much can also make the *misère.* You know? Once you get your mind on something you won't let go. Stubborn like your mother. Your sister too. My sister ruined you two that way. Always wanting more. Talking about what she didn't have."

"No guarantees in this world, huh?"

"This country is bad, *pas bon.* Too much Indians, too much cold, too much wind, not enough water, a war. Don't think that you're so special that nothing bad can happen to you. Maybe you find a fortune, or maybe you find you leave this country with less than you came with. Only God knows."

Her hand found one of the coins in her pocket — cool and smooth. "Let's go find Faro. He'll be having a fit wondering where we are."

"He's tougher than he looks, and foxier than I first thought."

She poked him in the ribs and gave him a playful smile. "So you do like him? What, has my gruff uncle gone soft?"

Armand scowled at her. "You never could mind your tongue. I just said he was tougher than he looks, but he still smells too much like a woman. I don't trust any man that doesn't smell like the swamp, or that combs his hair more than once a day."

"Do you think he can get us to the gold if it's really there?"

He looked at her like he had done many times over the years — like he could see through her and know that she was thinking something bad before she even did it.

"You listen to me, just this once." He stepped in front of her and turned to face her. "I will look out for you, but if something should happen to me, you stick with him.

He may be a fancy man, but he will not run when you need him."

"And you know this how? What makes him so brave?"

The serious expression on Armand's face was replaced with a smile, a rare thing for him. "Brave? Maybe not. But I promise you he is stubborn like you, and a stubborn man who won't quit is hard to stop."

CHAPTER 40

Rue was standing in her tent door watching the sleet and snowflakes slant downward between her and the campfire flickering outside. Something had woken her. Maybe the cold or the north winds flapping the tent walls. It couldn't have been much past midnight, and she was about to return to the warmth of her cot when she spied a figure trudging toward her.

It was General Sibley, although it was hard to tell until the fire lit his face. He had a blanket wrapped around his stooped shoulders and his hands hidden inside it where he clutched it to his chest. He smiled at her weakly, and took a seat on a campstool.

"You won't mind if I rest at your fire for a minute, will you?" he asked. "I think it might be good if I sat down for a while."

"Be my guest." She tugged into her coat and gloves, wrapped her own blanket about her, and took a seat beside him. Other than an occasional polite word in passing, he had never made any attempts to visit with her. She was curious what brought him to her fire, and it was plain that he was very sick.

"It's a miserable night," he said. "It's been a long hard pull to get here."

She looked to the starless sky, squinting against the tiny, hard bits of sleet stinging her face. "Any word from the north? I heard no cannon fire today."

"Colonel Green is retiring his men from the field and returning to camp. Those Yankees at Fort Craig won't come out and fight." The general shivered in his blanket and stared into the flames. The firelight reflected off of the beads of fever sweat, and the melting snow and sleet on his whiskers.

"You're too sick to be out in this."

He coughed and shook his head. "I'm getting better. Should have marched with the men today. Some kind of general I am."

Rue studied him. The nicest rumor was that Sibley was sick with pneumonia and unable to ride, and the harshest version going around the camps was that the whiskey was killing him. In truth, he did look like death warmed over.

Morale was low, and all kinds of talk was going around the camps, ever since they had started the march north from the Rio

Grande. First, the general had ordered his army to stick to the west bank of the river on their way to where the Yankees waited for them at Fort Craig. True, they avoided the ninety-mile waterless stretch of the Jornada del Muerto that way, but the trail was days longer and full of arroyo and canyon crossings, bog sand, and places where a path for the wagons often had to be cut with shovels and picks. And now, some of the men were beginning to believe that the general was reluctant to fight the Yankees, and was keeping them dawdling around camp while he tried to figure a way to detour around Fort Craig.

"I'm sorry if I woke you. I was restless and your fire looked inviting," he said.

"You didn't wake me."

The general turned his glassy eyes her way. "Miss McGaffney, pardon me for asking. I've got a war to fight, but what in tarnation is so important that you would suffer this journey?"

She debated whether to avoid his questioning by pointing out that he was prying, but decided against it. "My sister and I have business matters to attend to in Santa Fe. There is a matter of a small inheritance our father left us."

The general smiled in a way that made

him look like his mind wasn't quite in the moment. "Must be quite an inheritance, or you couldn't afford Faro Wells."

She immediately regretted saying as little as she had. "Is he such a mercenary?"

He tried to laugh, but it caused another coughing spell. He finally wiped his mouth with one sleeve and took a shallow, raspy breath. "Oh, maybe not so much. Don't believe all he lets on about. I've always thought it was the action he really craves."

"Him? He told me he quit the army because he couldn't see any sense fighting when there was no profit in it."

The general gave her a look like he was debating if he should say what he was thinking. "Faro was a good officer. It wasn't the fighting that caused him to muster out."

"Oh?"

"Faro's a warrior, even if the most unlikely appearing one you might ever meet."

"If he's such a warrior, then why did he quit the army?"

"He got himself into a little trouble while we were in Mexico."

"A court-martial, or was he invalided out because of his battle wounds?"

The general shifted uncomfortably. "Ma'am, I shouldn't have gone as far as I have. It isn't polite, and Faro's history is his own."

"I don't think you're belittling him, because I can tell you like him. Besides, you'd be doing me a favor by letting me know just what kind of man I've hired."

"This isn't exactly a polite story, or one that a gentleman would share with a young lady."

"I can handle whatever you tell me," she said. "Manners are admirable, but they often get in the way of the truth."

He cleared his throat and readjusted his blanket. "There was a woman in Mexico. Pretty woman . . . a rare beauty, in fact. I don't know just how it happened, but he met her in Veracruz while we readied to march toward Mexico City."

"And?" she asked after he paused for a long time, lost in his thoughts.

"The woman was the wife of a Mexican officer. He slipped back into the city one night and caught Faro with her in his bed. Shot Faro twice, left him for dead, and fled with the woman."

"The scar on Faro's face?"

"That's right. The first shot busted his knee, and he took the next one in the cheek. I guess that Mexican officer wanted him to suffer and beg, and then the last one was

411

meant to be an execution."

"All this time, and I thought those were war wounds."

"They are war wounds. Pardon me for disagreeing, but when you get to my age you learn some things." When the general looked her way, his eyes seemed to have cleared and a bit of anger pinched his face. "War isn't just about cannon shot and rifle fire, or men screaming on a battlefield. There is more than one kind of battle scar, and I don't think the ones that show are what wounded Faro the worst."

"He mustered out after that?"

"I saw him once before I marched out of Veracruz. I didn't think he was going to live. Didn't think he wanted to. I heard later that he survived and left the army. Didn't see him again until you showed up in San Antonio."

"Was he forced out?"

"No, like I said, he was a good officer, and a limp and a scar on his face wouldn't have kept him from serving later. The army would have been glad to keep him. Lord knows I could use his kind now."

"Why do you think he resigned?"

"You'd have to ask him. Maybe he needed to get out of Mexico."

"Is that all? I feel like you know more that

you aren't saying."

"You're an interrogator, just like my wife. Never could hide anything from her questions either." The general's wiry mustache crinkled in a smile. "Later, I heard from a friend stationed in Mexico City that Faro showed up there looking for the woman."

"Did he find her?"

"I don't know, but my friend said that there was a rumor that a certain Mexican officer was found dead along with his wife about that time. Apparently the officer had shot his wife and then himself. Murder and suicide all in the same breath."

"And you think that the woman was the same one?"

"Could be."

CHAPTER 41

Everyone had gone to their bedrolls, but Faro couldn't sleep. Another day on the trail, and a long, hard one at that. The Yankees at Fort Craig had refused to come out and fight Sibley's army, and the general decided that he would bypass them entirely by crossing to the other side of the Rio Grande and making his way north through the badlands until he could cross back to the west bank at Valverde Crossing north of the fort. The scouts had chosen a hard pull up one of the many gullies and dry arroyos running parallel to the river. Windblown sand lay deep between the outcroppings of black lava rock, and their wagon wheels sank deep — too deep. It had taken him and Caesar helping the wagon along with ropes snubbed to their saddle horns to even get their team to the top of the little mesa where the Confederates decided to camp for the night, barely four miles from where they started that morning. And to make matters worse, it turned out that there was no water between the two river crossings and damned little forage for the exhausted stock.

It was past time to get free of General Sibley and his war and go after the gold. The trick was going to be doing that without getting them all killed. The rumor was that the Navajo and Apache were raising all kinds of trouble with forts abandoned and the white soldiers focused on killing each other, and besides that, federal skirmish parties had been hounding their back trail all day. It was going to be hard to pass themselves off as anything but Confederate deserters or even spies if they were caught by the Yankees.

Restless, he decided to get up and take a walk. Maybe the cold night air would clear his mind. He ran into Jim just as soon as he came around the end of the wagon. The Cherokee was sitting on the wagon tongue with his elbows resting on his knees. His horse was saddled and standing by him.

"Just come in from scouting?" Faro asked.

It took Jim too long to answer. "No, I've been in camp since before dark."

"What's the matter?"

"I'm done with scouting. No more army

for me."

"Okay. Have you told the officers that?"

Jim stood and tightened his cinch. "I'm riding out. I figure I can slip across the river in the dark without the Yankee pickets spotting me."

From the way Jim's hands were fumbling with his saddle, and the sound of his voice, Faro could tell something had scared him or upset him.

"So you're going to run out on me?"

"I know it isn't right, but I'm just honest enough to admit that I'm a coward."

"You're no coward."

Jim climbed on his horse. "No? We're awful close to being in a battle, and the thought of it almost makes me wet my pants. How's that for ya?"

"I promise you, we'll get out of this the first chance we get. Strike out on our own. It's time."

"It's past time, Mr. Faro. I'm done."

Faro scrambled for something to say to calm the boy. "We've already been through several scrapes together, and I could always count on you."

"It's those cannons that get to me. I can't take 'em," Jim said. "Not again."

"You've been under cannon fire before, haven't you?"

"I snuck off last year with Unc' and a bunch of Cherokee volunteers. They were going to Missouri to help General Price whip the Yankees up there."

"I take it that it wasn't what you expected."

"I thought I was as brave as the next fellow, but it turned out that wasn't the case." Jim paused. "Little place called Wilson's Creek. We were going to show those Yankees a thing or two, but they caught us in camp. I woke up with bombs going off around me. First thing I saw was a bouncing cannonball take off my cousin's head just as soon as he sat up in his blankets."

"Things like that don't ever leave you," Faro said quietly. "You just have to learn to live with them as best you can."

"I can live with that. It's what I did afterward that I can't stand," Jim said. "The men I was with threw themselves against the Yankees three times that day. Fought 'em tooth and nail — rifles, hatchets, knives, and fists. Gave grapeshot and canister round back as good as they got. Good men, real men, died running those Yankees back to Springfield while I hid behind a log in the woods, laying on my side with my hands cupped over my ears so I didn't have to hear those awful cannons."

Faro knew Jim wasn't finished. Saying it wasn't going to fix what ailed the boy, but getting it out in the open was a start.

"I couldn't face Unc', nor anybody else after that. Thought about shooting myself, but I wasn't brave enough for that either. Ended up catching a Yankee horse and heading south. Rode him until I drowned him swimming a big creek. Walked after that and then I caught a flatboat ride down to New Orleans," Jim said. "That Mississippi can be a slow river. Had a lot of time to think. Faced up to what I am."

"And what's that?"

"Damned sure not a soldier."

"I think you're being a little too hard on yourself. Lots of men don't perform well in their first fight. I've seen some men who did heroic things later lock up their first time under fire."

"Won't matter what I do, there's still the shame. How could I go back home and face my family?"

Faro stepped closer to Jim. "Is that a pretty good horse you're riding?"

"He doesn't look like much, but he's the best I've had. Little mustang won't quit, and he's as quick and handy as a jackrabbit."

"You think he's so fast that you can

outrun your past?" Faro put a hand to the mustang's neck.

"That's easy for you to say."

"How's that?"

"Everybody knows that you're some kind of war hero."

"Me? I got these war wounds because a man caught me sleeping with his wife. While I was lying in an infirmary trying not to die, he killed that woman because of me," Faro said. "Think I'm proud of that? We've all got scars, and we aren't too proud of some of them."

"You've had time to work it out. Nothing you can say is going to change my mind."

Faro reached into his pocket and took a wad of Confederate scrip and a few coins. "Take this, then. See if you can slip across the Valverde ford. Strike out for Albuquerque or Santa Fe from there. Maybe you can hire on with a freight outfit headed back to Missouri."

"You don't have to do that." Jim took the money reluctantly.

"No, but I want to. I just hope the time comes when you figure things out. I've got to believe that we can make up for some of the wrong things we've done, or there isn't a bit of hope left for any of us. You run out on me, and it's just going to be another thing you're ashamed of."

"I'm scared, can't you see? I can't quit thinking that I'm about to be back there in that Missouri fight all over again. I don't know. Maybe I'm more scared of doing what I did all over again than I am of some cannonball smashing me."

"Come tomorrow or the next day, when the fight comes, every one of these soldiers will be scared. The thing about war is that you usually have somebody to stand with you — the man right next to you on the line," Faro said. "You get down off that horse and I'll stand with you, and then we'll get shuck of this army as quick as we can."

Jim started to turn his horse, but it was plain that he was wavering.

A huge explosion and a ball of fire at the foot of the mesa rocked the night, and Jim's mustang reared. Faro tripped over the wagon tongue getting himself clear of the frightened horse and scrambled to right himself. Already, the mustang's hooves were clattering over the rocks as Jim fled off the mesa — two runaways, a half-wild boy and a half-wild horse.

"What was that?" Armand almost stepped on Faro in the dark.

The McGaffney sisters came running up, all of them searching the dark in the direction the explosion had come from. Seconds later, a squad of Texas troopers trotted by their wagon on their way back to the camp's defense perimeter.

"What's happening?" Faro asked.

"Those damned Yankees are bound and determined that we don't get any sleep," one of the soldiers answered.

"Was that cannon fire?" Faro asked. "Didn't sound like it."

"No, the word is some crazy Federals tied boxes of howitzer shells on a couple of mules, lit the fuses, and stampeded them toward us," the same soldier called back. "Good thing those mules only made it halfway up the hill before they turned around and tried to go back to their handlers."

"Did I just hear that man say that the Yankees are tying bombs to mules and running them at our camp?" Rue asked.

Zula cut Faro off before he could think of any kind of answer. "Nothing to worry about but mules running through our camp with bombs tied to their backs. Nothing to worry about at all. Isn't that right, oh, wise leader?"

Faro was about to tell them both where they could go, but the sound of stampeding livestock and the frantic shouts of soldiers cut him off.

"Stop those mules!" somebody shouted.

Faro had just a split second to imagine a whole herd of bomb-toting mules about to run him down before the first of the animals charged out of the black. He shouldered into the women and knocked them both under the wagon just in time to avoid being trampled. All three of them watched the tangle of churning legs passing them, trampling their tent before thundering off the mesa edge.

Faro realized he had been gritting his teeth, expecting at any moment that bombs were going to go off and blow them to Kingdom Come. It soon dawned on him that it was the Confederates' own mules that were stampeding, and that not one of them had a bomb strapped to its back. He was just climbing out from under the wagon when a group of Rebel horsemen charged past at a run.

"Catch those damned mules!" one of them shouted.

Faro had just helped both of the sisters to their feet when a hand grasped his arm. He expected it to be Armand, but it was Caesar's voice that spoke.

"Those bombs going off frightened the mules," Caesar said. "About a hundred of them broke loose from the picket lines."

"The Yankees will have them soon," Faro said.

"Not if you and I catch them first."

CHAPTER 42

Faro knelt behind the sharp crest of black
rock and peered through the morning's gray
light at the herd of mules drifting slowly
down the ravine paralleling the one he and
Caesar had camped in to wait for daylight.
He adjusted his French binoculars and
scanned across the spiny ridges and broken
country for any signs of Yankee activity.
From his elevation, he had a good view all
the way to the river, and after a long search,
he felt confident that the enemy was elsewhere. It looked too easy, at least for the
moment, but there was still plenty of time
left in the morning for things to go to hell.

"Looks like about fifty mules, give or
take," Caesar said. "I say we find a way to
cross over this ridge and trap them in that
narrow bottleneck." Caesar gestured with
his rifle at a point where the walls of the
ravine narrowed to no more than twenty
yards apart.

"You find a place to get your mule over this ridge below them, and I'll find a way across somewhere above them." Faro started back down the badlands outcropping to where he had left Old Scratch hobbled, trying not to roll any rocks. Caesar came along behind him, as quiet as the Indians he used to hunt. The Mexican muleteer was a likeable sort, but he could be a little spooky sometimes and moved like a ghost.

They separated at the bottom of the wash, with Caesar heading downslope and Faro turning back the way they had come. It was a quarter mile before the lava bed ended and Faro was able to wind his way through a small patch of sand dunes and over into the head of the next arroyo. He turned down it and followed the mule herd's tracks in the sand. By the time he came within sight of the mules, Caesar was already blocking their path on the other side.

"Sibley's boys will just take them back from us if we herd them back to camp," Faro called out as loudly as he dared.

Caesar was down off his little mule and untying a large coil of grass rope from his saddle. "I think we catch a few of them and string them together like you gringos do. I'll lead them, and you can drive the rest behind me."

"And then?"

"Then we find a place to hide them."

"Never thought I'd be stealing mules from the army."

Caesar already had his knife out and was cutting lengths of rope and fashioning them into crude halters. "Better we have them than the Yankees."

"I never took you for a Secessionist, Caesar."

"How do you say?" The Mexican shrugged. "I am practical. The spoils of war, no?"

"And maybe you're thinking about a share of the gold?"

"Some gold would be nice, but I would settle for these mules when we are through. You have your treasure, and I have mine."

The mules were a little fractious at first, but settled down after a few minutes. Faro helped Caesar move among them and place halters on those they could catch. After half an hour they had a dozen mules caught and haltered. Caesar tied the lead rope of each mule to the neck of the one in front of it.

"That's a pretty sight," Caesar said, admiring the string of mules.

"I won't be happy until we get out of here." Faro put a boot in the stirrup and climbed on Old Scratch. "There's bound to be Union scouts pilfering around."

"Uh-oh," Caesar's voice went a notch quieter.

Faro knew from the sound of Caesar's voice what that meant, even before he looked down the arroyo. Five men sat on their horses there at the narrowest point between the walls of the dry wash, some fifty yards away — three Mexicans wearing outsized sombreros, and two bearded white men. None of them wore uniforms, but all of them were armed to the teeth and pointing rifles at him.

"Buenos días," Caesar called out to them.

"Ain't it a good morning?" the biggest of them answered, the one on the right with a matted beard hanging down over his chest. His eyes were little pinpricks under the drooping brim of his leather hat. "Looks like we just caught us some Rebel trash and a fine string of mules."

"Now, that's no way to be friendly." Faro edged Old Scratch closer to the wall of the wash, trying to put the mule herd between him and the Union scouts, if that's what they were.

"Johnny Reb, you keep that mule still if you don't want to get shot." The bearded man cocked his rifle and propped the butt on his thigh.

Caesar was caught in a bad spot closest to the scouts and afoot on the downhill side of the mule herd. However, he had managed to put his little saddle mule between himself and the scouts. The old shotgun he carried was hanging off his saddle horn closest to him.

"That's pretty ballsy to ride down here in the middle of us by yourself," the bearded man said again.

"Was that you boys who tried to blow us up last night?" Faro asked, stalling for time.

"Pretty crafty piece of work wasn't it? You can thank Captain Paddy Grayson's Independent Spy Company for that," the scout said. "Too bad those mules got to longing for home before they made it all the way up to you."

One of the loose mules passed in front of Faro, and he took the opportunity to unsnap the flap on the holster of his Walker Colt at his saddle swells. "Lucky for us. Not so lucky for those mules you blew up."

"Mule lover are you?" The talker's gray horse was a little fidgety and was going to be hard to shoot from.

"I don't suppose it would do me any good to tell you that we aren't soldiers and that we're just traveling north with the army for protection against the Indians," Faro said.

"Not a bit."

"Then would you believe that these are our mules?"

"Not a chance." The scout dropped his rifle barrel down a little farther toward Faro, "What say we quit this jawing and you ride that black John over here closer. We can take you prisoner or make you a corpse. Makes no never mind to me."

Two of the Mexican scouts stepped their horses forward, edging up the opposite side of the wash on Faro's left. A few more feet would have them past and behind Caesar.

More mules shifted in front of Faro, giving him a chance to slide the Walker from its holster. He wasn't so sure that the scouts wouldn't kill them even if they surrendered, for it was a pretty hard-looking lot of cutthroats staring back at him. He lifted the heavy revolver, cocking it as he leveled it on the nearest Mexican scout. He tried to move fast, but his gun hand felt clumsy and as slow as molasses in wintertime. The click of the cocking hammer was the loudest thing in world.

Two rapid gunshots from somewhere above and behind him sounded before he could even pull the trigger. Old Scratch whirled and tried to bolt away up the wash, and Faro only caught a glimpse of Jim Tall

Tree up on the banks of the gully, dodging from rock to rock, his pistol smoking.

Guns roared all at once, and somebody was cursing at the top of their lungs. The mule herd was trying to stampede, but those haltered were all tangled and trying to go seven different directions at once, stirring up the dust and milling wildly. Faro got Old Scratch pulled down and parked broadside in the bottom of the wash in the midst of it all. He knew he needed to shoot somebody, but Old Scratch wouldn't be still long enough for him to take aim. It was about all that he could do to stay in the saddle.

Caesar was down on one knee with his shotgun to his shoulder, his little mule on its side and dying beside him. The shotgun jerked and the muzzle rose, and one of the Mexican scouts reeled limply in the saddle. Faro snapped a shot at the scout nearest to him, but Old Scratch's antics caused him to miss badly. The Mexican scout was having his own problems with his horse, and he had dropped his rifle and was clawing wildly at the pistol on his belt.

The mules finally surged in the same direction and stampeded down the wash right through the Union scouts. Faro spotted the scout who had done all the talking with a rifle leveled at him an instant before the man's gun boomed. Something whizzed by him, and Old Scratch shook his head wildly and scrambled backward on his haunches, threatening to rear and fall over. Blood flew everywhere. A cluster of shotgun pellets rattled off the rocks like a rain pelting a tin roof.

The black mule had gone crazy, but he took a giant, high lunge forward instead of cutting loose and bucking. He charged down the gully at a dead run with Faro fighting to right himself in the saddle. The Mexican nearest him was still trying to get his pistol out of his holster. Faro shoved the Walker across his saddle and snapped off another shot as the scout came up on his left, missing for a second time. No matter, Old Scratch brayed and veered dead-on toward the Mexican and his frightened mount. The giant mule and the horse collided with an impact that nearly sent Faro flying over Old Scratch's neck. Man and mount went down under them, and Old Scratch snaked his neck out and bit a chunk from the Mexican's leg and double kicked at the poor horse.

Caesar ran toward them, firing a one-handed shot behind him without looking. Faro shifted his pistol and extended an arm, and the muleteer took it and swung up behind him. The Mexican scout had a hold of Faro's leg and he clubbed down with the Walker's heavy barrel and felt the steel crack bone. The hands on his leg let go, and Caesar whipped Old Scratch on the hip with his hat until they were free of the downed horse and running again.

Faro tried to slow the mule as they banged into the back of the running herd, but Old Scratch didn't respond to the bit and seemed to go faster the more he pulled on the reins. It probably didn't help that Caesar was still fanning him with his hat. Faro did his best to keep his seat over the rising and plunging ground, cursing the day he had ever decided to ride that loco mule or befriend a crazy Mexican.

Two of the Union scouts had shifted over against each side of the coming bottleneck in the arroyo, and out of the way of the stampeding mule herd. Both men fired simultaneously, each vanishing behind a cloud of black powder smoke. Neither bullet found its mark, and the two scouts were only a blur as Old Scratch barreled past them. Two more strides and they were through the bottleneck and into more open country. A horse with an empty saddle raced up beside them, and before Faro knew what was happening, Caesar braced one foot on the saddle skirt and leapt from Old Scratch's back. He landed in the middle of the horse's back, never missing a beat, and whipped it forward.

More men appeared in the distance, far down along the river near the crossing. The Yankee blue of their uniforms was plain, even from afar.

Caesar passed along the side of the running mules and herded them toward a gap in a stretch of lava to the south. Guns were still going off behind them, and Faro turned in the saddle and saw that three of the Union scouts were whipping their horses in pursuit.

Another mile and the herd passed through a wide gap between the point of the lava rock badlands and a line of mesas and little mountains that lined the river. Caesar hauled his horse to a stop and waited for Faro in the pass. Old Scratch was finally winded enough for Faro to handle him, and he bounced to a reluctant stop alongside the Mexican.

Faro cast an anxious glance back behind them. "We had better keep going. They don't look like they want to quit."

Caesar snatched the Sharps from Faro's saddle and flipped up the ladder-back sight, adjusting it for range. He shouldered the cocked gun and took aim at the cluster of Union scouts coming their way.

"That's too far for accurate rifle fire," Faro said.

Caesar ignored him, and the rifle boomed in his hands. "I might not hit them, but I intend to give them cause for concern."

Faro lifted his Walker, steadying Old Scratch under him long enough to let off two quick shots. He didn't hit anything, but true to Caesar's assumptions, the trio of pursuers pulled to a stop several hundred yards from them.

Caesar held out his hand for more paper cartridges and primers for the Sharps. Old Scratch pinned his ears and made a half-hearted attempt to bite Caesar's arm off.

"Watch out," Faro said. "All this shooting has him in a terrible mood."

He finally had time to notice that Old Scratch was wounded. The mule shook his head, flopping his long ears and slinging tiny specks of blood everywhere. Faro wiped at his face and then leaned out over the saddle for a closer look at the back of the mule's head.

"They shot him right through the ear." Faro pointed at the neat, round hole bored just below the tip of Old Scratch's left ear. "No wonder he's pissed."

"Lucky it didn't hit you."

The Union scouts were no longer firing, but it was plain that they were talking amongst themselves and deciding what to do next.

Caesar nodded to the south through the gap in the lava beds. "Jornada del Muerto. No water that way for two, three days, maybe more."

"Well, we've got our mules, but we're in a tough spot, aren't we?"

"Throw me up that rifle, and I'll keep them bayed while you two gather those mules," Jim Tall Tree called out.

Faro turned to see the boy sitting his horse on the rocks above them and working hurriedly to reload his pistol. "Nice to see that you decided to lend a hand."

Jim shrugged. "Just don't go getting your hopes up. They break out any cannons and I'm liable to run on you."

"I can live with that."

Jim capped the last nipple on his pistol and holstered it. "We catch those mules, and maybe we can outrun those soldiers until nightfall and then slip down to the river. Shouldn't be much problem to sneak around that fort in the dark."

"No problem, huh? Just like that."

Jim's face broke into his old, cocky grin.

"No step for a stepper."

Faro looked at Caesar. "I thought we were done for back there."

Jim laughed. "Like you always say, the day ain't over yet. Looks like all the shooting has brought us more company."

The kid was right. Faro could barely make out more men riding in their direction from the river.

"Never thought I would die over a bunch of mules," he said.

"I thought it was the gold you are after," Caesar said.

"Thanks, it does sound better that way."

CHAPTER 43

The main body of the confederate army broke camp at dawn and started off of the mesa, leaving the supply train and a guard to the rear. Much of the livestock had been half a day without water, and the beef herd bellowed pitifully.

Rue twisted in the saddle to look back at the campsite. Thirty wagons full of tents and bedding were left behind, for the loss of two hundred head of mules the night before meant that there wasn't anything to pull them with. Their silhouettes on the skyline of the little mesa looked like burnt carcasses.

She rode her horse in tight against the wagon and made sure there was no one close enough to hear her before she looked up at Zula. "This is beginning to feel like a death march."

"They say the river crossing is only four miles ahead. Once the Texans win the crossing, at least we'll get a drink," Zula answered. "You're the one that kept saying this wasn't going to be easy."

"Go ahead, say I told you so, but I admit I never imagined this."

"Are you saying you want to turn back?"

"What I'm saying is that maybe it's high time we consider other options."

"You mean leaving the Army of New Mexico, or do you mean leaving Faro?" Zula asked.

Rue bit her bottom lip like she did when she was trying to look determined. "Maybe both. Faro has gotten us this far, but the whole trip has been a circus. There's bound to be a better way."

"I'm listening."

"What if we could get Captain Lacey to guide us?"

"You haven't told him about the treasure, have you?"

Rue winced at the mention of the gold and looked around again to see if there was anyone listening. "No, it was just a thought."

"Faro said last night that we're going to strike out on our own soon. According to him, we can't be more than two weeks' ride from the gold."

Rue's face was turning redder than the chill morning air made it. "I've heard more than enough of his big talk. We don't even know where he's at right now. The Yankees could have captured or killed him, for all we know."

"He was trying to get us some pack mules. It's going to be hard to haul Daddy's treasure on our own backs."

"Trying is all he ever does. Sometimes I think he's a bumbling fool," Rue threw back. "Have you decided you don't want the gold? That you aren't willing to do what it takes to get it?"

"I want it just as bad as you," Zula studied the look on her sister's face closer, "Or maybe not."

"Money isn't everything," Armand said.

"Tell that to somebody that doesn't have any," Rue said. "Do you want us to end up like Mother?"

Zula twisted around in the wagon seat so that she was facing her sister. "Don't you dare drag her into this. You weren't even around when she died."

"I loved Mother too, but I'm sick of you portraying her like she was a saint when we both know different."

"She did what she had to do after Daddy left for good," Zula said. "She was a lady."

"Yes, a lady, but everyone knew how she kept up the appearance. How she kept herself in a fine house and those dresses of hers."

Zula perched herself on the edge of the wagon seat, threatening to leap on her sister. "Don't you say it. Don't you dare."

"What? You of all people are bothered because our mother was a high-class whore?" Rue stopped her horse, her voice plainly taunting.

Armand barely had time to stop the team before Zula jumped off the wagon.

"She sent most of her money to you so you could go to that fancy school of yours. And never a word of thanks from you, Miss High and Mighty," Zula said.

"You haven't answered me. Just how are you going to make a living if we don't find that gold?" Rue asked. "Neither one of us knows how to do anything but look pretty and provide stimulating conversation for whatever man happens to come along. Maybe we would make pretty good whores at that."

"Shut up."

Rue ignored the look on Zula's face. "Mother may have thought that a rich man was the only way to make it, but Father left us another way."

Zula produced a tiny knife from some- where in her coat. "You take back what you said about Mother, or I swear that I will cut your icy heart out."

"Try it." Rue cocked her riding crop above her head, ready to chop downward.

Zula started to charge forward, her eyes wild, but she only managed two steps before Armand's hand clamped around her wrist and jerked her backward. She thrashed wildly, but he snatched the knife away effortlessly, as if she were a child.

"Stop," he said, stepping between them. "My sister was what she was. I loved her so, but curse her, I think she ruined you two with all her talk of money. Money this, money that. All she ever thought about was money."

"Stay out of his," Rue said.

Armand turned her way. "You're both acting like spoiled fools. Arguing over a woman that's long dead, and that gold . . . gold that might not even be there."

The two women glared at each other.

"Bitch," Zula growled.

"Slut," Rue threw back at her.

"Such fouls words from your pretty mouth. Did you learn that in finishing school?"

"You're such a tramp," Rue said.

Zula charged again, windmilling her arms and crashing into Armand in an attempt to get at her sister.

Armand grabbed her around the waist and lifted her to the wagon seat. He stepped back and pointed an accusing finger at one of them and then the other. "There will be no more of this. You'll act like family. Like sisters, or I'll knock some sense into both of you. You think I spend all my time looking out for you just to see you kill each other?"

"This isn't over yet," Zula said, but made no attempt to come down off the wagon again.

"Not at all." Rue quirted her horse up the line without a single look back.

Cannons began to boom to the north, coupled with volleys of small arms fire. It was plain that a battle was raging near the river crossing.

Armand took a quick glance at the bitter look on Zula's face. "This gold is no good. *Pas bon.*"

Zula shaded her eyes with one hand and pointed to the south with the other. "Is that Faro coming up the trail?"

CHAPTER 44

Valverde crossing was little more than a shoal at the beginning of a wide, shallow stretch of the river. The looming bulk of Mesa de Contadero stood sentinel on the bank of the Rio Grande where the steep canyon walls of the river channel gave way to a narrow valley dotted with stands of cottonwoods and willow thickets. Nothing more and nothing less, except for the fact that General Sibley wanted his army to cross the river there, and the Yankees had decided that they wouldn't allow it.

Faro and Rue rode alongside the pink wagon through the failing evening light toward the sheen of the river in the distance, following the rattling Confederate supply wagons. All around them, the valley was dotted with bloating horse carcasses, bits and pieces of gear, cannonball craters, and the twisted bodies of soldiers, blue and gray, who would fight no more — the grisly remains of the battle that had raged for most of the afternoon.

The Texas Confederates they passed were a somber lot, scavenging equipment and tending to the wounded and dead, their somber faces giving little evidence that they had sent the Yankee army fleeing back to the safety of Fort Craig.

Faro noted that Rue kept her eyes locked on the river, willing herself not to look at the horror around her. Zula was doing the same on the wagon seat while Armand mumbled to himself.

"Tell me that we're leaving this army right now," Rue finally said when they were almost to the river.

"I told you. Jim and Caesar are going to cross the mules we gathered at Paraje tonight and meet us at some little settlement to the north called Socorro."

"I want to strike out on our own now," Rue said. "No waiting for this army. On our own."

Faro noted a lance sticking up beside the trail they followed and leaned from the saddle to pluck it from the ground. The red pennant hanging below the lance head marked it as belonging to Captain Lacey's Company B.

A Texan trying to hook a team of horses

up to a captured Union field piece near the crossing noted the lance Faro was carrying. "Damnedest thing I ever saw. Captain Lacey led those lancers of his head-on against a company of Colorado volunteers. It was sheer suicide. Those Colorado boys opened up with buck and ball at forty yards. More than half of Lacey's men dead or wounded."

"Captain Lacey?" Faro stopped Old Scratch to hear more.

"He survived, but he and Colonel Scurry had a big falling out," the Texan said. "The colonel accused him of ignoring orders and threatened to court-martial him. Said he was going to dismount the lancers and give their horses to some of the other companies needing them."

"I don't imagine Captain Lacey would take too well to being turned into a foot soldier," Faro said. "He's too proud for that."

"Captain Lacey pulled out with some of his men before any of the officers got wind that he was deserting. Said he would fight this war, by God, on his own. Said these greasers and Yankees didn't know what war was, but he would show them. Fire and the sword, he said."

Faro tipped his hat to the Texan. "Congratulations on your victory."

The Texan spat in the dust. "Tell that to them that didn't make it. I wouldn't give you a squirt of piss for all of New Mexico."

Faro rode on after the pink wagon, splashing across the river behind it. He spied General Sibley wrapped in a blanket and sitting on the tailgate of a nearby ambulance. The general's eyes were bloodshot and he looked about to die. He lifted a whiskey bottle above his head in salute to Faro and almost fell off the tailgate in doing so.

Faro didn't wave back. Armand had stopped the wagon and was letting the supply train pass him by, waiting for Faro to catch up.

"And how do you know that Caesar and Jim will show?" Rue asked when Faro rode up to the wagon. "What's to keep them from running off with those mules?"

"They'll be there. I trust them, just like you'll have to." The Confederates were already setting up camp on the west bank of the river, but Faro's eyes were turned to the north. "Armand, start that wagon up the trail. We can make several more miles before dark, and Santa Fe isn't more than a week away."

"Danged if he doesn't sound different

today," Zula said as she watched Faro turn Old Scratch away from the Confederate camp and start upriver.

"I've heard all his talk before," Rue said. "He's just feeling bossy."

"I kind of like him that way."

CHAPTER 45

Faro rested his rifle across his thighs and braced both palms on Old Scratch's withers, wincing painfully and propping himself up off the mule's back. The inside of his legs were chafed raw, and his backside felt like somebody had taken a club to it. Two days of riding bareback hadn't exactly been a pleasure, and to say he could use some relief was putting it mildly.

The fact that the women were in a foul temper and still blaming him for the latest bad turn of fortune didn't help matters any. They sat their horses to either side of him, both of them with their shotguns propped on their thighs. If it hadn't been for their dresses and their ladylike airs, it would have been easy to mistake them for some kind of *bandidas* or women revolutionaries.

They had all left Sibley's army with high hopes that the going was going to get easier, but the pink wagon had become stuck in

the mud two days out from Valverde Crossing and a few miles short of Socorro where
they hoped to meet up with Jim and Caesar.
A branch of the trail that crossed a semi-
marsh along the cottonwood-strewn riverbank looked frosty enough to bear the
wagon's weight but turned out to be nothing but a bog. Despite a Herculean effort,
the wagon wouldn't come free.

With no other options, they loaded what
they could on the spare mule, and Faro put
his own saddle on one of the wagon horses
for Zula and flung blankets on the back of
the other horse and Old Scratch for him
and Armand. After leaving the stuck wagon,
they had arrived in Socorro at daylight, only
to find that an advance party of Confederate
cavalry had surrounded the village and was
in a standoff with the small Union garrison
there. There was no sign of Jim or Caesar.

Getting involved in more war business was
the last thing Faro wanted, and his party
continued north. And now, he could feel
every one of the seventy-odd miles he had
come upriver since then. Other than a meal
of beans and tortillas they had bought from
a sheep herder at Los Lunas, that stretch of
trail had been nothing but cold camps,
sleeping on the ground, and entirely too far
to ride on a round-backed mule with only

blisters and saddle sores between your tender parts and his hide.

He studied the settlement a half-mile up-river from where he and the rest of his party sat their horses. Albuquerque lay on a broad plain that looked more like a basin lying between the escarpment west of the river and the towering, bare rock heights of the Sandia Mountains. There weren't any soldiers of either color uniform visible to his naked eyes. In fact, the place would have looked quite peaceful if it weren't for the big cloud of smoke pouring from its midst.

"Do you think Sibley's men have already come and gone?" Rue asked.

"No, must be some other kind of trouble," he answered. "I haven't seen a single sign of any of the Rebels riding ahead of us since we left Socorro."

"Well, what's that smoke?"

He shrugged. "How am I supposed to know? Maybe those people up there are just as sick of this winter weather as I am and decided to burn the town down to get warm."

"You've been so grumpy today." Rue gave him a mild version of her pouty look.

"He's just worried that Jim and Caesar might have deserted us and run off with the mules," Zula said. "That's what they should

450

have done if they were smart."

Faro didn't respond. In truth, the fact that Jim and Caesar hadn't been at Socorro weighed heavily on him. He didn't for one minute believe that they had run off on him, but he did worry that something bad had happened to them. Maybe they had been captured while trying to sneak around Fort Craig or ambushed by Indians or renegade deserters. It was a hard country and hard times, and there were a jillion ways that a man could get himself killed.

He shook his worries from his mind and turned his attention back to the town. He figured he had about five dollars burning a hole in his pocket, and what he wanted was a decent meal, a bath, and a real bed to sleep in for the first time in better than a month . . . and a saddle. On second thought, he had gotten used to being hungry, he had about given up on ever looking presentable again, the bathwater would probably be muddy, and the bed would probably give him a dose of bedbugs. He would settle for a saddle.

He started Old Scratch up the trail.

"Are we going to ride in there, even though somebody has set the town on fire?" Zula asked.

"Maybe the whole Union Army's there,

murderous bandits, or a thousand blood-thirsty Indians. I don't care," he answered.

They made a half circle around the little town until Faro was satisfied that they weren't riding into some kind of ambush. Using the column of smoke as a beacon, they finally rode into the main plaza. Somebody had stacked a huge pile of goods in front of the military storehouse and trading post and attempted to burn them. However, the pile wasn't burning well. Instead of raging flames, most of the intended bonfire was no more than a smoldering, smoking mess. Furthermore, a large mob of Albuquerque's inhabitants was dragging plunder from the stack just as fast as they could.

The next thing they saw was Jim leaning against an adobe wall and watching the chaotic scene as if it were great entertainment. He had one thumb hooked in his gun belt and was sucking on a stick of candy he had managed to find somewhere.

"I didn't think you were ever going to make it here," Jim said.

"I thought we were supposed to meet in Socorro," Faro said.

"Took us longer than we thought to get by Fort Craig, and then a bunch of Navajos *confiscated* half of our mules."

"Is Caesar all right?"

"We both came through alright," Jim said. "We've got the rest of the mules penned here in town, and Caesar's tending to them. That Mexican sets more store by those long ears than he does people."

Faro pointed at the crowd and the fire. "What the hell is going on?"

"Yankee soldiers came this morning intending on hauling all the supplies to Fort Union. Trouble was, they couldn't fit everything into the wagons they had. Then some officer gave the order to burn everything else so the Rebels wouldn't get it when they show up," Jim said. "They must have been in a hurry, because they didn't make sure their fire was going good before they left. They weren't even out of sight when the locals swarmed in."

"Somebody ought to put a stop to this. Looks like nothing more than looting and stealing to me," Rue said.

"To these poor folks, it probably seems foolish to let that stuff burn when they could make use of it. The army obviously didn't want it, or they wouldn't have tried to burn it." Faro gave her a wry look. "Think about the time you were the hungriest on this trip. Would you have pulled food from that fire if it meant getting something to eat?"

"I promise you that I have as much or more compassion for poor people than you do, but they should have enough pride not to dig through the army's refuse." Rue gave her horse a tap on the hip with her quirt and trotted away with a stern look on her face.

Zula sat her horse beside Faro and watched her sister leave. "Don't mind her. What you said was true, and she knows it. But watching those people fighting over those storehouse scraps scared her, that's all."

"I didn't think she was scared of anything," Faro said.

"Nothing scares Rue as much as being so poor that she might not be able to afford her pride. That scared our mother too," Zula said. "To be a southern lady, you have to look like a southern lady. You have to act like you don't care about money, but you better look like you have plenty of it. Rue knows that doesn't come cheap, and she feels like she's not too far from having to dig in the scrap heap herself."

"Jim, see if you can find a place for the ladies to lay their heads tonight."

"Will do," Jim said.

"And I see a few McClellan saddles in that bonfire," Faro added as he started to ride off, "See if you can drag one of them out for me before it burns."

"Where are you going?"

"I'm going to find a hot bath and a good meal."

He rode down a side street until he was out of sight of his party before sliding painfully from Old Scratch's back and tying him to a hitching rail. He looked up and down the street for anything that looked like an inn or a station that might offer shelter and comfort to a weary traveler. He hadn't taken two tender steps when he spotted the Mexican sitting under the brush roof in front of a little, flat-topped adobe house.

A broad sombrero was tilted down over the man's face, and all that Faro could see of him besides his chin were the two hands that protruded from a wool serape and rested on the small table in front of him. Thin lines of sunlight leaking through the brush roof overhead painted stripes on the shadowed table.

"Buenas tardes." The Mexican raised his head and Faro could just make out a pair of wizened eyes twinkling under the hat brim.

"Good afternoon to you." Faro moved his attention back to the Mexican's hands and to the three, upside-down clay cups on the table. He watched as the man shuffled and slid those cups around nonchalantly, pausing to lift one and reveal a small, white bean under it, and then covering it again and shuffling the cups some more.

"Interesting, no?" The Mexican smiled and left the cups lined up in a neat, evenly spaced row before him on the table. "You look like you have sharp eyes. Care to guess where *el conejo* hides?"

"El conejo?"

"The rabbit," the Mexican explained, "Can you follow the rabbit and find where he hides? Every time his burrow is a different one."

Faro pointed to the cup in the middle, and the Mexican smiled again before lifting it to reveal that the bean was indeed where Faro had guessed. "I knew I couldn't fool you. Perchance, would you care to venture a bet that you can spot *el conejo* again?"

It was Faro's turn to smile. The shell game was as old as they came. With a little sleight of hand, a willingness to cheat, and the proper sales pitch, a shyster like the man in front of him could make a little profit, providing he had plenty of suckers passing by.

"It has been a very slow day for travelers," the Mexican said, shoving his sombrero farther back on his head and running a hand across his mustache. "And it is cold enough that I think my hands are a little slow and stiff today."

Faro wasn't under the false impression that the location of the bean would be as easy to guess the next time, especially if he placed a bet. Letting the customer guess right the first time was a part of the act that he had seen a thousand times.

On second thought, he decided that he might as well take advantage of his experience. He laid a dollar on the table. The Mexican studied Faro carefully, almost friendly like, but to a fellow gambler, it was plain that he was gauging just how much money his latest victim had to lose. Faro guessed that he would be allowed to win one more time if the first wager were small enough.

The Mexican's hands moved faster this time, shuffling the cups with both hands in a confusing pattern, all the while keeping them against the table. Once he was through, he leaned back against the wall and made a dramatic gesture with his open palms, as if to invite Faro to pick.

Faro took the time to make a show of pondering his selection, as if his choice were a grave one, although he was instantly sure of which cup the bean was under. He pointed hesitantly at the one on his right. The Mexican tried to appear saddened when he lifted that cup and revealed the bean.

"Like I said, you have good eyes," he said.

Faro picked up the dollar that the Mexican pulled from a leather purse on one end of the table, and pocketed it with his own. The little roadside gambler had let him win again in hopes that he would place a larger bet. Picking the bean wouldn't be near as easy the third time, and it might even be impossible if the Mexican was good enough at cheating. His kind could work magic with their hands.

"I am a poor man," the Mexican said, "Perhaps you wish to bet again and give me a chance to win my money back."

Faro started walking away. He knew better than to fall into such a trap. The meager money in his pocket was the difference between going to bed with a full belly and going hungry that evening. A man shouldn't bet what he couldn't afford to risk.

"Maybe we only bet once more," the Mexican said. "I think I can fool you this time."

Faro was telling himself the safe play was to walk away with the Mexican's dollar and not be baited in. He was still telling himself that when he stopped and went back to the table.

Six dollars was all he had except for the clothes on his back, the guns on his hips, and a mean black mule. Not much to lose to some, and little to risk for a high-rolling gambler used to wide-open riverboat games. But those six dollars were more than enough to buy a man a bath and a meal, with enough left over for a drink or breakfast. Then again, he'd be dead broke the next morning whether he made a bet or not, and he'd be damned if he wanted go to the O'Hell sisters asking for money to feed himself when they got to Santa Fe. Doubling his money might even give him enough to buy some new clothes.

"What the hell," Faro said. "This isn't the first time I've let everything ride, and probably won't be the last."

He didn't know where the sudden optimism was coming from, but he did feel good. He hadn't had any luck in years, but that couldn't last forever. Maybe his luck had already turned and he didn't know it yet.

"And this." Faro pulled the vial containing his lucky gold nugget from his pocket and put it with his six dollars. "It's worth about six dollars."

The Mexican picked up the vial and held it up before his eyes. After a cautious study he counted out ten dollars of his own and stacked the coins beside Faro's. His smiling demeanor changed as soon as his hands touched the cups again. He lifted one cup to prove that the bean was present, in what was meant to be evidence that his game was honest.

"Shall we play?" the Mexican asked.

Faro nodded and the Mexican gambler's first shuffle and shifting of the cups was three times as fast as his last performance. Faro strained to follow the bean while the Mexican did all manner of fancy moves, flourishes, and distracting gestures. Faro was so intent on keeping his focus on the right cup that he failed to notice the Mexican's hands slow for the briefest instant. Nor did he notice the Mexican looking over his shoulder with a frown on his face.

"Let's see if it is your lucky day." The Mexican finally leaned back against the wall once more, offering the pick of the cups before him for Faro's pleasure.

It quickly dawned on Faro that he didn't have a clue which cup the bean was under. For an instant, the old depression that sometimes came over him started to rear its head, but he fought it down. The worst he could do was to lose, and he had done that before, often in fact, and survived in spite of it.

He hesitated for only an instant before placing his hand on top of the middle cup. Better to get it over with than to wait any longer. He was already starting to feel his luck fading away. Luck was a wispy thing and hard to hang on to.

CHAPTER 46

Jim Tall Tree leaned against the corner of the store and watched Faro and the Mexican shill man across the street trying to outfox each other. He saw Faro win the first bet and had a pretty good idea what was coming next. It kind of surprised him that Faro was making another bet when anybody could tell at a glance that the Mexican gambler made his living suckering anybody he could. An honest game was the last thing Faro was going to get.

Jim cocked his head to better hear what was being said.

"Go ahead and turn it over," Faro said.

Even from across the street, Jim could see enough of the Mexican's face to tell that Faro hadn't picked correctly.

Jim slid his Colt Army from its holster and waved an arm to catch the Mexican's eyes. Faro's back was to him, and his attention was locked on the cups. He wasn't even aware that Jim was anywhere around.

The Mexican was quick to spot the gangly Cherokee boy standing across the street. Jim shook his head slowly, pointed at Faro with his free hand, and subtly pointed the Colt in his other fist at the Mexican. The roadside gambler had been long at his trade, had seen many things, and was quick to get the gist of Jim's threat. He nodded slightly and his lips compressed into a subtle sign of surrender. He never took his eyes off of Jim's gun while he reached forward and lifted the cup Faro had chosen.

Jim could tell by the straightening of Faro's posture that the Mexican had managed, by whatever sleight of hand or tricks such men manipulated the game, to make sure that bean appeared under the middle cup and that Faro won.

"How about we go again?" Faro's voice carried across the street. "Let it ride one more time."

The Mexican looked across the street again, and Jim nodded.

Once again, the cups were shuffled until the Mexican finally let out a sigh and offered for Faro to pick. Faro chose the cup on the left end.

"Your eyes are too quick for me," the

Mexican said, revealing the bean under the cup.

"How about one more go?" Faro asked.

The Mexican glanced over Faro's shoulder, and Jim shook his head and holstered his pistol.

"I think I will quit before my purse is empty," the Mexican said. "You are too lucky for me. I think maybe someone is looking out for you."

"Don't take it too hard," Faro said. "Out here, they say there isn't a horse that can't be rode, and there isn't a man who can't be thrown."

Faro started down the street, stuffing his winnings into his pocket. Jim took his eyes off of his friend and gave the Mexican a courteous nod. The Mexican nodded back, cautiously. Jim crossed the street and pitched two double eagles on the table while the gambler clutched his money bag to his chest.

"Thanks for the favor, amigo," Jim said. "That ought to make us even."

The Mexican didn't answer him and Jim tipped his hat and hurried up the street to catch up to Faro.

Faro noticed Jim after several steps and slowed to let him catch up. A broad smile lit his face, and it was the first time Jim had seen him smile like that in many weeks. Faro had a good smile, almost a Cherokee smile.

"What were you doing over there?" Jim asked, trying to appear as nonchalant and innocent as he could.

Faro put his hand on Jim's shoulder. "Come on and let me buy you a drink and something to fill your belly."

"Well, my, my, if you aren't in a good mood. Did you skin that gambler out of his money?"

"No, just a few dollars, but that isn't what matters."

"What's got you so chipper then?"

Faro got that old twinkle in his eye that Jim had seen the first time he met him in the gun store back in New Orleans. "Kid, my luck's finally turned. I can feel it. I think things are going to be all right."

"Glad to hear it."

Faro started along the edge of the street, expecting Jim to follow. "Soon as we eat, what say you we trade the wagon horses for a couple of good riding horses for the girls and go get us some gold?"

Jim took one last look at the Mexican peering at him from the doorway of the adobe. Maybe what he did wasn't right, but it didn't feel that way. His mother had always told him that it was wrong to cheat, but Unc' also said that sometimes such rules didn't fit every situation. He hadn't lived long enough to sort out the world, but he was already pretty sure that a man needed to win every now and then. A gambler like Faro Wells needed it more than most. So, maybe it was okay, like Unc' said, to bend the rules every now and then to help a friend.

CHAPTER 47

"I'll say it again. I want to see the letter that your father sent you and have another look at the map." Faro leaned over the table until his face was in the pool of light thrown by the lantern hanging overhead.

Rue McGaffney passed her sister a guarded look, and then another at Armand, who merely grunted and shoved another mouthful of beans onto his fork with a piece of tortilla. She glanced nervously to where Jim sat alone at a table closer to the door of the restaurant.

"Don't mind Jim. I brought him along to watch the door so we could have a little privacy," Faro said. "And it isn't like he doesn't know what we're after."

Zula took her own look around the dark room to make sure that the owner was still back in the kitchen. "Let him see the letter."

Rue shook her head. "Faro, you've already

seen the map more than once, and our agreement was that you didn't get to look at the letter until we reached Santa Fe."

"Things have changed," Faro said. "I'm not taking you one more mile until I see that letter. I can't do my job any longer unless I have all the details."

"Faro," Jim's voice called out softly, "Caesar's coming down the street with the pack mules."

"Let me see the letter," Faro said again.

"We'd better ride. The word is that General Sibley's boys aren't ten miles outside of town." Jim had finished his meal and was standing in the doorway looking worriedly up and down the street. "We don't want to explain to the general how we came by his mules."

"Here." Zula unbuttoned the top button of her shirt and reached down into the realm of her ample cleavage.

Rue put a hand on her wrist. "My gosh, keep your clothes on. If he's going to see it, he might as well see the original."

Zula chuckled. "Sister, you don't have anything to show him that I don't have more of and better."

Rue ignored the jab and pulled an Indian medicine bag from inside her coat — the very same one that Faro had seen when they showed him the golden eggs back in their New Orleans apartment.

She pitched the bag on the table in the middle of their empty dinner plates. "Are you happy now?"

Faro opened the medicine bag and laid its contents before him. He only gave the deerskin map a quick once-over, already having it down to memory long before. However, he carefully removed the yellowed letter paper from the envelope beside the map, unfolding it and spending several minutes poring over what he read there — two pages of the scrawling, crude, and sometimes illegible handwriting of Tin Pan McGaffney. Faro took a couple of deep breaths after he had finished reading.

"Well, what do you think?" Rue said when she saw the smoldering look on his face. "Haven't we told you the truth?"

"What does this say?" Faro shoved the second page of the letter into the weak pool of lantern light and thumped a finger on two words about halfway down the page.

Rue slowly slipped the paper out from under his finger and turned it so that she could read it. "Bring some good mules for forty loads of gold."

Faro jerked the paper back from her and ground his finger into it just below the words he had pointed out. "Zula, what does this say?"

Zula leaned forward and craned her neck until she could read what he was pointing out. She took longer reading it than her sister had. "Bring some good mules for forty loads of gold?"

"You aren't sure, are you?" Faro asked.

"That's what it says," Rue snapped back at him.

"Maybe, or maybe it says four loads, or five loads, or something totally different," Faro hissed. "Who can tell?"

"It says 'for forty loads,' " Rue repeated. "Believe me, Zula and I studied those very words far more than you have, and both of us agree it says 'forty.' "

Faro pointed again to the letter. Somebody, apparently Tin Pan, had scratched out a couple of words and scribbled in replacements — the very ones that he had doubts about. Tin Pan's penmanship, and the fact that the whole thing was written with a blotchy pen, made it an iffy proposition to accurately read. To top that off, a large spot of what looked like blood or grease partially blurred part of the words being debated.

"It looks like 'forty' to you, because you want it to," Faro said. "And I was as big of a fool as you two for not seeing the letter

470

myself before I ever agreed to this deal."

"I don't believe that, and I won't," Rue threw in, "but say you're right. Worst-case scenario, maybe there isn't forty loads of gold, but four loads of gold is nothing to sneer at."

"There's a big difference, especially when you're trying to talk a man into risking his neck to help you get it."

"Who's the greedy one now?" Rue smacked her palm on the tabletop. "Afraid you won't get a big enough cut of our gold? Calculating your ten percent? Is that what's eating you?"

"Every damned one of us has been risking our lives for what we thought was a king's ransom, including you. I don't know about you, but I put a pretty high price on my head."

"You said yourself," Zula interjected, "there is no telling how many pounds of gold Father was talking about putting on each mule. Even four loads might mean four hundred pounds of gold."

"A few months ago, I'm guessing you would have done just about anything to get your hands on that much money," Rue added. "I bet that's more than a third-rate gambler like you has seen in a long, long time."

"Third-rate gambler?" Faro stood to his feet.

"I'm sorry. I didn't mean that."

Faro went to the door to stand beside Jim with his back to them.

"All right, Mr. Mercenary, what are you going to do now that you think we aren't worth millions?" Rue asked.

Faro waited to answer her. "I'll take you to your gold, because it's what I promised to do and because I'm as gold crazy as you are. But this third-rate gambler is going to be the first to tell you that the kind of living you want will run through a lot of money in a hurry. Believe me, I've been there."

"Faro, we're risking just as much as you are, and you can't make me believe it isn't worth it," Rue stood to her feet and met his stare. "Stay here if you don't want a share."

Faro took his blanket poncho off the wall and slipped it over his head and buckled his gun belt over it to keep if from flopping. He could see Caesar coming down the street with the string of mules following him. Not forty mules, but they would have to do. They had almost managed to salvage enough good army packsaddles and other gear from the failed Union bonfire to outfit the string. What they couldn't find by looting, they had traded a few of the mules for or the sisters bought with the last of their money.

He didn't have much use for mules, but he had to admit that a dozen of them coming down the street in the dusky evening light was almost a pretty thing. In the Southwest, pack mules weren't usually tied together like they were in other parts of the country, or as practiced by army muleskinners. The little animals followed along of their own free will, herd instinct, and training. Those that didn't could be herded along until they learned to do so. The practice worked better on rough mountain trails, because a mule that might slip off the edge of a bluff wouldn't drag any more of his friends along with him.

"I see you got yourself a new hat," Caesar said as he rode by.

Faro took the hat off so that he could look it over one more time. It was just a cheap felt hat with an open-topped crown and a three-inch brim, but it was a far cry better looking than the battered sombrero he had been wearing. The rest of his outfit, from the wool poncho down to the new rawhide-soled boots he'd bought from the cobbler across the street would have looked better on a Mexican vaquero, but he could live with it. A fresh shave and a good hat always made him feel at the top of his game.

Old Scratch was waiting for him at the hitching rail, with a McClellan army saddle on his back, the Sharps rifle hanging from it, and two good Navajo blankets rolled up and tied behind. They had traded the wagon team for a pair of shaggy horses and bare-bones Mexican saddles for Armand and Zula to ride. Those horses stood saddled and ready beside Old Scratch, along with Jim's mustang.

"Come on, ladies," Faro said over his shoulder as he tightened Old Scratch's cinch, "We've come this far, so we might as well see this thing through."

He started to put a foot in the stirrup, but Old Scratch blocked him by craning his neck around and putting his head in the way.

"Is he still trying to bite you?" Jim asked as he got on his horse.

Faro reached in his pocket and pulled out something that he offered in his open palm to the black mule. "No, but he's decided that he likes mesquite beans. You still can't trust the devil, and now he's turned into a beggar."

"So, you're buying mesquite beans for him now? I think he's growing on you," Jim said.

"Don't kid yourself. I'm just trying to

bribe him," Faro shoved Old Scratch's head out of the way while the mule's jaws worked at a mouthful of beans, "We'd better hurry up and catch up to Caesar before he's halfway to Santa Fe."

Zula rode up beside him when they reached the edge of town. "Maybe it was all too good to be true. That much gold, I mean."

"A lot of things are too good to be true, or at least only half as good as you hoped they would be," he said. "But you might be right. Even a little gold is more than most people have to dream on."

"You mean make the best of it?"

"If we find some gold . . . well, that's just gravy on the biscuits."

"Back there in the restaurant, you were starting to sound like you had given up."

Faro gave a deep chuckle. "Don't count me out yet. Not while I've still got a seat in the game."

"You want that gold as bad as I do, and that's saying something." Zula leaned back in her saddle and gave him an odd look, as if she were seeing him for the first time. "You might want it as much Rue does, just for different reasons."

"We all have our reasons."

She gave him that cat smile again — the

one that always made him feel a lot of different ways at once. "What are you going to do with your share of the gold, whatever it is?"

"I was thinking I might go to California," he said.

"And then what?"

"I'm still working it out."

"Don't have a clue, do you?"

"I'm weighing my options," he said. "First, Rue knows everything, and now you. For your information, I intend to start some kind of business. Maybe I'll grow some oranges or put in a dry-goods store."

"You, a farmer? A shopkeeper? Please. You would be a lot more interesting if you would quit trying to be who you aren't."

"And what are you going to do with your money?" Faro asked.

"Me? I'm going to buy a big house and fill it full of pretty serving boys to attend to my every whim. They'll pour my bath, massage my feet, and walk around the house naked and scatter lilac petals wherever I go."

"Zula, you're a bad girl."

"Being naughty is sort of a hobby of mine."

"Why are you looking at me like that?" he asked.

"I was just trying to imagine what you

would look like with your hair curled, your skin oiled up, and nothing but an olive leaf wreath on your head."

"Oh, Queen, forgive me if I don't have any lilac petals to spread before you on the trail." He tried to hold back the snicker that was building in him, but couldn't. "And I think it's a bit too cold to be wearing nothing but a wreath on my head."

Her laughter joined his own. "I might enjoy counting the goose bumps on you."

"Not me. Find another toy."

She clucked her tongue and gave him a sad, dramatic shake of her head. "Tut-tut, Monsieur Wells. So boring. At times you show such promise."

CHAPTER 48

Rue had slept in late and woke up to find Zula already gone. The fire in the stove had burned out, and the hotel room was almost frigid. She laid some kindling on the coals and went to stand at the window, hugging herself.

A long train of freight wagons lined the street below, as the Union troops prepared to flee Santa Fe for Fort Union with their commissary and anything else that the invading Confederates might use. Around the old plaza square and the Palace of the Governors, officers were kissing their wives good-bye, leaving them behind because they were ordered to retreat to a new post. Those civilians wealthy enough or scared enough to leave were lining their loaded wagons up with the soldiers' caravan. Santa Fe was going to have a lot less people in less than an hour, and if the grain-laden wagons were any sign, a lot less to eat too. She could see

Faro down there, talking to a Yankee officer.

Her stomach growled, reminding her that she could use a little breakfast. Dressing quickly, she started out of the room, but realized that she had forgotten her coat. Hers lay across the room on her bed, and she grabbed Zula's hanging on a peg by the door without thinking. Shrugging into it, she shoved her chilled hands into its pockets, only to find Zula's handbag stuffed in the right pocket. She tossed it on the dresser, but the sound of clinking metal gave her pause. She went back and opened the purse, standing there for several minutes thinking about the coins she found — three hundred dollars' worth.

They had spent almost the last of their money in Albuquerque to resupply, and barely had the price of the hotel room and meals when they finally arrived in Santa Fe two days later. Why was Zula holding out on her? What's more, how had she come by so much money?

Zula was always secretive and could be more than a little manipulative when there was something she wanted. It was high time she and Zula had a talk.

Rue went down the stairs quickly and crossed the lobby to the hotel entrance. She barely set foot on the street before she saw the party of horsemen coming from the south. There were a dozen of them on hard-ridden mounts. The town was on watch for Rebel scouts that might signal the arrival of General Sibley's army, and the civilians on the street whispered among themselves and more than a few of them slunk back into their doorways to appraise the newcomers. The Yankee soldiers near the supply train went to their rifles and kept a cautious eye on the men.

Rue didn't recognize any of the party but didn't need anyone to tell her who the tall man in the eye patch at their lead was. True, there were many stories about King Brou-let, but one glance at him was all anyone needed to see that he was pure poison. He rode at the head of his men, slumped in the saddle atop a nervous Thoroughbred so dark brown that it was almost black. His caped overcoat flapped in the wind on either side of the horse, slapping its flanks and making it nervous enough to push against the bit and trot sideways. His long hair hung in two strands over each shoulder, and all that could be seen of his face below the slouching brim of his hat was a long jaw and hollowed cheeks above a wide, thin-lipped mouth. It was the kind of mouth that story villains always had. It was the kind of mouth that ate children and never smiled except to laugh at someone else's misery.

She fought off the urge to go back inside the hotel when his horse came opposite her, and managed to stand her ground. So that was the man who had tried to ambush her in the swamps outside of New Orleans and tried to kill Faro in San Antonio. More important, he wanted to steal her gold, and had ridden all those miles in her wake with that one intention. Strangely, she could almost understand a man like him. Not the meanness that must be there, but the single-mindedness. Nothing was going to stop him until he had what he wanted.

He was going to have to be dealt with. Seeing him made her so very sure of that. Up until the moment, he had only been a rumor amongst all manner of worries. Now he was very real.

His head slowly cranked her way. She lifted her chin defiantly and peered into the shadowed recesses of his hat brim, ignoring the sneering looks on the faces of his men as each of them appraised her in turn.

When he had passed, her attention moved across the street to where Zula stood with one arm hugging a porch post. Rue was reminded again just how beautiful her sister truly was, more beautiful than any woman had a right to be. In some strange way, she loved Zula but hated her too. It was only a tiny bit of hate, but there was no denying it. Funny, she had felt the same way about their mother.

King stopped his horse in the middle of the street, and a long moment of silence passed between him and Zula, as if they were old acquaintances. Finally, he reached up one hand to bend the brim of his hat before riding on. He waved to the Union soldiers and called out greetings to them as he passed alongside the army supply train and disappeared into a side street several blocks away.

Rue's eyes went back to the other side of the street and found that Zula was staring back at her. Rue knew her well, at least as well as anyone could know her, and recognized the look on her face. She had seen it a thousand times. Zula always looked that way when she had been caught doing something wrong . . . something sneaky.

The sun was almost down by the time Rue left her room for a second time. She stayed in the shadows until she could see campfire flames reflecting off of the adobe walls of the livery corrals ahead. She paused across the street, trying to will her heartbeat to

slow and clutching the Philadelphia derringer she carried in her coat pocket for re-
assurance. A tiny thing, but it was a real
Henry Deringer, silver inlaid, and its stubby,
single-shot barrel loaded with a .41-caliber
round ball. It had been her mother's gun,
and that seemed somehow fitting.

She stayed there for the better part of half
an hour, watching while most of King's men
left the fire after their meal for another go
at the cantinas and saloons. Her view of the
campfire wasn't great, but as near as she
could tell, only one man remained in camp.
That tall shadow cast against the corral wall
would be King Broulet.

The money in Zula's pocket and the look
that passed between her and King kept running through Rue's mind. Another question
also bothered her. How had King known to
be waiting for them back in the swamps
outside of New Orleans? So much gold —
enough to tempt even a temptress like Zula,
who was never one to curb her appetites or
hesitate to get what she wanted. Sisters or
not, had the rift between them grown so
large that Zula would betray her?

A twinge of guilt rose up in her, for the
thought of betraying Zula, if it came to that,
had popped into her own mind more than
once. What if there wasn't forty loads, but

only four as Faro had threatened her? Four loads would barely be enough to take care of one person.

She remembered the look of King and his men riding into Santa Fe. There was no way that Faro Wells was any match for them, no matter how good his intentions were. The Indian boy was just a boy. Armand was loyal, but he was only one man. There was nobody else she could turn to, or count on except herself. She was going to have to be hard, and she was going to have to be stronger than ever . . . she was going to have to be like Mother.

She remembered the words so often spoken when some bully had knocked her down, or when she was disappointed and shattered by some turn of childhood events, sometimes spoken in English and sometimes whispered in her ear in soothing French like a Creole nursery rhyme. *Look out for yourself, dear, for nobody will do it better.*

She crossed the street and stepped into the firelight.

King rose from where he sat on his bedroll beside the fire. "Good evening, mademoiselle. I must admit this is unexpected."

She had miscalculated. He wasn't the only one left in their camp, although the man beside him was obviously sloppy drunk and

484

only mumbled and rolled over in his twisted blankets, the empty whiskey bottle in his hand falling to the ground beside him.

Rue pulled the pistol from her pocket and pointed it at King's head. "Tell me, what's so good about it?"

King smiled at her and then at the pistol. "What is it about you two sisters? I'm beginning to think you both like to play with guns."

"Just how well do you know my sister?"

"Ah, so that's it." King squatted slowly and held his hands to the fire to warm them. "Care to warm yourself, or are you afraid to come closer?"

Rue kept an eye on his hands. "No, this won't take long."

"Just what have you come for? To threaten me? To kill me?"

"I'm going to make sure that I get my gold." Rue extended the pistol to arm's length.

"And you think by killing me that you will guarantee that you get it?" He laughed to show his disgust. "Do you think my men will give up just because I am dead?"

She had never seen a man so damnably confident, or one so plainly what he was. She knew that she should have already shot him and realized how foolish she had been to even consider, however shortly, that she could scare him away, or talk with him like someone civilized.

Every second she let him live was a chance for his men to return or for a witness to show up. Murder? If she didn't kill him, he would be waiting for her somewhere up the trail. His death would be nothing more than pure self-defense, and the difference between her being rich or going back East in poverty.

"And I thought you were supposed to be the good sister," he said to the flames. "Killing seems such an easy thing, doesn't it? But you don't want your gold bad enough, and that is why you won't get it. You are just a spoiled little girl playing games, like your sister."

"You are an evil man."

"Maybe you should send Faro down here to shoot me. No? Maybe you think he isn't man enough to take care of you. You want to get your way, but you don't know how."

"Shut up."

"You can go ahead and cry if you want to."

"You are wrong if you think I won't kill you." She wanted him to keep talking. She wanted to be mad enough to carry out her threat.

"Maybe we can strike a deal that makes us both happy. Isn't that what you really came for?" he asked.

"A deal with the likes of you?"

"How much of that gold are you going to have to pay Faro? What about a share for the Indian kid and the Mexican?" He stabbed the fire with green stick and the sparks flew up between them like some kind of spell. "You can't even trust your sister to leave you any of the gold."

"At least *you* won't get my gold." Rue cocked the pistol in her shaking hand.

"I would say that a two-way cut would be much better for you." He looked up at the pistol barrel again, not even blinking.

"God forgive me," Rue whispered as her finger tightened on the trigger.

CHAPTER 49

"Put down that pistol." The drunk in his bedroll was suddenly awake and very alert. He was propped up on one elbow and pointing a revolver at her.

"You had better do as he says." King yawned and stretched his long, thin arms like the wingspan of some kind of vulture. "Black Jack kind of has this thing about women."

She lowered the derringer, letting it hang beside her leg. A little sigh escaped her, and she realized that she had been holding her breath.

"It's funny how things turn out." King held out one open palm for her gun. "I wasn't leaving here until I had at least one of you ladies, but I never would have guessed that it would be you."

She uncocked the pistol and pitched it to him, wondering how quickly help would come if she called for it.

"I see the little gears turning in your mind," he said. "Rest assured, if you scream, I will cut your throat."

She had no response, for she believed he would do just what he said.

"Sit." He gestured to a stool across the fire from him.

She did as she was told, gathering her dress about her and doing her best not to appear terrified.

"Black Jack, you go find the rest of the men," he said to the man in the bedroll, "Tell them to get back here and saddle up."

The big man with the beard staggered to his feet and holstered his pistol. "Don't kill her before I get back. I'll give you twenty dollars for her if you don't want her."

King slapped the dust from his hat on one knee and ran his other hand through his hair. "You have come a long ways. That took guts, but you didn't want it bad enough."

Still, she said nothing. He was right. She knew the threat he presented, yet her willpower had failed her. To come to his fire without killing him was worse than having not come at all.

He pointed to his eye patch. "There is a price for all things. Anyone who comes to bargain unwilling to lose something cannot bargain at all."

He paused as if savoring his own voice. "When I was young a man held a knifepoint to my eye. He laughed at me. He wanted me to beg and he wanted me to fear him. I let him laugh while I slid my own knife out and spilled his guts on the ground."

"I suppose there is a moral to this story." She strained to catch the sound of anyone passing by.

"The moral is that I got what I wanted."

"You lost your eye."

"I wanted to kill that man very badly and had searched for him for a long time," he said. "He could pluck out my eye if it gave me time to draw my own blade. That is commitment."

"Am I supposed to applaud you?"

"You know that I will hurt you."

"Are you such an animal as that?"

"I am committed." He stood quickly, looking down at her across the fire. "Give me the map. Now."

"I don't have the map."

"You lie."

She did her best to meet his stare. "It's back in my hotel room."

The knife appeared in his hands as if by magic. "I'll cut that dress off you until I find it, and if I don't find it, I'll keep cutting until I do."

"I'm telling you the truth." She kept her voice as steady as she could. "But the map wouldn't help you anyway. The directions to the claim aren't on it."

"And where are they?"

"They were in a letter my father sent me, but I burned it."

In what seemed like one quick step, he was around the fire and beside her with his knife at her temple, the tip of it pressing against the corner of her right eye. His other hand wrapped around her throat and shoved her chin up and back.

"You really want me to hurt you, don't you?"

The knife tip was already cutting into her eyelid. She strained to watch the gleaming steel, tears running down her cheek because she was afraid to lose sight of it.

"Half the gold," she gasped. "I'll take you to it and you get half the gold."

The increasing pressure he was putting on the knife blade ceased. "And I won't find the letter?"

"Not unless you can cut my memory out."

He pressed lightly on the knife again. "How committed are you? Will you give your eye?"

"Go ahead."

"Maybe you won't talk when I take the

first eye, but what of your other?"

"That is my gold. Kill me if you will."

He waited, silent while the tip of the knife caused a single drop of blood to trickle down her cheek. "I think you are bluffing."

He sheathed the knife and stepped away as quickly as he had come. Suddenly, she was so weak that she reeled on the stool and almost toppled from it.

"You understand that this is no game?" he asked.

She nodded.

"You had better be able to take me to that gold. No bobbles, no pretending to be lost. The first time I think you are playing me I will finish what I started here," he said. "Do you hear me?"

"I hear you."

"I'll give you to my men, and then when they're through with you, I'll have them cut you up so that no man will ever look at you again. They will hurt you in places you wouldn't even dream of in your worst nightmare."

She nodded, trembling.

"Say it!"

"I understand," she said.

"How far is it to the gold from here?"

"Less than a week's ride to the north. Take me to Maxwell's ranch. They say that it is

492

right on the trail south of Raton Pass."

He pointed at a Dutch oven beside the fire. "You had best eat while you can. We ride as soon as Black Jack gathers the men."

She wiped the tears and the blood from her cheeks but ignored the food. She knew that she had done nothing more than buy a little time. Even if he kept her alive until they found the gold, they were going to have the same conversation again. The next time, she would have nothing left to bargain with.

CHAPTER 50

Faro helped Caesar and Jim saddle the last pack mule by lantern light. King Broulet had them outnumbered and the handful of Union soldiers had left that morning. The best thing to do was to try and slip out of town and outrun King or lose him somewhere in the mountains. Maybe they could catch up to that Union supply train and ride with it for protection.

He made his way across the plaza to the hotel and knocked on the McGaffney sisters' door. Just when he was about to knock again, Zula answered from within.

"What do you want?" she asked.

"Wake your sister up. It's time to ride."

Seconds later, Zula cracked open the door. "She's gone."

"What do you mean she's gone?"

"I mean she's not here. I haven't seen her since before I went to bed."

Faro took the stairs down to the lobby two

at a time. The whole town knew that King's men were camped at the livery corrals, and he ran in that direction. He made no attempt at stealth and ducked through the open gate to the first corral, only to find nothing but the faint, glowing embers of King's campfire.

He took a quick walk through the heart of Santa Fe, coming back to the corrals after a half hour search that netted him nothing. The sun was already rising.

"What are you looking for?" A bow-legged man in high-water pants and straw hat that looked like it had been run through a corn sheller leaned on his pitchfork in the middle of the corral.

"Where did the men go who were camped here?"

"Beats me, but I can't say that I'm sorry that they're gone," the man said, the sharp knot of his Adam's apple bobbing up and down. "That was a nasty lot. I'm still not sure they weren't Confederate scouts feeling us out. The army boys should have arrested them."

"When did they leave?" Faro asked.

"Nigh about midnight I heard horses outside my shack. I clumb out of my bed and went to the window. Saw them riding past. Looked like they were headed east."

"Was there a woman with them?"

"Didn't see no woman, but it was dark, so that don't mean nothing." The liveryman pulled a pipe from his pocket and began to tamp fresh tobacco in it with his thumb. " 'Course, there was a woman who came to visit them last night. Pretty thing. Blond hair. I seen her watching them across the street just at dusk, and then I heard her talking to one of them later."

"Thanks." Faro started at a high walk back to the hotel.

"Hey, you sound like one of those southern boys yourself," the liveryman called after him.

Zula met Faro in front of the hotel with her bags packed and on the ground beside her. "Did you find her?"

"I think King got her," he answered.

"What are we going to do?"

"I don't know, but at least we know where they're going," he said.

Armand picked up Zula's bag. "It's my fault. I should have kept a closer eye on her."

Caesar was already starting the mules out of town. Jim was sitting his mustang on the edge of the street watching Faro and holding the saddle horses and Old Scratch.

"How much of that did you hear?" Faro asked.

"Enough."

"Getting here may have seemed hard, but that was child's play compared to what's coming. I wouldn't blame you if you quit."

"What do you intend to do?"

"I'll get Rue back, and if I can, I'll get the gold."

"I'll kill that King," Armand added. "He's mine."

"Jim, I'll pay you a bonus in gold if you stay with us," Zula said.

Jim stepped off his mustang and checked and tightened his cinch without saying a word.

"What about you, Caesar?"

"Do I still get to keep these mules?" The Mexican stopped his saddle mule while the pack train continued down the street.

"And I'll pay you a bonus too," Zula said.

"I'll stick with you." Caesar kicked his saddle mule after the pack train. "The mules were enough, but some gold too wouldn't be bad."

"What about you, Jim?" Faro asked. "You still haven't answered."

Jim swung up on his horse and gave them a wry smile. "I'd say y'all are spending too much time talking when we should be riding."

Old Scratch was especially willing to travel

that morning, and he pinned his ears and led the treasure party out of town at a jig. By the time the sun popped over the mountains they were riding toward Glorieta Pass and points beyond.

CHAPTER 51

Rue tried not to cry and swore to herself more than once that she wouldn't give her captors the satisfaction of seeing her break. They had left Santa Fe at a high lope and rode that way for the better part of an hour. Since then, they had alternated between a walk and a long trot, occasionally taking breaks to let the winded horses blow. Apparently, King intended to put a lot of miles between them and any pursuit, even at the risk of their horses.

The pace at which they covered the miles gave her a new understanding of just how quickly Faro could have gotten her to the mining claim, instead of dawdling around with the Confederate army. Had he chosen to go up the Mississippi and hired a strong party of guards to make a forced march over the Santa Fe Trail, she could have had the gold months before. She had been a fool to hire him and blamed him, most of all, for her predicament.

The ropes that bound her wrists were tied so tightly that her hands had swollen to twice their size, and the pain was almost more than she could bear. She missed her own horse greatly, for the one she was given to ride had a trot that jarred her teeth. To make matters worse, she was forced to ride astride on a man's saddle, something her dress wasn't well suited for, and that the inside of her thighs weren't at all prepared for. She hurt all over, but the only good thing about the pain she bore was that it kept her awake. She didn't understand how such men could ride so far and fast with so little rest. They had already been almost eight hours in the saddle, and she had long since given up looking behind them for a sign of a dust cloud that meant someone was riding to rescue her.

"Really, I expected a woman of your breeding to be a better conversationalist." King threw a frown at Rue riding beside him.

She fought down a bitter reply. Anything she said might get her into more trouble than she was already in. "My hands hurt."

"Poor thing," Black Jack said.

Rue looked at him, and then just as quickly looked away. He was always nearby and watching her. He leered and made no attempt to hide the fact that he would rape her in an instant if King would allow it. Not that he was any better than most of them. More than once she had caught them undressing her with their eyes or passing some rude comment about her.

"If you promise to be good, maybe I'll untie you," King said.

It galled her to have to ask again, for it felt like begging. She held out her bonds when they slowed going up a steep grade.

He studied her swollen hands. "I warn you, it's going to hurt a lot worse when I untie you."

"Just do it."

For once, he spoke the truth. Seconds after he untied her, the blood began to course through her hands. First, like pinpricks of glass trying to erupt through her skin, and then solid, agonizing fire. He watched her face as if to gauge how much she was enduring. She would have loved to keep that pleasure from him, but she couldn't hide just how bad it hurt.

The pain, when it was over, seemed to clear her mind. No matter how foolish it was to try and make a deal with the likes of King, it was plain to her that Zula had been working with him all along, intending to cut her out of her share of the gold. The thought that Zula might have paid King to kill her would have once seemed preposterous, but the more she considered it the more she knew that it was likely true.

An hour later they made camp high in the hills above the trail. The horses were unsaddled, and after a quick meal, the men scattered out from the fire and unrolled their bedding under the trees. Rue sat on a rock beside the fire and stared listlessly at the bowl of beans in her lap. She was too hungry to sleep and too tired to eat.

"You act like you don't appreciate our cooking." King walked up and pitched her a thin blanket. "You will eat when you are hungry enough, silver platter or not."

"I'd much more appreciate you letting me go pee without sending one of your men along."

"And have you run off? Maybe trip and fall and break your neck?"

She glared at the bowl of beans. Even considering all of the pain and discomfort she had endured at their hands, perhaps worst of all was squatting behind a trailside bush while one of his minions stood on the other side, and trying to relax her bladder while hearing the splatter of the men urinating in the trail.

"It's time you give me directions to the gold. No more bargaining." He glanced over his shoulder, as if checking to see if anyone might be listening before he spoke.

She knew it had been coming and was surprised he had waited that long to broach the subject. "What, and have you kill me right here and now?"

He clucked his tongue and shook his head. "Do you think I can't hurt you worse than you can take?"

"I've told you enough. I won't tell you more until we are closer to the claim."

"I'm going to count very slowly to three while you think about that, and then I'm going to wake Black Jack and call him over here."

"Is he so bad as that?"

"You don't even know."

Fear was his stock and trade, and she tried to keep her face bland. When she finally answered him, she raised her voice above a whisper and was pleased to see him cringe slightly. "I don't think you want to torture me in front of them and have them hear where the gold is at. Splitting the gold with so many men doesn't set well with you, does it?"

He glanced over his shoulders and hissed to cut her off. "Do you still think this is a game that you can win?"

"I intend to stay alive." She forced herself to take a mouthful of the beans and made him wait until she swallowed them. "And I intend to have my inheritance."

He studied her. "How committed would you be if I stuck your feet in that fire?"

"I'm sure I would shout out the directions to the mine very quickly." She crinkled her toes in her shoes and avoided looking at the coals.

"Then tell me."

"Why don't we ride for the mine together, just you and I?" she whispered. "I think it would be more profitable that way."

"Do you think you can play me like that?"

"What kind of deal did you and Zula make?"

One of the men tossed in his blankets and mumbled something. King watched him for a moment until he was sure that he had gone back to sleep.

"And what if you and I ended up with the gold? What does that solve for you?"

She tried to match his callous, smart-ass smile. "Why, I'm sure you would want to kill me just as much as I would want to kill you. That's the beauty of it — one of us ends up with it all."

"And you think you could best me?"

"At least it narrows the odds."

"You little Goth."

"Perhaps we might grow on one another, given time. You'll find that I'm much better at sticking to a plan than Zula is."

" 'Fortune is a woman, and if she is to be submissive it is necessary to beat and coerce her.' "

" 'For it must be noted, that men must either be caressed or else annihilated,' " she replied evenly.

"A lady who reads Machiavelli? I would have thought you would enjoy French poetry and depressing English novels."

"I am no more surprised that a man like you should quote the Great Prince."

"I admit, that in my more respectful days, I focused more on a gentleman's skill at arms than I did literature," he said. "But that cold-blooded Italian always tickled my fancy."

"Think on what I suggest."

"I think I should kill you now. You are beginning to remind me of me." He turned and disappeared into the timber.

CHAPTER 52

King stopped his horse and the rest of them followed suit. The trail ahead passed between an adobe way station on one side and a blacksmith shop and saloon on the other. Nobody was in sight, not so much as a single horse tied anywhere. The place looked peaceful enough, but that didn't stop his men from giving it a cautious study.

"What do you think?" Black Jack asked.

"I think we could use some fresh horses if there are any to be had." King stared at the adobe corrals beside the trading post, as if he were wishing that he could see what was inside them.

"I could use some wuh . . . whiskey," Willie chimed in.

"We'd best hurry," King said, "I don't like the look of that dust cloud behind us."

"We ought to be a lot farther ahead of those Yankee freight wagons than that," Black Jack said. "Could be a patrol."

"Look sharp. This place looks too damned quiet to suit me." King spurred his horse forward.

Black Jack followed suit, keeping his horse close to Rue's. The rest of them lined out abreast of one other behind them.

They were only fifty yards away when the first volley of rifle fire knocked four of King's men from their saddles. No warning, nothing, just shooting and shooting and killing. Black Jack grunted and Rue saw little cuts of thread flying off of the coat over his belly where the bullets hit him. King was already charging forward at a run, and Rue kicked her horse after him. The guns wouldn't stop and everyone was dying, and the only place she could think to be was someplace else.

Whoever was shooting at them was hidden in the buildings ahead, and Rue gritted her teeth as her horse followed King's right through the heart of the little roadside station. She wasn't used to riding with split reins and her sore, still swollen hands dropped one of them and her horse stepped on it. The bit jerked its mouth viciously and it squatted on its hindquarters and reared. She rolled out of the saddle and hit the ground hard.

The fight was over almost as quickly as it

began and the sudden change to dead silence made the ringing in her ears even louder. She waited until well after the sound of running horses ceased before she chanced rising to her feet, not quite sure how she was still alive. King Broulet was nowhere to be seen, and the first thing she saw was Captain Lacey coming out of the front of the trading post swapping the empty cylinder in his pistol for a fresh one.

"Did anybody get that one-eyed fellow?" he called out. "That man must have nine lives."

The lancers filtered out of the buildings cautiously, their guns still at ready. Rue could see riderless horses and dead men scattered up and down the road. It looked as if none of King's men had survived the fight.

"They were like sitting ducks," a mounted soldier pulled up in front of the captain.

"How many did we lose?"

"Clyde stuck his head up when he shouldn't, and Hopkins took a ricochet in the guts."

The captain holstered his pistol and turned his attention to Rue. "Care to tell me why you're worth kidnapping? Not that pretty women aren't scarce out here, but I think it's time you came clean with me.

Especially since you've cost me any chance of ambushing that Union supply train coming behind you."

Rue was still too shaken to think of a quick answer that might appease him. It was hard not to look at the dead men everywhere, and the sudden, shocking violence of the afternoon and the gunfire had taken her wits. She was still struggling to think of a good lie when a bugle sounded in the distance.

The captain studied the dust cloud coming their way. "My guess is that's a Yankee cavalry patrol scouting ahead for that supply train. A couple of you men ride down the trail and pop off a few shots to slow them down and buy us time."

Two of the lancers raced off in the direction of the dust.

"Gather what you can, and then let's ride," the captain added.

One of the lancers brought the captain's horse to him, while a couple of more led a pack train of horses out of the corrals. Rue wondered what had happened to the civilians who manned the outpost, but thought better of asking.

"Miss McGaffney, I would like to stay here and chat with you, but as you can see,

I have more pressing concerns," the captain said.

"You can't leave me here."

"Those Yankees will be here soon. I'm sure they will see you safe and sound to Fort Union."

"Captain Lacey, I have a proposition for you," she said as she attempted to knock the dust from her dress and gather her composure.

"Hopkins just died," one of the lancers passing by, said to the captain.

"Captain Lacey, are you listening to me? I would like to hire you to take me to my gold claim," Rue said, swallowing the nervous lump in her throat and trying not to dwell on what she had just done. There was too little time to think things out.

Gunfire sounded back down the trail, followed soon by the sound of a bugle. The captain swung on his horse and cast one last look at the dust cloud.

"A gold claim, Captain," she said.

"There are a lot of gold claims out here, Miss McGaffney." The captain was too busy to even look at her. "Get those damned packhorses moving!"

"I could pay you and your men quite handsomely."

"Set fire to that haystack!" the captain

shouted. "Excuse me, but what makes you think you could bribe me away from my duty? In case you haven't noticed, I'm in the middle of a war."

Rue looked down the trail. Somewhere back there, Zula was coming, and King was somewhere ahead of her. "Not just a mine, Captain. I have a considerable amount of refined gold waiting for me."

"How much gold?"

"A lot."

The captain walked his horse over and stopped it beside her. "There, now that wasn't so hard to say, was it?"

"You'll never know."

"Get Miss McGaffney a horse," he called out.

"What about that Yankee supply train you are so worried about?" she asked. "You know, duty and war and all of that."

The captain looked down at her from the back of his horse and dressed one end of his mustache before he gave her a broad grin. "What kind of scoundrel do you think I am to ignore a southern woman in distress?"

CHAPTER 53

King's winded thoroughbred staggered and barely made it up the side of the mesa. He tied the lathered animal to a pine tree and went back the way he had come until he could look down the slope for signs of pursuit. Stuttering Willie spurred his horse past him just as he gained his vantage point. He heard Willie fall off of his horse behind him but made sure they weren't being followed before he glanced that way.

Willie crawled over to the nearest tree and managed to roll over and lean back against its trunk. There was blood all over him.

"I'm hurt bad, King." A bullet had passed through the side of Willie's face, shattering most of his teeth, and his jaw sagged crookedly when he tried to speak, "I think they got me in the guts."

King lifted his greatcoat from his sides and counted three bullet holes punched through it. "I'd like to know who in the hell that was down there. I owe them one."

"Where are the rest of the boys?"

"They're all done for." King rose and went to catch Willie's horse. He loosened its cinch and readjusted the saddle on its back before he led the Thoroughbred over beside it.

"What are you doing?" Willie fumbled for his pistol, but another bullet had mangled the fingers on his good hand so badly that he had to use his left. "Can't you see I need a doctor?"

"You're already dead, you little runt. You just don't know it yet." King went to Willie and jerked the pistol from his belt before he could get a hold on it.

"Damn you, King."

King mounted Willie's horse with the Thoroughbred trailing behind. "I can shoot you, or you can lay there and suffer. Your choice."

"Piss on you."

"Have it your way," King said as he rode off.

"Do you think there was really that much gold?" Willie called after him.

King never answered him, and Willie watched him disappear, winding the horses through the timber.

"Your time will come," Willie whispered.

The pain wasn't as bad as it had been and he tried to pull one of his boots off by rubbing the other against it. But something was wrong with his legs and he gave up the effort and leaned his head back against the tree.

He gasped and tried to keep from swallowing the blood filling his mouth. The feeling that he was drowning was the worst part of all. He wished he had the energy to take his knife and blaze the tree trunk above him. A mound of stones, a stick in the ground, anything to mark his bones when he was gone so people could say that was where Stuttering Willie died.

"Forty loads," he whispered. "Forty loads."

It dawned on him, before he took his last, ragged breath, that he wasn't stuttering anymore.

CHAPTER 54

Faro could barely understand the trader's broken English, and the fact that the man was so excited and that the Union cavalry lieutenant was questioning him again didn't help things any. Faro leaned against the bar and nursed his whiskey while he eavesdropped. Out the door, he could see the Yankee troops tending to the bodies left by the ambushers.

Jim walked into the saloon carrying a lance that he leaned up against the bar beside Faro. "That look familiar to you?"

"Do you know something that I don't know?" the Yankee lieutenant asked from across the room.

Faro shrugged. They had arrived at Pigeon's Ranch right after the cavalry company, and like any Yankees they encountered, the suspicion of being spies was immediately cast upon them. Having Zula along helped alleviate some of the lieutenant's suspicions. Most scouts and spies didn't drag young ladies on maneuvers with them. However, the dead men in the street had the lieutenant upset.

"The same ones that did this shot my sergeant a mile down the trail before they ran off," the lieutenant added.

"Rumor is that one of General Sibley's lancer companies deserted," Faro said.

The lieutenant took a drink of whiskey. His white hair and lean, almost scrawny body looked far too old to be leading a cavalry patrol, but he had the air of a hard, veteran campaigner. "Not many days ago, we lost a supply train being evacuated out of Belen to a lancer raid."

"Well, those deserters might be who you're looking for."

"Any idea who those dead men in the street are?"

"Not a clue." Faro tried to decide if the lieutenant was buying that but couldn't get a read on him.

"That trader said that he saw everything. He and his hired hand ran up in the rocks when those lancers showed up," the lieutenant said. "Said there was a woman riding with the deceased, and that she rode off with the lancers after it was over."

Faro knew that the lieutenant was fishing.

He debated telling the man about Rue's kidnapping, but that would lead to too many questions and wouldn't help her at all. "You don't say?"

"Kidnapping white women — I hate to think what the world's coming to," the lieutenant said. "Since this war started there have been some bad things happening to folks out here, and I can't say it's all due to the Indians raiding again. Somebody burned a little village south of here and killed damned near every man in it. Shot women and children too. Killed a priest, for crying out loud. Can you believe that? A priest. Made what the Apaches can do look tame."

"You sound like you think it might have been this same bunch of lancers."

"The Mexican rumor mill says it was Confederates that did it, but who can tell? This country has gone to hell since the Rebels showed up."

"It might get worse before it gets better."

"That's what I'm afraid of."

"Good luck, Lieutenant."

"Corporal, get the men mounted as soon as those bodies are buried," the lieutenant called out as he headed for the door. "I want us in the saddle and on the trail of whoever did this in half an hour. I won't have those renegades threatening the supply train, and maybe we can get that woman back."

"Do you think Captain Lacey has gone renegade?" Jim asked when the lieutenant was gone.

"He never was far from it."

CHAPTER 55

Rue looked to the snow capped mountains to the north and west. Her heart swelled. It didn't matter that she was tired, filthy, and had worn the same dress for almost a week. No matter how bad things had turned, the gold was still up there waiting for her. She could even see the gray, hazy outline of the high, bald mountain to the northwest that had been in her mind since she first received her father's letter.

She turned her face to the sun and the wind sweeping across the high plains, thinking back on the three hard days of riding at the foot of the Sangre de Cristo mountains: through the sleepy village of Las Vegas, across the Mora River skirting Fort Union, up the west side of Wagon Mound to Ocate Crossing beneath the looming crater of an ancient volcano, across the Rayado near the ruins of an old fort, and all the way to the Cimarron.

"There's too many farmers around here to suit my tastes," Captain Lacey said beside her. "I'd rather get in and get out without being seen."

True, she had to admit that she had envisioned the gold claim in a far less inhabited place. While the terrain surrounding them certainly looked wild enough to be termed a wilderness, for the past few miles they had passed flocks of sheep and scattered herds of cattle. Little farms dotted the creeks draining from the mountains above, and before them, just visible in the distance, was a house like she hadn't seen since she left the South — a giant, two-story home with double chimneys, glass windows, and dormers sprouting from the roofline, laying along the sandy, shallow waters of the Cimarron River. The whitewashed adobe bricks all but gleamed. Around it were sprawled all manner of outbuildings and corrals, and a crew was busy constructing what looked like a gristmill.

"That must be Maxwell's ranch," Captain Lacey said. "They say he owns two million acres or more, and has six hundred peons working for him. Every wagon coming down the trail from the Raton Pass stops there, and every Indian on the east side of the mountains comes to him to trade."

"How could one man acquire so much?"

"I don't know the all of it, but this Maxwell was some kind of mountain man. He came to Taos back years ago and married some Canadian fur trader's daughter. That Canadian had political clout, and the Mexican government gave all this to him and a partner of his as part of some kind of land grant."

"Maybe we should stop there for the night," she said.

"You want a man like that to find out you have a gold mine nearby, and possibly even inside his holdings?" the captain asked. "I don't know him, but rich people can smell a profit a mile away."

Rue started to snap something back at him, but stopped herself. She admitted that what he said made sense. Perhaps that was why her father had worked so hard to keep the mine a secret. Being so close to the mine had excited her, and she mustn't forget that the gold wasn't hers until she could find it and get it back to civilization.

The thought caused her to look again at Captain Lacey. Was it just paranoia, or had he changed? Much of the arrogant, smiling dandy she had known back in Texas was gone from him, and he seemed somehow harder around the edges.

There had always been a dangerous feeling that went with the captain. Her one hope had been that he was so enamored of her that she might be able to keep a handle on him, but she wasn't so sure anymore. While he had been polite enough since rescuing her, he was more gruff and less flirtatious. More than once, she smelled whiskey on his breath, and his eyes were red-rimmed and his face haggard as if he weren't sleeping well. At times he talked to his men as if they were dogs.

And his men were another matter. While she had grown used to the rough ways of men on the trail, Company B was a harder lot than she remembered. At first she had thought it was because they had been in the field so long that made them look more roguish than they really were. Lord knew, she didn't look her best. However, they were too quiet when in her presence, almost calculating, like King's men had been. To add to her worries, their second day on the trail she noticed that a couple of the men carried what she was sure were human scalps on their saddle strings.

"Don't worry about them," the captain said. "They're loyal, and the gold you promised them has their spirits up."

Rue realized that she must have been staring at the men riding ahead of her. She didn't say it, but the lancers' enthusiasm to take her to the gold was what was worrying her most. That, and the fact that it was the captain they were loyal to and not to her.

Just how much gold would the captain settle for? She had promised him the same ten percent that Faro had asked for, to be divided amongst him and his men as he saw fit. At that, he only shrugged. Either he was truly honorable, or he didn't think any negotiations mattered because all the gold would be his if he wanted it, once they found it.

"Captain, I know I've said it many times, but thanks again." She rode her horse closer to his. "It's good to know that there are still men of honor in the South."

"My men and I are deserters. Plain and simple as that," he said. "Don't act like you don't know. Unless I'm careful, we are just as apt to get hung back in Texas as we are if the Yankees run us down out here."

Her mind raced. "Maybe we could go somewhere else."

"We?"

"Captain, you embarrass me." She turned her head away but managed to keep a look at him out of the corner of her eye. Back on the trail with Sibley, the captain had fawned over her, and several times hinted that he might propose to her. Even though he had grown colder, she still caught him looking at her sometimes.

"Captain, were you just toying with me?" She tried her best to look hurt. "Have you forgotten all those things you said to me while we were in Texas?"

"I have not."

"I even let you kiss me."

"Things have happened since then that are beyond my control."

It was only a glint in his eyes, but she could see that he still wanted her. That wasn't much, but it was all she had to work with. The trouble was, did he want her more than the gold, or as least as much?

"I think it is you who toys with me," the captain said.

"Me?"

Some of the captain's foxy old smile came back to him. "Worried that I'll steal your gold? You played coy with me back in Texas. All prim and proper and acting like you were better than anybody else."

"Captain, I assure you . . ."

"I bet you would kiss me now, and I wouldn't have to beg for it either."

"I won't be insulted. You can take me to Maxwell's right now."

He pulled up his horse and gave her a cold grin. "I could do that, but maybe I won't."

"Am I your hostage, then? Have I judged you wrong?"

"What I am is your only chance. You ought to keep that in mind." He kicked his horse to a trot and rode ahead.

A cold fear clamped around her stomach, and she knew then that the captain intended to take all of the gold. He hadn't said it, but she knew it just the same.

Rue slammed her fist down on her saddle horn. Why did it have to be so hard?

CHAPTER 56

Faro led them down to Maxwell's ranch just before sundown. Several Mexicans called out greetings or lifted their hands and waved as they drove horses and small bands of goats and sheep to the corrals for the night. Several tepees and brush huts stood across the river from Maxwell's house, and Indians lay on the riverbank wrapped in blankets and watching the newcomers arrive.

A flock of speckled chickens on their way to roost scattered in front of the mule string as they neared the big house, and a man with a heavy mustache and flat-brimmed Spanish-style hat came out of a side door and waited for them. The front of his beaded, buckskin coat was open, revealing a ruffled shirt and a string tie. He drew on a fat cigar and squinted at them.

"We were hoping we might find shelter for the night, and perhaps buy a meal if we cannot buy a bed," Faro said after he pulled up his horse.

"You can have both here for free," the man said. "I'm Lucian Maxwell and my home is your home. Some news from the south would be a welcome thing."

Faro introduced himself and the rest of his party, and Maxwell gave each of them a careful study in turn. His attention went back to Caesar once he was through.

"That's a fine-looking string of mules, Caesar," Maxwell said.

"*Buenas noches,* Don Maxwell," Caesar said. "It has been a long time."

"I hear that you quit hunting Indians," Maxwell said.

"It was time."

Maxwell must have noticed the look on Faro's face. "Your *arriero* was once a well-known man in these parts. Are you an Indian fighter too, Mr. Wells?"

"I'm a speculator."

Maxwell stepped over to Zula's horse and offered to help her down. "Well then, Mr. Wells, would you care to speculate over some good food, and maybe a glass of wine?"

"Finally, a gentleman," Zula said.

"And because of it, he won't stand a chance with you," Faro said under his breath as she passed him.

A Mexican woman came from one of the out buildings and Maxwell pointed at Zula. "Would you show the young lady to the dining room?"

"She won't be dining with us?" Faro asked.

"My wife has some peculiar notions about etiquette. We have a dining room for the women and a separate mess hall for the men," Maxwell said. "I can assure you that my wife and her help will make sure that Miss McGaffney is quite comfortable." Maxwell gestured for the men to follow him to a long, low building twenty yards from the big house.

Faro cast another look at the Indians across the river. They were still staring.

"Don't worry about those Indians," Maxwell said. "Just a few friendly Jicarillas and Utes camped here for the winter to trade and get their government allotments."

Several travelers, freighters, farmhands, and other bachelors were already digging into the plates of food scattered down the length of the plank table. Maxwell took an open space on a bench and gestured for his new guests to do the same.

Faro sat down and stabbed a pork steak off of a platter passed around the table.

Maxwell seemed to have forgotten them and was engaged in conversation with the other men in the room. Faro listened to the talk of wool prices, winter weather, and war conditions while he ate his supper. He knew little of Lucian Maxwell beyond rumors, but it did shock him that such a wealthy man with a fine house would take his meals in a common mess hall.

Maxwell was a quick eater, but drank a cup of coffee and continued his small talk until Faro, Jim, and Armand had their fill. Afterward, he led them back across the yard to his house and into a large front room with fireplaces placed diagonally in the corners at opposite ends of the room. Couches and chairs were scattered before each fireplace, and Maxwell gestured to one of them. A young Mexican man brought a bottle of wine and some glasses to them on a silver platter. Faro assumed he was some kind of butler by his actions, but the man was the first butler he had ever seen wearing spurs with gigantic rowels and a Colt Dragoon on his hip.

Maxwell took a seat on the fireplace hearth and sipped at his glass of wine before speaking. "Just what do you speculate in, Mr. Wells?"

"This and that. You know, whatever I can

find a profit in. Santa Fe and points south have been my focus as of late."

Zula walked into the room wearing a dress that Faro had never seen before.

"Don't let me stop your talk," she said, obviously enjoying the looks the men were giving her. "The ladies suggested that I sit with them, but I wished to check on my friends."

"Please sit." Maxwell rose and seated her and then resumed his place in front of the fire.

"I thank you, monsieur, for a chance at a bath, and your wife was kind enough to loan me a fresh dress while my wardrobe is laundered," she said. "We've been so long on the trail that I had almost forgotten what it feels like to wear a new dress."

"You are welcome, Miss McGaffney." Maxwell's accent was an odd mix of French, Spanish, and other things Faro couldn't put his finger on. "McGaffney, that seems a familiar name."

"It's a common enough Irish name," she replied.

"You wouldn't by any chance be related to Tin Pan McGaffney, would you?"

"He was my father."

"I hated to hear that the Utes had gotten him." Maxwell set his glass aside. "He showed up here occasionally for supplies, and I always enjoyed visiting with him."

"Oh?"

"The last year he started trading to the south in Las Vegas or Mora, and I didn't see him much."

"Father was always hard to predict," she said. "First one place and then another. You never knew where he was going to be."

Maxwell leaned back and crossed one leg over the other. "Yes, a lot of those old prospectors are like that. The Mexicans thought he was looking for gold in the mountains, and I assume they were right."

Zula shrugged. "He always had gold fever."

"The Indians sometimes bring me small amounts of placer gold to trade, but as far as I know, no white man has ever found color in paying amounts around here."

"Father always said that he panned a lot more dry holes than he did paying ones," she answered.

"Kit Carson and I drove a herd of sheep to California one time. I met your father out there right after he made that Feather River find."

"He was proud of that."

"He told me that he had come through this country on his way to California, and that he was sure there was gold in the San-gre de Cristos and on the south end of the Rockies."

"I wouldn't know."

Maxwell watched her for a few seconds. "Where are my manners? All this talk of prospecting, and I haven't even learned anything about you. What brings you to New Mexico, Miss McGaffney?"

Zula passed a quick look to Faro before she answered. "I'm returning from Santa Fe. I went there to see to some of my father's things, and these men were good enough to escort me back East."

"We're headed back to Missouri," Faro added. "Delivered our goods to Santa Fe, and headed for another load."

"Wouldn't freight wagons pay much bet-ter?" Maxwell asked. "Such a small mule train can't let you haul much."

"All businesses have to start somewhere, and it is our first trip out here."

Maxwell nodded. "If General Canby can run those Confederates out of the territory, maybe we can all get back to business. With the soldiers all busy, the Indians are starting to make trouble again."

"This war is so horrible," Zula said.

"And what's your story, young man?" Maxwell aimed his question at Jim.

"Story?" Jim repeated.

"We all have a story."

"I just work for Mr. Wells."

"And you?" Maxwell looked to Armand. "Do you just work for Mr. Wells?"

Armand growled something in Cajun French, but Maxwell only smiled and spat something back at him in the same language.

Faro stood up and stretched and yawned. "It has been a long day. I thank you for your hospitality, but I think I'm ready for bed."

Maxwell walked to a desk on the other side of the room and opened a drawer in it. He piled two bags of coins on top of the desk, and turned around with a deck of cards in his hand. "I had hoped that I might interest you in a game of cards, Mr. Wells. A little *speculation,* as you call it, might help pass a winter night and give me a chance to get to know you better. I assume you might be coming through here regularly after this, and we could talk business."

Faro made a show of yawning again.

"No?" Maxwell asked. "I guessed that you might be a sporting man. I detect a touch of the Big River in your accent."

A little warning bell was going off in the back of Faro's mind. Maxwell seemed friendly enough, even magnanimous, but he was way too sharp. "Thanks for the offer, but we need to get an early start in the morning."

"Very well." There was a touch of a smile at the corner of Maxwell's mouth. "Miguel will show you to the bunkhouse. Miss McGaffney has already been given a room upstairs."

Miguel, the spur-wearing butler, showed them to the bunkhouse and offered them their choice of the empty beds lining both walls. He left the lantern he carried, and went back to the big house without another word.

From the sound of the snoring, it was plain that several men were bunked up there for the night. Faro tossed his bedroll on an empty bottom bunk and sat down on it to pull off his boots.

"You think that man knows what we're after?" Jim whispered from the bunk beside him.

"Maybe," Faro answered just as quietly. "Or maybe he's just speculating."

"Do you trust him?"

"No."

"I think we ought to ride off in the wrong direction tomorrow morning," Jim said. "We can double back once we've gone a few miles up the trail."

Armand was already snoring like the bear he was. It was amazing how fast the man could go to sleep.

Faro adjusted his blanket and rolled up his coat for a pillow. "Jim, are you still awake?"

"I am."

"I'm thinking you're right. That might not be a bad idea at all."

CHAPTER 57

Miguel wrapped his horse's reins around the hitching rail and went into the house. Maxwell looked up from his desk at the sound of spurs clanking across his floor. He took a moment to glance out the window at the sun just beginning to climb up out of the east before he slipped his reading glasses off of his nose and turned his attention back to Miguel.

"Which way did they go?" Maxwell asked.

"North toward Clifton's."

"How far did you follow them?"

"Far enough to see that they ducked off the trail about five miles north of the river and headed west." Miguel kept his hands stuffed in the pockets of the sheepskin coat he wore. "They are very cautious for some reason, *Patrón.*"

"Old Tin Pan found himself something up in those mountains, or I miss my guess."

Miguel shuffled his feet. "There is something else."

"Oh?"

"Some farmers came in this morning and said they had seen Confederate soldiers riding near their fields yesterday evening."

"How many?"

"Eight men with lances, and a woman . . . a pretty woman."

"And which way did they go?"

"Up the river toward the mountains."

"It seems that this country is suddenly very popular, Miguel."

"So it would seem."

"Why don't you take your cousins and ride up the river a ways," Maxwell said. "Maybe you can kill a cougar or a bear, or maybe you can read a little sign up there."

"I understand."

Maxwell cracked his knuckles. "Tin Pan had a reason to be sniffing around up there for so long, but he was better than an Indian at hiding."

"There is little snow this year on the mountain, but enough to make good tracks."

"I'm counting on that."

CHAPTER 58

"What has you so nervous?" Faro stirred up the fire with a stick and then drew his coat tight about him. Since hitting the higher country, the temperature seemed to have dropped ten degrees, and a thin covering of blown snow lay on the slopes and it was deeper in the low places.

Caesar was standing with his back to the flames, staring up the dark mountain. "Indians."

"What makes you think there are Indians about?"

"I can feel them. Not just Indians." Caesar took up his rifle from where it leaned on a packsaddle. "Apaches."

Faro twisted his neck around to scan the steep slope of the canyon rising up on either side of their camp, but he couldn't make out anything in the dark except the blanket of stars overhead visible through the narrow strip in the treetops. "Do you think it's some of those agency Indians we saw back at Maxwell's? Why, the youngest one of them had to be at least eighty years old."

"Not them."

"I thought you said those tracks we saw today were made by white men."

"Yes."

"How can you be sure they weren't Indian tracks?"

"Because I can read sign better than you, and Apaches don't make tracks when they don't want to."

"Say you're right, and it's Indians. How do you know it isn't Utes prowling around, or maybe Cheyenne, Arapahos, or even Comanches?" Faro asked. "The freighters on the Santa Fe Trail are scared to death of Comanches."

"It's Apaches. Mark my words."

"I thought this was too far north for anything but the Jicarillas, and the New Mexicans say they've been peaceful for almost ten years."

"Real Apaches are like the Comanche. They go where they want to."

"Where are you going?" Faro asked.

"I'm going to get Jim to help me bring the mules in from the meadow and tie them closer to camp."

"I thought Apaches aren't supposed to like

to fight at night," Faro threw after him.

"Maybe some don't, but I bet if you looked hard enough you could find the skeletons of a few men who thought that same thing," Caesar said.

"I don't like the sound of that," Zula said from her bedroll. "Do you think he's right?"

"He thinks he's right," Faro answered. "And it won't hurt to play it safe."

Jim helped tie the last of the mules to the picket line strung between two bull pines and came back to the fire. "Caesar thinks we're being watched, and I can feel it too."

"And those tracks we saw this afternoon?" Faro asked.

"Captain Lacey's men. I found where they camped the night before."

"Did you see any sign of Rue?" Zula asked.

"She's with them. I saw her shoe prints, plain as day."

"How far ahead of us are they?"

Jim shrugged. "Half a day, or maybe less."

Faro nodded at Jim's bedroll. "Get you some sleep. I'll stand the first watch."

Jim gathered his own rifle. "I think I'll stay up tonight. Something has the mules nervous. Maybe a panther, or maybe whoever Caesar thinks is out there."

Caesar walked back to the fire and pitched

more branches on it. "It's no panther, amigo. Those mules smell Apaches."

Armand hadn't said a word. When he saw that the conversation about the Indians was over he grunted and propped his saddle up against a deadfall log for a backrest. He drew his blanket up over him and then laid his shotgun across his chest. They all heard the sound of him cocking it as he closed his eyes.

"That isn't an exactly safe way to sleep," Faro said.

"Well then, be careful how you wake me," the Cajun said with his eyes still closed.

Faro took up his Sharps and headed up the side of the canyon to someplace out of the firelight and where he could listen and think. Captain Lacey was somewhere ahead of them, Caesar thought Apaches were following them, and the last thing he wanted was for that land baron, Maxwell, to get wind of what they sought, not with the manpower he had to call upon. He had been nice enough, but his kind of men didn't get wealthy missing such opportunities.

And then there was King Broulet, still alive and out there, somewhere. Faro didn't believe for a second that the man had given up on the gold — not until he had it or somebody punched his ticket.

He took a stand in the pines on a point hanging out over the picket line and settled down on a spot of ground free of snow with his back against a giant tree trunk. If anything prowled around their stock, he should be able to hear it.

One more day, or two or three at most, was all he needed, and then he could get the hell out of New Mexico. Gold. How much were riverboats going for? Not a big one, just something that could haul enough goods upriver to pay its own way, with berths for forty or so passengers, and just fancy enough for people of means not to snub their noses at. A good cook and a plush dining area would be a must, and he could steal a competent staff from other riverboats by offering top wages. A good pilot and captain were hard to find, but it could be done. If run right, he would have plenty of time to sit in on a hand of cards occasionally. Side-wheel or stern? Now that was something to think about . . .

CHAPTER 59

Captain Lacey cocked his pistol under his blankets but didn't move and kept his eyes slitted while he tried to decide what had woken him. His bedroll was several yards uphill from the rest of his men where an aspen thicket blocked most of the wind. He heard the snow creak under someone's foot and slowly began sliding the pistol free from the blankets.

"Captain," a voice whispered.

He could see her silhouette coming to him, with her hair as pale as the snow, and floating through the trees like a ghost. He waited and watched until she stood only two steps from him, wrapped in a blanket and shivering.

"Captain?" Her voice was unsure and scared.

He propped himself up on one elbow, keeping the pistol cocked, although he wasn't sure why. "What is it?"

The blanket dropped from her shoulders and the rest of her was as pale in the starlight as her hair. He lifted his blankets with one arm and she slid under them and pressed the cool, naked flesh of her body against him.

"What . . ."

"Sshh," she whispered with her lips close to his ear and her breath warmer than the press of her palm against his cheek.

CHAPTER 60

"Top of the world." Captain Lacey pulled up his horse on the windswept summit and looked down the mountain. The spine of the ridge was barren and free of trees. One end of it pointed down to the Cimarron River miles to the southeast, and the fat end of it ended just below the bald, talus crest of the mountain sticking up like some kind of volcanic ruin.

Below him, the lancers were stretched out in a long, single-file line, rolling rocks and straining up the narrow goat trail snaking through the spruce timber. Some thousand feet below them, at the canyon's bottom, the frozen ribbon of Ute Creek shined like a mirror.

"I think we made a wrong turn somewhere," the captain added.

Rue watched him, and when she shivered she knew it wasn't just because of the cold wind blowing over the mountaintop. The captain glanced at her, and even though he didn't have the sneering, arrogant smile on his face that was there earlier that morning, the possessive look was still there, as if he owned all or part of her. That look reminded her of what she had done the night before and what she needed to forget. Shame washed over her like mud, leaving her filthy and unclean and knowing that no amount of gold should be worth that. If she could take a bath, she would scrub herself a thousand times; scrub until the feel of him was gone from her.

"This old mule trail is as plain as day," the captain said. "That cabin must be close, although I don't know why a man would want to build his shelter up on this bald ridge top."

"Maybe we didn't go far enough up that creek. The letter said the cabin is where that canyon heads up below this bald peak," she said.

Although they had barely been on the trail an hour, already he was angry. They had argued over the directions in the letter, and then one of the horses slipped on a patch of ice and fell down the mountain and broke a leg.

"I didn't see any trail going farther up that canyon. This one was the only one, and here we are," he said.

The men were in as bad a mood as their captain, but they fell in behind him without a word when he led them over the ridge and down a gradual slope toward another canyon to the north. The tall spruce and fir trees had given way to stunted, dwarfish versions of themselves scattered with loose rock and some kind of shale. The wind had swept patches of ground free of snow, and they picked their way carefully.

They had only gone a short ways when they came across an elk skull tied to a dead bush. Just beyond it was a hole — more like a depression some thirty feet in diameter and waist deep. The downhill wall of the hole was pushed up as if by some geologic force, and the slope steepened below it until the mountain fell away into an almost sheer drop into the next canyon.

"I don't see any mine," one of the lancers said.

"I think there's our mine." The captain pointed to the hole and then dismounted.

He left his horse ground-tied while he went down into the little crater, and several of the men followed suit. The snow was knee-deep at the bottom, and they began to scrape it back with their feet.

"If this is her daddy's diggings, I don't see

any tailings piled around it," one of the men said when he took a break from clearing snow.

Captain Lacey was walking to and fro examining the ground his men uncovered. After a while, he stopped and dug at the hard ground with the toe of his boot and bent over and picked something up that he studied closely before getting down on his knees.

"You boys take a look at this," he said.

Rue joined the rest of them and clambered down into the hole to stand over him. The captain held up a chunk of rock and the men passed it around.

"Is that gold I see?" the captain asked.

None of them seemed sure.

"Doesn't look bright enough for gold," one of them said. "Might be pyrite."

"Well, how about this?" the only man still clearing snow called out, holding something out to them in his hands.

They ran to him like children, staring at the flat chunk of dark rock he held. A thick vein of gold ran through it, and smaller rivulets laced out from that. The rest of the ore was dotted with sparkles as if it were embedded with glass.

"This quartz stuff is rotten." The man crumbled the rock in his hands as if it were made of dried mud. He held up what was left — a thin strip the size of a finger and looking like there was almost nothing left but gold.

By the time they cleared the bottom of the hole, they had built a snowbank taller than their heads. The streak of rotten rock they had found was only six feet long, and from three other, much longer strips that someone had dug out in the past parallel to it, they assumed that they had found where Tin Pan had mined his high-grade ore.

"How much do you think this ore will pay?" someone asked.

"I don't know anything about mining, but when there's enough gold that you can see it like this, I would guess that it's worth a lot," the captain said. "Somebody get that pick and a shovel."

Rue's heart was beating wildly. Everything she had dreamed finally felt possible. "We need to find that cabin."

The captain gave her an impatient look. "We will, but I can't see leaving this behind."

"This isn't what we've come for," she said. "Even if there is more of this here, we don't have enough packhorses to carry enough ore off of this mountain to matter."

"I'm not leaving gold lying here," the

captain said.

Already the men were carrying armloads to the pack-horses and filling the panniers. They threw the supplies and plunder from their raids on the ground to make room for the ore. The sun was high in the sky by the time the vein of rotten rock they found played out. They had managed to dig a hole a little over a foot deep and six feet long with nothing more than one pick, a shovel, and their bare hands when necessary. Some of the men even used their knives and their belt buckles to dig. The panniers on the four packhorses were all full and sagging heavily from the packsaddles, and the men went so far as to stuff their pockets with the best of their findings.

The captain sat on the edge of the hole beneath the elk skull, out of breath. "Darling, we are rich."

She fought down the unclean feeling again when he called her that and forced herself to focus on the task at hand. "We need to find that cabin. This will seem like nothing when we find what Father really left for me."

The men went quiet and every one of them looked to her.

"He worked this claim for over two years, and took the best of it," she said. "He made his own gold ingots and there's a stash of them close by. A lot of them."

"You fool," the captain hissed so quietly that only she could hear him.

The men tightened their cinches and mounted, chattering amongst themselves. The excitement over the gold ore hadn't left them, and they were obviously ready to go find more of it.

"Why didn't you keep quiet?" The captain lingered behind as the men started across the ridge. "They didn't know about those ingots. They were so excited they would have ridden all the way off of this mountain with that ore and never a question asked."

"That isn't what I came for," she said.

"If you're going to be my woman, you're going to learn to listen to me," he said. "Do you give a dog the steak if he's just as happy with only the bone?"

His woman. She tried to push away the image of his hairy, stinking body pressed against her as he grunted and pawed at her like some animal, thinking she enjoyed him and thinking he deserved her. *Never again. Never.*

"When I ride down the mountain I want what I came for with me. I've waited long enough," she said.

He slapped her so hard she almost fell from her saddle. "You dumb whore. Did you think that sleeping with me was going to make me take orders from you? For a greedy bitch, you don't have the sense God gave a goose."

She could only stare at him while a trickle of blood poured from the corner of her mouth. Shame and anger choked her like a hand about her throat, but there was also some kind of justice in the pain. Maybe that was because she knew in her heart of hearts that she deserved to be slapped.

A gun was what she needed. A gun and just one good chance.

CHAPTER 61

It was beginning to snow — big flakes tumbling and fluttering and slanting down like butterflies.

"It looks like they turned off too soon." Faro studied the horse tracks pointing up the steep slope to their right.

The rest of them looked up at the high ridge above them. The trail had led them through a series of glades and meadows and patches of timber, following the creek at a steady but tolerable climb. Finally, the canyon walls had choked back down again until only fifty or sixty yards wide, with the trail clinging to the north wall.

"Maybe they know something we don't," Zula said.

"Your father said to follow the right hand fork of this creek all the way until the canyon heads up."

She considered the directions given in the letter. "I counted five little lakes we've passed. That's right."

"If we're following the right creek," Jim said. "There are more canyons running off this mountain than you can shake a stick at."

"This is the right one," Faro said. "I'm guessing that mule trail going up there leads to the mine, and I'm guessing Captain Lacey hasn't figured that out yet."

"What are you going to do about Rue?" Zula asked.

"I don't know. Something," Faro said.

"From the sign I've seen, they aren't treating her like a prisoner," Jim mentioned what they had all been thinking but hadn't voiced to that point.

"I've worried about Rue my whole life, but there's nothing we can do right now without getting us all killed, and maybe her too," Zula said. "And if Jim's right, she's working with Captain Lacey to beat us out of the gold."

"I won't ride off this mountain without her," Armand said.

"One way or another, we're going to have to worry about Captain Lacey chasing us down the mountain," Faro thought out loud.

"Don't forget those Apaches," Caesar said from the head of the mule train.

"Yeah, and there's that to think about," Faro said.

"What do you say, Faro?" Jim asked. "Do we go the way the tracks lead?"

As if to answer him, Faro rode past the trail pointing up the side of the ridge. The canyon narrowed even more a little ways ahead, and a heavily timbered hump of ground almost created a little saddle across it. The creek was now nothing more than a dry gully, and Faro picked what he thought was the easiest way along the side of the ridge above it with the others following him. A hundred yards further along the timber thinned out and a well-worn trail appeared again. Not far beyond that, the barren, eroded face of the head of the canyon came into sight and a small cabin lay on a bench of flat ground just downhill from it.

As they neared it, Faro saw that it wasn't much of a cabin, barely the size of a good smokehouse, with gaps between the little logs where the mud chinking had fallen out big enough to pass your head through, and the roof so short as to make a normal sized man nearly bend over double. A lean-to shed extended off of one side of it, and under its roof was a miniature version of a Spanish-style *arrastra*.

Like most such devices, a bed of flat

stones was laid to form the floor of the basin, with other stones forming the lip or border around the outer edge. A pivoting wooden arm was attached to a post in the center, and a chain connected the short end of the arm to a large, flat-bottomed rock inside the basin. A mule or a donkey was usually hitched to the long end of the boom arm and used to walk around and around and drag the crushing rock over the top of any ore placed in the *arrastra*.

The *arrastra* in the shed was small enough that it must have been built for a man to move by hand, plus there was no room under the roof for a mule to work. There was a ditch beaten into the ground around the basin, and the slope in front of the cabin was littered with tailings.

In addition to the little *arrastra,* there was what looked like a large mortar and pestle setup mounted on a pine stump. The pestle was made from a cupped-out, water-worn rock, and a rusty shop hammer served as the mortar. Such a setup was a ponderous, almost ridiculous way to crush any large amount of ore.

Jim came out of the cabin carrying two cast-iron ladles and a strange, long-handled mold. He stopped beside the rock-ringed fire pit in front of the door and showed the mold to Faro. "Here's where your egg-shaped ingots came from."

Faro went to the tailings pile and took up a sample in his fist. The grindings and a few larger pieces were almost as soft as chalk. Tin Pan must have found a vein of rotten quartz and high-grade stuff.

Zula was off her horse, but ignored the cabin and was headed toward the bluff at the head of the canyon where a talus slide spilled down from the summit of the mountain. He followed her to where small deadfall logs, rocks, and other debris littered what must have once been a landslide at the bottom of the bluff. One such log lay farther up the side of the canyon, lodged in an exposed ledge of rock.

Faro watched Zula making a beeline for that log. Surely, it couldn't be so easy.

Zula stood over one end of the log, staring at it for a long time. He went to stand beside her, patient only because it was hers to discover.

Zula tapped the log with one foot and gave him a curious look. "It's just like he wrote."

"Go ahead."

She raised her foot higher and brought it down on the log with force. The log was as rotten as it was hollow, and broke to pieces.

Both of them stared at the three leather bags the size of a human head lying amidst the splintered wood.

It was Faro who gave the log a second kick, and then another, tearing it apart completely and revealing two more bags. He reached down and picked one of them up, hefting it and guessing at its weight — maybe twenty pounds. He could already tell what was in it before he untied the string holding it closed and offered the open top to Zula. She reached inside and pulled forth a golden egg just like the ones he'd seen back in New Orleans.

"Not exactly forty loads, is it?" she asked.

"No."

"But it's really something, isn't it?"

"Yes, it is."

She rolled the egg from one hand to the other. "So much gold. Father was telling the truth."

"He left it for you."

"I wish he were here." She wiped at her eyes. "And I wish Mother could see this."

"I'll go get a couple of mules. Why don't you sit here until I come back?"

She only nodded.

Faro went back to the cabin and found Jim sitting on a stump whittling a stick. Caesar was standing several yards downhill, cradling his rifle against his chest and watching their back trail. Armand was still sitting on his horse, staring up the mountain the way the lancers had gone.

"Was it there?" Caesar asked when he noticed Faro.

"It was."

Caesar whistled low and soft. "I didn't think it would be there. This is the third treasure hunt I've been on."

"The third?" Jim paused his whittling long enough to cock one eye in Caesar's direction.

"Yes, the third," Caesar said. "The first time I was very young and the Apaches killed almost all of us before we even got close to where we thought the treasure was. The second time we hunted for half a year, thinking we would find it any day."

"Did you find it?" Jim asked.

"We were sure we were very close, but the men became suspicious of each other and two of them killed each other in an argument. Then we ran out of food and horses, and then we ran out of money to buy more food and horses. With treasure, there is always something that keeps you from finding it — desert, mountains, bad directions, Apaches, landmarks that have changed and where nothing looks the same as it should.

Maybe even somebody came before you and got the treasure."

"Who knows? Fortune is a fickle thing," Faro said.

"Sólo Dios sabe," Caesar said so quietly that they could barely hear him.

"What did he say?" Jim asked.

Faro put a hand on Jim's shoulder as he passed him on the way to the mules. "Only God knows."

Jim put his knife and stick away and followed on Faro's heels. "How much gold is there?"

"One hundred pounds or so."

"How much money is that?"

"I don't know . . . at nineteen dollars a troy ounce, maybe a little short of thirty thousand dollars."

"You're good with numbers," Jim said.

"No, I've just been thinking about gold a lot."

"Should we load it on two mules, or spread it out amongst all of them?" Jim asked.

"Load it all on two mules," Zula said as she walked up with a sack of gold hanging from each hand. "At least we will know which mules to fight for the most."

Faro looked to Jim and Caesar. "She's right."

They carried the rest of the gold back to the cabin and loaded it on two of their best mules. They were Caesar's picks, just two plain brown mules.

"This is for you." Zula pitched an egg apiece to Jim and Caesar. "I want you two paid, even if we lose all of the mules."

"Thanks." Jim tucked the gold away in his coat pocket.

"Gracias." Caesar did the same.

"What about you two?" Jim nodded at Zula and Faro. "Don't you want to stash away a little insurance? You both have more to lose in this deal."

Faro shook his head. "Rue isn't here to make the cut, and I won't take my ten percent until the job is done."

"Suit yourself, Don Quixote," Zula said. "Armand and I will settle with you when the time comes."

"I know you might like to stay here longer, but it's time we ride," Faro said to her. "We don't want to get caught up this high if it keeps snowing, and there's still Rue to think of."

Zula shrugged sadly. "I've seen enough. Maybe someday I'll go across the mountains to Taos and visit Father's grave."

They mounted their horses and started back through the timber. They were almost back to the point where they had left Captain Lacey's tracks when rocks rolled from the ridge above them.

CHAPTER 62

Another horse slipped and fell and came up lame, and the lancers were busy trying to shift its load to another horse on the steep side of the ridge. Rue made use of the time by dismounting to stretch her legs and try to walk some warmth into her feet. Her walk led her fifty yards past the men to a point where she could almost see the bottom of the canyon through the trees. She was standing there when Jim Tall Tree came into view and rode his horse directly below her. Armand, and then Caesar and the mules followed, with Faro and Zula coming behind.

She counted the mules and noted the packsaddles on them, absorbing the ramifications of that. She looked over her shoulder at the men behind her. None of them seemed aware of the party passing along the trail below them.

She felt everything slipping away again.

She had been the one with the willpower and the smarts to get them so close to the gold, yet Zula was going to get it all — naughty, hateful, treacherous Zula. Where was the justice in that? If anyone deserved their father's gold, it was her. She was the one who had done everything she was supposed to. She was the one who had sacrificed so much.

She knew that there was no way Faro and his friends could rescue her. It was time to make a decision. Her jaw trembled. All of it was slipping away. Zula was going to leave her behind and take the dream with her.

"Captain!" she yelled and pointed down the mountain.

CHAPTER 63

At the sound of the shout Faro threw up his rifle, but the first thing he saw was Rue standing on the side of the canyon above them and pointing at him. Before he could get his mind wrapped around that, the lancers were already coming downhill, some on foot and others mounted. Faro knew that they should have run, but it was already too late for that.

Captain Lacey stopped his horse forty yards uphill from Faro. "I can't say that I didn't expect to run across you up here."

Faro noticed how the captain's voice cracked, and the man sounded and looked like he was on the raw edge.

"I was glad to find out that you rescued Rue." Faro stalled for time. "We owe you a debt of thanks."

"You owe me more than that."

Faro shifted in the saddle and looked at Rue. "Why don't you get your horse? I'd like to be off the mountain before the weather gets worse."

Rue stood where she was, only turning so that she could watch both the captain and Faro.

The captain laughed bitterly. "Why beat around the bush? You came up here looking for the same thing we did, and I'm guessing that you already found it."

Faro hated it that he couldn't see all of the captain's men. Most of them were either out of sight or only partially visible where they had taken cover behind tree trunks or boulders. That wasn't a good thing, considering that Faro guessed that he was outnumbered three to one.

"You come down here, Rue," Armand called up to her.

Rue didn't even look at her uncle. "Captain, have them leave those pack mules with us and let them go."

"Like hell," Zula called back to her.

There was barely time for what Rue had said to really dawn on Faro before the captain raised his pistol from where he had held it on the far side of his horse. A gunshot cracked and reverberated off of the canyon walls, and it took Faro a bit to realize that it wasn't the captain or his party either who had fired the first shot. Seconds later, Apaches were filtering through the trees, shouting war cries. Captain Lacey's horse reared with a bullet in its neck and fell on its side with the captain's leg pinned underneath it. One of the other lancers tumbled like a ragdoll down an especially steep section of the mountain, two arrows in his chest.

Jim and Caesar were shooting, but Faro couldn't tell if they were shooting at the Apaches or the lancers. Everyone was firing and shouting in the confusion.

Rue screamed and ran down the hill with her hands clutching her head. "Faro, wait!"

Faro kept a firm hold on Old Scratch, looking up the hill, not at her but at the captain a little to one side of her. Still with his leg pinned, the captain grimaced and rested his pistol on his dead horse's rib cage. Faro couldn't get his rifle sights on the man quickly enough, and knew that he was about to get shot.

"Faro!" Rue called out again.

She ran in wild, lunging strides down the steep, broken ground. Faro watched her coming as if it were in slow motion. He found the captain in his sights just as Rue stepped between them. He saw the black powder smoke rise behind her and watched as the impact of the captain's bullet threw her shoulders back. She made two more wobbly strides with her chest thrust out and crumpled to the ground.

"Rue!" Zula screamed.

Faro knew that Rue was dead the instant she fell. He fired, but the captain ducked low behind the horse. An arrow glanced off the tree limbs beside Faro and he turned Old Scratch in time to see an Apache ducking and dodging through the cover on the opposite side of the canyon and nocking another arrow on the run. He snapped a one-handed shot from the hip with the Sharps at the Apache, but Zula's horse crashed into Old Scatch and he didn't get to see the effect of his bullet. Zula's horse had gone half mad, and it scrambled on the rocks and almost went down.

Armand screamed something himself and tried to fight his horse up the slope to Rue's body. He didn't even have a gun in his hand, as if he intended to kill the captain with his bare hands. An arrow was already protruding from his side. He let out one more strange, impassioned war cry, deeper and sadder than those of the Apaches, before a bullet knocked the snow from his chest and tumbled him from his saddle.

Faro slapped Zula's horse on the root of its tail with his empty rifle. "Run!"

Caesar and Jim seemed to have arrived at the same conclusion as a matter of self-preservation, and the pack mules were already charging down the canyon. Faro hung his rifle off of his saddle and drew his right-hand Navy. The Apaches were among the lancers, and the fighting was now hand to hand. For a brief instant, he saw Captain Lacey amidst the confusion, still pinned beneath his horse. Two Apaches were upon him, hacking and cutting.

Faro took one last look at Armand's lifeless body and then turned Old Scratch loose. In four strides they were ten horse lengths behind Zula and gaining.

It was no kind of ground to be running a horse — or even a mule — over, but they stampeded down the trail single-file, popping their guns at anything that showed above them. The little pack mules ran with them, their ears pinned and their noses outstretched, finding footing on the uneven ground as surely as a bounding deer. Zula was fumbling to get her shotgun off of her saddle, while Faro kept Old Scratch reined in behind her.

Half a mile down the trail they reached the point where the canyon opened back up some, and a little farther on the timber gave way to the highest of the mountain meadows along the creek. A gun boomed ahead of them and one of the mules flipped end over end. Four Apaches rose up from the ground a little to one side of the trail where a strip of trees pointed out into the meadow. Faro knew that there was no stopping, because there were bound to be more Apaches coming behind him.

Jim kicked his horse to run even harder and dropped his reins over its neck and held his rifle in one hand and his pistol in the other. One of the Apaches dropped, as his horse blew by them. Caesar had the two treasure mules on lead ropes, and it was hindering his ability to fight on the run. The loose mules were racing three-wide, and one more of them fell dead right in front of Faro. He barely managed to rein around it and snapped a wild shot at the Apaches moving like phantoms through the falling snow.

The trail passed the shores of a tiny alpine lake, and the elk and deer watering there the previous fall had churned the mud with their hooves. That mud had frozen with the onset of winter, and the rough, bare ground was slippery and uneven. Zula's horse lost its footing and went down, and it took Faro several strides to get Old Scratch pulled down on his hindquarters. He reined the black mule back around in time to see Zula trying to pick herself up from the ground, apparently no worse for her tumble. Two Apaches were charging on foot toward her. Faro parked Old Scratch broadside and thumbed three rapid shots from his pistol in a wild attempt to slow their approach and to buy her some time.

Running footsteps grated on the frozen mud and he turned his head barely in time to see a large warrior, almost a giant in fact, running at him with a spear. He cocked the Navy and leveled it on the Apache's chest, but the hammer fell on an empty chamber with a sharp snap. Hurling the empty pistol at the warrior, he struggled to draw his other Navy in time.

The big Apache sunk the spearhead into Old Scratch's neck with a sickening puncture of flesh. The mule reared high, jerking the spear from the warrior's hands. Faro kicked out and his boot caught his attacker square on the chin, knocking him down.

Faro tried to find the butt of his other Navy again, but Old Scratch bawled and made a huge leap forward, pawing at the spear still buried in his neck. He lunged and ran wildly, staggering and pawing, until finally the spear fell free. He took a few more slowing strides and finally stopped with his great body quivering with pain.

The mule's maddened flight had carried them all the way to one side of the meadow and under a great rock bluff. Faro looked back the way they had come and saw the Apaches take hold of Zula. A war club flashed and she crumpled to the ground.

More Apaches began to show up across the meadow and they started toward him on foot and at a dead run. He slid out of the saddle, putting Old Scratch between himself and the Apaches. He was caught in the open. The bluff was too steep to climb, and there was no time to find other cover. Somehow his other Navy was missing from its holster, perhaps bouncing out during his ride, and he drew the Colt Walker from his pommel holster and rested it across the saddle seat. Old Scratch's trembling had lessened, but it was still enough to make the long pistol barrel shake — or maybe that was because of his own pounding heart.

He eared the hammer back and let off one booming round, and then another. His bullets must have come close for all but one of the Apaches turned back. That one was a young brave, lean and swift on his feet, and foolishly courageous. He came on across the open ground, zigzagging and whooping and shaking the short-barreled musket in his fist as if it were a club instead of something to shoot. He finally fired the musket from the hip when was less than fifty yards away, and a bullet knocked a splintered chunk out of the swell of Faro's saddle. Old Scratch took a staggered step, and Faro waited for him to still again and for the recoiling Walker to settle. He cocked the hammer on the down stroke and brought it to bear on the Apache's chest. The .44 bullet struck home like a thunderbolt and the Apache was dead before he hit the ground.

Faro cocked the pistol again, watching the other Apaches across the meadow, and trying not to look at the ugly exit hole in the dead boy's back. A few potshots were fired his way, but the Apaches apparently had poor guns, or were poor shots, for none of them hit close to him. He could hear other gunfire still coming from the head of the canyon, and it sounded like some of the lancers had forted up and were putting up a staunch defense. When that was over, Faro was going to have a lot more Apaches coming down to pay him a visit. Caesar and Jim had disappeared, and he just hoped that they were far away and still running.

He ducked under Old Scratch's neck and made a quick examination of the wound. The hole was half the size of his fist and steadily seeping blood. He stuffed the hole with a handkerchief, and dodged out of reach of Old Scratch's teeth when the mule, surprised by the sharp stab of pain, tried to bite him. He hoped that stuffing the wound would slow the bleeding.

The three Apaches across the meadow shouted and tried another set of shots at him, several of them coming close enough to make him flinch and get back on the other side of his mule. He peered over the saddle again in time to see the Apaches, now mounted, starting back up the canyon. To Faro's horror, one of them, the giant who had stabbed Old Scratch, had Zula on his horse in front of him. What's more, she was still alive, although reeling weakly.

He knew little of Indians, much less Apaches. Caesar loved to talk about his most hated enemy, and a thing he had said once came to Faro right then. *Don't let them take you alive. Save the last bullet for yourself if you're of a mind to. A bullet to the head is a far kinder death than the Apaches will give you.*

If he counted right, he had only two rounds left in the Walker. He took a fine aim on the white-painted Apache clutching Zula before him, his hands shaking more than before. He couldn't make himself pull the trigger. The falling snow made it hard to see, and the Apaches were going too fast and were too far away. What if he hit her? He never had been able to shoot well at any distance to speak of.

He wiped at his eyes and then took a two-hand grip on the Walker. A snowflake stuck to his right eyelid and his front sight was nothing but a blur. It was an impossibly long shot for a pistol, and the Apaches kicked their horses to a run. *Be still, you damned mule.*

The Indians were nearing the timber, getting farther away by the second. Two hundred yards and growing — he didn't have a prayer. *You'll never get her back, and she's as good as dead even if you don't shoot.*

He closed his eyes and opened them quickly to clear the snow away. *A kinder death, at the worst.* He guessed how much lead to take and how high to hold at such a distance. *Shoot, damn it! Shoot now!* He squeezed the trigger, thin and cold against his finger, and the Walker belched hellfire.

CHAPTER 64

The Walker Colt slammed hard against Faro's fists, but the big Apache stayed on his horse. Faro cocked the pistol again, but knew he didn't have time for another shot, nor did he have it in him to pull the trigger again if there was time. He stared at the fleeing horsemen, feeling drained and cursing under his breath.

As if by some magic, both the big Apache and Zula fell from the running horse just short of the timber. Neither one of them moved, and he couldn't tell if one or both of them were dead. His greatest fear had been hitting Zula, and that old feeling of bad luck hanging over him came back again. *No, by golly, you're due, Faro Wells.*

The other braves had charged into the timber, either unaware that the big warrior had fallen, or going too fast to turn around quickly. Faro knew that he didn't have much time, if any. He took up his reins and climbed into the saddle.

"Damn you, you black devil," he said to Old Scratch, "I need you to give me one more run."

Old Scratch went from a standstill to a dead run all in one movement, his stride unfaltering, as if his lifeblood weren't pouring out of him, and as if there wasn't a hole torn into him. Faro kept his eyes on the timber, expecting at any moment for the Apaches to reappear.

The other two Apaches rode out from the timber when he was still a hundred yards from where Zula and the big Apache fell. Gunshots sounded from behind him, and one of the Apache horse's knees buckled. Faro looked behind him and saw Jim and Caesar charging up the meadow, shooting on the run. The Apache on the wounded horse left it and jumped up behind the other brave. They fled back into the timber riding double.

Faro leapt from the saddle and hobbled to the bodies before Old Scratch was completely stopped. Zula was lying on her back and there was blood all over her forehead.

Jim and Caesar pulled up around him, searching the timber for targets.

"We'd better pull out of here," Caesar said. "We surprised them, but it won't take long for them to get their courage back."

Faro looked at the big Apache lying beside Zula with one of his arms flung above his head, as if he had been dramatically posed. A bullet hole just under his armpit was leaking red all over his war paint.

"One hell of a shot," Jim said.

Zula moaned and ground her shoulders into the snow in pain. She opened her eyes and looked up at him. "Good shot."

He lifted her like a child and put her up behind Jim. "Get her out of here."

Caesar rode over to the dead Indian and looked down at him and spat. "Apache."

Faro got back on Old Scratch, wincing again at the sight of the wound in the mule's neck. Jim tore off with Zula clutching him around the waist, and Caesar raced to catch up. Faro hated to do it, but he kicked Old Scratch one more time and hoped the mule wasn't dead on his feet and just didn't know it yet. Old Scratch took out after Jim's horse like the racehorse he thought he was.

You tough, glorious bastard. If you weren't so ugly, I'd hug your neck.

CHAPTER 65

The Vaqueros rode up the canyon carefully, rifles at ready. The little snowstorm of the day before hadn't been enough to completely cover the tracks of many horses, at least three separate parties of men. They argued amongst themselves whether some of what they saw was Indian sign, and some of them wanted to go no farther up the canyon.

They found where Apaches had camped and butchered a mule and cooked it. Two miles above that, they came upon the battle site. The ravens and buzzards had found it first, and they flew up into the treetops when the vaqueros rode up, protesting the interruption of their dinner. Dead horses and mutilated soldiers scattered all over the side of the canyon littered the snow. Most of the bodies had been stripped of their clothes and the weapons and other gear scavenged.

The story was easy enough to read to the Mexicans' skilled eyes. They rode among the bodies and carcasses on the slim chance that one of the soldiers might still be alive, but they found nothing but the dead. The Confederate soldiers hadn't stood a chance. The Apaches' ambush was almost perfect — firing down on their enemy from the heights above, and the only escape from the trap being either up the steep side of the canyon or down its narrow confines.

"There was a woman among them," Miguel said.

They all stared at the dead woman he had found. The Apaches hadn't cut her up, but there was still something pitiful about the way she lay. There was a look of surprise and terror on her face, as if the cold had frozen the muscles and flesh at the very moment she had died.

One of the vaqueros dug into the panniers on one of the dead packhorses. He brought one of the strange rocks he found to Miguel. "Is that what I think it is?"

"I think you might be right," Miguel said.

The vaqueros passed the gold ore around, clucking their tongues and speculating on where it might have come from. When they were done admiring the thing, Miguel stuffed it into his saddlebags.

"Don Maxwell will want to know about this," he said.

Most of the men were already dismounted and going from dead horse to dead horse and picking out the likeliest looking bits of ore for their own keeping. One of the older men warned them that it was blood gold, and that no good could come from it. The rest of them listened politely, but did not believe in such a thing. They had no packhorses of their own, but loaded their coat pockets and the *mochilas* on their saddles. Unable to carry but a small portion of the ore, they made a pact among themselves to come back to the site with plenty of tools and packhorses when the snow melted off that spring. That would give time for the ravens and other scavengers to do their work, and only the bones would remain to testify to what bad thing had happened there.

They buried the woman alongside a fresh grave they found in the uppermost meadow and rode toward home. All they had seen and the hint of so much gold had them all wanting to talk.

"You know, when word of the gold leaks out, there will be many men on this mountain," Miguel finally said. "They will come from all over and far away."

"Who will tell? Not me," one of the vaqueros said. "We can all keep a secret."

Miguel shook his head. "Gold cannot be kept secret. She is like an unfaithful woman and will find many lovers."

CHAPTER 66

Faro and his party rode into Maxwell's ranch for a second time on the evening of the fourth day since they had ridden for the bald mountain. He traded an Apache horse and a spare rifle for supplies. Before they were loaded out, Maxwell walked up to the trading post and leaned against the front wall.

"You look like you had trouble," he said.

Faro helped Zula up onto her horse, while Caesar and Jim started the mules up the trail. He examined the bandage and poultice on Old Scratch's neck and checked that his cinches were tight before he looked Maxwell's way.

"Ah, what trouble?"

Maxwell looked at Zula, but she said nothing, her face drawn and her eyes bloodshot. Faro mounted and rode in between her and Maxwell.

"How's the trail to Missouri?" he asked.

"Cold and dry and full of mad Indians," Maxwell said. "You'd be asking for trouble to try it before spring. Winter isn't over, and you don't want to get caught in a blizzard out there."

"We'll see," Faro said.

"Did you find what you were looking for?" Maxwell asked.

Faro didn't know just how to answer that.

"There's a man down there by the river that I believe is waiting for you," Maxwell said.

"Oh?"

"He's been hanging around here since the evening after you left."

"One-eyed fellow?"

"That's him."

Faro started up the road and Zula swung in behind him. They passed the big house and several small jacales belonging to the Mexicans that worked for Maxwell. Ahead of them, near the crossing, a horse was tied to a pole of a garden fence, and a man stood beside it. Faro recognized him, even at a distance.

Jim pulled up and waited for Faro to ride up beside him. "That's a bold devil to think he can take us all."

Faro pulled the brim of his hat down a little lower, his shaded eyes never leaving the man waiting down the road. "Keep your hand off of that gun butt, kid. This is my trouble."

"I can't help it. It just keeps inching up there," Jim said. "You know that he's too good for you."

"Probably."

Faro slid the Walker from its holster and let it lay on top of his thigh as he rode down to the river. King Broulet hung his greatcoat over his saddle and stepped out into the trail. His LeMat was hanging from his hand alongside his leg.

"You are a troublesome man, Faro Wells, and you're either the luckiest man I ever met or better than I gave you credit for."

Faro stopped Old Scratch ten yards away. "I'm here."

"Kind of a like a dueling ground, only better," King said. "Don't you think? No seconds giving us silly last minute advice and no one to call the shot. We just talk until we think we have the advantage, or until one of us loses his nerve and can't stand it anymore."

"King, you're playing a stacked deck. You can't get the gold, even if you kill me," Faro said. "I imagine that boy back there has his carbine out by now, and if I die he's going to put a bullet in your liver."

"Thinks a lot of you, does he?"

"Not necessarily, but I paid him a hundred dollars to kill you if I couldn't. I gave the Mexican another hundred just to make sure."

"I don't kill easy."

"And I won't let you have the gold."

King chuckled. "This isn't just about the gold. I mean to have that too, but you and I have been riding to a reckoning for a long time."

Old Scratch shifted his feet and swished his tail, and a goat bleated somewhere in the distance. Faro took a cigar from his pocket with his left hand and shoved it in the corner of his mouth. He struck a lucifer against his saddle swell and held it to the cigar, squinting over the flame.

King was rubbing his pant leg between one finger and the thumb of his free hand. "Are you a reading man, Mr. Wells? Did you ever read *Beowulf*?"

Faro clenched the cigar in his teeth. "Are you going to stand there all day talking, or are you going to lift that pistol?"

King's gun swung up, and Faro shoved the Walker forward. Their pistols went off as one. The Creole staggered forward, straining to get his gun arm to mind his will. Faro's second bullet split King's belt buckle and he fell to his knees, staring at his pistol lying in the dust before him.

Zula rode past King, not even glancing at him. Faro kept Old Scratch where he was while Jim led three of the pack mules after her. Faro let them wade the river before he rode closer to look down at King.

The Creole was still on his knees, breathing in short, ragged gasps and still staring at the ground. Faro holstered the Walker and waited.

"You're no hero," King said without looking up.

"I didn't have the sun in my eyes this time."

Old Scratch brushed against King and the highwayman fell over, his one good eye staring lifelessly at the sun high overhead.

Caesar was waiting for him with most of the mules not lost in their run from the Apaches, and leaving Faro three to carry the gold and gear. He offered Faro his hand. "I'm going to miss you, gambler."

"You still think too much of your mules."

Caesar looked at Old Scratch and smiled. "They grow on you."

"I wish you would take more pay. Five sorry mules is a far cry from what we agreed on."

Caesar patted the golden ingot in his

pocket and waved a hand over the mules. "They are fine mules, and more than enough."

"It didn't work out like I planned," Faro said.

"No man can plan such things."

"Where will you go?"

"*Quien sabe?* Maybe back to Mora. There is a pretty widow there that might look at a man with gold in his pocket and a string of fine mules."

"Adios, Caesar."

"Adios, my friend."

Faro watched as the muleteer made his way down the windblown trail through the settlement and eventually disappeared into the distance.

CHAPTER 67

"You know, this is about as pretty a country as I've ever seen," Faro said.

"We could have ridden farther," Zula said.

"I felt like going into camp early." Faro nursed the cup of coffee between his hands, liking the smell and the warm steam rising up to his face.

Zula looked out across the high plains at the gray mountains in the distance. "It's pretty enough. I wouldn't mind coming back fifty years from now when it's civilized."

"You don't think that would ruin it?"

"Maybe it would," she managed a weak smile, "and I don't think Father would want it tamed."

"They say we can make Missouri in two weeks or thereabouts, even traveling easy."

She didn't seem to hear him. "I saw her die. Armand too."

"I couldn't help her."

"Nobody could. She didn't want that, but it doesn't make it easier," she said. "I don't have anybody left."

"I'm sorry."

She turned her face away from him and wiped at her eyes.

Jim brought a load of buffalo chips and dropped them beside the fire. "I buried those picket stakes deep, but you had better keep an eye on Old Scratch. He'll find a way to turn himself loose before the night is over."

"I'll do that."

Jim busied himself trying to cook them some supper. "I never showed you, but I make the best cornbread and beans you ever ate."

"Kid, I think you ought to go back home once we get to Missouri."

"I've thought on that some."

"Good."

It was dark by the time Jim finished cooking, and Faro was sopping up the last of his beans when the sound of horses came to his ears. He set the plate aside and reached over and picked up his rifle. Zula came to stand by him.

The riders spread out and stopped at the edge of the firelight. They were Indians, but dressed in white men's clothes. Some of them had their hair cut short, and the broad man in the middle on the chestnut horse was wearing a Confederate uniform jacket with a colonel's insignia.

"Why don't you put that gun down?" the stocky man asked almost politely.

There were at least twenty of them visible, and more behind them, every one of them with a rifle in his hands. Faro set his gun down. At a nod from the stocky man, several of the Indians headed for the mules, while a few of them dismounted and went to the packsaddles stacked beside the fire. Faro felt Zula stiffen, and he put a hand on her shoulder.

"Hello, Unc'," Jim said.

"Hello. I had about given up on finding you," the stocky Indian said in perfect English.

"The gold is in those two packsaddles there," Jim said.

The dismounted Cherokees looked inside the two he pointed out and nodded at their leader before the mules were led up. They quickly saddled two of them, while the rest of the Cherokee kept watch on Faro.

"Mr. Faro, this is my uncle, Colonel Stand Watie," Jim said.

"Jim, I never thought you would be a traitor," Faro said.

Jim ducked his head. "You've been good to me and always treated me square. Believe me, I hate this, but it has to be done."

The Indian colonel watched the interplay between them and waited until they both had no more to say to each other. "The war has been hard in our nation. Crops burned, farms abandoned, fathers killed in battle, whole families gone. Tribe against tribe, Cherokee turning against Cherokee, and sometimes brother against brother. We need that gold. We need food for our families until we can grow crops again, and guns and bullets to fight the Federals."

"You're stealing, no matter how you say it," Faro said.

"Yes, but the Confederate States of America and the First Mounted Cherokee Rifles thank you for your donation to the cause."

"How did you know about the gold and where to find us?"

"I sent word upriver to Unc' the day before we left New Orleans," Jim said, still looking down at the ground.

"I've had scouts out on the trail for months," the colonel said. "We'd about given up on you, and thought maybe you had taken another way. We were hunting for a federal wagon train supposedly heading to

Fort Union and were just about to give up on it too when we saw your fire. It was pure luck that it happened to be you sitting here."

"Luck," Faro scoffed.

"We're going to take your guns, but we will leave them up the trail a ways. You can keep the other two mules and the horse. Jim thinks you are a good man, and I have no trouble with you."

"Well, I'll have a bone to pick with you if we ever meet again."

The colonel smiled, and when he did he looked a lot like Jim. "You'll have to wait your turn. The Federals already have a price on my head, and I don't know if any of us will live through this war."

"I'm sorry, Faro," Jim said. "They're my people, and I can't not help them."

"Come, Nephew," the colonel said. "We need to be going, and your family will be glad to see you again."

"I don't know if I can go home," Jim said.

"I don't know why you ran after the fight in Missouri, but that was a bad day for many of us. No one will think badly of you."

One of the Cherokees took Faro's rifle and plucked his Walker Colt from his saddle scabbard. They led up the horses, and as soon as Jim was saddled and mounted they all disappeared into the darkness.

Faro poured himself another cup of coffee and stood with his back to the fire. "I didn't expect that."

"You don't sound too bothered that they just took all of the gold," Zula said.

He turned around and smiled at her. "They didn't get all of the gold. Look in my saddlebags."

Zula did as he asked. She pulled two more of the leather bags of gold from them.

"I found those in your father's cabin. Thought it might not hurt to have a little insurance."

"You were going to cheat me."

"The thought crossed my mind once or twice, but I would have told you I had them once we got to Missouri."

"I don't believe you."

"That makes no never mind. Think what you will, but be glad that you didn't lose all of your gold."

"I just lost a hundred pounds of it."

"Forty pounds is a lot better than a poke in the eye."

"The gravy on the biscuit, huh?"

"Just the best that we can do."

He walked up the trail and groped around in the dark until he found where they had left his guns. Back at the fire, he pulled off his boots and laid out his blankets.

"How can you go to sleep after what just happened?" she asked.

"There's nothing that can be done about it. I might as well get some rest. We've a long ride ahead of us in the morning."

"I would do something terrible to you right now if I thought it would make me feel better."

"Go to sleep."

Sometime later, after the fire had burned down, he felt her crawl under his blankets and sidle up against him.

"Hold me," she said.

He wrapped his arms around her. "You realize that you are naked, don't you?"

"I can feel that you noticed."

"Quit moving. You're letting the cold air under the blankets."

She giggled. "Want to count goose bumps?"

"There are about a hundred reasons why this is a bad idea."

She kissed him lightly. "It's going to be a long way to Missouri."

CHAPTER 68

The cold was seeping through a crack in his blankets and he woke to find that he had one leg sticking out from under them and his foot felt like a block of ice. It was already well past daylight, and he sat up and scratched his head and squinted at the sun hitting him in the face. Zula was gone from his bed, but she had stoked the fire up and there was a pot of coffee sitting on some coals she had raked out to one side.

He stood and pulled on his clothes as fast as he could, shivering and swearing that if he ever made it back to civilization he was going to stay close to a stove and never be cold again. He sat his boots by the fire to warm them and poured himself a cup of coffee. He was taking his first sip when he realized that Zula's horse and the only pack mule left to them was gone.

The next thing his groggy mind realized was that his saddlebags were gone too. He could see for miles in any direction, but couldn't spot so much as a speck of her anywhere. He tugged on his boots and brought Old Scratch to the fire. At least she'd had the decency to leave him something to ride. He swung his saddle up on the mule's back and discovered that she had cut his cinch in two.

"Zula, dear. You're a real sweetheart."

There was no telling how much of a head start she had on him, and she was smart enough to know that he wasn't going to catch her on a mule still too stiff and sore to travel far and fast. The least she could have done was leave him a little gold and not cut up his saddle. Missouri was a long damned way to ride bareback.

Old Scratch shook his head and yawned.

"What are you laughing at, you lop-ear? Don't tell me you never let a woman make a fool of you."

Old Scratch shook the dust from his back and blew snot on him.

"Dumb mule."

Faro patched the cinch with some rawhide string, but it was never going to hold his weight. It would work good enough to hold his saddle in place with his meager belongings lashed to it. He brushed the snow from his hat, then took up his rifle and shoved the Walker Colt in his belt.

"She was really something, wasn't she?" He worked the kinks out of his bum knee and turned in a slow circle. "Which way, partner?"

CHAPTER 69

Lucian Maxwell was supervising his black-smith shoeing a horse when Faro arrived at his ranch for a third time. He was leading the black mule, and it looked like he had walked himself right out of his boots.

"You look like hell," Maxwell said.

"I feel worse."

Maxwell took Old Scratch's reins and handed them to the blacksmith. "If I ever saw a man that needed a drink, it's you."

They were halfway to the big house when Faro glanced down the street and saw a Union cavalry patrol coming his way. When they were closer he noted that the officer leading it was the very same lieutenant he had met at Pigeon's Ranch the day Captain Lacey ambushed King's bunch of cut-throats.

"Morning, Lieutenant," Faro said as they passed.

The lieutenant stopped his horse. "We

haven't seen a sign of those lancers or that woman. Not even a hint. They seemed to have slipped off of the map."

"It's big piece of country."

The lieutenant pulled his hat down farther after a gust of wind. "I hope that woman is all right. That trader that saw her said she was a pretty thing."

"I bet she was."

"Damned this war," the lieutenant said. "But at least it's about over now, at least out here."

"How's that?"

"Haven't you heard? Our boys took it to those Rebels at Glorieta Pass. Burned their supply wagons and sent them running back to Texas with General Canby nipping at their heels."

"No, I hadn't heard."

"That Sibley bit off too big of a chunk."

"It was a big idea."

"Well, I'd best be riding. So long."

Maxwell stood with Faro and watched the soldiers ride away, and then took him inside and poured them both a healthy dose of whiskey. He pulled up a chair in front of the fireplace and motioned for Faro to do the same.

Faro lifted his glass in a toast. "To women and fortune."

Maxwell arched one eyebrow and downed his liquor. "You aren't going to tell me any of it, are you?"

"What good would it do me?"

"I'll trade you a new pair of boots and a week's worth of grub for your story."

"You wouldn't believe it if I told you."

"Try me."

Faro finished his whiskey, already feeling warmer as the alcohol settled in the pit of his stomach. "My father used to say that whiskey was a damned fine prescription for life's ailments, but the trick was getting the dosage right."

"I hate to see a man fall on hard times," Maxwell said.

"Don't you feel sorry for me. I'm in my prime." The desk on the other side of the room caught Faro's eye. "Have you still got those cards in that desk?"

"You don't look like you have anything left to gamble with."

Faro held up the vial containing his lucky gold nugget. "I've got this, and I've got a good black mule."

"That nugget isn't worth two dollars, and I own more mules than I know what to do with. I'll give you a hundred dollars to start the game with if you'll tell me your story."

"Two hundred."

"This had better be a good story."

"You'll make money from it."

"How can I be sure of that?"

"Speculate."

"Table stakes?" Maxwell shuffled the deck.

"Suits me. Can you get somebody to bring us something to eat?"

Maxwell dragged a table to the center of the room and sat down at it with a bag of money in front of him. He counted out two hundred dollars and shoved the coins to Faro's side of the table. "What are you going to do when that runs out?"

"I intend to clean you out," Faro said. "I'm feeling lucky."

"You, Mr. Wells, are an optimist." Maxwell shoved the deck forward. "Care to cut?"

Faro made a thin cut off of the top of the deck.

"Where is that lovely Miss McGaffney?"

"She couldn't afford me anymore, or maybe I couldn't afford her."

"Does five-card stud fit your pistol? Dollar ante, five-dollar bets, and three raises?"

"Deal away."

Faro looked to his hole card — the ace of hearts and the ace of spades faceup on top of it — and tried to keep from smiling. "How far is it to the Mississippi from here?"

"A thousand miles, maybe," Maxwell said.

"A damned long ride, anyhow."

Faro counted out the coin and pitched five dollars into the middle of the table. "I'm going to buy a boat . . . a big one."

"For a man with nothing but a mule to his name, I'd say that's a long shot," Maxwell said. "I'll raise your bet."

"It's a matter of perspective. I'll raise you another five."

"Call."

Faro watched Maxwell flip another card across the table. It was a third ace. He placed another bet into the pot. "Are you going to call?"

"No."

"See, that's the thing about this old world." Faro dragged his winnings to him. "You never know when your luck is going to turn."

"The glass half full, huh?"

"Speaking of glasses, you've let mine run empty."

Maxwell shoved the bottle to him. "You'd best go easy on that whiskey. It's liable to be a long game."

Faro shuffled the deck and made a fancy one-handed cut. "One thing you'll learn about me is that I'm a runner, not a sprinter."

Epilogue

The banker took a careful look about the room, appraising the fine furniture, the carpets, and the paintings on the walls. He stopped in the middle of the office and made an entry into his ledger before going to the table where the old man sat shuffling a deck of cards. The banker cleared his throat, but the old man didn't look up.

"You won't make problems, will you?" the banker asked. "I have the papers with me if you should care to look at them."

The old man began to deal himself a hand of solitaire, his fingers working smoothly for a man of his years. He grunted occasionally when he couldn't find the card he needed, but other than that, he seemed lost in his own world.

The banker walked over to the hideous bronze statue displayed on a Grecian, marble column as tall as his waist. It was one of the most ugly pieces of art he had ever seen, but the column was worth some-thing. He entered another figure into his ledger and snapped it shut, hoping to get the old man's attention.

"Where did you get that awful sculpture?"

The old man set the cards aside and straightened in his chair. He brushed at something on the lapels of his coat and adjusted his tie. "I had it custom made. What do you want?"

"You're bankrupt and we've foreclosed on you. I suppose you don't know how this works."

"I've been bankrupt before, twice a year a couple of times."

"Very well. I've come to see your ship and to appraise its value," the banker said. "I hope you won't mind my clerks taking inventory before the auction."

The old man finally looked at him, and the banker was a little startled by the pair of cold blue eyes. Or maybe it was the dimpled scar that was so disconcerting.

"Is that all? I'm too damned old to put up with any more from you. Be gone, and good riddance." The old man pulled a massive pistol from under the table and slammed it down on the tabletop. It was obviously of an antique vintage, the old cap-and-ball kind. The banker thought his father had once owned a similar pistol, yet not so ridiculously large.

"I assure you that you can't intimidate me, and there is no need to be hostile, sir. This is purely a matter of business, and I'd hate to have to call on the high sheriff," the banker said. "The auction of your ship should pay for a good part of your debt, unless I miss my guess. She's old, but she's really in quite good shape."

"You wouldn't know a riverboat from a hole in your head."

"Like I said, it's just business."

"Business?"

"Yes, business. Your vessel is too small and too old and behind the times to pay for its upkeep and operation. Nobody rides riverboats anymore. Trains are faster, and they say that the horseless carriage will one day make even the train obsolete."

"You've got it all figured out, don't you?"

"I know that you've gambled too much. Cards and liquor do not mix well with sound business practices."

"What do you know about gambling? Did you start that bank of yours?"

"I don't know if that is any of your business, but no, my father did."

"Sonny, I've made and lost three fortunes. I never made a dime without gambling, and if I make another fortune before I die, I'll gamble for that one too."

"I understand that risk . . ."

"You don't understand anything but ledgers and pencil sharpeners. They didn't teach you anything in business school, did they?"

"I will just be on my way," the banker said. "Again, I'm sorry for your losses."

"Don't you feel sorry for me. Not your kind."

"Good day, Mr. Wells." The banker started across the room, but paused at the door, taking one more look at the sculpture, "What made you choose such a subject, or was that the artist's concept?"

"It's a mule, you penny-pinching prick. Haven't you ever seen a mule?"

"But what was the meaning of the naked woman on its back supposed to be?"

The old man picked up the pistol and pointed it nonchalantly but steadily in the banker's direction. "Not another word."

The banker hurried out of the room, and when he was gone the old man took up his cane and went to the hat rack beside the door. There were several hats hanging there, and he made a studied selection, pausing to look in the mirror after he sat his choice carefully on his head. He opened the door and stepped halfway through it before turning to look back at the room. His gaze fell last on the sculpture.

"Glorious." A chuckle far younger than the lines in his face came from his lungs and he limped down the gangplank to the riverbank and points beyond.

HISTORICAL NOTES

- Sibley's Brigade, also known as the Army of New Mexico, invaded New Mexico Territory during the winter of 1862. After an indecisive victory at Valverde Crossing, the Confederates drove all the way to Santa Fe. By spring, a portion of the brigade was marching to take Fort Union. Federal forces met them east of Santa Fe in Glorieta Pass (where Captain Lacey's lancers ambush King Broulet's men in my novel). The Confederates won the battle but a detachment of Colorado Volunteers made a hard climb over a mesa and surprised the poorly guarded Confederate supply wagons and burned them. Even though they had not yet been driven from a battlefield, the underequipped and starving members of Sibley's Brigade decided they had had enough of New Mexico. They retreated back to Texas, hounded most of the way by the federal army, and leaving a trail of abandoned wagons and dead draft stock all the way to Fort Bliss.

- Although my portrayal of Brigadier General Sibley is fictional and I have taken many liberties with his personality, his contemporaries and modern historians agree that he was an alcoholic and not one to lead from the front. After his failure out west, he served in south Louisiana. His drinking led to accusations of cowardice and a court martial in 1863. He would later end his military career in the Egyptian Army as military adviser and artillery general. He sued the federal government for unpaid royalties for his invention, the Sibley Tent, but died in poverty in 1886, despite the fact that the Union army used approximately 44,000 Sibley Tents during the Civil War.

- My naval battle in Matagorda Bay never took place; however, such a thing could have happened and did happen in Galveston Bay on January 1, 1863, when two Rebel cotton-clads, the CS *Neptune* and the CS *Bayou City,* sailed boldly into the bay and engaged six

Union ships.

- The last and only lancer charge of the Civil War, and possibly in US military history, took place during the Battle of Valverde. Captain Willis Lang and his lancers of Company B made a wild run at Captain Theodore Dodd's Colorado Volunteers. The Coloradans opened up with buck-and-ball at forty yards and finished their defense with bayonets. The Texas lancers were turned back with severe casualties. Captain Lang himself was mortally wounded in the valiant but antiquated charge. Legend has it that, several days later he requested that a slave bring his pistol to him and ended his own suffering. Texas organized and sent other lancer companies to the Confederacy in the east, but they were never equipped as lancers and saw service as regular cavalry or were even dismounted due to a lack of horses. Although Willis Lang was no villain like the fictional Captain Lacey, his charge did inspire the similar event in the novel.

- Mount Baldy lies just to the west of Cimarron, New Mexico, and the gold is very real. Lucian Maxwell founded the famous Aztec Mine there, and from 1868 to 1910, it is estimated that an excess of four million dollars' worth of gold was mined from the peak and its drainages.

- Golden eggs — the famous Texas cattleman, Charles Goodnight, claimed that Lucian Maxwell once owed him a large amount of money for a herd of cattle he had purchased. Goodnight rode to Maxwell's home and the land magnate took him to the Aztec Mine on Mount Baldy. The mine was only in its infancy, but was already pounding out high-grade ore. Maxwell took Goodnight over to a hollow log and pulled forth a stash of gold. Perhaps more interestingly, the gold ingots in the log bank were shaped like eggs instead of the usual bars.